Creations

Creations

William Mitchell

COSMIC
EGG
BOOKS

Winchester, UK
Washington, USA

First published by Cosmic Egg Books, 2014
Cosmic Egg Books is an imprint of John Hunt Publishing Ltd., Laurel House, Station Approach,
Alresford, Hants, SO24 9JH, UK
office1@jhpbooks.net
www.johnhuntpublishing.com

For distributor details and how to order please visit the 'Ordering' section on our website.

Text copyright: William Mitchell 2013

ISBN: 978 1 78279 186 7

A CIP catalogue record for this book is available from the British Library.

Design: Stuart Davies

Printed and bound by CPI Group (UK) Ltd, Croydon, CR0 4YY

We operate a distinctive and ethical publishing philosophy in all
areas of our business, from our global network of authors to
production and worldwide distribution.

For Emma, Thomas and Phoebe

Part I

Chapter 1

Rot in hell you sick piece of shit. In any righteous world you would be hanging from a rope by now. Do you have no idea what you're up against? Or do you think you can pour your Godless filth down innocent children's throats and get away with it? Because I am going to make sure you don't. Chile and Brazil are God-fearing countries, we have many friends there. You will pay for feeding them your lies.

To think your wife betrayed her faith to be with you. I await the day when pigs like you and her get their throats cut. I will be praying for your salvation.

Max Lowrie sat in the marble-floored reception area and winced as he read those words again. He was projecting them from his omni, using the surface of the table for want of a better viewscreen, scrolling through the scanned copies sent to him by a campus security staff now well accustomed to the attention that his extra-curricular activities were generating. The first had arrived almost a year previously, this latest, two weeks ago, sent in hardcopy, with no clear sign of who they were from, only a series of far-flung and blatantly random mailing points to show just how widespread his fan club's membership must be.

Except now, if the latest one was to be believed, they knew about the South America trip, and the school talks he planned to give between research assignments. And that meant he had a serious choice to make. He did what he did for a reason, but people like him had received more than just threats before now and he had his safety to consider. Maybe Indira was right, maybe scrapping that trip and taking this other job wouldn't be such a bad idea after all.

"We've had an invitation to put you forward for a project," she'd told him when she'd called him into faculty management the week before. "It's a marine engineering company called ESOS. They haven't told us what the job is yet but they're asking for you by name, and they're willing to pay big numbers."

Big numbers. Big enough to fly Max and his wife right across the country to meet him in person, giving them a free trip to Washington in a time when corporate flight quotas meant non-essential journeys were effectively illegal.

Getting bids for commercial work was nothing new, but Indira was pushing this one for good reasons. The welfare of her staff had always come first.

"I know you don't want to hear this, Max, but I have some grave concerns about sending you to Chile. I've yet to consult with our security experts but I think exploring other options might be advisable. I'd like you to go to D.C. You'll be meeting a man called Victor Rioux. Talk to him, find out what he wants, then report back to me."

Max looked round the ESOS lobby as he waited, and tried to imagine the money that must have gone into the place. A huge screen at the far end was showing company promotional clips, endlessly looping testaments of glossy self-congratulation for the many and varied achievements that had brought the Echo-Sounding and Ocean-Surveying company to its current position. Outside, beyond the reach of the aircon, ornamental lawns sat between the road and the building. Max even recognised one of his own creations in amongst the mist from the sprinklers, the Jardina-San maintenance machines, small six-legged robots cutting and pruning the borders until they had to return to their storage site to recharge. Products of the design codes Max made his living from, for six whole months they'd only existed inside a computer while seven million generations of simulated evolution turned them into something more compact and efficient than a human designer could ever have created.

He didn't know what made him look across the room at that point. Maybe he knew he was being watched, but he saw her straight away, sitting on the other side of the waiting area with her head to one side, frowning at him as if trying to remember his name. Her frown turned into a smile when she saw him looking back, and she got up and walked over to join him.

"Something tells me I should know who you are. Didn't you do that Space Sciences conference a few years ago? Optimised satellite design, right?" Her accent was somewhere between Georgia and Northern Florida.

"You've got a good memory. Yeah, that was me." He thought back to the people he'd met at the conference, or rather seen across the telepresence link from his office in L.A. He didn't remember her, but then there'd been over two hundred researchers connecting up at one time or another, attending in virtual form now that travel restrictions had made mass gatherings a rarity. "I'm Max Lowrie."

They shook hands. "I'm Safi. Safi Biehn. Hi."

She was about the same height as Max, and slim framed with it. Her hair was straight and shoulder length, and very fair in colour, fair enough to almost look white at a distance. Her age was hard to place, mid to late thirties perhaps, fine lines just starting to show around her eyes. Her eyes also gave away her intelligence, something Max could spot easily whenever he met someone. It was a skill often found in salesmen and diplomats, but rarely in biologists.

"So what are you here for today?" he said.

She laughed. "I wish I knew. I just got this message a couple of weeks ago asking me to show up. They paid for me to get here though, said I'd regret it if I didn't."

"Could be we're here for the same thing then. My faculty head had something similar, asking for me to come. From a guy called Victor Rioux, right?"

"You too? Wow, curiouser and curiouser, I wonder what the hell this could be."

In fact in the ten days since they'd asked Max to come, they hadn't once given any clue what they wanted him for. Even when Indira passed on their invitation, all she knew was that ESOS were citing the Turin Protocol, a sure sign they had something valuable on their hands, something they would protect like a state secret, and take to the World Intellectual Property Court in Turin if anyone used it fraudulently.

"So that genetic design stuff you were showing at the conference," Safi said. "Do you reckon this could be something to do with that?"

"It could be," he said. "It's been my day job for the last eight years. That's how the department makes its money, designing things by evolution."

"But you're a biologist aren't you? Is that right?"

She obviously had a good memory for details. "Among other things, yes," he said. "I was a palaeontologist at first though, that's how I started."

"So isn't satellite design a weird sideline for a fossil hunter?"

"I guess it might look that way. But I've studied evolution all my life, now I'm using it as a design tool. It's a natural progression when you look at it. And we use it for all kinds of design jobs, not just the SatComms work that you saw."

"So what are you working on at the moment?" She leant over to get a drink from the table's water dispenser as she spoke, revealing a bracelet on her wrist, a slim silver band topped with a large oval of amber. Presumably her omni; it was always interesting to see where other people wore them.

"Well, it depends," he said. "I'm meant to be in South America in two months' time, doing biodiversity studies, part of the GRACE controls. But my faculty head is thinking of dropping me from that."

"So you can take this job instead?"

"Not just that. This job came at the right time, but she has other reasons for not wanting to send me out of the country."

"Like what?"

"I, ah, I'm part of the campaign to see the teaching of evolution reintroduced into schools. Most of South America has followed the US lead in faith-based education, and not everyone likes the idea. I'd been invited to give some lectures as part of the study trip. Let's just say there are people out there who would prefer it if I kept quiet."

She seemed to know where he was coming from. For the past year he'd been visiting schools with sympathetic biology departments unhappy with the government-sanctioned material they were given to teach. At each one he gave the same talk, a seemingly harmless how-I-got-where-I-am account of why biology and natural history were worthwhile subjects to pursue, that he would then seamlessly transition into the life story of Charles Darwin and a beginner's guide to the theory of evolution. If he was honest, threats to his life should have been no surprise.

"What about you?" he said. "What do you do?"

"I'm a pilot at the moment, last couple of years anyway, doing regional cargo routes out of Atlanta. And before that I was working as a systems engineer up at —" Then she paused, and looked thoughtful for a second. "Now that's interesting, bringing both of us here." She'd said it more to herself than anyone else, a frown reappearing on her face.

"What's the matter?" Max said.

She started to answer him, but seemed to think better of it. "Forget it," she said. "I'm probably wrong."

Max wanted to ask her more, but then they were joined by a third person. It was Victor Rioux's assistant, the woman Max had spoken to when finalising his travel arrangements. She was still the closest he'd got to talking to Rioux himself.

"You must be Miss Biehn," she said, marching across the lobby with her hand outstretched. "Jane Glenday, good to see you at last. And Dr. Lowrie, I don't need to ask who you are! Welcome to Washington. Did you have a good journey?"

"Yes, we got in yester—"

"I am sorry to have kept you by the way. We're still waiting for one more person, but I think we should go ahead. If you'd like to come this way?"

She led them out of the reception area and into a wide, wood-panelled hallway. The bright sunshine outside was visible through slit windows at the top of the wall, but not much light was getting in and the corridor was lit by antique looking lights high above them. Even then it was still quite dark and almost completely silent. It felt comfortably cool compared to the heat and traffic outside.

"Have you seen anything of the city yet?" Jane said as they walked. "But then you only got in yesterday, didn't you?"

"That's right," Max said.

"Well you'll have plenty of time for that. Did your wife come with you?"

"Yes, she's here too."

"Taking in the tourist sites I presume?"

"Yes. Well, sort of, she's seen most of them before. She has relatives not far away."

The pace was fast, and even Max, with height on his side, was having to take large strides to keep up with her.

"Right, we're here," she said suddenly. She stopped outside one of the rooms and held an access card up to the door, causing it to swing open silently. "If you'd like to go in, I'll leave you with Mr Rioux. Drinks are in the corner there."

Two other people were in the room when they entered, both men, one young and one old. They approached Max and Safi, the elder of the two taking the lead, and beaming broadly.

"Safi, Max, wonderful to see you!" he said. "I'm Victor, Victor Rioux."

"Mr Rioux," Max said, adding to the day's tally of handshakes. "So does this mean we're finally going to find out what this is all about?"

"Please, call me Victor. And yes, you'll know what's happening very soon. Can I call you Max by the way? We try to be a bit informal here."

"If you want to, yes. Go ahead."

Max hadn't known what to expect of this man who had so successfully orchestrated his trip across the country without even once showing himself in person. Victor was a lot shorter than Max, definitely in his mid fifties, with thinning grey hair and filled-out waist. His eyes were his most prominent feature, piercing blue eyes set into a pale round face. ESOS was a Swiss company but despite his name, Victor's accent was almost as English as Max's own.

"I see you've met Safi here. Can I introduce you to Ross? This is Ross Whelan from our materials department."

Ross was a New Zealander, Max could tell once they'd made their greetings, and must have been the youngest one in the room, mid-twenties by the look of him, easy going, tanned and casually dressed. He reminded Max of himself ten years previously, when a relaxed attitude to appearances in the workplace was a deliberate show of being gifted enough to get away with it.

"We're only waiting for one more," Victor said. "Shall we sit down?"

They found themselves places round the central table, Victor at the top, a large wall-mounted screen behind him, and everyone else down the sides. They each had a small screen set into the table in front of them, a never-ending loop of corporate video clips and animated logos, brand reinforcement raised to saturation levels.

Victor touched a few controls and brought the room lights down, leaving them with small reading lights and the glow of their screens. The door swung shut, its access latch clicking into place.

"I think we ought to make a start," he said. "I'm sure our missing colleague will join us as soon as he can. Well, Safi and Max, if I can start by thanking you both for turning up so promptly. I understand you must feel a bit messed around with all this cloak-and-dagger act, but as I've said, you won't be kept in the dark for much longer."

Max had heard that more than once as he'd prepared for this trip, trying to glean even the most fragmentary information from ESOS to see whether their confidence in him was as justified as they seemed to think. Every attempt had been met with the same promise though: wait and see, we picked you for a reason.

Victor continued, "Ross here, as you'll find out later, has already been with us in Marine Extraction for, what? Five months now?"

"Going on six," Ross said.

"Six months, yes. Long enough to become probably one of the world's leading experts on the particular exam question we've set ourselves this past year. Though none of us could claim to be *the* leading authority, of course." He looked over to Safi as he said that, a meaningful smile on his face as if teasing out the mystery of their invitation as far as he possibly could. She looked at him quizzically in return.

"If we want to get the formal introductions out of the way first, my name is Victor Rioux and I head the Marine Extraction division of ESOS. This division has sixteen offices, in four different countries, run jointly from Zurich and here in Washington. Our main business is offshore mining, but lately we've been looking into marine chemical extraction techniques, something you'll hear more about later. Max, do you want to tell us a bit about yourself?"

"Okay, I'm Max Lowrie, and I work in the evolutionary studies department at UCLA. Most of my work concerns the use of simulated evolution as an engineering design tool, but I'm also a biological researcher with a place on the GRACE programme."

"And you're the Cambria man," Ross said with a grin.

Max looked over at Ross, surprised to hear that name mentioned out of the blue. "And I'm the Cambria man, yes."

It wasn't something he liked being reminded of, even though

most people couldn't see why he regarded it as a failure. It had seemed so simple at first: take the same simulated evolution code he worked with every day, then run it endlessly, with no design goal in mind other than that the things it produced should survive to the next generation. But the things it had led to, albeit contained in that little virtual world: to call it carnage wouldn't even begin to describe it.

They carried on round the table.

"I'm Safi Biehn, and I used to work as an engineer for a major research corporation based out of Florida." She was softly spoken, but her words were clear and deliberate. "Most of my work was into advanced manufacturing techniques and production systems. Since then I've been working as a commercial pilot."

Victor had a wry smile on his face. "Okay, Safi, I think you're holding back a bit on your real achievements there, but let's carry on. Ross, do you want to go next?"

"Okay, hi everyone, I'm Ross Whelan. Oceanography is what I do, what I'm trained in, marine chemistry and that kind of thing. I was at the University of Hawaii before I came here, and I work with the kind of extraction techniques Victor here mentioned earlier. But that's probably all he'll let me say on the subject, so I don't give his little game away, is that right Victor?" He looked over at Victor and grinned, and got a smile in return. "So that's me basically. Any more you want to know, just ask."

Ross had hardly finished speaking when the door opened and the final attendee walked in, a tall heavy set man with thick black hair and an air of imposing gravity that would have drawn all eyes to him even if he hadn't just turned up late. He smiled round at the room in general as he strode in, while Jane Glenday stood behind him making apologetic faces at Victor. Then he walked over to the table, choosing the first seat he came to even though it was at the far end from the others, before looking round at each of them in turn. The last person his eyes fell on was

Ross, who he looked up and down a couple of times before saying, "Dressed for the beach are we?" and smiling at the rest of them as if expecting a laugh in return. Ross sat back heavily in his chair and looked to Victor, seemingly unsure how to react and looking to his boss for guidance.

Victor turned to the door, thanked Jane, and hit the control to swing it shut. Then he turned to face the newcomer. "Professor Rudd?" he said.

"That's right. You're Rioux, I'm guessing?"

"Victor Rioux, yes, thank you for joining us. We were just going round doing the introductions."

He indicated for the newcomer to speak, but he didn't take the invitation. In the end, Victor spoke for him.

"This is Oliver Rudd from London, England. He's a professor of mechanical engineering, and he works in robotics and cybernetics. He's acted as a consultant to some of the world's largest manufacturing companies, and sits on the boards of two major professional bodies. Do you want to add anything to that?"

"If I knew what I was even doing here, I might be able to answer that," he said, smiling again as if the wit of the reply should have been lost on none of them.

The others then had to go round and introduce themselves again, something that Ross looked less than impressed about — and Safi too, though as far as Max could tell she was doing her best to hide it. That was interesting, he thought, her attitude to lateness. In fact everything about her suggested an uncompromising attitude to organisation: her clothing, a simple light coloured suit with not even a sign of a crease, the way she spoke, articulate but never wasteful of words. She wore no make-up, and her hair was cut simply, hanging straight down over her shoulders. Attractive she certainly was, but exploiting that fact seemed to be a low priority for her.

Once the introductions were finished they managed to move on. "In front of you, on your screens, you'll see a standard commercial confidentiality agreement," Victor said. "You may have come across forms like this before, but I want you to study it carefully because you each need to sign one before we can go any further. If any of you object, then I'm afraid you can't stay any longer than this part of the presentation."

"Is this ratified?" Max said.

"Yes," Victor said. "All our confidentiality measures adhere to the Turin Protocol."

"And if we sign this form of yours, but don't like the sound of what you tell us later? What then?"

"The agreement is binding, whatever you decide. Once you've signed this form you'll be trusted with some very sensitive information, and you'll be held liable if that information is passed to the wrong people. Beyond that, you're under no obligations at all."

The agreement was a standard one; Max had signed others like it countless times before when various companies, all with their own sets of secrets, had wanted to hire out his skills. He read it from end to end, checking for any surprises, then picked up the pointer and signed the box on the screen.

Victor waited until all their signatures were confirmed, then brought up the first video clip of his presentation. It flashed into view behind him, and on the small screens in front of them. "Right," he said with a smile. "Let's get started."

The scene was a grim one. Like an open-cast wound in the planet's crust, a vista of spoil heaps and automated ore-decks filled the screen, barely visible through the haze of smoke and dust kicked up by an endless procession of dumper trucks.

"Think about this," Victor said, getting to his feet and taking a position beneath the main display. "All the gold ever mined out of the ground, in the whole of human history, would fit into a cube eighteen metres on a side."

He paused for effect, then continued.

"Eighteen metres. That's five thousand years of digging, with a whole planet to work on. Not very much, is it?

"Now, we all know how sought after this material is, not only for its intrinsic value, and its use as a store of wealth. Those new fusion plants that are coming online in Japan, and the others in development around the world: the gold-coated deuterium spheres that are central to their operation are going to open up an entirely new market for this material, with demands on purity and availability that have never been seen before. And what's becoming obvious, is that over the next hundred years, land based mining will not be able to meet the demand. This —" he pointed to the image over his head "— will not be enough.

"So what are we to do? Well, it's worth noting that mining operations to date have suffered a slight handicap. They've limited themselves to one third of the Earth's surface: the land. The oceans and seabeds remain untapped. Until now.

"As you'll probably be aware, this company is no stranger to extracting materials from deep marine environments. In fact it's only in the last decade that technologies have been developed which allow us to start exploiting these resources while still remaining profitable, and I'm proud to say that this division of ESOS has been instrumental in perfecting some of these techniques. I won't go into details, but the recent growth in our company has been entirely due to successes in this field.

"Seabed mining is only one approach, however. For this particular application, another opportunity presents itself: not what's under the oceans, but what's in them."

By now Victor had stepped up to a raised dais at the foot of the screen and was gesturing at the images as he spoke. The video clips had been changing constantly and were currently fading between shots of rolling waves and wind-whipped seas.

"For as long as the oceans have existed, rivers have been flowing into them, bringing whatever materials they've picked up on the way. For almost as long, life has populated the seas and made its own contribution to the content and composition of the waters. As a consequence, most of the fifty-eight elements that are widely used by industry today are held in solution in seawater in one form or another, sometimes in surprising amounts. Once you know how to extract them, there's no need to go looking for the richest deposits, no need to laboriously dig them out. You can tap into this vast, chemical reservoir from anywhere. And that's what we intend to do.

"Ladies and Gentlemen, consider this. The oceans of the world contain one ton of gold in every five cubic miles of seawater. They cover two thirds of the surface of the Earth, and at their deepest, they're over seven miles deep. Think how much water that represents. Think how much gold is just sitting there for the taking. It exceeds that eighteen-metre cube by a factor of almost five hundred. In our view, extracting gold from the sea is the only viable option.

"This isn't a new idea. However, though the idea is nothing new, putting it into practice is another matter. With conventional processing plants, the cost of extracting just one gram of gold far outweighs the price that gold could be sold on for. That's why it's still there now.

"But I want you to imagine something. Imagine you had a machine that could get at this gold, built so that its energy costs were zero. It could be solar powered, say, or it could run on tidal energy. And let's keep this machine small, so that it's easier to build. So, to be realistic, let's say the rate of production was low, maybe a dollar's worth of gold for every month of operation. That's not much, but once you've paid for the machine, every-thing it produces is free.

"Now imagine that gold isn't the only thing it's taking out of the water. Imagine it taking iron, and copper, and silicon, in fact, whatever else you want it to take. Imagine then that it has some kind of manufacturing capability, so that while it's processing the gold it can also be building something. Building, in fact, a copy of itself, identical in every way, including its ability to make further copies. Where you had one machine, you would then have two, and if they continued the process, your automated workforce would double at every step."

Victor paused as if to gauge their reactions, or maybe just to let the idea sink in. Max had plenty of questions, but he felt he should save them for the end. Safi, he saw, had been nodding intently all the way through and was still doing so in spite of the pause.

"This," Victor continued, "this is what we have been working on for the last twelve months."

And with a wave of his hand, it was as if the room transformed around them. The wall panels, no longer showing just the company logo, seemed to grow and merge into each other, taking on new depth and perspective as they did so. The floor, now down-projected from the ceiling, took on its own extra dimension, and even the table was included, the pseudo-stereo imagers using its upper surface as just another element of the scene being created around them, correcting for its shape and height so that the join was barely visible.

They were in a large enclosed space, like an aircraft hanger but with a pool beneath them, floodlit both from above and below its surface so that elusive shapes and reflections danced over the white painted walls. The space was large; there were people in the pool, around a dozen of them swimming in wetsuits and diving gear, and judging by their scale Max put the pool at almost two hundred feet in length. However it was the object they were clustered round that seemed to be the centre of their attention, and it was only as the viewpoint dropped toward the water that Max could begin to see what it was.

Two distinct memories of childhood came to him as he saw the thing floating there under the lights. The first was of the rafts he'd had to build at scout camp, four oil drums lashed to a platform of beams and slats, bobbing on the surface of the water as if ready to topple at any moment. The second was of the constructor sets he'd played with as a child, pre-drilled sections of metal and plastic held together with nuts and bolts, the same components used dozens of times over to make beams and levers and supports. The upper surface of the raft seemed to be covered with the stuff, boxy mechanical shapes studded with bolt-heads, parts of it operating with jerky, repeated motions, like the interior of a wristwatch magnified a hundred times. At one corner of the thing one of the swimmers was feeding it with sections of plastic, the same distinctive bar shapes it seemed to be built from, while another swimmer was helping to support a vague construction of girders and plates coming out of the far end. It was a flimsy arrangement, bowing and flexing even as the man tried to hold it steady against the slight surface waves of the pool. If these new components were meant to be a copy of the original, they were some way off.

"This is our development facility," Victor said. "And this," he added with what he seemed to think was justifiable pride, "is our third prototype: the SRS-3."

Safi had got out of her seat and had moved down the table, leaning over to try to see the machine better. As the viewpoint continued to descend the details became clearer, although the false perspective of the projection was distorting the overall shape. Max got up too and moved round to her side, also hoping for a better view.

"Is that some kind of rudder arrangement, on the back there?" Safi said.

"Not just rudders," Victor said. "That's the propulsion system: four fins, independently actuated, or they will be once we get the motors installed."

"So it's mobile?"

"That's right."

"Does it need to be? It's a lot of added complexity, given it's in a fluid environment. Why not just anchor it and let the water run past?"

This time Ross answered. "Space, that's why," he said. "The sea is almost a mile deep in the operating site. If we're limited to the shallows then we'll run out of room in no time."

"Why not anchor them to each other? Like a giant raft?"

"That's a no go too," he said. "If they're all crowded together then only the ones on the edge will be able to replicate. That'll slow us down too much."

"And they need to be surface based?"

"If they're going to get power. We've got wind or solar to choose from, that's all."

"Plus, there's another big advantage to making them mobile," Victor said. "It means they can bring the gold to us instead of us going to them. When the population gets into the millions, that'll make a real difference."

"Basically, we've just got ourselves into the boat building business," Ross said.

Safi was still staring intently at the scene in front of her. "Those guys in the water," she said, "It looks like they're giving the thing its feedstock straight out. That can't be right? Or is there another type of replicator that does all the processing and metalwork?"

"No, Safi, that's it in its entirety."

"But that's just an assembler, you give it its component parts and it plugs the bits together. That's a long way from something that can replicate in the wild, from raw materials."

"We're doing an incremental approach," Ross said. "We started simple. Next we're going to modify it to add raw materials processing, and finally, the kind of chemical extraction it will need to get those materials out of the sea."

"And you reckon you'll have a full end-to-end replication cycle? One hundred percent closure?"

"That's the idea."

"And what are you running at now?"

"Well, some way less than that. But we're working on it."

Max looked from Safi to Ross, and then to Victor. There was a lot of jargon flying around all of a sudden — assemblers, feedstock, closure percentages — and although Safi seemed to know the subject, Max was beginning to feel left behind. He looked at Oliver, who hadn't left his seat but was leaning forward watching the exchange with his face screwed up in a frown. He might have been dazzled by the projection lights, or maybe the finer points were making as little sense to him as they were to Max. On one point however, Max felt more than qualified to comment.

"Victor, there's one thing that concerns me here. When these things — these machines or whatever you want to call them — when they're building copies of themselves, how do you know those new machines will behave the way you want them to?"

"I'm not sure I understand the question. Their behaviour will be programmed into them, copied from one to another. We'll decide how the new ones will behave, exactly as we decide how the first ones will behave."

"But you're talking about a copying process, and copying always involves errors. Usually they're small but they're always there. I don't think you can take it for granted that every machine that gets made will do exactly what you want it to."

"You're certainly right, Max, copying does involve errors, but errors can be corrected for. Whatever replication method we choose, we'll ensure that the appropriate checksums and digital protection schemes are in place. Built-in error testing is a well established technique. If a machine's program gets copied incorrectly, we can make it shut itself down."

Max wasn't so sure. "Victor, you obviously brought me in on this for a reason. It's up to you whether you listen to me or not, but my advice would be to think very carefully about what you're planning here. It's a lot more complex than the way you're describing it. Maintaining control isn't the foregone conclusion you think it is."

"The reason I asked you to come, Max, is to use your experience in evolutionary design to help refine the plans for these machines. Once we've done that, we'll freeze the design, build the first one, then set it replicating, as close to flawlessly as we can get it. We know very little about how we're going to achieve these objectives, but we know that the design task which is ahead of us will require some very advanced skills, which very few people are in a position to provide. Of course any views or advice you have will be listened to, but we want to hear about how we can do this, not how we can't."

He was making it sound so easy, Max thought, and yet they must have run into problems of some kind, otherwise why call this group together? Why recruit new faces at this late stage, when a company this size should have more than enough brainpower on their regular payroll? He didn't get the chance to ask any more though; Victor had already climbed down from the dais, his sales pitch complete. He struck Max as someone who liked to play the enthusiastic showman, but his breathlessness and the sheen of sweat on his forehead suggested that he rarely had the opportunity to get up and perform.

"Ross, why don't you go next?" he said as he retook his seat.

The room was still acting as one giant projection screen, but now the viewpoint had left the pool facility and was flying low over blue sunlit seas, the coast of an island to one side, a small tropical outcrop covered in thick vegetation from the shore right up to its peak.

"This is the place, folks," Ross said, standing up to take Victor's place. "If it looks idyllic, well that's probably because it is. I've not been down there myself yet but I'm told there are worse places to earn a living. We don't own the island, we just lease it, but we've worked with the government down there before and we have a standing arrangement, including free and exclusive use of over four thousand square miles of water. This is where you'll be living."

The island was small, barely four miles from one end to the other. On one side some small white buildings were visible, but the other side was dominated by a large, grey office building. It was built on terraces cut into the rock, like four huge steps leading away from the water. The lowest seemed to be a harbour; five or six vessels of various sizes were docked there. Elsewhere beaches were visible as little patches of white, tracing the outline of the coast. Max leant in, trying to see the facility better, to see what kind of place he was being asked to go to.

And then the view was gone, as the projectors switched off and the room's original decor returned. Max found himself suddenly incongruous, up out of his seat, staring at bare wall for no reason. He went back to his place, and Safi did the same.

"So, a few facts and figures," Ross said. "Basically, what have I been doing for the last six months? Well, if you look at your screens you'll see some predictions for material production rates, given the kind of extraction techniques I've been looking at. Algal cellulose and silicon, that's what we seem to have most of, so let's start there..."

By now the words were just washing over Max as he considered the implications of what was being planned. He looked round the others at the table and tried to guess what they were thinking. Victor was smiling and nodding at Ross's enthusiastic presentation. Safi was leaning forward, looking straight at Ross and hanging on his every word. Oliver was leaning toward Ross as well, but he was frowning and his brow was creased right up to where his reading light was reflecting off the grease in his hair. Nobody said a word as Ross took them through his part of the plan, a spirited and authoritative discourse on the usually tiresome subjects of marine chemistry and industrial materials processing.

By the end of the talk the spotlight was on Victor again, who spent the final ten minutes detailing contracts and terms of employment, the lengthy but necessary logistics relevant to anyone about to make a career-changing decision. When that discussion drew to a close, Victor called a halt to the proceedings, and called for Jane Glenday to come and lead them back to reception.

Max was last to leave the room as they filed out. He was almost out of the door when he stopped, and went back in to where Victor was shutting down the presentation.

"I want to make sure you've thought about what you're getting into here," he said. "You're talking about building something — and you still don't know exactly what that something will be — that's going to sit in open water with no constraints or safeguards other than what you decide to build into it, and that's going to spread exponentially as fast as you can make it spread. Doesn't that sound dangerous to you?"

"But Max, it's not as if we'll have our eyes closed while we're doing this. Any controls or safeguards that are needed will be in place from the start. That will be part of the job that we've set ourselves, planning for every eventuality we can think of."

"Yes, but it's the ones you can't think of that worry me."

"If this concerns you so much, Max, then surely that's all the more reason to join us. If you could see things done your way would that make you happier?"

"Implying that if I didn't sign up then you would go ahead anyway?"

"Certainly. That's true of Safi and Oliver as well as you. You'd all be assets to the programme, but there are always other people we could call in."

"Then I guess I'll have to let you know," he said, and headed for the door.

* * *

He called Indira as soon as he was out; an open-line omni link wasn't the place to discuss what he'd learned, but he'd promised her a courtesy call to at least tell her they were done. She smiled at him warmly when the call linked up.

"Max, it's good to hear from you. Do I take it you've spoken to Mr. Rioux?"

"Yes, we're finished," he said. "I just got out now."

"And do you think you can help them?"

"I'm not sure. In terms of the technical aspects of the project, maybe, but I'm going to have to think about what I've heard today."

She frowned slightly. "So what's your gut feeling?"

"If I'm honest? That bringing me, Gillian and two other people to Washington for a one-hour meeting was a flagrant waste of their flight quota."

Indira knew how he felt on the subject. Without intervention the GRACE point would have come just ten years previously, but already people were treating the measures that held it at bay like some kind of marketplace, as if the catastrophic extinction that formed the last two words of the acronym was something for governments and corporations to barter over. And if he took this job, he'd be giving up his place on the international monitoring programme that stopped things sliding back even further.

"But in terms of the project itself," he continued. "I'll have to let you know."

Indira nodded slowly, but didn't press him for more details. "So is Gillian looking forward to visiting her family?"

"She is, yes. We're driving out there tonight."

"Good, I'm glad. She must be as shaken up as you by those letters, some time away will probably do her good. How has she taken it all?"

Max hesitated; he knew the true answer wouldn't be received well, but the hesitation was obviously answer enough.

"You still haven't told her? Max, you must! If my husband kept something like this from me I'd be furious. Please tell her."

"We've never had one delivered at home, only at work. I don't want to worry her unless I absolutely have to."

"That's your decision of course." To Max that didn't sound nearly as judgmental as it might have done.

"So if I give you my report when I get back, we can take it from there?"

"Of course. Have a good journey Max."

Chapter 2

Max met up with Gillian later that day, picking her up from the hotel where she'd already checked out to get them on the road as quickly as possible. Then they headed away from DC, out toward West Virginia, the low sun already turning orange ahead of them.

"So, this hush-hush job offer that's so secret you couldn't even tell your own wife what it was about," she said from the passenger seat. "If you do end up saying no to it, what then?"

"Then we're back to the original plan," he said.

"So that means you're still going to Chile?"

He thought of the monitoring programme, and the school talks, and what might be waiting for him down there. "Yeah, it does," he said.

"Well, at least that's the option I'd prepared myself for. Six months away with one home visit, that's still the arrangement I assume."

"It is. Are you still okay with that?"

"I guess. I have stuff planned at least. Preparing for that San Diego exhibition will keep me pretty busy. It's still a long time for you to be away though. Especially if we want the go-ahead to start a family sometime soon."

"I know it is," he said. The hardest part about joining the GRACE programme had been the prospect of spending so much time away from home. It was important work, something he believed in just as passionately as the school talks he worked into each monitoring schedule, but leaving Gillian for months on end to go off counting endangered creatures was a big sacrifice.

"I'll be back before you know it," he said without conviction.

They drove another half hour or so before the freeway forked, one branch heading toward Charleston, and the forests to the east.

"Here we go," Max said as they got into lane. "No backing out now I guess."

"Oh, Max, try to make the best of it. It's been so long since I saw my family, if they knew I was so close and didn't visit they'd be really upset. I know you don't want to even go near the place, but please — one night can't be that hard can it?"

"And do I have to spend that one night sitting there with my mouth shut whatever gets thrown at me?"

"I'll talk to my dad when we get there if you like. If you want I'll say nothing, but I'll try my best."

"I'll let you know," Max said. He could see the dilemma she was in; opportunities to travel across the country were few and far between and her separation from her family was hard on her. Marrying Max had been an unpopular decision with some of her relatives and the chance to show she still valued them and wanted to be close to them wasn't something to give up lightly.

"I'll be with you the whole time," she said. "You can rant and rave all you want once it's over, just not tonight. I know it's hard."

For Max though, just being in the same room as people like that was hard. "I don't know, Gillian," he said. "I just can't get my head around people who live in the most enlightened, technically advanced age the world has ever known, but somehow manage to think the earth was created six thousand years ago. I mean, there are cave paintings in France older than that."

Gillian didn't answer, staring straight ahead as they drove, as if she hadn't heard what he'd been saying. Or maybe she knew what he was *really* saying, and didn't want to look him in the eye.

"Like that 'Freedom in Faith' book," Max said. "The one your dad always brings out. How many people have read that now? Swallowing every word of it as if it was true? If we have a child, do we really want them growing up in a world ruled by superstition and fear of the unknown?"

This time she answered. "What are you trying to do here, Max? Make me rise to the bait?"

"No, this isn't bait. I'm genuinely trying to understand what makes people believe things that bear no resemblance to the facts they supposedly explain. I've never been able to understand it."

"Because maybe there's more to this world than facts and conclusions and scientific method?"

"And that's the gap that religion fills? A system of belief in the supernatural so arbitrary and undefined that it comes in over a hundred different forms? Most of which have been at each others' throats at one time or another?"

"It's people who make wars, Max, not religions."

"But if those wars amount to little more than an argument over who's got the best imaginary friend? The responsibility has to lie somewhere."

She went silent again. The things he'd said were things he genuinely believed, but Max knew he'd pushed it too far, treated her unfairly. They'd agreed long ago not to let The Big Difference be the thing that defined their relationship, and for year after year it had worked. But in recent months the threats had strained Max's resolve like nothing had before and now he was breaking those rules, taking it out on her. Which was even worse considering he still hadn't been able to tell her about them. And still he couldn't say why.

Would she worry? Certainly she would, but that wasn't enough of a reason on its own, not for keeping something like this from her. Maybe it was more to do with what those people claimed to represent, what they claimed to be upholding, and how close that came to what Gillian herself believed. Was he protecting her from the realisation of what those who could be considered her allies were capable of? No, that didn't fit with his feelings either. There was a truth in amongst those feelings, a truth he was reluctant to face. Deep down he knew he was only protecting himself from the way she would react if she knew what his actions had brought upon them: actions aimed at furthering a view of the world which she saw as fundamentally flawed. There were a lot of old arguments on that subject, arguments they'd put behind them long ago, and opening them up again to explain why his choice of career had led to people threatening his safety, and hers, was not a course of action he wanted to take. But if she ever did find out — for the past year Max had tried not to think what that would be like.

They were halfway to her parents' place, the scenery outside dimming to shades of grey, when Gillian's omni rang with an incoming message. She checked the listed sender, then bit her lip and stared straight ahead. Max could tell she'd seen something she didn't like.

"What is it?" he said.

"It's the medical board," she said. "They've decided."

Max waited for her to open the message, unwilling to rush her when something so important was at stake. Eventually she plugged the omni into the car's viewer and brought up the message on the display in front of her. It took only seconds to read what was there.

"They said no, Max. We've been rejected."

Her voice was flat, emotionless. From that alone, Max could tell how hard the news had hit her.

"Did they say whether we can go through another round?" he said.

"We can, but it gets less likely each time."

"That's no reason not to try."

"No, you're right, it isn't."

Her tone however suggested she already saw it as a lost cause. And that at least was something Max would find hard to argue with. They were only thirty-five years old, but the longer a childless couple spent trying to get the go-ahead the less likely it became that the process would come down on their side.

"So what do we do?" she said.

Max paused. This had the potential to be a long and difficult conversation. "We can apply again," he said. "In fact we should do, no matter how unlikely it is. But if our names don't come up — I don't know what we'd do then. I'm starting to wonder whether we should just go for it, find somewhere we can pay for the treatments ourselves."

She shook her head, her usual stoic resilience obviously dented by the news. And with good reason; almost twenty percent of conceptions needed some kind of medical assistance these days, to counter the effects of the sea of chemicals and leaked synthetic hormones that made up the environment, and tests had confirmed that Max and Gillian were in that category. With the world's population already at unsustainable levels, the opportunity to ration those treatments was too tempting for those in control to pass up. The government had targets to meet: a decrease of twelve million people in the next fifty years, a twenty percent cut in industrial output. Sometimes it seemed they lived in a world defined by its rules: who could fly, who could drive, who could have children. They were necessary rules, internationally agreed between the free world nations, and Max more than most could see the need for them, but the restrictions were a strain that left few unaffected.

"Pay for them ourselves?" she said. "Where?"

"We go abroad and get treatment. Asia, North Africa, there are plenty of places."

"And how do we get there? Walk? No, Max, we'd never get a warrant to fly there, and they'd cripple us when we got back. I've seen it happen. Asha, that woman I exhibited with last year, she had to sell her home to cover the penalties. She thought it would be okay, but it wasn't."

Max looked over at her and nodded slowly. He was trying to look as sympathetic as he thought she expected him to be, but really his mind was on more practical matters, searching for things they could actually do to solve the situation they were in. Right now, he had no answers.

They went over it again after that, cycling through the

familiar territory of the barrier they'd come up against, suggesting then discounting one course of action after another, knowing that they'd have little new to add compared to the last time they'd discussed it, or the time before that. And all along they knew the answer was a simple one: just one little implant, fitted under Gillian's skin to monitor and modify her blood chemistry over the course of six months, to make normal conception and development a possibility.

"We can't do anything tonight," Gillian said eventually, a glimmer of her usual fortitude returning to her voice. "Let's get the griddex for the next application and try for that. We'll play up your qualifications and the job you're in, that might count for something."

Max was glad it was her that had decided to postpone further discussions. He knew how she felt, seeing their chance to start a family taken away so unfairly, but without firm suggestions, practical answers, he was lost.

"I'll find it when we get to your dad's," he said. "We may be able to get our names down early."

"Yes, do that," she said. "We'll be there in ten minutes. I'll call him now to say we're close. And Max, when we get there, try to keep things friendly, okay? My sister's bringing her fiancé over. He's from the church as well, but she says he really wants to meet you. And don't let my dad get to you. If you think he's trying to make you rise to it, then just — just don't, okay?"

"I'll do my best," Max said as she made the call. "That's all I can promise."

The house was up a forested hill, timber-built, like a large alpine cabin, with the steep slope to its rear and tall trees overhanging it on all sides. Theirs wasn't the only house here; the nearest neighbours were just a few hundred yards away, but the foliage and curving road hid any other signs of habitation. Max and Gillian got out of the rental car and climbed the short steep pathway to the door.

"Gillian, my girl," her father said when he answered. Ira Letz was a stocky white-haired man, his face creased and ruddy, thick arms covered in more coarse white hair. Even the backs of his hands and fingers had that same wiry coating. He held Gillian tight, then took her by the shoulders and held her facing him while he looked her in the eyes. A protective gesture, but one of protection by restraint. "Everything okay? You keeping well?"

"Yes, Dad, I'm fine," she said. "Really good."

Then she moved inside leaving Max on the doorstep facing her father.

"Max," her father said, looking him in the eye. They shook hands, but from a distance, leaning in to avoid coming too close and never taking their eyes off each other. Then Ira went inside, leaving Max to bring in the bags and close the door behind him.

The interior was dimly lit, low-level table lights illuminating the dark woodwork and quilt-draped furniture, a musty smell in the air. A haphazard collection of pictures lined the walls, some paintings by Gillian, others were family photographs, many of her brother, Luca, before his death. Max dropped the bags by the door and went over to where Gillian was greeting her mother. Derry Letz remained seated — they'd heard she was weaker now — and held Gillian's hands in her own.

"Max, it's good to see you," Derry said when Max went to Gillian's side. Her voice sounded as frail as she looked. "I hope you're taking good care of my daughter."

"I am, Derry, as best as I can."

Derry turned back to Gillian, still holding her hands. "Your sister wants to introduce someone," she said. Laura was sitting on a sofa off to the side, and stood up as Gillian approached. They hugged, gushing greetings, but it was Laura's companion, standing behind her, who caught Max's attention. He'd heard the guy's name was Roy, but beyond that hadn't known what to expect from this tall, smartly dressed young man, all broad shoulders and thick sandy hair. Though it was the pin he was wearing on his chest that told Max exactly where Roy's priorities lay, with its green and purple design of hands and stars encircling the world. "The Children of the Faith", Max immediately recognised that high profile, well-funded group, whose ability to get whole laws redrafted in line with religious teaching had brought them to his attention a number of times.

"Max, hi, I've heard a lot about you," Roy said when they were introduced. Max wondered exactly what he had been told; the greeting was friendly enough, but tinged with a look of curiosity, a hint of 'so this is what a Darwin worshipper looks like.'

They stayed in the lounge, drinking coffee and juice, while Gillian's parents caught up on what she'd been doing and where she'd been exhibiting her artwork. Max sat out of that part of the discussion, allowing them their family time before the conversation moved on to other things. It was when Ira brought up the subject of children that Max knew the first potential minefield had been reached.

"Are you ever going to make us grandparents?" he asked Gillian. "Your mother and I have waited so long, it's what we've wanted for you for such a long time."

"I want to, Dad, Max and I both do," Gillian said, the strain of the situation evident in her voice. "But we'd need treatments, most people do these days, and it only ever gets harder to get through the process."

"Excuse me, what process?" Roy asked from the far sofa.

"California runs a lottery-based treatment programme. It's not all random, you can get a preferential weighting, but you still need to get your name selected if you're going to have a child."

"But if it's going to be loved, isn't that all that matters?" Roy said. "Are you suggesting you should deny a child its chance at life just on someone else's say so?"

"We're not suggesting that at all. But they're trying to get the population down, and they can only have so many millions of births a year. These fertility treatments aren't something normal people can just pay for, they're controlled."

"It seems a messed up kind of law that tells a mother she can't have the children she's always wanted," Ira said.

"We keep applying," she said. "With Max being in such a good job, that gives us a better chance than most."

"Sounds pretty ironic to me," Ira said. "An evolutionist being told he's not allowed to have children unless his number comes up. Survival of the fittest? Or the luckiest?"

"I wouldn't say that," Max said, pretending not to have noticed the jibe. "The laws have to be the same for everyone. It's just the world we live in now."

"The world that science has given us you mean," Ira said. "Ice caps half melted, hurricanes in every state, oceans turned to poison. Is that 'just the world we live in' too?"

Max sighed inwardly; it hadn't taken long. "It was men with axes and chainsaws that deforested Brazil, nothing more. It's greed that's got us where we are now, unconstrained industrialisation. We're the generation that has to put the brakes on, put those constraints back in place. It's not pleasant, but there we are. The kind of work I do helps us develop new technology without doing the damage. That's what science has to be for."

"So that's why you just flew across the country, when most people will never get to fly in their lives? Why you're flying to Chile in a few weeks' time?"

"The Chile trip is part of the GRACE controls, it's vital work. It's one of the world's hotspots for new extinctions, and there have to be biodiversity surveys if we're going to minimise the damage."

"Or maybe if you'd never tampered in the first place, you wouldn't need to."

Max didn't reply. He had plenty he could say, but the talk of GRACE controls and tampering with nature was getting dangerously close to the subject of the Children of the Faith, and the reasons for that group's establishment, and it wasn't somewhere he wanted to go. Fifteen years ago, when the point of no return seemed unavoidable — the Geometric Rate of Catastrophic Extinction itself, just around the corner — the advent of apocalyptic religious groups was an almost inevitable consequence of human psychology. The idea that God's Earth was about to be destroyed by the activities of those same scientists who denied God's creation in the first place must have been irresistible to those predisposed to such beliefs. Including, judging by his lapel pin, Gillian's soon-to-be brother-in-law.

"So, Max, where did you grow up?" Roy asked. The question was harmless enough — an attempt to defuse an uncomfortable discussion, maybe, or to move on to other things — but Max had been on edge since the moment he'd entered the house and couldn't help looking for an angle, or speculating on what Roy had already been told.

"I was born in London," Max said. "But we lived in Toulouse for a few years, then my father's job moved to Palmdale when I was four."

"What was your father like?"

"He brought me up well," Max said, wondering what kind of answer was expected. "As well as I hope to bring up any children I may have. He taught me to think for myself, think rationally and objectively, not just follow the herd." He wondered if he'd been too obvious with that last comment, but it reflected his mood. None of Gillian's family seemed to react.

"And what did he do?"

"He was in the space programme. He designed science packages for space probes, planetary landers." That was less overt, but if anything more likely to get a reaction.

"Spreading man's corruption into the cosmos too then," Ira said.

"Most of what we know about Callisto and Europa is due to instruments he designed," Max said, as calmly and flatly as he could manage.

"So tell me this," Ira said. "With the world like it is, and rules about who can turn their lights on and who can take a plane ride and who can have children, why are we still sending people up there? Why do we have these space planes and bases on the Moon and people going to Mars?"

The answer was a simple one, and one that Max was prepared to stick to for as long as it took whenever this question came up. "Humanity needs to be a multi-world species," he said. "If there's one thing we've learned in the last fifty years it's that one world isn't enough. It's too fragile. Even if we didn't have these problems with industrialisation and pollution, all it would take is one big asteroid strike and we'd be gone, like the dinosaurs. We need to spread out. The world being in this state only makes it more urgent, not less." He hadn't had to mention the dinosaurs, but sitting among people who believed giant reptiles died out in Noah's flood, it was hard to pass up the opportunity.

"And why did you fly here?" Gillian's mother hadn't spoken a word throughout the whole exchange, sitting next to Ira, watching Max intently. "It's good to see Gillian and all, but what could be so important that they fly you here just for four days?"

In fact Derry and Laura had both maintained an obedient silence throughout the discussion. It seemed to be lesson number one of being a Letz family female: keeping quiet while the men talked grown-up. It was something Max was glad Gillian had left behind her.

"Max has had a job offer," Gillian said. "They wanted him to come to Washington to talk face to face about it."

"Does that mean you'll be living here?" Derry said.

"No," Max said. "It's not a job as such, more a project that UCLA could have contracted me out for, but I won't be taking it."

"Why not?"

"I don't agree with what they're doing."

Ira visibly stirred at that; the idea of the Darwinist having principles must have seemed out of place.

"What exactly are they doing?" Roy again, another probing question thrown in from the far side of the room.

"They're, ah, they're testing a new technology, but I think it could do more harm than good."

"Like technology always has, you mean?"

"What do you mean?"

"Nothing, apart from the fact that this 'progress' as it's called has only ever brought suffering to the world. And men like you have been at the forefront."

So Roy was making more than just polite conversation; there was an angle after all. "I don't think the people whose lives have been saved by vaccines and medical scans and clean water supplies would think so," Max said. "Or maybe you'd prefer to have lived when average life expectancy was thirty and infant mortality ran at fifty percent?"

"Compared with now? When no one can have children at all without a say so from the government and a gut full of medicines?"

"We've got problems," Max said. "The world has a lot of problems. But I'm not the one who made them. Previous generations who didn't know what they were doing, maybe. Those who did and should have known better, sure. But right now you have to look further east for the real culprits. Half the restrictions we've imposed on ourselves as a society are because the Chinese are refusing to cut back, and they know they can afford to defy us because if we pollute as much as they are then the whole biosphere will die out. It's a dangerous game they're playing, but they know we can't afford to oppose them, that all we can do is fix the damage they're doing as they're doing it and try to keep our own half of the world functioning. They're not getting off lightly either — those Shanghai flood defences couldn't last forever — but they know they've got us cornered. They're having the same problems as us, as far as we can tell — heavy metals and hormone analogues in the water, epidemic infertility — but they can afford to stonewall us when we try to make them play fair. So don't blame me for the mess. If we switched off all the power stations and went to live in the forests, we would *not* have a better life."

There was silence after Max had finished. He hadn't meant to turn it into a lecture, but it was hard to keep it in when he felt this challenged. He felt he'd crossed a line though, and Gillian would find it hard to forgive him if he let a full blown fight develop.

"Anyway, I'm tired after the drive," he said. "I'm going to head up early. Derry, it's been good to see you, Gillian, I'll see you later on. Goodnight."

* * *

He checked his work messages and news updates on his omni as he lay there, fishing the small black tablet out from around his neck to open up its viewer. Then, remembering something Ross had said back in the ESOS presentation, he went to the UCLA site and opened up the Cambria page. And what he saw on that sunlit, rock-strewn landscape didn't surprise him one bit.

Down below him, framed by the soft green glow of the view-screen controls, the creatures were swarming. The gathering was one of the largest he had ever seen, at least twenty thousand on each side, covering the slopes and valley floor which lay between the two groups. That they had come here to fight was beyond doubt.

He descended, taking in the individuals, counting off the species and castes that were present: the shielders with their low, squat bodies flaring out like barricades; the mantis-like throwers, their elongated upper limbs as accurate as they were strong; and the chargers, their blood-red crests curving outward and downward like devils' horns.

And then it began. As if some invisible signal had spread

down the lines the front ranks advanced, immediately fanning out to broaden their front and increase their speed. Like avalanches of armour and muscle they raced down the slopes towards each other and onto the valley floor, as the volleys of rocks from the throwers thickened overhead. Even when they collided, piling up like tectonic ranges of roiling, seething carnage, the charge barely slowed. By the time the last fighters reached the middle, half their predecessors were dead and the count was still rising.

For six years now the experiment had been running, a vast digital ecosystem playing out like some enormous game where the only players were the simulated organisms who inhabited it. It was partly a research tool into the emergence of biodiversity, partly a UCLA PR exercise with interested members of the public offering up spare processor time to help run the code. Though for most if its time it had been the scene of one pitched battle after another as the surviving species savaged each other for the limited food supplies that remained.

This was what this place had produced. From those simple beginnings, those blind, stupid creatures with barely enough brains and body parts to keep themselves alive, this was what the rules of the game had created. Increase the mutation rate, accelerate the divergence, and suddenly a simulated ecosystem that should have rivalled the Amazon rainforest turns into a bloodbath.

Was this why the ESOS proposal made him so uneasy? On the surface there was no comparison — their machines would be built *not* to mutate, *not* to evolve — but still something about it was gnawing at him.

He closed down the viewer and made the sign to switch off the omni altogether. Then he saw another message, this one from his colleague, John Olson, back in L.A. It wasn't long, just a cryptic note from John's UCLA address, something about the delivery they'd both been waiting for having arrived at last. Max smiled; at least he had something to look forward to. Then he shut down for good and turned off the light, hoping to get some rest.

He was still awake when Gillian came up. He wondered if she'd be mad with him for missing dinner, snubbing her family, but instead she lay down next to him and said "you okay?" She stroked his hair.

"Yeah, it was just getting to me, that's all."

"I know it was. I think Roy likes you, if it's any consolation."

Max snorted, genuine disbelief. "Really?"

"He said he hopes you didn't take anything personally, that you seemed a pretty regular guy."

Max couldn't think of a reply; he looked at the ceiling instead while she continued to stroke him.

"Did you see that company wrote to us?" Gillian said eventually. "The one you went to today?"

"What do you mean?"

"It was addressed to both of us, it'll be on your omni as well. Some kind of terms and conditions form for that job."

Max sat up and reached over. This time he opened the home account and sure enough the message was there: a document attachment showing more legal small print concerning the terms of the offer. Nothing confidential, just the dry output of the ESOS human resources department.

"Look at this bit," Gillian said, pointing to one of the items in the contents list. It was described as "Medical Aspects". Max squinted in, looking at the size of the font and its position near the top of the list. It had been done subtly, but it almost looked as if it had been placed there to be noticed.

He followed the link, and yet again felt his eyes drawn to one particular paragraph.

Full class II medical facilities are available at the Area of Operations (AO). These facilities are owned and run by ESOS, and are available to all employees, resident contractors and their families. Note that due to the location of the AO, these facilities are not subject to international regulations concerning corrective surgery, fertility treatment and genetic screening.

"Where is this place?" Gillian said. "I guess not Washington if they can get round the rules like that."

"No, it's in the South Pacific somewhere."

"And you said you'd be there for a year?"

"That's right."

"So they must let families go with people if it's so far, right? That must be why they sent this to both of us, because we'd both be going?"

Max nodded; he knew exactly where Gillian was headed.

"It means we could get treatment there," she said. "We could have children, without having to get through the appeals. Do you read it like that too?"

"I do," Max said. And that's exactly how we were meant to read it, he thought.

"Are you sure you can't go?" she said.

How presumptuous are these people? Max thought. How presumptuous to send this to Gillian? Do they know how much we want children? Is that why they're doing it?

"This thing they're planning, this job they're bringing people in on," he said. "I've got some pretty serious doubts about what they're doing. I'm not sure getting involved would be a good idea."

"You think it might not work? That doesn't stop you signing up if there are benefits like this though, does it?"

"I'm not doubting it'll work, quite the opposite. It's what happens after that. I think they're doing something that might get out of hand, out of control."

Her expression changed at that point, hope turning to hurt and disappointment. "Max, this could be the best thing that ever happened to us, and you're saying no because the job sounds like a bad career move? How can you do that?"

He realised how it must have sounded to her. He rolled over and put his arm round her, but she didn't respond.

"I can't tell you what they're doing," he said, aware of the need to choose his words carefully, "but imagine if someone said they were going to let a new virus loose and just cross their fingers that it didn't mutate: that's how much of a bad idea it is."

Gillian was just looking at the ceiling. "If it was that dangerous then it would be illegal. And anyway, if you think it's so stupid, why not go and make sure they do it right?"

Max all but jumped; Victor had said almost the exact same thing. "I don't know Gillian, my gut feeling is to say no. I've had a bad feeling about it ever since that meeting."

"And you're willing to take away our chance of having children based on a gut feeling?"

Again the consequences of saying no had been brought home to him. He marvelled at how effectively he'd been railroaded; just minutes ago he'd been dead set against going, and now, with this one message, that choice would bring more pain to him and Gillian than he could imagine.

He thought about the job again, about the scale of the project and the likely consequences. Could copying be carried out flawlessly, time after time after time? Almost certainly yes, but to do those replications in parallel, with a population in the millions? How many opportunities for error did that make? And how bad could they be? A sudden image filled his mind, inappropriately comedic, of Victor's machines swimming round endlessly until there was nothing left of the sea except distilled water and a few boulders.

"I'll think about it," he said.

* * *

Max went into work the day after he and Gillian got back. He knew Indira wanted to see him to talk about the ESOS job, and he knew he had more preparations to make for the GRACE trip, but neither of those was at the top of his list. Instead he went straight to the lab block where John Olson was waiting.

"Well," Max said, as soon as he was through the door. "Where are these new arrivals of yours?"

"I didn't think you'd be able to stay away," John said, smiling. "Come with me, I'll show you where they are."

They left John's office, and went down to one of the labs in the basement. "It's a pity you picked this time to leave," John said as they walked. "If you weren't Gracing the South Pacific with your presence this project would have you written all over it."

"Tell me about it. It's been too long since I did any real research."

John nodded. "Ever since the Australians started digging this stuff up we knew we had to get our hands on some of it. Sure you don't want to cancel the Chile trip and stick around?"

Max smiled thinly. "You never know."

They got to the lab and John led them inside, stopping at one of the benches that lined the room. "Right, here we are," he said.

In front of Max, only just unpacked from the protective case in which they'd arrived, was a pile of rocks. Max walked over to the lab bench and picked one of them up in one hand. It was about the size of a house brick, dull, grey, and completely nondescript in shape. If it wasn't for what they knew about its origins on the muddy seafloor of an ancient ocean, it wouldn't have been worth a second look. However its age, and the stunning level of preservation of the bacterial fossils inside it, made it easily the earliest example ever found of recognisable terrestrial life. How close to the beginning it really was, and what form that mysterious first ancestor may have taken, were questions that John and his colleagues were about to try and answer.

"How much material have they got now?" Max said.

"About twenty tonnes so far, with bacterial fossils all the way through. But it's the diversity that's really got people worked up.

They're too varied for something this old. I mean *way* too varied."

"How accurately do we know their age?"

"Almost four billion years. It's the closest thing to the beginning we've ever seen."

"Yeah, and the closest we're ever likely to see. So what are you going to do next?"

"Radiological scans first, then we'll start layering them and loading them into the 'scope.'"

"Well, just make sure you tell me first if you find anything."

"Of course I will."

* * *

Max went home after that, going in through the garden entrance where he knew he'd find Gillian. She was in the small workshop she used as a studio, doing the roughing-in for a forest background on one of her latest pieces. Max drew up a stool and perched off to the side where he wouldn't get in her eye line.

"So you've seen your lumps of rock then?" she said, a sarcastic edge to her voice. "We've got more out there in the flowerbeds if you're really interested?" That had pretty much been her tone ever since Max had said no to ESOS: subdued rather than angry, distracted rather than argumentative, her rarely-seen cynical side coming to the fore. He knew she still wished he'd said yes, as much as he knew she understood his reasons for saying no.

"Yeah, I've seen them," Max said. "It looks like they've got some interesting times ahead of them."

"Do you wish you were there too?"

"Maybe. I seem to have no shortage of projects I could go for right now, one more choice wouldn't hurt."

Max was inwardly glad that his transition from evolutionary biologist to evolutionary engineer had happened so smoothly.

Even now it let him cherry pick interesting jobs from his old line of work, when time permitted.

"Did you get everything done today?" he said, watching her work.

"Pretty much," she said. "The bigger canvases are in the gallery's store room, they'll be slotting the smaller ones in today and tomorrow. Friday was our last proper day. Busy though. Must have had fifty people come through just in the afternoon."

"Some kind of last minute rush?"

"Maybe. Someone was trying to take pictures though, it set the detectors off. No way of telling who with that many people in there."

"Is that even a problem if the show's almost over?"

"It's gallery policy. And anyway I'd prefer it if I didn't see unauthorised prints turning up on the grid, don't you think?"

"Yeah, I suppose. You do have to sell the things after all."

She didn't reply.

"Do you want a drink?" he said. "I'm going to get some juice."

"No, Max, I'm fine."

He got off the stool and made his way out into the garden, then in through the back of the house. And that was when he saw the envelope, sitting on the mat under the front door.

He knew what it was the moment he saw it up close, its printed address label showing the source point somewhere in rural Idaho. The location seemed a random one, almost deliberately random when compared to the previous ones, as if whoever was sending them was going out of their way to avoid any telltale patterns.

Though, until now, they'd never sent one to his home.

He listened out for Gillian, the unopened letter in his hands; she was still out there, busy on her picture. He offered silent thanks that she hadn't got to the letter first, then looked over the outside of the envelope while he decided what to do.

He felt its weight and flexibility; there was no indication of anything other than paper in there. He thought about taking it to the campus for the security staff to check it over, or even straight to the police, but something inside him wanted to know what it was right now, without delay.

The letter was open and unfolded in front of him before he even knew what he'd done, his hands having made the decision for him. The realisation of what it said — and the cold, dead feeling in his stomach — weren't far behind.

January–February 2040: Atelognathus Nitoi / Dromiciops Gliroides habitat survey, Valdivian forest Protected Zone

February 15 2040: Colegio Gregorio Quinteo, Puerto Montt

February–March 2040: Rhodopis Vesper population study, Azapa Valley

April 10 2040: Colegio San Martin, Santiago

April 18–May 4 2040: Myotis Atacamensis survey

May 10 2040: Escuela Preparatoria Internacional, Antofagasta

The list continued, a comprehensive account of every research trip, every study and field assignment he'd planned, worded the same way as his own equivalent lists and records, including the school visits and Darwinist lectures he'd be fitting in between them.

There were pictures too though, of him and of Gillian, the ones of him taken in and around the campus, the ones of Gillian taken at her recent exhibition. The last of them even showed her standing next to one of her paintings, a crested caracara on a Baja California tree branch. The photographer in the crowd, the one who'd set off the detectors — they'd actually walked into the gallery and stood right next to her. They'd got that close.

The final line of the note simply read: *Three times already we've got close enough to kill you both. Still feel safe?*

Max dropped the papers to the floor, and leant back against the doorframe for support. Who are these people? he thought, again and again. Who is doing this to us?

Then his omni rang, the office number showing in its display strip. He answered, hands trembling.

"Max, it's Indira, you need to be aware: we've had another of those letters delivered."

She looked genuinely concerned, as she had been all the way through the ordeal.

"I've had one too," Max said. "It's about the GRACE project."

"It sounds like the same one. Look, Max, I can't send you to Chile now, not after this. It would be too much of a risk. I want you to take that ESOS position. I haven't had your report on it yet but they've been in touch today to reiterate how much they want you. I can't imagine you being unsuitable for the post."

Max hadn't given her his report because he hadn't written it yet. He simply couldn't think of what to say, how to take the limited amount he could tell her and boil it down to the "yes" or "no" she wanted to hear. Or the "no" he wanted to give her.

"Do I get a say?"

"You do, of course, if there's a burning reason not to go."

"Well, I'd be working away from home for a year, we'd have to rent the house out, I mean —"

"We can help with that, Max, you know we can. You wouldn't be the first person we've sent on external detachment. Why, are you thinking of turning this down? I need to give them a good reason if so."

Again he thought about the incentives they'd shown him, the medical package, and how much it would mean to Gillian and to him. It felt like bait though: bait that he was about to walk in and take with his eyes wide open. The decision was hard, but inevitable.

"I'll do it," he said. "I'll go."

He told Gillian as soon as Indira had rung off. Gillian's yell of joy was still ringing in his ears minutes later as they stood in her workshop, her arms fast around him, holding him tight.

Chapter 3

The pool building was large, a wide echoing structure of metal frames and sheets enclosing the ESOS marine test facility. It was hot too, the same punishing humidity as the rest of the island, but here, confined, amplified. Victor led the four of them in then took them over to one corner where the SRS-3 prototype was sitting high and dry on its support rig. There they stopped, Victor and Ross to one side of the machine, Max, Oliver and Safi to the other.

In a way Max was surprised that the other two had signed up. He didn't know their backgrounds, but for Safi and Oliver to have made the break and come all this way for a year couldn't have been easy. Neither of them seemed to have close family though; they'd both come out alone, unlike Max and Ross whose wives had shared the plane ride down with them.

"So, here we are," Victor said. "Here's what you're going to be working on. Quite an opportunity, I think you'll agree."

Max stepped up to the rig and examined the machine more closely. It was even more makeshift than it had looked in the projections, roughly formed lengths and sheets of plastic bolted together to form gears, levers and pushrods.

"Okay, I can kind of see what you were aiming at," Safi said, having also come in for a closer inspection. "You're trying to keep the parts count down, that's a good first step."

"Exactly," Victor said. "There are over two thousand components to this machine, but they're drawn from a parts list of just thirty: we have three sizes of bar, four sizes of sheet, just one bolt design used universally, plus peripheral items like motors and flotation cells."

"And have you demonstrated a replication cycle yet?"

"To an extent. This is a third generation machine: SRS-1 built SRS-2, which then built this one."

"But it's still just an assembler, not a true replicator, right? It's not going to perform closed-cycle replication out there, in the wild?"

It was like the Washington meeting all over again, a sudden influx of jargon between Safi and Victor, with Max and — judging by the frown of confusion on his face, Oliver — both none the wiser.

"So what are we saying here," Max said. "Assemblers? Closed-cycle replication? If this machine isn't the answer you're looking for, then what is?"

"Sure," Safi said. "Excuse me, I guess I'm racing ahead here because I've been through this before. An assembler replicator is what you've got here: it works fine if you feed it ready-made components, but if you dropped it into the ocean, literally swimming in its raw materials, it wouldn't even know where to start. So you need to design in extra features, like the ability to pull materials out of the sea, and refine them. But there's a problem: if it's going to replicate it needs to be able to make everything it's made from, and every feature you add runs the risk of a snowballing effect. You add a furnace to the design for heat treating metal, you need to be able to *make* that furnace too. So you add a machine for making high current heating coils, but you need to be able to make *that* machine as well, and so on."

Max nodded; it made sense, and he could see it wouldn't be easy.

"So I'm assuming Payne's law has never occurred to you in all this?"

It was Oliver who had spoken. He'd stayed back from the machine, leaning nonchalantly against the wall, his look of confusion having turned to one of amusement, even smugness.

"Payne's law?" Safi said, "I'm sorry, I'm not familiar with that."

"The law saying that manufacturing machines can only make things less complex than themselves? Come on, you claim to be

William Mitchell

an engineer, you must have heard of it."

"I've got to be honest Oliver, I haven't."

"Well it should be fairly obvious on its own I would have thought."

"Okay, so, complex things only making simple things, I agree it kind of sounds like it should be true, but really it isn't. There's nothing fundamental to prevent machine replication from taking place, no laws or principles. You just need the technology, and the know-how. And the last one at least, I can provide."

"With all due respect to your abilities," he said, "I don't believe you can." Max felt the tone change at that point; the smile on Oliver's face suggested that respect was the last thing he had. "If something is fundamentally impossible, then nothing can change that."

"But machine replication has always been possible in theory," Safi said. "John von Neumann showed that over a century ago. That's even what people call replicators: von Neumann machines."

"But what good is theory if no one's ever done it?"

"Because someone has to be the first? Von Neumann developed the template, the outline, of how you could build a machine that would replicate itself. Building one for real wasn't possible then, and it wasn't possible for a long time afterward, but we can do it now."

"*That* I seriously doubt."

"But the work that von Neumann did —"

Oliver suddenly stood upright. "Von Neumann was an overrated crank! Just because he wasted his time building adding machines, everyone seems to think we owe him the world! I'm not surprised this idea was one of his. I'd have thought people nowadays would know better!"

Max couldn't help being slightly alarmed at the reaction Safi was getting. A simple design discussion had taken a turn for the bizarre. Victor chose that moment to intervene.

"Professor Rudd," he said calmly, "tell us what makes you think this is impossible."

Oliver sighed heavily. "Look," he said, pointing at an intercom box attached to the wall beside him. "I could design you a machine today that would build as many of these units as you wanted, but could you use one of those terminals to build the original machine? Could a hundred of them do it? Of course they couldn't. It's stupid."

Max had to think hard to see how this contributed to the argument. He couldn't.

"But what's that got to do with what we're talking about here?" Safi said. "If you want to build a machine that can copy itself then you design it to do just that. You don't design it to sit there pushing out comms terminals."

"But it cannot happen!" Oliver said. "It's never going to happen!"

"But that's what we've come here to do," Victor said. "To make it happen. As I said before, that's our aim, to design a self replicating machine that can extract gold from seawater."

"And as *I* said before, just how are you hoping to achieve that? If it's so easy, why bring us here, if your own people have been on it for months now?"

With that at least, Max agreed.

"Alright, I'll be honest," Victor said. "It's true we've hit problems. We're a marine company, our expertise is strong, but in a narrow field of engineering. We've got as far as we can with this. Full closure from raw materials is going to be tough. All three of you have something to offer, you, Oliver, plus Safi and Max. That's why I asked you to come."

Oliver leaned back against the wall, looking to the roof. "You want to build a machine to take gold out of seawater. Just standing here I can think of half a dozen ways of doing that: electrolysis plants, molecular filters, vapour centrifuges. Magic perpetual motion machines that can build themselves out of thin air aren't on that list. I can help you with the first ones, but no one can help you with the last one."

"But we're not talking about perpetual motion," Victor said. "And we're not trying to build things out of thin air. The methods you described will form part of what we design, just as they have done when people have tried to extract gold in the past. But without replication there's no point even trying because it'll cost more money than it makes."

"Then what are we doing here?"

"What are you doing here more like?" Ross said under his breath.

"Oliver," Safi said, quietly but persuasively, "I can prove this is possible because I've already done it. I've worked with replicating systems before. I can show you them operating if you want."

"I doubt that very much."

Safi paused. Max looked over to see how she would react.

"Okay, Oliver, would you class bacteria as capable of reproducing?" she said.

"Yes, of course I would," he said cautiously.

"But bacteria are simple compared to other living things. We understand how they work. We understand how they reproduce. You can write down all the chemical reactions that go on inside them and appreciate fully how they do it. There's no mystery there. Doesn't that make them a kind of machine?"

"Of course they're not machines!"

"So what are they then, supernatural? They follow rules, cause-and-effect physical laws. You could call them biological machines if you wanted to, but they're still machines. Replicating machines. Reproduction in animals and plants is the same, just more complex. Trust me, there's no magic to this."

Oliver didn't answer, and there was an uncomfortable silence before Victor stepped in.

"Safi, do you have anything you could show us from

Earthrise?

"Yes, sure." She seemed caught off guard in the wake of her exchange with Oliver, but collected herself immediately. "Just give me a moment and I can show you the whole thing."

* * *

The setting was unmistakable. As the five of them watched the projection from Safi's omni on the pool hanger wall, and saw the low rounded hills of the lunar landscape panning across the scene, it was as if those hills were close enough to reach out and touch, though equally there could have been miles between them. In fact the horizon itself was barely two miles away, but with no atmosphere to distort the scene, there was no indication of the distances involved.

The foreground however, when it panned into view, was a different matter. The six people who were now visible in the shot gave a very clear indication of distance, from the closest pair, just twenty feet away, to the furthest, barely visible on the screen as tiny white figures, standing by an open-topped rover. Behind them though, even further back, was the sight that really dominated the scene: the factory itself, a vast open framework of girders and struts, filling the screen from one side to the other and stretching just as far toward the horizon. It must have measured hundreds of yards in length if the perspective was to be believed, and was well over fifty feet tall at its highest point with a bewildering tangle of pipework, storage tanks and other machinery housed inside. Only when Max spotted the crew quarters clustered at one end did he accept the scale of what he was seeing. At first he hadn't believed that those tiny pinpricks of light really were windows, but now he could see the individual modules, and the pressurised walkways climbing up among the processing stacks. He was amazed he'd never heard of this place before.

"Okay, what you're seeing here is one of the Earthrise research sites," Safi said. "They set this up a few years after the base itself was established: twenty plots of real estate hooked up to the power and water lines, all set for anyone who wanted to do research there. My company rented one of the sites, and I was lucky enough to go."

"A real life astronaut," Ross said. "Nice one!"

"No, Ross, I was just a passenger, nothing more. My job started once we got there and did the engineering work."

"Safi here is being too modest," Victor said. "Going to the Moon back then wasn't an easy journey. Not that it's a day trip now of course, but Safi was one of the first real explorers. She was only the thirteenth woman ever to set foot there. I think you played more of an integral role in those expeditions than you're admitting."

She nodded, but didn't say anything.

"So what were you doing there?" Max said.

"Building a replicator," she said. "We wanted to build a self-replicating lunar factory. We figured it would revolutionise the way off-Earth mining and production is carried out: you start with one factory, and you end up with thousands, all working away under your control. Compare the situation at the moment. There isn't a single mining or factory project anywhere on the Moon that's managed to break even, but the resources available there are huge."

"And that's just one factory, what we're seeing there?"

"Yeah, that was our first site, the grandfather site, it would have been."

"Would have been?"

"There was an accident a couple of years in. We shut things down after that."

"What kind of accident?"

Safi went quiet for a second as if considering how best to answer. "A fatal one," she said. It was clearly not a subject to dwell on.

"So can we see you there?" Ross said, pointing to the image on the wall.

"Yeah, you can see me, in the middle distance there. Look for the one with the yellow ID patches."

"Oh yeah," Ross said, straining to make her out. "Cool. Who's that with you?"

"That's Niall West, he was the project leader."

"So how far had you progressed when this was taken?" Victor said.

"We'd finished Anchorville a couple of months earlier. Excuse me, Anchorville was what we called this place. We were using this one to build Bakerville, then that was going to build Cooperville. We always built replicators over three generations, ever since the first lab tests."

"How come?" Max said.

"I'm assuming, the same reason they built three of these things," she said, indicating the ESOS machine beside her. "You need to prove that any copy you build can go on to make further copies. That way the ability to replicate gets passed down along with everything else. It's an important test."

"So, tell us what we're seeing there," Victor prompted.

"Oh, okay, that's one of the mining trucks." A large six-wheeled vehicle had just emerged from an opening at one end of the structure and was heading off to the side of the shot. As it did so another one approached in the opposite direction, loaded to capacity with rocks and soil.

"We had a couple of mining sites out to the east there. We had to shift a lot of dirt to get the materials we needed."

"From lunar regolith? Yeah, I can imagine," Ross said.

Then the picture changed. The setting was similar, but where there had been a fully functional factory, now all they were seeing was a bare skeleton. It was easy to recognise as a copy of the first site, but was far from complete. For almost half of its length it was a mere outline, pillars and supports driven into the ground but so far unconnected. More vehicles were visible in this shot, but these were clearly construction vehicles, equipped with earth movers, cranes and robotic manipulators. They could be seen fitting sections of machinery together as other vehicles brought the parts in from elsewhere.

"Okay, this is Bakerville," Safi said, "about two months into construction. When we built Anchorville we had to ship every part of it in via the Crisium base, but everything we're using here is coming from Anchorville itself. Even the power is free."

"How far apart are the two sites?" Victor said.

"About half a mile," she said. "Not far at all."

They could almost see the new site taking shape, even as they watched.

"Impressive," Victor said, nodding.

"Right, a couple of things occur to me here." It was Oliver; he'd moved round to see the projection but was still standing back from the others. "Those mobile fabricators. What kind of automation were you using on them?"

"None at all, they were operated by the drivers," Safi said.

"They were what? I thought you said these things were meant to work autonomously?"

"Yes, they would have done, eventually."

"And how exactly was that supposed to happen?"

"Easy, we'd have installed a central computer, running all the production lines and vehicles. Just like —"

"Easy? Have you any idea how much work it takes to automate something that size? No, no, it's a massive job. You'd have given up within weeks."

"We built it precisely so that we *could* automate it. Niall wanted to run it as a crewed facility for the first replications, then let it self-replicate later on."

"What? The mining operations, the chemical extractors, the fabricators? You thought you could just flick a switch and suddenly it would work on its own?"

"Yes, Niall designed it that way himself."

Oliver snorted contemptuously. "In that case this Niall character was either very intelligent or very deluded. And I think I know which."

Safi looked at him icily. It was almost as if she couldn't believe what she'd just heard. Again Victor stepped in.

"Safi, thank you for showing us that, I'm sure your experiences will be very useful to us in our work here." He sounded as if he was trying to reassure her: maybe not something she'd appreciate, Max thought. Then Victor turned to the others. "Let's all take a break now shall we, we can carry on later."

Then he reached over to the screen and paused the clip, which had been running continuously as they'd talked. It was now showing the inside of the Anchorville airlock, as the crew re-entered and began to remove their suits. The chamber looked crowded with all of them in there, especially the two at the head of the group, the tall, crew-cut man at the front and the woman standing next to him. His head was almost touching the ceiling as he looked into the camera, a broad smile on his face and the name badge, "Niall West", fixed to his chest. She looked young, fresh faced and attractive, with her long fair hair spilling down the back of her pressure suit now that her helmet had been removed. Her name badge wasn't visible, but as she stood there next to her team leader, smiling up at him warmly, she wasn't hard to recognise.

* * *

"Hi, Max! I thought I'd start the unpacking without you. Hope you don't mind."

Gillian had come to the door to meet him when he got back. The house was a single storey villa, with a living area leading out to a terrace, and a kitchen in a large alcove. The shelves and refrigerator were already stocked up when they'd arrived. As a home it was comfortable, but nothing special. They'd only been able to bring a few cases of possessions with them, but she'd found places for everything and already it felt more like a home.

"Looks like someone's woken up since this morning," he said, squeezing her tight. "So what have you been doing today?"

"I got up just after you left and went off to do some exploring. Did a few pictures too. No one here to sell them to, but what the hell. In fact there's not much of anything round here is there? Oh, and I met Tess down on the beach, we must have walked at least a mile without seeing another person. Did you know she's a journalist? A pretty successful one too. I'd wondered why her name was familiar."

She was talking fast, gabbling even, as if brimming over with excitement. She'd pinned a lot of hopes on their arrival there, like it was a kind of salvation for the ambitions that had been so mercilessly thwarted over the last few years.

I hope she's not in for a disappointment, Max thought. It's a long way to fall. "Yeah, Tessa Whelan. You're right, I've heard of her. Is she going to carry on working while she's out here?"

"I don't think so. Sounds like the job was getting too much for her and coming out here with Ross was a good excuse to get away from it."

"Good, I'm glad you're not the only ESOS widow." That had been one of his fears, that despite her eagerness to come here, being yanked out of her normal existence would leave her feeling isolated.

"So, how did whatever-it-is go today? Are you making any progress?"

"I don't know, it was an interesting start. Oliver Rudd caused us a few problems. I've got a feeling he's going to carry on that way."

"Oliver? He hardly said two words to us on the way down. What did he do?"

"Tried to start an argument, basically. Seems like something touched a nerve. I don't know, he's either very very clever or very very stupid, I've not figured out which yet."

"Unlike you to not have judged his IQ on sight. Has your ESP deserted you?"

"It must have."

"So what about Safi? What's she like?"

"She's the one telling us how to do everything, so far anyway."

"I take it she's not married if she came here on her own?"

Max shook his head. "I don't know, I haven't asked. I saw your new car outside by the way."

"Yes, it was there when I got back from my walk. It was a bit of a surprise, you didn't tell me I'd be getting a car."

"I didn't know until today either, but we've all been given one. Looks like everything on the island is too spread out for walking anywhere."

"Well, it's good I can get around the place, because there's something else I did while you were away."

"What was that?"

"I found out where the company medical centre is, and got us booked in for a consultation. We're seeing them on Saturday morning, I hope that's okay?"

"Yes, sure, that's more than okay. Did you find out what they can do for us?"

"Everything. The full hormone course, IVF if necessary, full monitoring right through to term."

"That's great," Max said. "That's wonderful." And seeing how happy she was, he meant it.

"So, if we're going to be trying soon, why don't we get some practice in?"

She didn't need to ask twice, but smiled instead, and led him through to the rear of the house.

* * *

When Max turned up at the ESOS facility the next day, Safi was there ahead of him. She was in an alcove away from the poolside, with some kind of engineering drawings projecting onto a nearby screen. At first it looked like she'd come in early and was keeping herself busy until the others arrived. It was only when he asked how long she'd been there that he found out she'd never actually gone home.

"I could see some faults with their assembler design, so I thought I'd fix it for them. It didn't take long, just a few hours once I'd realised I had to start from scratch."

Max hesitated, wondering if she was joking with him. There was no sign of sarcasm on her face, but no sign of tiredness either. And behind her, on the wall, a very different design was being projected: the schematics had zoomed out to something more like a streamlined catamaran than the ramshackle raft ESOS had created.

"You're serious? You were in all night?"

"Sure. That's normal for me, I can never sleep when I can see a problem that needs fixing, so there's no point trying."

"So, hang on — that design they've been working on for almost a year — you're saying you did the same thing but better, single-handed, in one night?"

She didn't seem to want to say yes in a way that might sound conceited, but had to admit that it was true.

And Victor and Ross, when they arrived with Oliver, were similarly impressed. Although the design only existed in her omni, she could simulate a replication cycle clearly enough to show the thing in action. It was still no closer to a raw material replicator, but just looking at it working showed how much more elegant it was than what had gone before.

"The through flow of components is much more natural this way," she said, pointing out features of the machine. "When we add materials and extraction, we'll have a much easier time linking the process up."

"And you really did this overnight?" Victor said, showing the same disbelief that Max had done.

"Well, remember I've done this before. Whether you're in a lunar or marine environment, many of the principles are the same: parallel fabrication, production line streaming, that kind of thing. Fifty percent of the problem is how you lay out your factory floor."

"Or in this case your deck plan," Ross said.

"Exactly."

"So, Ross, what do you think of this?" Victor said. He seemed to hold Ross's abilities in high regard, see him as a valuable advisor on all matters technical.

Ross was nodding, looking at the design appreciatively. "Well, my part in all this is materials, so anything that makes my job easier is a good thing. I don't know, Victor, I don't want to criticise anything Mayaan and his team did, but somehow this design just looks right. You know how if something looks right, it usually is? And having seen it go through a rep cycle, seen how it works; I'm feeling better about this already."

"This could be the answer we needed?"

Ross nodded again, considering his reply. Max still wasn't sure what kind of problems ESOS had run into, what issues had led to his and the others' sudden recruitment, but it was clear the programme had hit hard times. "It could be," Ross said. "It could well be."

"In which case we're four weeks ahead of schedule right from day one," Victor said.

"Yeah, I guess we are," Ross said. "So, Safi, bearing in mind we're paying you by the day here, you might want to slow down some!"

She smiled and looked down, as if slightly embarrassed by the praise, but didn't answer. Oliver too was silent, looking at her design schematics with what seemed to be mild disdain.

"Why don't we go and meet the teams?" Victor suddenly

announced. "Meet the people you'll be working with. And show them what we've got here."

* * *

The rest of the morning was spent away from the pool facility, walking round the design and fabrication offices, seeing the various teams that were housed there.

"There are eighty people working here," Victor said as they walked to the first of the departments. "Most of them are on the SRS project now, so you'll be getting to know them pretty well. We have a skeleton crew on the manganese beds but the locals seem to be running that for themselves now."

It seemed to be the main reason the facility existed as far as Max could tell, some kind of ESOS breakthrough ten years ago bringing the Pacific seabed's manganese deposits within reach for the first time and starting a mutually beneficial relationship with the local island states' governments. Sufficiently beneficial for ESOS to be allowed to stay and run whatever other projects they wanted to run, no questions asked.

"So we'll be meeting the sim group first," Victor said, "then the mech engineers, then materials and chemistry, then the control group. And you'll be meeting Garrett Gentry later on as well. He's our resident helicopter pilot, he'll be on hand to take you to and from the other islands. And just let me know if you want cleaners or housekeepers, we have people to do that as well."

Victor seemed to like reeling off the list of people who worked for him, revelling in his role as emperor of his island domain. But ESOS was a big company, and Marine Extraction only one of its divisions, so Victor must have had his own superiors, people to whom he had to explain himself. Max tried to imagine where this replication idea had first come from: was it decreed from above, or was it Victor's own pet project? Was he told to do it, or had he had to justify it, make the case for its funding? And if it failed, would he be the one feeling the heat? Suddenly Max had a suspicion he and the others weren't just here to help the project to stay afloat; they were keeping Victor's career intact too.

By the time they'd toured the offices, meeting the personnel whose talents they'd be drawing on over the next few months, it was lunchtime. They'd been taken round seven separate departments, including the modelling and simulation group Max was told he'd have working for him, but everywhere they went the reaction was the same: polite curiosity, greetings and handshakes traded all round but tempered by mild wariness as to just what these newcomers were about and how they were going to change things. The reaction to Safi's new design was similar: no overt sign of resentment that twelve months' work had just been overturned, but plenty of searching questions on the technical side which she fielded ably while Victor looked on, smiling with appreciation, as if watching his latest asset fulfil her potential.

Oliver had been silent for almost the whole walkabout, saying little more than hello, even when he was introduced to the control and mechanical engineers he'd be working with. It only was when the five of them finished up at the canteen that he had anything more to say.

"A machine which builds a copy of itself," he said as they sat down at one of the tables. He spoke slowly, almost as if the words didn't belong in the same sentence together. "Is that really what you've got us doing here?"

"Yes, that's the aim," Victor said.

Oliver shook his head as if in disbelief. "What a waste of time."

"Oliver, can you take us through your specific objections?" It was clear that Victor wanted to get Oliver's views out in the open, and was doing his best to keep the discussion civilised, but the contempt emanating from Oliver for everything he'd heard was unmistakable.

"Okay, point number one: making them copy themselves. I've already made my position clear on this, so there's little more I can say. Point number two: controlling them. You're describing these things as behaving autonomously, yet you don't have the faintest idea how you're going to keep them where you want them. What's to stop them just wandering off when you're not looking?"

"We know exactly how we're going to do it," Ross said. "We haven't got to that part of the design yet, but that's actually the easy bit."

"So what are you planning?" Max said.

"A chain of short-range acoustic transmitters, all around the operating zone. We'll need a few thousand of them but they're easy to mass produce. We could start making them today if we wanted. We just build our machines so that whenever they pick up the signals they turn away from the barrier. It's that easy."

Max hesitated, running what Ross had just said through his mind.

"Max? What do you think about that?" Victor said. Max's thoughts must have been showing on his face. Either that or Victor had read his mind. "I don't know," he said. "I can see the reasons for making them mobile, but the containment issue worries me." He was having to be careful with his words, aware he was echoing what Oliver had said, but not wanting to seem like his ally. "We need to be absolutely sure we can keep them where we want them."

"We will be Max," Victor said, "I can assure you." He seemed eager to move on to a different subject. "So then, we know what these machines will look like, pretty much, and we're starting to understand how they'll work. The only other question is what we're going to call them. I'm getting tired of all these 'SRS' designators we've used until now. Any fresh ideas?"

"Factory ships?" Ross suggested. "Sail barges?"

"Prospectors," Safi said firmly. It was obviously an idea she'd brought with her.

Victor repeated the word to himself a couple of times. "Yes, I like that. The old word for gold miners. Prospectors it is."

Oliver, however, just shook his head. "Can you people hear yourselves?" he said, looking round and smiling as if he was the only one who could see the joke. "Making up fancy names before you even know if you can do this." He stood up from the table. "Look, if you want to get gold out of the sea, I'll help you. But the sooner you realise this approach won't work, the better it will be for all of us." Then he left.

"What was that all about?" Ross said once Oliver was gone.

"I don't think he understands where we're coming from on this," Safi said. "He's convinced himself it's impossible and nothing's gonna shake him."

"So why come here?" Ross said. "Why did he even turn up if he thinks the project is worthless and all he's going to do is make a pain of himself?"

"I'll be honest, Ross," Victor said. "Oliver Rudd is a highly respected man when it comes to designing robotic systems. His knowledge and experience will be invaluable later on. He does have a reputation for, ah, not suffering fools gladly, but once we've won him round you'll be glad he's here. I promise you."

And that, Max decided, he'd have to see to believe.

* * *

For the last ten days the view from the ESOS facility hadn't changed: the same bright blue sky, the same turquoise sea, the same sweep of land where the flat part of the island curved round to form the harbour. But now, for the first time, Max could see something different. A cloud had appeared in the distance, a small smudge of white on the horizon, but a cloud all the same. He was amazed how something so simple was managing to hold his attention.

"So how much have you told Gillian about what you're doing here?" Ross said. He and Max were sitting on a low wall with one of the island's beaches ahead of them and the pool hanger loading bay behind them. They'd come out for a break while the machine shop fitted the final few components to the half-scale demonstrator model: Safi's new design being realised at last.

"Very little, unless I decide to bend the company rules. The contract said 'complete non-disclosure', but there may be some leeway for families. How about you, what does Tess know?"

"About the same, Victor's rules are pretty tight."

"How does she feel about that? You not being able to tell her anything about the job?"

"She kind of understands. Lots of people are in jobs where they can't talk about the details. With this job even the overview would be a giveaway. She knows that limits what I can say. Unless she starts working here herself of course."

"She told Gillian she was trying to get a job here."

Ross nodded. "Yeah, something in information management ideally. Victor's going to see what he can do for her. I think the sudden lack of connections is starting to freak her out. She liked the idea of the seclusion out here, but the reality is boring her senseless."

Gillian on the other hand seemed to be relishing her time there: a whole new nature trail to paint, plus their ongoing appointments with the medical centre. It took a bizarre set of circumstances to make a trip to the company doctor feel like a dream come true.

The sound of a jet flying over made Max and Ross look up. It was one of the ESOS company planes, heading along the coast at low altitude, ready for its turn to final approach.

"That'll be Marie," Ross said. "Victor said she might be getting in today. In which case I guess the party's on."

* * *

The invitation was for seven, with dinner itself — courtesy of Victor's wife — not long after. Ross and Tess had decided to ride over with Max and Gillian, mainly because none of the roads had auto-guidance markers for the cars and Gillian had volunteered not to drink for the night. She took them down the unlit zigzag road that led to the bottom of the hillside they all lived on, then drove through the residential zone used by the other company workers. The small white painted villas weren't much different to their own places.

"So how is everything with Oliver now?" Gillian asked Ross over her shoulder. Oliver seemed to be the main topic of conversation whenever Ross felt free to vent: whatever working relationship the two might have had seemed to have died on day one, and what had started as simple animosity now appeared to be verging on hatred.

"With Oliver? Pretty awful, same as usual. The guy's offensive, that's all there is to him. You should hear the way he talks to his backroom team. God knows why Vic brought him out here."

"His reputation must be better than the rest of him," Max said.

"Maybe. So what's your theory on the guy?"

Max paused before answering. "He's someone who's spent his entire working life using technology that just fifty years ago would have seemed impossible, but he takes it for granted because it already exists and he can see it round him every day. But as soon as you ask him to look ahead, at things that seem impossible now but one day won't be, it's as if some kind of mental block comes down. If he hasn't seen it done already then there's no point trying."

"But didn't you have your doubts when we started this?"

"Yes, and I still do, but I never doubted it was possible. We just — we need to be careful, that's all."

They remained silent until they reached Victor's house, halfway down the coast road on the beachfront. There they filed inside and joined Safi and Oliver at the table where Victor was helping his wife lay things out.

"You're in for a treat tonight," he told them when she was out of earshot. "Marie used to cook for a living. She studied in Brussels for six years."

Another five minutes later everything was ready. Victor and Marie said grace in French, a family tradition according to him, and then they started.

"So what do you think of our little island?" Marie asked Gillian across the table. Her accent gave away her French-Swiss origins much better than Victor's did.

"It's certainly warm enough," Gillian said. "I'm only just getting used to it. We soon learnt to stay indoors after midday."

"But that hasn't stopped you building up quite a tan, I can see. Of course, you may have been that colour when you arrived here for all I know."

"No, I've done all this since we got here. I'm spending most of my time outdoors at the moment. I'm a painter, I do wildlife pictures."

Even Oliver, who had spent more time indoors than anyone, was several shades redder than when he'd arrived.

"We spend as much time here as we can," Marie said. "Usually it's a nuisance to have to pack up and follow Victor off around the world, but coming here is always a treat."

"So you travel round a lot with work, do you?" Tess said.

"Here and there," Victor said. "Usually more there than here. I don't like to think how many times I must have circled the Earth by now. A few I'd imagine."

"Victor claims he's going to retire here," Marie said, "but somehow I doubt it."

"Why, what do you think?" Max said.

"I don't think he'll retire at all," she said, laughing. "He'll just keep on going, dragging me after him."

"Of course, this place isn't always quite so warm," Victor said. "We're building up to the storm season at the moment. I'd be getting ready for a couple of weeks of rain if I were you."

"Huh, rain," Oliver said from where he'd been tactfully placed opposite Victor. "I could have stayed at home if that's what I wanted."

"So is that why I've been seeing clouds lately?" Max said.

"It is," Victor said, "though I'm surprised you noticed them. They're blown off the lee sides of the neighbouring islands, and the nearest ones are over five miles away. If you can see them from here then it's a sure sign the rains are coming."

"Are they like cloud tails, or vortex streets? Is that what they are?" Safi said.

"Yes," Victor said. "That's exactly what they are. Sometimes they'll stretch for miles, always downwind of land. The old Polynesian sailors used to navigate the whole ocean using them. It's called wayfaring, not a map or a compass in sight."

Safi was nodding. "They're amazing when you see them from orbit. They're like little whirlpools being swept downstream, coming off each side of the island. I once saw a whole chain of atolls giving them off, like a hundred tiny volcanoes all erupting at once. It was breathtaking."

She raised her eyes as she was speaking, with a faraway look on her face. It was something Max had noticed her doing a lot when she was talking about things she'd seen on her travels. A few moments later she returned from wherever her mind had taken her and came back down to earth.

"Well if someone working for me spent their time staring at the scenery, they wouldn't be working there much longer," Oliver said. Then he looked along the table, yet again laughing as if at some witticism he'd just made, and seemingly unconcerned that no one else was joining in.

Gillian and Max immediately looked at each other, Gillian

mouthing the words, "what did he say?" as if unsure she'd heard him right. Safi herself said nothing, simply pausing for a moment before she carried on eating. For Ross however, the few seconds' silence which followed seemed to be just too much of a temptation.

"So, Oliver," he said. "I heard the other day that these two guys from Ohio are going to stick an engine on a big kite and fly themselves around in it. Are you planning to head over there and tell them not to bother?"

"What are you talking about?" Oliver said, the smile vanishing from his face.

"It just occurred to me that it's never been done before, so you might want to tell them it's impossible. And when you've done that, there are three guys in Florida trying to fly to the Moon in a rocket ship. You could save them a lot of hassle if you talk to them now."

Tess was giving him a warning look from across the table. Ross pretended not to notice.

"At least I don't sit around dreaming up new ways to waste time and money," Oliver said, teeth gritted. "Or fall for every moronic idea that gets waved in my face."

"So how many real ideas of your own have you ever had?" Ross continued. "Or do you always just shoot down other people's ideas, knowing that the law of averages will make you right nine times out of ten?"

Oliver didn't answer.

"Sounds like a good way to build a career," Ross said. "All that money you save by never taking risks, and making sure no one else does either. Is that the safest way for you?" He looked Oliver in the eye. "Is that what you used to do in your old job?"

"What do you know about that?" Oliver shouted. He got up from the table, his face red. "What do you know about anything!" Then he turned and left the room, heading for the entrance hall. Victor got up and went after him.

"I guess I hit a nerve there," Ross said. No one answered him.

Max could hear Victor and Oliver talking in the hallway, but couldn't make out what was being said. Then he heard the front door open and close again, and Victor came back alone.

"Oliver has decided to go home for the night. He said he was feeling tired. Safi, I don't think he meant to offend you just then, or anyone else for that matter."

Max wondered if Oliver had said that himself, or if Victor was saying it for him.

"Victor, I'm sorry I let it get out of hand there," Ross said. "Would it be easier if I left too?"

"No, you stay where you are, Ross. We shouldn't let this spoil things." Then Victor retook his seat and beamed at them all, getting back into his role as host for the evening. "So, how's the food?"

They carried on for the next half hour, the bad atmosphere eventually clearing, then moved into the lounge. Victor brought in more drinks and joined them.

"Now then, here's a little game I always like to play with my guests," he said. "I've got a question I want to try out on you. We're all intelligent, educated people, college degrees or equivalent, so this should be no problem at all. So, as accurately as you can manage, and according to the latest estimates, what do you think is the age of the Universe? Ross, do you want to go first?"

Max knew the prehistory of Earth inside out, but was ashamed to admit that he knew next to nothing about events in the wider cosmos leading up to it. Looking at the blank faces around him he realised that the others were none the wiser too. Ross's answer, when it came, was obviously a guess.

"I don't know, twenty billion years?"

"Okay," Victor said. "How about you, Tess?"

She shrugged. "I'll say a billion."

"I won't ask Marie because she's sat through this little discussion before, so, Gillian?"

"Er, five million?"

"And Max?"

"Well, life started around four billion years ago, we're pretty sure of that, and the Earth itself isn't much older, so I'll say four times that. Sixteen billion years."

"Good thinking from Max there. And finally, you, Safi."

"I think the best estimate is thirteen point seven billion years."

"So there's quite a spread of answers," Victor said. "Anything between five million and twenty billion years. How many of you were just guessing?"

A couple of them murmured that they had been.

"But I don't think it was really a fair question," Ross said. "None of us are astronomers, so why should we even need to know? And aren't people still arguing over it anyway?"

"No," Victor said, "the answer has been agreed for a few decades now. And you shouldn't need to be a trained astronomer to know it. It may not be something you use every day but it's still a fairly significant number."

"So what is the answer?" Ross said.

"Safi got it right, it's thirteen point seven billion years. I thought she would know. But I liked your approach Max, starting with something you were sure of and working back from that."

"But what was the point of the question?" Ross said.

"Well it shows that none of you are particularly religious for a start. Even though your answers varied by a factor of twenty, you were still all going for the scientific big-bang answer. You could easily have said the universe was created in four thousand BC or whatever."

"No, hold on," Gillian said. "I wouldn't say that's true at all. I'm a Christian, I have been all my life. You can't say I'm not religious just because of how I answered that one question."

"That's interesting," Victor said, turning to face her. "You say you're a Christian, but you still gave an answer in millions of years. Does that mean you don't believe in the Bible's version of creation?"

"The six days story? I could have gone with that answer if I'd wanted to. It's just as likely to be right as any other."

"But what about all the evidence for the big-bang? The expansion of the universe, the background radiation? Do you accept those?"

"I don't doubt them, but that's not the issue here."

"So, what don't you like about the big-bang idea?"

"Nothing, it may well be true for all I know."

"Which implies you think it might not be."

"No, I never said that. Look — I don't have a problem with the idea at all, but you shouldn't just accept it as absolute truth. Scientists are always claiming they've got the one true explanation that brushes everyone else's beliefs out of the way, then changing their minds again a couple of years down the line."

"What do you mean, changing their minds?"

"Like, I don't know, like when Newton thought he'd figured out gravity, and everyone called it the 'Law of Gravity', as if it couldn't work any other way, then all of a sudden Einstein came along and it turned out the old version was completely wrong."

"That's putting it too strongly," Safi said. "Einstein's ideas didn't replace Newton's altogether. In most situations you get the same answers from both."

"But scientists are always saying that their version of the world is the 'right' one, and half the time they can't even agree among themselves. How can that be if they only ever deal in facts?"

"Well," Safi said. "Any scientist who says that any theory is the absolute truth isn't doing their job properly. The most you can ever say is that it explains everything it's meant to explain and it's passed all the tests people can throw at it. But if an exception comes along that can't be explained, then you need a new version of the theory."

"Doesn't that mean that they've wasted their time?"

"Not at all. If people increase their understanding by comparing old and new hypotheses then that's a step forward, not backward. That kind of progression is a strength of science, it's just easy to portray it as a weakness. But everything is based on real observations of the world. That's the bottom line: none of it is just made up."

"So, Gillian," Victor said. "If you don't believe the Bible story of creation, and you're not convinced by the scientific one either, then what do you believe? And where did your answer to the original question come from?"

Gillian was the centre of attention now, and even though the others were reacting with genuine interest, she looked as though she was starting to feel singled out.

"I don't think evidence is everything," she said. "You can show me all the evidence you want that the universe is this many years old or the Earth weighs that many tons, but what happens if something completely different turns out to be 'true' the next day? You can't build your life on things that could be overturned like that; only compassion and morals and faith are solid enough to build your whole existence around. I don't think that scientists can ever give us the full picture of what the universe is or how it was created. There has to be something more to it, some higher power. Science can do a lot for us, but trying to work out why we exist by doing experiments and testing things in labs is never going to work. It's just not something we're equipped to understand."

"And what about the origins of life, and evolution?" Victor continued. "What's your view on that?"

"The same. I can see how all the evidence supports it, but it can't be the full story. When I look around at all the life on this planet, especially in a place like this island, I can't think of any other way that something so amazing could have been created except by some deliberate plan. If life has changed and adapted over millions of years, then that ability must have been part of the plan too."

"But if you don't buy the scientific view, then what stops you from believing the biblical six days story outright?" Safi said. "It sounds like you're trying to find some kind of compromise."

"The fact that something exists that is bigger than me, bigger than all of us. That's defined by the love it holds for us and expects nothing but the same in return? There's no compromise there."

"So do you object to children being taught the scientific explanation?" Victor said.

It was an inevitable question, still as relevant now as it had been decades before, and Gillian paused before answering. "I'm not against children being taught about science," she said, "but I think that if they're taught to see the world as something cold and amoral, that doesn't care about us or what happens to us, they'll live their whole lives in a cold, amoral way. And I just can't imagine why someone would knowingly set children down that path."

A few of them cast curious glances at Max at that point, obviously wondering whether those sentiments were aimed at him.

"Don't worry," he said laughing, raising his hands in mock defence. "We don't spend our lives waging some pitched religious battle or anything like that. I do believe that a rational, evidence-based approach is the best way to comprehend the universe, and I think the curiosity and drive that led the Newtons and Einsteins and Darwins of the world to find out what really makes things work is anything but cold and amoral. I think everything we see around us can be explained without resorting to some intelligent creator, and I genuinely think a day will come when people will look back on this age of superstition and shake their heads in disbelief. Gillian knows I think that; it's not meant as anything personal against her or people who share her beliefs. For what it's worth, I think Jesus was a genuine historical figure who had a lot of good things to say about how people should live their lives, and you can quite justifiably celebrate his birth and his life, without resorting to the supernatural. And personally, I'm happy to be part of that."

"And what will you do if you have children?" Marie said. "How will you raise them, and teach them what to believe?"

"We're going to let them decide for themselves," Max said. "It's the only fair way. It's not going to be straightforward, but we've agreed to raise any children by example, and the fact that people who think different things can still get on is one of the examples we hope to set."

It was good to be able to think in those terms again. Many people had expressed surprise that two people with such differing views of the world could work so well together; many other couples got on fine despite such glaring differences, and the fact that he and Gillian did too was probably one of their greatest strengths. Now that the threats were no longer a constant feature of his life, now that they weren't preying on his mind and tainting the relationship he had with Gillian, it was like being back to the way they had always been.

Which made him wonder why Victor had chosen this lame "age-of-the-universe" party game to spring on them, almost calculated to prompt this very discussion. There was something of the manipulator about Victor, despite the charming exterior. He also found himself wondering how Gillian and Safi would get on in future. There was certainly no hostility, but maybe they were just too different for anything more to develop.

"So where did the first life forms come from?" Tess said suddenly. "I mean, we all know about evolution, and survival of the fittest, but what got it started? Can anyone answer that yet?"

She'd been silent for almost the whole discussion, but Max could tell she'd been taking in every word. And now she'd come out with one of the biggest questions there was.

"That's a tough one," he said. "In fact I've got some friends back in L.A. who are trying to find the answer even as we speak. It wouldn't have been a plant or animal as we'd understand it, more like a primitive single cell, filled with a few molecules that could copy themselves if they were surrounded by the right chemicals. And it probably appeared in the sea, that's the most likely place for it. Once evolution took over, the rest was history."

"Yes, but you haven't answered the question. What made it appear in the first place?"

"It just appeared on its own. The sea already had the right chemicals to form it, and once you added sunlight and lightning strikes all sorts of substances would appear and disappear at random; they're still doing it now. One day the right arrangement appeared, and that was it."

"That doesn't sound very likely to me."

"Well, it isn't. In fact it's probably the single most unlikely thing that's ever happened on this planet. But we're talking about a whole ocean's worth of chemicals here, with billions of years' worth of chances — and it only had to happen once."

"But that one time it did happen, the Earth had only just been formed, right? You said it yourself when you were answering Victor's question. It happened almost as soon as the conditions were right, not billions of years later. How likely is *that*? How does the 'Karman-Lowrie' number explain *that* away?"

Max looked at her, suddenly realising that she'd known the answers all along, and was leading him on just to see how he'd respond.

"The K-L number is certainly something to bear in mind," Max said. "But it's not the final answer. We know something led to that precursor life form, we just don't know what."

The Karman-Lowrie number was something Max took great technical pride in, but which had returned to haunt him ever since he'd published the work which produced it. It dated from his less politically aware days, when the idea that he could be vilified for simply writing up the results of an honest scientific investigation would have been unthinkable to him. All he'd done was apply his biological and chemical knowledge to try and calculate the entropy, the necessary complexity, of the simplest possible self-replicating molecule. Whatever started life on Earth, the logic went, was at least this complex if not more so. Then followed a probability analysis, an estimate of how many randomly recombining atoms and molecules would be needed to produce something this complex within the known lifetime of the Earth. The answer was a concerning one: an ocean five thousand times the volume of all those on Earth would need to be left for four billion years before the probability reached even fifty percent. For the specific case of DNA-based life, the odds were even worse. Max and his colleague, Sheldon Karman, hadn't meant it to demonstrate that spontaneous abiogenesis was impossible — their own conclusion was that some previously unknown chemical catalyst must have been at play — but that hadn't stopped those with a political motivation from jumping on the result with fervour, yet another sign of how the scientists were tying themselves up in knots with their lack of faith.

"But once it did happen," Victor cut in, "it would have spread exponentially until it covered the world. It would only have taken a few years before the planet was teeming with them, whatever 'they' were."

"Exponentially?" Tess said. "Is that enough for something that small to cover a whole planet? In just a few years?"

"Don't underestimate how fast something will grow if you double it time and again," Victor said, smiling. The fact that their presence on the island hinged on that very principle was obviously foremost in his mind. "There's a little story I could tell you about someone who did that."

Marie sighed as if she'd heard it before, but Victor carried on regardless.

"It's a story from India," he said. "About a king called Shere Khan, who ruled at the time that chess was invented. Now he was so impressed with the game, so the story goes, that he ordered his whole army to find the man who'd invented it and bring him back with them. Eventually they tracked him down, and his name was Buddhiram. Now, he wasn't rich or powerful, just an ordinary man who made a living by teaching, but the king greeted him with open arms and promised that whatever reward Buddhiram asked for, he would get it. And back then a king was supposed to be a man of his word: if he promised something he couldn't deliver then he would lose face. Now I think Shere Khan must have had a reputation for being a bit pompous or stupid, because Buddhiram decided to play a trick on him. He said, 'This will be my reward. I want you to take your chessboard, and put one grain of rice on the first square. The next day, put two grains on the second square. Then every day after that, put down twice as many as the day before. I'll come back in sixty-four days and take what you've collected as my payment.'

"Shere Khan looked at the small chessboard in front of him, thought of everything else Buddhiram could have asked for and decided the man was an idiot. But he had to stick to his promise, so he called his advisors and asked them how much rice he would need to give him. He was the richest king in India, so he didn't think it would be a problem. It was only when his advisors worked through the night and came back the next day that he realised what he'd agreed to. 'There is not that much rice in the whole world,' they told him. 'To meet your promise you would have to level every mountain, drain every ocean, and grow rice there for years, and even then you would not have enough to pay him off.' And he looked again at the sixty-four little squares in front of him and knew how clever Buddhiram really had been. So you see?"

Victor beamed at her, obviously impressed with his own storytelling skills. Tess forced a smile in return. "I'm glad I asked," she said.

Chapter 4

"So you're the guys who are going to make us all millionaires, right?"

"I don't know who told you that," Max said. "Is that really what people think?"

"Ha! No, but there's a few people who wish it was true. Here, mind your head."

Max ducked into the cabin of the helicopter and strapped himself in. Garrett Gentry checked the harness was fastened, then walked round to the other door. The tall, heavily built pilot almost had to bend double to squeeze through, but once inside he got the rotors spinning and the machine in the air in no time.

Max took a few moments to enjoy the view once they were up. The colours were what stood out most. Last time he'd seen the island from the air it had been almost night-time, the night of their arrival, but this time the sun was right above them. The rich green of the vegetation, with the rust red of the dirt roads cutting through it, contrasted sharply with the bright white beaches and the pale grey cliff faces. Max couldn't take his eyes off it; as an example of what nature could produce, it was breathtaking. Then there was the sea itself, thick bands of colour going from clear to turquoise to green, then suddenly turning dark blue as the seabed dropped away into the Pacific depths. Max looked into the blue, trying to see the underwater canyon he knew to be running there right under their flight path. It was invisible, lost in the murk and oceanic solutes which had become a feature of tropical seas over the last two decades.

Once the island was behind them Max turned back into the cabin. Now all that surrounded them was featureless ocean. He switched on the microphone on his headset and spoke to Garrett.

"So how much have they told you about what's going on here?"

"Just that there's gold in them thar waters," Garrett said. He didn't have to change his Western States accent much to make the line sound right. "And you guys are gonna dig it out for us."

"Yeah, that's the plan. I guess you weren't brought here just for this bit of work then."

"No, I've worked for Victor's little outfit for a few years now. I was here when this place was built."

Most of the people that Max and the others were working with had been there from the start, working on the manganese mining project that had seen ESOS first arrive on the island. Some of them still got called away when that project needed them, sometimes for days at a time.

"What did you do before then?"

"I was in the military for ten years," he said. "That's where I learned to fly. Then I did a couple of years in Southeast Asia, and then I came here."

"Which part of Asia were you in?"

"Singapore and the floating cities, mainly. But I got tired ferrying tourists around between the islands so I took this job instead."

"And now you're ferrying us around."

Garrett looked over at Max and grinned. "That's right," he said.

They carried on in silence for another five minutes, then one of the other islands came into view. It was tiny, no more than a barren rock sticking up out of the sea.

"What do you want me to do?" Garrett said. "Just follow the boundary at low level?"

"Yeah, that's right. I want to make sure the boats have laid the buoys out in the right places. And that none of the gaps are too large."

"Okay, no problem."

The flight lasted about fifty minutes as they took in all the small islands and reefs that formed the boundary inside which the Prospectors would be operating. Their almost ring-shaped distribution formed a convenient natural enclosure for the area, sealed off by the acoustic boundary markers strung between them.

At one point a tanker was visible in the distance on one of the shipping lanes to the west. They could only see it because of their altitude, Garrett explained. And with the local territorial waters extending many miles beyond the island chain, that was the closest anyone was expected to come.

* * *

When Max arrived back at the island he headed up to the top floor, to the room Oliver had chosen as his office. On the way he passed a group of three ESOS workers from Oliver's engineering team, striding purposefully as they came round a corner. One of them was talking animatedly as they approached, a young engineer called Mayaan who had worked on the original ESOS replicator design. He just had time to say, "Who do those people think they are, coming out here —" before he saw Max and shut up quickly. The three of them passed him, then carried on in silence. Oliver must have made an impression on them, Max thought.

Oliver was sitting hunched over his desk, peering at a schematic display on his screen. Max walked over and took up a position just behind him, waiting for him to look up from his work.

"Yes?" Oliver said, not taking his eyes off the screen.

"Hi, Oliver, I need to talk to you about something. Mind if I sit down?"

Oliver sighed heavily, shut down the program he was using, and pulled another chair up to his desk. "Go on."

"I've just been out to look at the boundary chain. The spacing looks fine, there's no gaps or anything, but I'm starting to think we need something else, another layer of protection. I'm not the expert on this, but I think it needs to go into the navigation system."

"And you want me to do that for you?"

"I'd like your advice on it first of all, you or one of your staff. Right now I just want an idea of what's possible, how we can contain these machines if the boundary fails. I remember you mentioned this as a concern yourself, right back at the start."

"Look, I know what you're saying, but I'm really busy with everything else right now. If you want to do this you'll have to figure it out for yourself, okay?"

He looked back at his screen again. As far as he was concerned, Max might as well not have been there.

"Right, I'll leave you to it then," Max said.

Max was halfway down the corridor when he heard footsteps behind him, not running, but walking fast, trying to catch him up. He turned to see another of Oliver's staff, a young South African called Isaac, gesturing for him to stop.

"I heard what you were saying to Oliver," Isaac said, keeping his voice low. "I think you've got the right idea, doubling up on the controls. Look — Oliver's got us stretched pretty thin right now, but what if I took a look at this for you? I think it's worth spending some time on at least."

"If you could, that would be really helpful. Do you have any ideas for what we could do?"

"A couple. I've got to get back now, it's probably best if Oliver doesn't know we're talking, but, how about if we meet up this afternoon? I can come to your office, about two pm?"

"Sure, I'll see you then."

Max went to his own office after that, wondering what working for Oliver must be like if half his staff were either ranting about him in the corridors or sneaking around so they could talk to other people without getting in trouble. It didn't suggest a happy workplace.

He got to his desk, then sat down and dialled John Olson's number back in L.A. John's face erupted into a broad smile when he saw who it was.

"Max! We thought you'd disappeared! How are you doing?"

"Really good, John. And you?"

"I'm good too. So are you going to tell me where you are this time? Or are you still being mysterious about this new project of yours?"

Max was having to concentrate to hear what John was saying; the audio was crackling for some reason, and the image kept flickering on the screen.

"Oh, I'll tell you one day. I don't want to spoil the surprise just yet."

"Well, whatever it is, they must have made a good offer. What are you doing, making diamonds for a living?"

Max winced slightly. "Yeah, something like that."

"So what can I do for you?"

"I was wondering how things were going back there."

"You mean the Eden rocks, I guess."

"The Eden rocks? Is that what they're called now?"

"It was a good name to use in the press releases. Someone thought so anyway. But yeah, we're seeing some pretty spectacular stuff in there."

"Like what?"

"Well, there's the kind of bacteria you'd expect to see, but with completely different species mixed in, types we've never seen before. It's really weird, Max. Whatever they were they obviously died out pretty fast. There's nothing like them anywhere else in the fossil record."

"How different are they?"

"See for yourself, I'll send down some of the images we're getting."

One by one, the grainy x-ray images appeared on Max's screen. Also included were chemical analyses of the material, plus a selection of electron microscope shots, tiny segmented structures familiar to him as bacterial fossils. He could see at a glance that John had been right about the diversity in there; the range of organisms was far too large. Rocks more than three billion years old usually showed nothing more than cyanobacteria or fossilised algae, not the menagerie he was seeing here.

"What are those other structures?" he said. "Those narrow streaks and lumps?"

"On the x-rays? Crystalline deposits mostly. We opened up a couple of the rocks and that's what we found running through them."

"Could you do a chemical scan on them? See if they have some catalytic effect on RNA formation?"

"Still trying to get that Karman-Lowrie number down? Don't worry, we're already working on it."

"Good. And you're absolutely sure about the age?"

"The age is a dead cert, it's definitely early Archaean."

"That's good work, John, keep it going. And thanks for the pictures. I'll keep calling you back for updates. If you need any help just let me know."

"Sure thing."

Max was about to break the connection when suddenly he remembered the other reason he'd called.

"Before you go, John, there's something I wanted to ask you."

"Yes?"

"Have you ever heard of the Earthrise program?"

John thought for a second. "Yeah, I think so. Isn't that the research site on the Moon? Where they had that accident?"

"What do you know about it?"

"Just what was on the news at the time. There was an explosion in an airlock, I think, five or six years ago. A couple of people got killed. Why? That's not where you've gone is it?"

Max laughed. "No, I've not quite gone that far! It just got mentioned recently, that's all."

"Oh, okay. Anyway, keep in touch, Max. And say hi to Gillian."

"I will do. Bye, John."

He'd already broken the connection when he saw a message waiting for him from Indira. There was nothing of note in there, just a request that he call her next time their time zones matched up. He dialled her number, waiting for the ESOS encrypted line to link up to California for a second time.

"Max, thank you for getting back to me, how are things going on the project?"

"They're good, it's, ah, exciting work." Again, the audio and video were distorted, not much, but enough to notice. Max made a note to check with the building support staff.

"That's excellent news. Look, Max, I wouldn't normally trouble you with this but I thought you should know, we've been getting more threats. They're delivering them to the department again, all in your name. Security have been opening them for evidence."

"And what do they say?" Max's mouth was dry; he thought he'd left those problems behind when he took this placement.

"Well, they know you changed your plans, whoever had got hold of your GRACE schedule seems aware of that fact. But don't worry about this at all. Our security have spoken to ESOS security and they've assured us you're in a safe location."

"Well, it's pretty remote, assuming that equates to safe."

"Good, good, I'm glad. I just wanted to keep you informed, even though, God willing, this won't have any direct effect on you."

"No, I'm glad you did," Max said. "Thanks for letting me know."

"No problem at all, Max. Just take care of yourself. And of Gillian too, of course. You have told her I presume?"

"I will."

"Make sure you do."

Max got up to go for lunch after that. He had to go back past Oliver's office, right next to the transmitter room where all calls, including the ones he'd just made to John and Indira, were coded and sent out by anonymous satellite link. He went in briefly, looking for anyone from the support team. No one was in there, so he logged in and left a quick message noting the audio problems before continuing to the canteen.

It was an hour or so later that he was back in his own office with Isaac.

"So you've worked with Oliver before?" Max was saying.

"Yeah, a few years ago, in a previous life. Quite a piece of work, isn't he?"

"Is he really as useless as he seems?"

"No, he's brilliant. I mean really brilliant, but a pain in the ass to work with. I've been involved with him on two projects now, that Pan-African desalination site was one of his, and also the inter-island mass transit line for Japan, and on both of them he was the same. But he got the job done, both times."

"I really can't imagine anything useful coming from him, I'm sorry."

"That's because you've only seen him here. He thinks this is a load of bull, the whole project. He's only doing it because of what he'd lose if he walked out. But there's more to him than you've seen."

Max nodded silently, trying to fit Isaac's description to the boorish arrogant fool they'd seen so far.

"And you're willingly working with him again?"

"Well, you need to be pretty thick skinned, that's for sure."

"I bet you do," Max said. "Anyway, the boundary chain, what have you got for me?"

"Okay, it's an interesting problem, but like most problems there are good ways and bad ways of approaching it. If we put additional measures in, it's best if a number of them are autonomous, like independent navigation programming that each Prospector follows, in addition to global measures like the boundary chain. A mix of autonomous and global will give us the most robust solution."

Max nodded in agreement, it made sense; make each Prospector responsible for keeping itself in place, and then draw a line around the operating site as well: controls within controls. "Okay, so let's start with the autonomous features. What kind of thing are you thinking of?"

Isaac didn't even have time to answer. The door opened, and Oliver strode in, face livid as he looked from Max to Isaac and back again.

"Just what the hell do you think you're doing?" he said, marching over to Max and bearing down on him.

"We're discussing the control system," Max said. "I asked Isaac to —"

"So you thought you could come and steal my staff off me, just because you've hit a problem you can't sort out for yourself?" Oliver was close to shouting now, rage filling his face with blood.

"Professor Rudd," Isaac said, "Max asked me to help because this kind of control system design is outside his area of expertise."

"And you don't think the jobs I've given you are important enough? Is that it?"

"No, it's nothing like that. This work runs alongside those tasks, not instead of them. That's why I'm —"

"If I'd known you were going to pull a stunt like this, I would have had you thrown out of my group right at the start. Give me one good reason why I shouldn't do it right now!"

Isaac hesitated, clearly lost for words. Oliver made for the door as if he'd had enough. He was about to leave when he turned to face Max. "Don't think this ends here, Lowrie," he said. "People who cross me end up regretting it." Then he stormed out of the room.

Isaac hurried out of his chair to follow him. "Let me talk to him," he said to Max as he left the room. "I'll sort this out."

Max decided that was about enough for one day. As he left the building he met Safi going the same way. He told her about the exchange of words that had just taken place.

"Now why doesn't that surprise me?" she said. "What is it with that guy? If ever anyone needed a session at charm school, it's him."

"He certainly does have problems," Max agreed.

They walked together down the road that led alongside the complex. On the way they passed Ross, helping himself to one of the bikes that were used for getting to the off-road areas of the island. He had a rucksack on his back and was wearing a black baseball cap with "New Zealand" written across the front.

"Going anywhere good?" Max asked him.

"Just exploring," he said. "I've got my backroom team doing my job for me today, so I thought I'd take a look round the south side of the island. Where are you two off to?"

"I've got some samples to pick up from the test beds," Safi said.

"And I'm finished for the day," Max said. "So I'm going home."

Ross joined them as they walked down the hill, pushing the bike along beside him. Max gave him the Oliver story as they went. Once he'd finished Ross just shook his head and said "unbelievable" a few times, but like Safi he had to admit that it didn't really surprise him.

"I wish I could figure him out," he said. "Just when I think he can't get any worse, he does. He was trying to argue with me about my own job the other day."

"In what way?" Safi said.

"There's some anaerobic bacteria on parts of the seabed round here that could mess up some of our extraction processes. He reckoned they don't count as being alive because they don't use oxygen. I told him I'd been an oceanographer long enough to know the definition of whether something was alive or not."

"Anything that can reproduce and mutate," Max said. "That's the one I use."

"Exactly. But he wouldn't take it in. He'd made up his own mind and that was that."

"Maybe he was worried you'd try the same test out on him," Safi said. "See what kind of life form he counted as."

"Yeah," Ross said, laughing. "Genetically unique, that does kind of sum him up."

They walked on a little further. Then Safi frowned for a second and turned to Max. "Are you sure that's how you'd define life? That simply?"

"Yes," he said, taken aback slightly. "If you want a good definition, then the simpler the better. If something can spread, but can also change over time, then that's all you need to call it alive. Multiply and diversify, life is as life does."

"But I can think of things that fit that description but aren't alive," she said.

"Like what?"

"Like jokes and stories. They get reproduced when people pass them on, and they always change each time they're told. I guess if the best ones get told the most, then they even undergo natural selection. Does that mean they're alive?"

"In a way they are, yes, but they've got more in common with viruses than living organisms. It's because they need help from us to get passed on to a new host. But every time a new joke appears it spreads like an epidemic. People who've heard it before are immune so it needs fresh minds to infect."

"To infect? Are you serious?" she said.

"Sure. You've heard of 'memes' I guess. People used to call them mind viruses. It's all for real, I promise you."

At that point the road forked, the left branch heading out toward the extractor test beds where Safi was heading, and the right branch continuing down the hill to the coast road where Ross would start his ride. The three of them stopped, and Ross climbed onto his bike and got ready to set off.

"Well, it's been great," he said grinning. "But I think I should leave you two and your mind viruses alone, in case anything's catching, so if you'll excuse me, I'll see you both tomorrow."

"Okay, Ross, have a good ride," Safi said.

He pedalled the first few yards, then freewheeled the rest of the way to the bottom, turning his baseball cap round backward so that it wouldn't get blown off as he gained speed. Once he was out of sight Safi turned back to Max.

"Do you want to help me carry these samples back?" she said. "I don't know how much there'll be this time."

"Okay, I'll give you a hand," he said.

This road was shadier than the one next to the complex, as if a tunnel had been cut into the vegetation that flanked the building. It was much cooler under the trees, and the building was soon out of sight behind them. After a while the paved road gave way to a dirt path, and eventually led to the extractor beds themselves. They were in a low windowless blockhouse, a row of large troughs, fed with seawater pumped from the beach. In each one, different combinations of catalysts and electrode arrays were being tested, in an attempt to coax the various trace elements out of solution. Safi went to them in turn and started pulling out the accumulator plates, lifting each one out of its slot like a honeycomb from a beehive. Roughly half of them went straight back where they'd come from, but she piled up the ones that looked the most promising and handed some to Max.

"Here, take these," she said. "I was right, there's more than usual. We must be nearly there."

"Which one of these has got the gold on it?" he said.

She looked down the ones he was carrying. "Er, that one, but don't try running off with it, you're carrying less than a cent's worth."

"I wouldn't dream of it," he said.

As soon as they were back out in the open they could tell something was different. Max was the first to look up.

"Where on earth did that come from?" he said.

What had been a bright blue sky was now dark grey, the clouds almost low enough to reach out and touch. They both shivered at the same time as a gust of wind came in off the sea, and then the first splashes of rain started to fall through the treetops.

"Uh-oh!" Safi said. "We can't get rainwater on these! Come on, we'll have to run!"

They were about halfway down the path when the rain really started. In no time at all the pathway had turned from red dust to dark brown mud, and by the time they got back onto the road they were both splashed and stained up to their waists. They sprinted the last fifty yards, sheltering the sample plates with their bodies as they ran up the hill to the main entrance. Once inside they put the plates down on the floor and leant against the wall to get their breath back. After a couple of seconds they just looked at each other and grinned. Safi had got mud all the way up her legs and arms, and even had some on her face where she'd wiped her hand across her forehead. Max was about to point it out to her, but then she put her hand up toward him, obviously to tell him something similar. In the end they said nothing and just laughed at each other.

"I think we ought to get cleaned up," he said eventually.

"Yeah, I think you're right," she said, not taking her eyes off him. Her clothes were wet through, a light blouse that had been perfect for the morning's heat now clinging to her in patches that held close as she moved.

"I, er, I need to go and make sure Gillian's all right," he said. "I hope she's not been caught out in this as well. I'll see you tomorrow."

"Oh, okay, sure. I'll see you tomorrow, Max."

* * *

The next day was the same, and the day after that. The rain came and went, but the darkness was continuous. Within a week they were losing four hours of daylight from every day. The workload however went the other way, as the hours they spent in the complex got steadily longer. On days when Max was working in one of the windowless lab rooms he would often turn up before dawn and leave after dark, never having seen daylight in between. And with Gillian almost housebound by the weather, he could tell she was starting to feel the strain.

The feeling among the design teams was no better. The project had hit its first bottleneck, the part where the competing requirements of all its subsystems and assemblies first came together to struggle for their share of the design's space and power budget. There were no outright arguments, just heated justifications of why the electrolysis tanks needed that extra amp that the steering system was asking for, why parts machining needed more space than filtration. And for Max the balancing act was particularly fraught, as he kept up a discreet line of communication to Isaac, drawing on his experience to help shape the safety measures he was more convinced than ever they would need.

Inevitably, at some point, the time would come to come clean.

* * *

"Right, everyone, if we can get started now. Thank you."

Victor had called this meeting at Max's request. Now that he'd got everyone's attention, he was looking at Max expectantly, waiting for him to speak. Max took his cue and walked to the front of the room to face the crowd.

"I know it's not usual to get this many of us together," Max said. "But there's something we need to discuss."

Everyone was looking at him with interest, wondering what

he was going to say. He could see on their faces the signs of the hours they'd been working. Safi especially looked tired; if anything she'd put in more hours than he had. Now she was frowning at him quizzically, surrounded by her seven strong engineering team. In fact, all four of them had their backroom teams with them: Ross with his chemical experts, Oliver with his control engineers, and Max's own group of sim programmers and mathematicians. The meeting room had never been so full.

"As you know, my role in all this is design optimisation. Using evolutionary methods to make your system designs as efficient as possible. And I hope I'm doing that successfully." He said it in the knowledge that none of them would disagree. "But on top of that," he continued, "I've been looking at the design as a whole, and I have to say there are a few things concerning me, and one thing in particular. I'm afraid we're going to have to make some serious changes."

He paused to see if there would be any reaction, then continued.

"I've been looking at the navigation system for the Prospectors, and what we're planning so far just isn't up to the job. We're going to have to redesign it."

Suddenly there was a burst of noise from Oliver's group, followed by a short exchange of words among its members. Then one of them stood up, the young engineer, Mayaan, who Max had seen in the corridor two weeks earlier.

"Now wait a minute," Mayaan said. "Navigation is our job, not yours! And it's something we finished weeks ago!"

"I know, but it needs to be completely reworked."

"What for? It's one of the simplest systems on board!"

"Yes, and that's the problem. It's nowhere near sophisticated enough."

"But it doesn't have to be 'sophisticated'. If it detects the boundary chain it turns round, if it detects another Prospector they pass on the right, if it's time to replicate it just stops! What on earth are you trying to build?"

Max kept his voice level but firm. "I'm not happy with the safeguards we're using to keep these vehicles in place. The boundary chain is a good idea, but if it breaks there's no backup. It's a single point failure, and we can't afford to have any of those in a system like this. We need to rule them out. I've spent a long time working on this, and there's only one way to do it."

"And what exactly is that?" Mayaan snapped. In many ways Max could understand his reaction; Mayaan looked more tired than most, and working alongside Oliver the last three months couldn't have helped.

"We need a second navigation system, in parallel with the boundary chain turnaround rule. The Prospectors need to track their own motion through the water, and plan their paths to always stay safely within the zone. Then if one of them gets too close to the edge, the turnaround acts as a backup. It's a two layer system: two things need to go wrong for it to fail, not just one."

"So what are you suggesting?" Victor said. His face showed concern, as if willing to listen but yet to be convinced.

"Each Prospector needs to have a map of the local ocean stored in its controller. It will know the position of the islands, all the transmitters on the boundary chain, and all the major seabed features. It will measure its own motion through the water using flow sensors, and at the same time it will measure the local depth and compare that with its seabed map. And when it gets close to the boundary, it won't just turn around, it will recognise which transmitter it's being signalled by and add that to its positional data."

By now Mayaan was facing away with his eyes closed, as if trying to keep his composure. Max carried on regardless.

"In addition to that, we need some kind of warning system, in case one of these machines does go where it shouldn't, and we need to be able to override the navigation system and put it under human control. The whole thing has to be completely safe and foolproof. Watertight, in both senses of the word. We can't have anything less."

Now it was Safi's turn to look concerned. "Max? What are you talking about?"

"I've been looking into this for a while now, Safi. It's the only way to do this safely."

"But we already know the limits we're working to. That kind of computing power simply won't be available on board."

"So we'll just have to design these things so that it is."

"But Max, we've been through this already. We can't put anything on a Prospector that it can't make for itself, and that includes the kind of hardware you're asking for."

"I know the restrictions on controller design. But using the turnaround system on its own isn't going to be enough. We need something more."

"But we ruled out complex autonomy right at the start, it can't be done. So why are you bringing it up now?"

"Because I have to. I've told you my reasons."

"Max, you can tell us what you want for as long as you want, but it won't change the facts. Putting a system like that on board is completely out of the question. When are you going to realise that?"

"I know what you're saying, Safi, but you have to think about how dangerous all this is, what could happen if we get it wrong."

"For God's sake, Max, just listen to yourself!" Even through her arguments with Oliver, it was the first time he'd heard her get even slightly annoyed. "Don't you see why what you're asking for is impossible? Do you think I'm just making this stuff up?"

Max recoiled from the outburst, unable to think of a reply. This wasn't the calm, reasonable Safi he'd worked alongside for the past three months. If anyone was going to react badly he could have been sure it wouldn't be her. The stress of the situation must have been getting to her more than he'd thought. He sat back, wordless.

Mayaan however was not so easily silenced. Along with the rest of the room he'd been watching the exchange almost in disbelief and now took advantage of the pause to turn on Safi.

"You knew about this?" he said. "You've been talking about this between yourselves for weeks, and you didn't think to ask how it affected us?"

"Hey, this is news to me too," Safi said, raising her hands in defence. "Talk to Max if it's a problem."

"Too right it's a problem," Mayaan said. "Do you know how much of our work is wasted if we do what he wants? How much extra work we'll need to do?"

"So what are we talking about here?" Victor said, stepping in. "If we wanted to design it Max's way, what would that involve?"

"It can't be done using the low grade electronics we're using so far," Safi said. "We'd need something way more sophisticated, a whole order of magnitude better."

"That can't be difficult, surely."

"It is if these things are going to replicate. They need to be able to make everything they're made from. You can't put a high-grade processor in the design unless it can make one when it replicates, and that isn't easy."

Victor walked over to the far wall where the preliminary designs were displayed. They'd started off as neat, tidy graphics, but were now covered in two weeks' worth of alterations and amendments, with even older versions saved beneath them for later retrieval. Hitting the CAD board's backup function was like digging back through geological history. In the middle of the display were two long lists: the parts list showing everything that was needed to build a Prospector, and the products list showing everything a Prospector could make, given seawater and sunlight. Everything on list A had to be on list B, with no exceptions.

"How are these processors normally made? Can't we use the same method?"

Safi shook her head. "Think of how high grade chips are manufactured — clean room facilities, silicon purification plants — but even if we could make a chip builder small enough, the Prospector couldn't make one for itself, so we wouldn't have achieved anything. If we can't get one hundred percent closure we might as well give up now."

Mayaan stood up again and looked round the room. "So why bother with this at all?" he said. "Why not just ignore Max and build it the way we want to build it? We know it'll work, so why make it more difficult for ourselves, just because he says so?"

Max was ready for this. "You're right, I can't force you to do it my way, but as Victor said when he first explained the plan to us all, I was brought in for a reason. I know what can happen if exponential systems are inadequately constrained. You need to trust me on this one."

Again, the silence was broken by Victor.

"Safi, any thoughts?"

She threw her hands up into the air and shook her head. "What can I say that I haven't said already? We've got enough problems as it is building these things, and then this comes along. As if a high-grade navigation system is something you can just bolt on as an afterthought. It's ridiculous."

"But if we assume that Max is right, and we need one, then we need to find some way of making it. What are our options?"

"Okay, the electronics we're using now would have been state of the art in the nineteen-fifties, but they're good enough for the job and they're easy to build, relatively. But now we're talking about something way more ambitious. We'd need a whole new set of production systems, more complex than anything else on board, just for this one part of the design. And somehow the manufacturing plant has to be able to make all those things for replication. I have to hand it to you, Max, you know how to make life complicated."

By this point in the discussion no eye contact was taking place. People were just staring into their own private bits of space, speaking in turn. Max looked briefly to where Isaac was sitting, near the back of the room keeping out of the discussion just as Max had promised he could.

"So what do you suggest?" Victor said.

Safi paused. "I didn't want to have to say this," she said eventually. "But if we decide we need high grade processors, we may have to supply them as vitamin parts."

"What does that mean?" Ross said.

"It means we make them here on the island, and hand them over to each Prospector as it replicates. That way it doesn't need to make them for itself."

Victor was shaking his head. "No, we can't even consider that. It would completely destroy the economics of the thing. Full replication is the only way to make this worthwhile."

"Then I guess we're stuck," Safi said.

This time Oliver was the next to speak.

"I hate to say I told you so," he said. "But I seem to remember warning you all that this would happen."

"Did you now?" Ross said without looking up.

"On the very first day, do you remember what I said? That a machine can only make something simpler than itself? That machines reproducing themselves is science fiction? If you'd listened to me back then we would all have saved a lot of time and effort."

"That didn't stop you hanging around to collect your paycheques though, did it?" Ross said.

"Now you listen here!" Oliver snapped. "I've stuck it out through this charade for long enough! I knew right at the start it wasn't possible, so don't blame me because it's taken you this long to work it out for yourselves!"

"Enough!" Victor said. It was the first time any of them had heard him raise his voice. "You four, in my office now."

Safi, Ross, Max and Oliver left the meeting room and followed Victor down the corridor. They walked quickly and in silence. Once inside, they stood there uneasily while he shut the door and turned to face them.

"How are we going to achieve anything through a performance like that?" he said.

None of them answered.

"We've got more important things to worry about than you people arguing among yourselves. Now, we're going to go back into that room, and we're going to settle this properly. I will not see this program fail just because you can't agree on what we need to do."

"If you ask me, it's failed already," Oliver said, "and I've said that right from the start."

"Yes," Ross said, "and we've proved you wrong every time."

"Proved me wrong? What was that little discussion all about if it wasn't you lot realising this can't be done? You can dress it up with words like 'closure problems' and 'throughput deficiencies', but you're the ones who've been proved wrong!"

Victor rounded on him. "Oliver, what we're trying to do is not impossible, and we've shown that, many times. It's going to take all of us to make it happen, including you, but we *are* going to do it. Now are you with us on this?"

Oliver shook his head and walked over to the door. "I'm glad you're so confident," he said as he went. "Just don't ask me for help next time you get stuck."

"Don't worry, we won't," Ross said under his breath.

As Oliver got to the door he stopped and turned to face Max. For a second he looked as if he was about to say something else, but then he turned again and left for real.

* * *

Victor decided to abandon the meeting after that. Max went straight down to where his car was parked and set off home through the rain, the events of the meeting playing over and over in his mind. Safi's words had stung him more than anyone else's, maybe because her reaction had been so out of character. Her calm, level-headed approach to problems was one of the things he respected in her the most, and he'd come to respect her a lot. He hoped he hadn't done any lasting damage. Ahead of him he could occasionally see the lights of her and Ross's cars as the winding coast road took them round the island.

Once at the house he parked up and went inside. Even running the short distance from the car to the front door got him wet and he went straight into the bathroom to dry off. It was only then that he noticed how quiet the place was. He went into the lounge, then the bedroom, then back to the lounge, looking for any sign of where Gillian might be. It was then that he saw the red LED blinking on the home terminal. The display showed a message stored there, with Gillian's omni griddex as the sender.

"Do you know what you are Max?" she said when he set it running. She looked livid, as if barely able to control what she was saying. "You're pathetic. That's the only word I can think of after what you've done." She'd recorded it in that very room, with the doors out to the small deck behind her. The glass showed darkness outside; whatever this was, she'd recorded it recently. "You lied to me to protect yourself, and didn't think once that you were putting me in danger. How could you do that? How could any man do that? Some psycho gets within two feet of me, and still you keep quiet. Were you just hoping they'd never do anything? That I'd never find out? Or wouldn't it have mattered if they'd come after me for real? Well whatever it was, don't think you'll get the chance to do it again. I'm not staying here, not after this. I'll call you when I get where I'm going, but don't try to find me. And don't expect me to change my mind. I won't be calling with good news."

It was then that he saw the stack of papers, on the desk next to the terminal's keyboard. Knowing what they'd show before he even turned them over, he picked them up and began to read.

Your sick blasphemous lies will be with you to your grave, the first one said. *Evolution is a fraud, just as the LORD has said, and many false prophets will rise, Darwin and his monkey worshippers among them. Should this hateful idolatry continue, a well sharpened steel may find your neck at any time.*

How can you dare to mock your LORD and creator in this way? another said. *He who made all life on this Earth, everything of beauty, yet your refusal to believe the evidence of your eyes has made you unfit to be part of His creation. You will end your days kneeling in sight of the LORD, you and your barren wife, begging for forgiveness and another chance.*

And finally: *You have lost, and you know it as well as I do. If you had righteousness and mercy on your side, you would be in South America even now, conducting your campaign of deceit and indoctrination. Instead you hide, cowardly and afraid. Your home is inhabited by strangers, your office empty. Is this how you show the conviction of your beliefs, hiding away like a criminal? Or is this your admission that those beliefs are flawed, that your faith in Darwin and his hateful prophecies is treasonous to everything the righteous hold sacred?*

Max flicked through the papers a second time; every one he'd ever been sent was there, all of them dated and addressed, the threats to him and to Gillian, the photographs of him and Gillian, plus that final one, the one Indira had told him about but which he'd never even laid eyes on until now.

He went round the house in a daze after that. Her wardrobe was empty, everything of hers in the bathroom was gone. She'd even taken her painting materials, nothing was left. Then he went back outside and saw what he hadn't even noticed when he'd dashed in to avoid the rain: the empty space round the corner of the house, where her car was normally parked.

He sat in the lounge, trying to force himself to think straight.

If she was going then she had two options, the long boat journey to Samoa followed by a flight from there, or the ESOS jet that had brought them down in the first place. The Samoan flights would be subject to GRACE controls, just one flight every one or even two weeks. The ESOS flights were supply runs, every two weeks at best unless a special delivery or passenger transfer was needed. That would force her to take whichever went first, and if she'd left the house already then at least one of them must be departing today. He went over to the terminal and brought up the flight schedules, and there it was: the ESOS jet, leaving that evening, flying back empty after offloading its cargo of food and supplies.

He ran back out to his car and took the coast road again, past the ESOS complex to where the airfield and its small terminal building lay. He saw the crates of supplies as soon as he got into the building; the jet was either on the ground or had already left. It was when he ran through onto the tarmac that he saw the plane had gone. He looked into the sky to see if there was any sign of it, but all he could see was the rain clouds, emptying ceaselessly onto the archipelago.

He stood like that for a full ten minutes, ignoring the curious stares of the two ground crew as they shifted the crates into a store room. Then he went back to his car and made his way home, dead on the inside.

* * *

The first thing he did when he got to the villa was to open up his omni and call Victor.

"Max, what's going on? The airfield just called me to say Gillian had gone."

"Yes, that's right, she's gone. What did they tell you?"

"Just that there was some emergency back home, something to do with her family. Is everything alright?"

So that was what she'd told them to let her fly. "No, Victor, things aren't alright at all."

"Max, what's going on?"

"I need to leave, I need to go after her. Where is that plane going back to?"

"It's going to Washington, the same as always. Why?"

"I need to go too. As quickly as possible."

"But Max, we need you here, you said it yourself in the meeting. And why did she go on her own if you need to be there too?"

"She, ah, she's gone without me."

There was silence on the end of the line, probably the first realisation of what had happened. "Max," he said eventually, "what's going on?"

Max also paused. He couldn't see any way out of telling the truth. "We, er, we've hit some problems. There was something I should have told her about but didn't, and she's gone." It was uncomfortable talking to Victor about this. He was a different kind of boss to Indira; with her, Max felt he could bring up any subject he wanted. Victor on the other hand led from a more reserved position. "Please, Victor, just let me get off this island, whichever way's fastest. I'll try to sort this out and then I'll be back, but you have to help me go."

Again Victor paused. "Alright, Max, I'll see what I can do. Is there any way you can reach her?"

Max looked at her listing on his omni; her link was blocked to incoming calls. He hadn't expected any different. "No, I can't. But if you can get me back to the US then I can try to find her."

"Max, why don't you —"

"Victor, please, just do this for me. Tell me when the next flight is, or if you can bring it forward. I need to do this."

* * *

It was four days later that Max was able to go, taking the Samoan flight. He stayed in the house the whole time beforehand, trying Gillian's number again and again, but with no success. He didn't know what Victor had told the others, and really couldn't care. By the time the day of the flight came round, he was counting the minutes.

The flight stopped in L.A. to refuel, but Max didn't even bother looking there. Their own house was being rented, and although there were friends she could have stayed with, Max could think of only one place she'd go.

* * *

He parked up on the wooded hillside much as he had five months previously. Lights were on in the house, but there was no sign that anyone inside had heard him pull up. He hesitated on the doorstep for a full minute before he finally rang the bell. It was Gillian's father who answered the door.

"Go away, Max," he said. "You're not wanted here."

"I need to see Gillian."

"She doesn't want to see you."

"Ira, please, I wouldn't be here if I didn't think we could work this out. I need to talk to her, there are things she needs to hear me say."

Ira let him in, wordlessly. The front door led straight into the lounge, and it was there that he saw Derry, plus Laura and Roy, sitting round the room on the exact same chairs they'd been on for his last visit. It almost looked comical seeing them there as if they'd never even moved, though the expressions on their faces broke the impression immediately. Laura and Roy lived nearby, and had obviously come round to give Gillian moral support. The overwhelming atmosphere of the room was one of hostility.

Max didn't stay in the room, or even say anything to them. They weren't the ones he was here to see. He went through the far door and up the stairs, into the room they still kept for Gillian, and there he found her, sitting on the bed staring at the floor. Max wondered if she'd escaped up there when he'd rung the doorbell; she must have known it would be him.

"Gillian, it's me. How are you?"

"How do you think I am, Max?" She didn't even turn to look at him.

"I know you're upset, and you've every right to be. But please just hear me out on this."

"On what? You lied to me, and not just a small lie either. Were you ever going to tell me?"

"Yes, I would have done, eventually."

"Really? You get these letters, threatening you, threatening *me*, and you keep them to yourself? Just when would you have said anything? Did they have to burn the house down before it occurred to you to warn me?"

Max couldn't argue; it pretty much summed it up. "Look, these people," he said, and then faltered. He was about to say something about the religious nature of the notes, make her think about how close to her beliefs they actually were, but he'd already decided it wouldn't be a good idea. "I'm sorry," he said. "I was doing everything I could to make sure nothing happened, I had the university's security in on it and they were talking to the police. Everything that could be done was being done."

"Except telling me? Did that little detail escape you? That person taking my picture could have been anyone. No — not just anyone, one of *them*, and I have no idea about any of it until those notes turn up. Did you not think even then it might be a good idea to tell me?"

Max felt as if all the energy had been sucked out of him. There were no arguments he could put up, nothing he could say. She was right, and if he was honest, then this moment had only ever been a matter of time.

"Is that all you're going to do, stand there?" she said.

"Gillian, you're right, everything you're saying is right, but please try to understand."

"No, Max. I understand perfectly. And you know what? Those people got one thing right. You are a coward. You went out there to hide, not because of the opportunity it gave us, not because it would let us have a child, but to hide. And all along you pretended you wanted the same thing as me. I sat in that house day after day, while you worked ten hours at a stretch, doing something you couldn't even tell me about, all because we'd have a chance to be a family at the end of it. And all along it was a lie."

"That's not true, I took that posting for those reasons too. You know I've always wanted a family just as much as you. That job was the luckiest break we've ever had, why would I pass it up?"

"Lucky? Do you want to know what's lucky, Max? You were lucky that plane left the day it did — more ESOS wastefulness, why use a boat when you can fly a plane from Washington and back — but at least it got me out of there. That was 'lucky'. If I'd had to wait just one more day in the same house as you, you'd have been a dead man."

"But I did it to protect you."

Gillian was still looking at the floor at that point, but he could see her smiling to herself: a satisfied smile rather than a happy one, as if she'd finally managed to work out where he was coming from. It wasn't the kind of smile that suggested a pleasant conversation lay ahead.

"You did it to *protect* me?"

"Gillian, please, you've got to listen to me. I'm the one they wanted to scare, not you. It would have killed me to see you going through that. It would mean they'd won."

She didn't respond, but looked at him instead, a mixture of disbelief and fury in her eyes. It was the first time she'd so much as faced him the whole time they'd been talking. "No excuse. You lied, plain and simple. You put me in danger."

The tone she was taking with him was if anything more scary

than the screaming and shouting he might have expected. It's over, she was saying. This isn't just something to fight about and fix later. It's done.

He moved toward her involuntarily, as if to see whether she would respond.

"Don't even come near me," she said.

"What do you want me to do?"

"I want you to go."

"I won't do that."

"You're in my father's house. If I tell him I want you to go, he'll make sure you do." Max ignored the threat that implied; despite the calmness of her tone he could see the suppressed rage that was driving her.

"And what are you going to do?" he said.

"I think that's my business, don't you?"

It was then that the doorbell rang for the second time that night. Gillian reacted with a start; whoever it was clearly wasn't expected. It must have been Ira who went to answer it again. It was a man's voice at the door, someone Max didn't recognise, and given the look of concerned concentration on Gillian's face, neither did she.

"We're looking for Roy Hocker. We were told he was here."

"Can I see some ID?" A pause, then Ira's voice again. "Yeah, he's here. Why, is anything wrong?"

"We need to talk to him. This is important."

There was the sound of feet coming over the threshold, two men entering the house, people down in the lounge standing up in response. There seemed to be no resistance to their coming in.

"Roy Hocker?" one of the newcomers said.

"Yes, what's the matter? What's happened?"

"I have a warrant for your arrest. You're going to have to come with us."

"Arrest? What for? What's going on here?"

"We've received complaints of harassment, and threats to

commit bodily harm."

"What? No, no way, it can't be —"

"These are serious charges, Mr Hocker. This will go a lot easier if you just come with us."

"Excuse me, you're in my house now." It was Ira's voice, firm but not aggressive. "Just what is he supposed to have done? You owe us that much."

"The charge is under section 4 of the 2018 transmissions act. Mailing threatening communications."

Suddenly Max knew why they were here, even though he could hardly believe it. It appeared Roy had come to the same conclusion.

"Wait — did he call you? It was him wasn't it? Lowrie? Listen, there's a man up there now, he's in this house, he must have —"

"I'd advise you to co-operate, Mr Hocker."

Gillian left the bedroom at that point, rushing downstairs to see what was going on. Max stayed where he was, listening in voyeuristically as events unfolded.

"Are you talking about the letters my daughter's husband was getting?" It was Ira again: *my daughter's husband*, Max noted, not *my son-in-law*. "Just what kind of evidence do you have here?"

"I can't discuss that at this time. Mr Hocker, this way. Now."

Whatever was said next was indistinct as Roy was led from the house. Max heard Laura saying "Where are you taking him?" over and over, her voice close to cracking, Ira trying to console her the whole time, until the voices spilled out onto the street and were lost. Whole minutes later they came back in, Ira, Gillian and Laura, rejoining Derry in the lounge. Heavy footfalls announced Ira's climb up the stairs. He stopped when he was in the doorway, and looked at Max with contempt.

"If I ever find out that you were anything to do with this, I will kill you." Then he went back down the stairs.

Max couldn't leave, but in the current climate going downstairs was probably best avoided. Instead he watched the clock, trying to put events together in his mind. Had it been Roy, all along? It certainly fit Roy's beliefs, but by including Gillian in the threats he was acting against his own soon-to-be family. Could he really have done that?

Eventually Max decided enough was enough; whatever was waiting for him downstairs, hiding in the bedroom wouldn't make it any better. He got up, and headed for the stairs.

The lounge was in silence when he came down. No one said anything when he took the seat nearest the staircase, not even to tell him to go. He looked round at the others, but no one returned his gaze. He seriously considered leaving at that point; he'd run this evening over so many times in advance of being here, how he would resist leaving at all costs, but nothing had prepared him for this. He was about to get up and go when Laura's omni rang, the loud tone making everyone in the room jump.

She kept the receive side muted, a hushed conversation, most of which was carried on by whoever had called. It took three minutes in all, during which Laura did nothing but say, "yes", and, "I see", before finally hanging up. Then she turned to Ira, her face white, and said: "That was our lawyer. He's saying Roy should plead guilty."

She passed on everything she'd been told after that: the way someone at the savings bank where Roy worked had found a collection of documents hidden in his area of a shared terminal, the way she'd been concerned enough by the contents to call her supervisor, and the way he'd then called the police, who within hours had matched those letters up with the evidence from UCLA security.

When she'd finished talking nobody spoke. Gillian was sitting with her head in her hands, while Ira stared at the far wall. Derry was just looking at her hands, clasped together in her lap.

"Oh my God," Gillian said after an age. It was all anyone seemed able to say.

Max got up to leave. If anything there was even more that he and Gillian had to talk about, but this wasn't the time. Some cooling off period would be needed before they picked up the discussion again. "I'm going to get a hotel," he said. "Call me sometime and we can talk more."

He was halfway to the door when Laura stood up, marched over to him and slapped him hard enough to send him staggering backward. Then she ran up the stairs, sobbing copiously. Max watched her go then left, red heat spreading over one whole side of his face.

* * *

Gillian called him the next day, saying little but arranging to meet that afternoon. He couldn't read much from her tone, but the fact she'd called at all was significant.

He went down ten minutes early and found a quiet spot in the hotel bar. At first he wondered why the print on the far wall looked familiar, until he realised it was one of hers: a single golden butterfly, sunning itself on a tree branch, with the Sacramento woodlands behind it. The detail was exquisite, right down to the hairs on its body and the delicate veins running through its wings. He remembered the day she'd made that sale, her biggest yet, to a firm that supplied hotel chains around the country; there were a few by her, he saw as he looked round the bar, but for some reason the butterfly picture was holding his gaze more than the others.

Her almost photographic eye for detail never failed to amaze him, he thought. A couple of centuries earlier she could have been among the best of the botanical artists, recording the wildlife around her far better than any camera of the day. Even these days she attracted enough interest to make a living out of it. He tried to remember the butterfly's species classification as he looked at it, Nymphalidae something or other. He was sure it would come to him.

She turned up on time, her expression neutral as she approached and sat down.

"Max, there are some things I need to say."

"Sure, that's all I've ever wanted, to talk."

"Now what you did was still wrong, you need to admit that, but if I'd ever had any idea it was someone in the family —" She shook her head as if she couldn't find the words.

"So was it definitely Roy?"

"He's denying it, but even his own lawyer is telling him to plead guilty, to try to get the sentence down."

"And what about your parents? And Laura?"

"Laura's taking it badly. She's hardly talking. Dad's been onto Roy's C.O.F friends, to see if they knew anything about it. He can't believe it though, Mum can't either."

"The Children of the Faith": Roy had worn his badge for a reason when he'd met Max that time. Was it really so hard to believe that wasn't the only message he'd decided to send?

"I've given up being surprised, the lengths some people will go to," he said.

"I just can't understand it. I don't think I ever will. That's not what my faith is about, or anyone in my family. Even Dad, I mean he has serious problems with what you do, there's no point denying it, but to have this happen? He can't understand it either."

Max was prepared to believe that. He couldn't see Ira being in on this; Roy must have been acting outside the family, presumably with accomplices to mail the letters and take the pictures. That was the police's problem now. For Max though, there was still one question unanswered. "So where did you get the letters from?" he said. "Who sent them to you?"

"They came in on my omni. I didn't recognise the address."

"Can I see?"

She got her omni out, a broad silver-plated pendant, and

opened up the messaging page. The letters were all there as softcopy attachments, the same scans that UCLA security had made of the hardcopy originals, but the message that had delivered them to Gillian showed only "Tyrell-B UCLA" as the sender. Griddex names had to match your own name or your company name; misleading ones were seen as fraudulent, a carryover from the ground-up rebuild when the early twenty-first century internet was replaced by the worldwide grid, but Tyrell B wasn't a name Max had even heard of. A status check showed the address was dormant, closed to incoming messages.

"I'm going to find out who that is," Max said. "And why they did it. It's got to be someone in the department, no one else knew about this."

"So I wasn't the only one left in the dark?"

"No, you weren't."

"You should have told me."

"I know. If I said I was waiting for the right opportunity it would probably sound pretty lame, but I didn't know how you'd react."

"Max, I'm your wife, there should be nothing you're too scared to come to me with."

"Even this? I know you don't approve of the school visits, the talks I give. How would you react if I said out of the blue that people were threatening us both as a result?"

"You're right, I don't approve of what you do. I think you're force-feeding children a flawed and overly simplistic answer to probably the most compelling questions human beings can ever ask. You're teaching them to see the world the way you do: one life, once we die that's it, no consequences, no higher power, no nothing. I still can't understand how someone can live a moral life that way, and I don't think I ever will. But I married you for a reason, despite what my family thought: there's more to you than just your beliefs. You're a wonderful man, everything I could have asked for, kind, compassionate, honest, or so I thought.

That's why this hurt me so much. If you can be dishonest over something this important, what else have I got wrong about you?"

There was little for Max to argue with. "It was a mistake," he said. "I won't let you down again."

"I hope you don't."

"Does this mean you're going to come back?"

Just for a second, she seemed to consider her answer. "Yes, I'll come back."

Max felt as if a weight he'd carried for days was suddenly gone. "Thank you," he said, taking her hand. She didn't resist.

"But we're going to be honest from now on," she said. "No secrets, no sneaking around."

"Sure."

"Not even the stuff you're doing out there. I don't want to be kept in the dark on anything. I want to feel trusted, no matter what Victor has told you."

"So you want to know what it's all about?"

"Yes."

He'd been sworn to secrecy, but in the circumstances he felt she deserved the truth. So he told her, the whole gold extraction plan, the replicators, everything, including his reservations about the Prospectors and the argument the day she walked out.

"Is that why you were reluctant to go? When you were first offered the place?"

"Yes. I think it's a bad idea, and I can only see it ending badly."

"It sounds to me like they're trying to create something alive. That's just wrong. No one has the right do that."

"That's pretty much what I've thought all along."

"Really? You really see it like that?"

"Yes, but not for the same reasons as you. It's the physical consequences I'm worried about, not the blasphemy."

"So what are you going to do? If you've got to stick with a

project you don't agree with, where does that leave you?"

He hesitated, thinking through the situation again in his head. His was a scientist's viewpoint, everything was a problem to be solved, a broken thing to be fixed. The navigation system, that was it. He could see the dilemma in his mind, just as clearly as he had back on the island. How to get a robust, reliable navigation computer into something simple enough to be made from algal cellulose and filtered sediment.

He stared at the picture opposite, of the golden butterfly spreading its wings in the sun. *Nymphalidae Vannevaris*, he thought, its name choosing that moment to come to mind. But still something about the picture was nagging at him.

"Somewhere there's an answer," he said. "Somewhere there's an answer."

* * *

When Max called the island to say he'd be coming back, he found out he wasn't the only one with news.

Oliver's departure was a shock, but not really a surprise. He had left a few days after Max and Gillian, the aftermath of that day's arguments never really having been put behind him. No one on the project planned to see him again. They didn't see any point, and they didn't think Oliver would either.

"All he ever did was gloat when things went wrong," Ross said from his side of the video link. "Why should we give him a send off? I'm glad to see the back of him."

"It was a mistake bringing him out here," Victor admitted. "I should have known he was here for the wrong reasons."

And once Max had heard those reasons, he had to agree. The way Oliver had used his position in his previous job to abuse and then fire anyone who tried to argue with him, the way he'd then lost that job after a protracted disciplinary battle, and the way this project must have looked like his salvation: a chance to rebuild his career as well as his finances. Suddenly it made sense why he'd stayed so long in a job he thought was a waste of time. And suddenly the stories of near-mutinies in his backroom team weren't so hard to believe either. He'd be a hard enough person to work for even if he didn't think the whole thing was pointless.

"This doesn't solve our real problems though," Victor said. "Just because we don't have him around anymore, that doesn't alter the fact that we're in trouble."

Chapter 5

In a previous age she would have been called a journalist. Not a famous name on the newsfeeds, not a face to be recognised from the broadcasts, but a vital part of the gathering process, her far-reaching electronic presence filtering and collating anything which might be of value. Times, however, had changed. For Anna Liu and her organisation, feeding stories to the news channels was now only part of the job. Contract information gathering was the best description for her profession, and these days the job she did, and the techniques at her disposal, had more in common with espionage than journalism. As an investigator for one of the premier international information agencies, she was often required to spend hours sifting through the real time data that came in from her sources around the world, and the twenty-four hour nature of the job had long since made its mark on her life. But the rewards made it worthwhile.

She only knew him as "Tyrell". Three weeks ago he'd started sending her information from within the ESOS company, all low value data, but the kind of internal documents and communications that only an insider would have access to. The staff headcounts and departmental management plans were just a taster though, the proof that something more valuable could be provided if the price could be agreed. Three times she'd gone back to him with an offer, and three times he'd held firm, waiting for her to offer more. And then, for some reason, his messages had stopped.

She knew there was something good there, some new project or breakthrough. Her gut feeling was that something big was going on in ESOS, a kind of feeling she'd long since learned to trust. If Tyrell had gone quiet, she would need another lead.

It was half past two in the morning when the flag came in alerting her to a tip-off from one of her trawlers. Informants aside, the trawlers were her most profitable data sources: artificial intelligence programs trained to hunt through government and company press releases, open source publications and existing news material, looking for any connections or inconsistencies that might be of value. They also tapped into the global "grey market" of information: which national grids someone's omni account had hooked up to, whose messages certain keywords had appeared in: far from legal, but far from traceable too. But although the trawlers were useful, they would never learn intuition. That particular gift was hers alone.

Three names were listed at the top of the terse, computer generated statement when it arrived; Safi Biehn, Max Lowrie, and Oliver Rudd. None of them sounded familiar to her, and a quick glance at their résumés showed nothing to link them either. The first, a regional cargo pilot from Florida who seven years ago had abandoned a promising career in lunar surface engineering; the second, an English biologist living in California, making a tidy living out of "Darwinian design", whatever that was; and the third, a professor of robotics with a string of qualifications and a talent for getting himself fired. Obviously they had something in common that was more than just coincidence. Intrigued, she read further.

Then she saw it. Not only had they all stayed in Washington DC over the same week five months ago, the two that weren't already unemployed had both left their jobs very soon afterward.

Private addresses were harder to get hold of, even for the trawlers, but she could see that all three of them had left their previous residences in order to take up their new positions. There was, however, no indication whatsoever of them moving into new ones. It was as if they'd simply disappeared.

Somewhere, deep down, she knew the ESOS story was linked. And she wanted to know how.

* * *

It was the day before he and Gillian were due to fly back to the island that Max realised he had the answer. It solved everything — the Prospector design, the control system, the safety measures — and what was more, it had been staring him in the face just days before. All he had to do now was convince the others.

"Victor, how would you like a trip to Colorado?"

"Colorado? What are you talking about Max?"

"I want you to meet someone I worked with a few years ago. His name is Doug Chowdry, and I think he may be able to help us."

"How? What does he do?"

"I can't explain it here, you'd have to see for yourself."

"Are you talking about getting him down to the island?"

"No, we'd have to go to him. All of us, in fact. I can get there from West Virginia easily enough, you'll need to get there however you can. But once you've seen the kind of work he does, you'll understand."

"Max, I can't take everyone halfway round the world just on a whim. You're going to have to tell me more."

"No, Victor, you got us all the way to Washington before you told us why we were there, now it's my turn to keep you guessing. But trust me, you'll know what I'm thinking of soon enough."

* * *

They'd arranged to meet in the lobby of Artemis Technologies, in an industrial unit on the outskirts of Colorado Springs. It was the first time Max had met the others in nine days. In true ESOS style they'd flown all the way, even the continental leg, but Max and Gillian had rented a two-seat Z-Vec, tearing along the interstate channel at over two hundred miles an hour, in a convoy of eighty close-coupled vehicles. Once on the slow roads he selected the Zip code for the centre of the city, then dropped Gillian off at the hotel Victor had arranged for them all before joining another automated traffic stream out toward the Air Force college.

The Artemis building was just beyond the college, with a line-up of aviation relics flanking the road outside, static displays of F-15s and F-18s mounted on concrete pillars, plus a recently retired Boeing U-155, battered and scorched from its lifetime of excursions in and out of the atmosphere. Max's father had spent most of his working life shaving gram after gram from the space-craft science payloads he'd designed, never once knowing that these then-classified planes were running halfway to orbit and back as if it was a day-trip. Max sat in the reception area and looked it over while he waited for the others to turn up.

"Max, good to see you again," Victor said when he arrived with Safi and Ross. "Everything alright?"

"I'm okay," he said. "Ready to get back to work."

"So you're back on the project now?" Safi said. She was back in her meeting attire, the same plain suit she'd worn when he first met her.

"Absolutely." Max didn't know how much she and Ross had been told about why he'd had to leave, but he hoped he'd get the chance to explain it his way. Keeping secrets would have to become a habit of the past, and that included colleagues.

Once they'd booked in they were led to the second floor, to a room looking out over the Rocky Mountains. They took their seats and waited for their host to arrive.

Doug Chowdry was slightly younger than Max, with reddish coloured hair and red checked shirt. He recognised Max straight away when he entered the room, but he still did a double take when he saw the four of them sitting there. After three months on the island their heavily tanned skin and weather-beaten faces must have made them look like survivors from a shipwreck.

Once they'd been introduced, Doug turned to Max expectantly. "Well, this is your show I guess, Max. So what can I do for you?"

Max's answer was meant for all of them.

"I've deliberately kept everyone in the dark on this one," he said, "because I don't want to prejudice any of the decisions we may end up making. You've probably guessed that Doug here has access to some technology that could help us in our program, and Doug, you've probably guessed that we could find a use for what you do. But I think it should speak for itself, so, I'll let you take over."

"What do you want me to say?" Doug said.

"Can you show us the MAV?"

"Only a very early version, anything else would be classified."

"That's good enough for us."

Doug left the room and came back a couple of minutes later with a plastic box held protectively in both hands. He put it carefully down on the table and lifted off the lid. Then he stepped back and took a small black keypad from his pocket. It had about a dozen controls on it, with a screen set into one end. Once he was ready to start, he switched the unit on, and looked over toward the box. Everyone followed his gaze as he began to work the controls.

Max knew what was coming, so he looked at the others and watched the expectant looks turning to surprise as the box's occupant revealed itself. Slowly and silently, a large butterfly had risen out of the box, and was now hovering over the table, bobbing up and down with each beat of its wings. But there was no way that nature had designed this insect. No real butterfly would be silver in colour, nor would it obey every command of a radio control unit in the hand of a human master, as it so clearly was doing with Doug. Even less likely would be the video quality images appearing on the screen of the controller as it relayed its view of the world back along its command channel. Safi was the first to realise what she was looking at.

"It's a micro-UAV, an Unmanned Aerial Vehicle," she said.

"Well done," Doug said. "This one's just a prototype, but it shows the kind of thing we can do. Here, do you want to try it?"

She took the controller carefully, and soon got the hang of flying it round the room. Then she got it hovering in front of her face, and looked down at the distorted image of herself on the screen. Once she'd finished she passed the controller along so Ross could take over.

"What would you use it for?" Ross said, as he flew a slow circuit of the room.

"It's mainly a surveillance device," Doug said. "Though the model that actually gets used is much smaller than this. Like I said, this was an early version. They tend to get used for hostage situations, things like that, but we've had a fair few customers lately."

"And why is it disguised as a butterfly?"

"That's not a disguise, it has to be that shape. The way air moves round objects at this scale is very different to what you'd get round a full size aircraft. You can't just shrink a plane down to build a machine like this, you have to copy nature. Insect flight was the only model we had."

"Very impressive," Victor said as he took his turn at the controls. As the others had done, he found it easier to control if he used the view from the camera, rather than following it round the room with his eyes. "But how does it help us?"

"It's the way it's made that's important," Max said.

Victor made a bumpy landing on the tabletop and gave the controller back to Doug. Then Doug picked up the craft itself and let them look at it closely.

"Within the body of this thing there's over fifteen-hundred electronic components, plus twelve electric actuators for the wings. Add the camera and transmitter gear, and I think you'll realise the kind of complexity that you're faced with. Building something like this is a real challenge.

"We initially tried using conventional motors and components, highly miniaturised, and assembled the way any other machine would be. We even had miniature power cables, thinner than a human hair. But we soon realised the limitations of that approach, so we had to find something else."

He looked over at Max to see if his explanation was going along the right lines. Max nodded back encouragingly.

"So we developed a new way of making things," he continued. "Now what's the best way to explain this? Are you familiar with 3D printing?"

"Yes, for fast prototyping, model making," Victor said. "We've been using it for decades."

"Not like this you haven't. Fast prototyping is a good analogy, but it's crude by comparison. We build an object up in layers, that much is the same, and we do each layer using a printing process, but it's the way we formulate the layers which is special. We don't just use structural materials like plastics and resins, we lay down completely different materials, some of them conductive, some of them magnetic, whatever properties you want to give them. Put the right materials in the right places and you can form relays, capacitors, motors, almost everything you'd need to build the kind of machine you're looking at here."

Looking at the body of the thing, they could almost see the stepped shape of the layers it was built from. The wings were single layers of resin, inlaid with a fine tracery of aluminium conductors that let them act as aerials. The pattern was so fine that the surface of the wings diffracted any light that fell on them, giving an appearance that varied between rainbow colours at one angle and shiny silver at another.

"So if 3D printing has been around so long, why isn't everyone using it?" Safi said.

"No one's cracked the problem of getting the right variety of materials into a single print run," Doug said. "And even then it's slow — anything you can make this way can usually be made better another way. But if you need to miniaturise, or if you need the most versatile construction method imaginable, this is it."

"What does this printer look like, the one that made this?" Victor said.

"Come with me and I'll show you."

Doug led them down to the basement of the building, to where one of the machines was kept.

"This one works at a much larger scale than the one we used for the MAV," he said as they walked. "It'll make it easier to see. The technique is so flexible we use it whenever we can, even if the size of the product doesn't make it a necessity."

The machine looked like a large rectangular tub with a robotic arm poised over it. A cluster of thin, flexible pipes led up the arm, and ended with a nozzle arrangement at the tip. Doug went over to a control panel, and brought up a list of design files on the screen.

"What do you want me to make?" he said. "We can do most types of autonomous robotic devices, walleye projectors, domestic air and water pumps, even a frequency-agile gridcom if you want one."

Victor looked down the list. "A solar generator," he said, as if picking one of the items at random.

"You want one of those? No problem."

Doug selected the required data file, and set the printer running. They all looked over the edge of the tub to see the first layer being laid down. The arm was scanning back and forth, and as it deposited the resins they could see slight variations in the colour and texture as different physical and electrical properties were given to each part of the unit.

While it was running Safi backed away and had another look at the list of items the printer could make. The variety was impressive. Victor saw her, and moved over to join her.

"Is this one of von Neumann's universal constructors?" he asked her, just within Max's earshot.

"Not quite," she said. "But it may be close enough."

"This'll take about ten minutes," Doug said to them all. "I

suggest we go and sit back down, then come back when it's done."

They moved back up to the meeting room, and retook their seats.

"Right, does anyone have any questions?" Doug said.

Safi spoke first.

"Is there any limit on the size of machine you can produce like this?"

"No, not at all. Big things take longer than small things of course, but that's the only rule. And sometimes you have to make things in more than one section, then fit them together. But otherwise there's no limit."

"And I guess there's no limit on the complexity either," Victor said.

"The only limit is the accuracy and resolution of the printer head itself, the dots-per-inch, if you want to think of it in normal printing terms. One thing you should bear in mind is that the complexity doesn't affect the time taken. We can make a simple computer the size of a cinder block in two hours using this method, but a solid block of plastic the same size would take just as long."

"And how would that computer compare to one made the usual way?"

"Not very well, in fact a lot worse, but remember we can make almost anything we want this way. That versatility is our main advantage. In fact nowadays, whenever we need a new 3D printer we use one of the old ones to make it for us. It's like — what's the matter? What did I say?"

The other three had exchanged swift glances at that point, as the significance of Doug's last comment hit them. Max took it as his cue to let Doug listen to them for a change.

"I think at this point it's our turn to open up and let Doug in on a few secrets," he said. "We've asked enough questions of our own so far. Is everyone happy to do that?"

In the end it was Safi who gave Doug the story, starting with the initial Prospector concept, right up to the replication problems that had marred their recent work. In all it took her around ten minutes. When she'd finished, Doug just leant back in his chair and looked at the ceiling, as if trying to comprehend what he'd heard.

"Let me make sure I've got this right," he said eventually. "You want to take the kind of manufacturing diversity that most small countries would be proud of, and condense it down onto a vehicle the size of a small pleasure boat. Is that right?"

The analogy was hard to fault.

"My God," Doug said. "No wonder you people need help."

"But the question is," Victor said, "are you able to give that help?"

"Your chemical plant will be the biggest problem. You won't be able to make molecular filters or anything fancy like that using this method. You'll be looking at electrolysis and chromatography for most materials. And the ones we use are pretty exotic, you'll need to find your own equivalents, things you can easily pull out of the sea. But assuming you can get a good enough set of raw materials, then, yes, I think this method could help you."

"And what do you think?" Victor asked Safi and Ross.

"It looks promising," Safi said. "One manufacturing method that makes virtually everything we'll need on board — I'm for trying it."

"But you're right about the chemical plant," Ross said. "It would need to be looked at."

"So is that a yes or a no?" Victor said.

Ross nodded. "Let's try it."

* * *

Later that evening they sat round a low table in the lounge area of Victor's hotel suite. Victor was sitting in an antique leather armchair, turning his new toy over and over in his hands. The panel was fifteen centimetres square and about two centimetres thick, with no visible openings or fastenings. The upper surface was translucent and featureless, but the layer below contained a network of tiny tracks and channels forming an intricate pattern repeated again and again over the face of the unit. The next layer was laced with carbon powder, the matt black material positioned to capture the heat of the sun and transfer it to the water in the channels. A series of minuscule turbines took up the next few layers, and finally came the generators themselves, set into the back plate. Three systems, fluidic, mechanical and electrical, all buried in one solid-state block, all built in a single operation.

"It's not just the range of products you can make that's important," Max was telling him. "It's the efficiency of design that it lets you use. All the electronics that control that generator are built into the structure of the thing, set into the material itself. You can see some of the conductor tracks running down the side there. If we do the same thing for the Prospector control systems it means we can distribute them through the material of the hull. Then it doesn't matter that the electronics are all low grade because we can make it as complex as we want and never have to search around looking for space. It's a good solution."

Victor nodded. "You can put in all the safeguards you want, and all without using a chip builder. Would that make you happier?"

"Of course it would."

"So how did you know about this process?"

"Doug came to us about five years ago. They'd already developed the production technique by then, but they needed a way of designing their products to make the best use of it. The MAV was the one I ended up working on. It took over forty thousand generations, but eventually we found the best way to integrate all of its systems into one block of material. It's breath-takingly complex when you see how it's laid out in there, don't be fooled by the size. But really it was the same problem that's facing us: a single manufacturing process that can pack the widest possible range of intricate robotic systems into the smallest possible space."

"I wasn't fooled by the size at all," Victor said. "Though I'd worry about getting ahead of ourselves with this. We still don't know if we can make it work with marine materials."

"Well, that's in Ross's hands now."

"It's going to take some work," Ross said. "I think almost every material they're using back there will have to be changed. But the extraction techniques themselves will be pretty much the same as what we've used up until now, so I'm hopeful. Give me a week or so and I'll tell you for sure."

"Aren't we going to have to pay Doug to let us use this technique?" Safi said.

"There will be contractual issues," Victor said. "But I'll get our people talking to his people. We should be able to sort something out."

"And Doug owes me a few favours," Max said. "We're going to need his help and advice pretty much all the way through if this is the method we use, but I think he'll be willing to help us. I suggest we stay up here until the design is pretty much finalised. We can set up secure lines to the island and work with our teams that way, and still test out our ideas using Doug's facilities. Does everyone agree with that?"

"That sounds sensible," Victor said. "And I'm glad to see you're getting into the spirit of this at last, Max," he added with a grin.

"I never said I thought this was a good idea," Max said. "That's not why I'm helping you. Bringing Doug's techniques into this is damage limitation as far as I'm concerned. Don't forget that."

The next day they moved out of their rooms and into one of the hotel's business suites: four bedrooms, two offices and a meeting room, with independent communication links and full encryption capabilities. Ross would be going back to the island to test any changes to the extraction methods, but the others would stay, testing component designs in Doug's printers even as they were formulated. Gillian would be staying too, taking advantage of another, as yet untapped, source of subjects for her artwork.

For the first time in weeks they could see a way ahead of them, and now they had more than just the financial rewards to motivate them. "We've got to make it work," Ross said before he left. "Just to prove how wrong that idiot Oliver was." For Ross at least, that was probably more of an incentive than the gold itself.

Chapter 6

Tyrell was gone, that much was clear, and in all likelihood she wouldn't be hearing from him anytime soon. Anna didn't know what had caused him to pull out of negotiations, but whatever it was didn't necessarily detract from the value of what he'd been trying to sell her. She sat back from her latest trawler run and touched the window controls, letting the humid Singapore air mix with the output of the aircon. The traffic noise far below helped her calm her mind, organise her thoughts.

Lowrie: his was the name at the top of her list right now. For although Tyrell's information would have given her a valuable insight into whatever ESOS was doing, it wouldn't have been her only route into the company. Years ago someone else had contacted her, some underpaid low level manager in the ESOS Washington office, and ever since then she'd had a way into their systems, a limited view of the administrative side of their operations. He'd long since left the company, but the trawler socket he'd left behind for her was still running, and the through flow of résumés and contracts had been mildly profitable ever since.

That little hook had now scored a bigger bite, and Lowrie's name was all over it.

It seemed to have been some sort of company emergency that had prompted the sudden recruitment of those three names, Lowrie, Biehn and Rudd, some breakdown in a prestige project still hidden from the outside world. "Essential skills", was the phrase she saw on the internal messages, "vital that they are brought on board". The last two names were almost certain to accept, that much seemed clear to whoever was running the programme, but the first, Lowrie himself, seemed to be a different matter. And when she dug deeper, she saw her first hints of how they'd decided to persuade him.

She needed a new source, a willing accomplice on the inside, someone motivated to help her in her search. Just how would Max Lowrie react, she thought, if he knew the lengths ESOS had really gone to to recruit him?

* * *

The completion of the Prospector design was a surprisingly low-key event. Considering the number of weeks they'd spent passing plans and schematics back and forth along the secure lines to the island, it was almost an anticlimax when they brought all the subsystems together to form the final blueprints. The workload had been intense; for Max the only respite had been Roy's trial, his own contribution being limited to one day at the Colorado Springs justice court on a telepresence link to the hearing in West Virginia. He had little to add to the evidence already on file. Beyond that, he'd kept his head down and worked with the others.

And when Victor, Safi and Max saw the finished plans for the first time, it seemed hard to imagine just how much effort had gone into producing the pictures that were in front of them. When they called Ross to tell him the finalisations were on their way, he was even more surprised at their reactions.

"You could at least smile, guys!" he said. "I saw your faces and thought someone had died!"

"We're just tired," Safi told him. "It's been a long few weeks. We'll get the champagne out once we're back, okay?"

* * *

It seemed strange to Max to arrive back at the island the same way they had done all those weeks ago. This time, though, he wasn't a stranger here, and it felt more like he was returning home. The usual oppressive heat had returned, and the only sign of the storms they'd left behind was a few fallen trees, most of which had been cleared away. In fact now there was a real sense of excitement in the air, and even Max's reservations weren't enough to stop him picking up on it. They'd got so far with the work, and so many of his conditions had been agreed to, that part of him was eager to see just how well they'd met the challenge they'd set themselves.

* * *

The next morning they assembled at the complex again, this time in the workshops that made up the lower level. The ceiling was about twenty feet above their heads, and three huge sliding doors led out onto concrete ramps that sloped down to the harbour. Two of the doors had been shuttered down like blinds, but the far one was open, and bright sunlight was streaming in through the gap. But what really got their attention was parked just inside the centre door, surrounded by a framework of gantry lights and lifting gear. The Prospector itself, vehicle number one, ungainly and functional in appearance but impressive nonetheless. It measured almost twenty feet from bow to stern, and was almost four feet in height, though less than half of that would be above the waterline when it was afloat. Once the sails were attached it would be taller, but from the look of it, those were the only major components that were missing.

The grey-green colour of the hull gave the thing an almost menacing appearance, an artefact of the algal cellulose which, Ross had observed, would put the Prospector population somewhere within an existing food chain, though as an offshoot rather than a link. Once processed and purified, the substance found its way into almost all the non-electrical systems of the design. Compared to steel or conventional composites it was poor, but here it was plentiful and versatile.

Max was initially surprised to see it so close to completion, but then again it had been designed to be easy to build. Once out in open water it would be building copies of itself every eight days, using nothing but the facilities on board, so for a dedicated workshop staff to construct the first one so fast wasn't such a shock.

However it was still an experience, to see with their own eyes something that so far had only existed in their minds or on their screens. Beyond those first subscale prototypes, this was their first real, close-up, view. Safi's reaction was the most telling, as she slowly walked up to it and ran her hand along the hull, nodding to herself. It was easy to forget that more than eight years had passed since she'd last done work like this, only to see that project abandoned halfway through. In many ways she'd waited longer for this moment than any of them.

Once she'd completed her walk-round inspection of the craft, she turned to face Victor.

"When's the launch?"

"In five days time."

* * *

Launch day came round quickly, and the final tests and preparations filled the time right up to the last minute. When the roll-out itself was due it seemed as if the entire ESOS staff were there to watch. Victor himself began the proceedings, taking his place in front of the crowd.

"Anyone who knows the history of the technology that we've created here will know that this day is the culmination of far more than just the months and weeks that we've invested. The ideas that inspired this project can be traced back to the nineteen-forties, or maybe even earlier. And the name of the man whose work laid the foundations for us should also be familiar to us all. As Sir Isaac Newton once said, 'If I have seen further, it is by standing on the shoulders of giants.' And for the past year we have been privileged to stand on the shoulders of one of the greatest giants of them all, one who we are about to immortalise today with the launch of the first of our creations. However, the head start he gave us should not detract from the sense of achievement we all feel today. To take the theoretical analysis of self replicating automata — the hundred year old mathematical proof that such a thing is even possible — to take that proposition and turn it into hard physical reality, that is one of the greatest tasks any of us will ever be involved in. And we've done it. You've done it."

Victor was talking to all of them at that point, but it was Safi that he looked at directly.

"All I want to do now," he continued, "is to thank you, all of you, for the effort you have put in. So let me present the result of that effort, our first Prospector, the 'John von Neumann'."

At Victor's signal the craft emerged from the workshop bay, and was slowly backed down the ramp on a trailer. The operator had to take it carefully through the door now that the sails were attached. Like upturned airplane wings pointing at the sky they left barely inches of clearance, but they made it through unscathed. The only difference between this craft and those that would follow was the name on the side, highly visible in large white letters against the dark green background.

Once in the water it floated free of the trailer and was swiftly reined in by the two-man crew of a waiting boat, ready to be towed out to the operating area. There were cheers when it began its journey out to the open sea, and Max and the others stood watching it for over five minutes while it left the harbour behind and was lost from view. The applause continued even after it had gone, as the euphoria and pride in what had been achieved infected everyone who had worked on it. Victor was beaming, Ross was cheering, and Safi was just standing there smiling, nodding to herself in quiet satisfaction.

"Let's go inside and see how it gets on," Victor said. An operations room had been set up in the complex, and they all hurried in to watch the craft's progress as the time of activation approached.

The cordoned off region of sea had been termed "the box" for ease of reference, and the planned activation point was on the near edge of the area. In the complex they watched the large view screens in silence as the craft was manoeuvred into position, ready for the switch-on. Then at last the towlines were unhooked, the towboat was positioned alongside, and one of the crew reached over to put the bridge piece in place: the final component which slotted into the Prospector's hull and linked the generators to the controllers.

The act itself was as far from dramatic as it could get, but the tension in the operations room was unmistakable. No one made a sound as they waited for some sign of life from the machine. Then, finally, came the moment of relief as the craft took its first independent action, rotating its aerofoil sails to the correct angle to the wind, moving its rudder hard to one side, and preparing to head off on its journey.

The life cycle of the Prospector had been carefully planned. First, it would choose a position in the box where its material collection and replication phase would take place. Then, it would hold that position as steady as possible while it processed the surrounding seawater, extracting all the solid sediments, organic matter and dissolved chemicals that made up its raw materials. As these stores accumulated it would then begin to build, putting the right materials in the right places to form exact copies of the same structures and mechanisms that it itself was made from. And all the while, somewhere inside its chemical plant, its store of gold would be growing.

Once its copy was complete it would activate it, release it into the open sea, then head for a predetermined drop-off area near the island where it would deposit its harvest of gold into shallow water for collection. Then the cycle would be repeated, but this time with two Prospectors at work instead of one.

The first day of operation was uneventful, as the craft kept station against the slow surface currents, pumping water through its processing plant. Nonetheless, the boat crews kept a constant vigil over it, working in shifts, watching for any unexpected developments. Just over twenty-four hours later however, the next critical phase was due to begin, when the replication process itself would get underway.

There were so many unknowns about this process, so many ways it could go wrong, that it had to be observed up close by the people who had planned it in the most detail. And luckily, the first stages at least would take place in daylight. So once the boat had returned to relieve the last boat crew, Max and Safi were sent out in their place.

* * *

They found the Prospector easily enough, and pulled in alongside it. Not all of its upper structure was strong enough to walk on and the few secure footholds weren't marked, so for safety they had to get as close as they could with their own vessel.

"Right, let's drop back a bit and get a look inside the chamber," Safi said once they were alongside.

Max adjusted the controls slightly and the boat manoeuvred back toward the stern of the craft, while Safi peered round some of its superstructure to get a better view of the layering chamber, where the components for replication were made. It was difficult to see from the side; the actual workings of the vehicle were all nestled between the two flotation tubes, but eventually she saw what she was looking for.

"It's forming the first section all right," she reported back, both to Max and the others listening in on the island. Max came over to join her and see for himself. The layering chamber was really just a flat area sheltered from sunlight and sea spray where the printing arm laid down the materials to make each section. It wasn't completely enclosed, but it was still hard to see inside.

"Looks good from here," Max confirmed. "We'll have to wait until it starts the next one before we can be sure though."

This first section to be made was one of the least interesting and least challenging for the machine, just the rear end cap for the starboard floatation tube, a hemispherical structure with a honeycomb of stiffeners inside it. However it was a good first test for the process. From what they could see it seemed to be a third of the way through the piece.

"All right, just keep us informed," Victor said from the island, and shut down the link.

Sunset was less than an hour away, and out at sea the air was already starting to cool down. Now it was just comfortably warm. Max went over to the open-air console and sat down on one of the side benches. Safi followed him and took one of the facing seats.

"Max, there's something I need to say to you."

"Go on," he said, intrigued.

"I'm sorry I lost my temper when we were back in the complex that time. The things you were saying, about how we should be careful, you were right to tell us how you felt. I shouldn't have reacted the way I did."

Max laughed. "Hey, don't worry about it! It was a long time ago, a lot's happened since then."

"I know, but I've never had the chance to say it until now. I was under a lot of pressure then, we all were."

"Now that's true enough! But don't worry about it, it really didn't get to me."

"You sure?"

"Absolutely. I never take things to heart if they're said in the heat of the moment. It's something you soon learn when you're married."

"That's good." She leant over to the cooler at the back of the deck and got a drink out. "Want one?" He shook his head, and she sat back down.

"So how did you and Gillian meet?"

"We were in South Africa. I was there collecting data for my PhD, and she was in the same reserve working as a wildlife artist. The same job she does now. It turned out we had the same itinerary planned, so we hooked up and travelled together. I even used some of her illustrations in my thesis. Things just went on from there."

"I had wondered," Safi said. "You seem an unusual match. I don't mean that in a bad way of course."

"No, I know what you mean. A lot of people say the same thing. We have a lot in common though, we both deal with the natural world, we have the same fascination with it. And the differences between us just make things all the more interesting."

"You do seem to have fairly different views of the world. That must be tough."

"It is and it isn't. I think my way of looking at things comes across as a bit soulless sometimes, that's all. You know what I mean?"

"No. Like how?"

"Like, okay, look at those clouds over there."

He pointed off into the west where the sun was still above the horizon, partially hidden by a bank of clouds. The light was streaming through the gaps, forming distinct sunbeams radiating toward the sea, lighting up the cloud base with shades of red and orange.

"People call that the 'Fingers of God' effect, like he's reaching down from the skies to touch the ground. It can be pretty breathtaking sometimes."

"You're right, it can," Safi said.

"Well, I tried to explain to her once how it actually works, how the perspective makes the rays spread out like that, and how the dust particles in the air mean that some colours are scattered more than others. But she just didn't get it. She believed me of course, but she couldn't see how I could explain it in scientific terms and still see it as beautiful at the same time. It was as if the two ways of looking at it cancelled each other out: you can have one or the other but not both. But for me, the fact that something as amazing as a sight like that can be the result of such simple rules, that just adds to the beauty. And I see things like that everywhere I look in nature, from rainbows to rainforests." He smiled at the unintentional alliteration.

"I could tell you some similar stories," Safi said. "My roommate at college was convinced you could prove telepathy was real by looking at how animals behaved. She was an engineer too, the same as me, but she had this one obsession. Whenever she saw flocks of birds going over, all wheeling and turning at the same time, she said there was no way that could be explained rationally. They had to be thinking as one.

"But around the same time, one of the guys in my faculty was researching emergent behaviour in robots — how you can take lots of simple robots following simple rules, put them all together and suddenly they do something clever — and he had a simulation of how flying robots would move in formation. One of them acts as the leader, and the others just follow it but avoid each other. And there it was: the way they moved was identical to the birds. Nothing spooky about it at all."

"And what did your roommate think of that?"

"She wasn't convinced. But she didn't mention it again."

Safi finished her drink and put the carton in the waste box.

"So what did Gillian think about coming out here? There can't be much for her to do."

"This is our chance to start a family, probably our only chance. That's the real reason we came. It's been tough for her though, definitely. Especially during the rains when she couldn't get outside. But she spends a lot of time with Tess, and she's getting loads of her own work done. And I try not to talk about my work too much when I'm with her. She's fine, really."

"So what have you told her about what you're doing here? Does she realise how important all the work you've done here has been?"

"She knows I needed convincing to even come here. That now I am here all I really want to do is see it done properly."

"Done properly?"

"Safely, so it doesn't blow up in our faces. You know what I'm talking about. But that thing out there is your baby more than anyone else's, so you probably don't want to hear about that."

"I know what you're saying, Max, believe me. I know why you're concerned. But remember I've been through this whole process once before. This isn't an unknown subject to me the way it is to you or the others. I know what's possible and what isn't. You're right to be cautious but don't take it to extremes, please. Especially as it's thanks to you that we've got this far at all."

Max nodded, but didn't reply.

The sky was darkening rapidly, so Safi got up and went to check on the Prospector again before the light failed completely.

"It's done it!" she called back. Max went out and joined her.

The completed end cap had been lifted out of the chamber, and lowered into the water behind the right-hand side of the vehicle. It was held in place by an extendable arm that would gradually move it back as more and more sections were slotted in ahead of it. This way the new machine would be built back end first, always held close in behind its parent. The layering chamber was already at work on the next piece, another identical part to form the rear of the left tube.

"I think we can leave it to it now," Max said. "See how it looks in the morning."

"I think you're right," Safi said. "I'll let them know back at base."

Once she'd called in with the news, they sat back down again.

"So let me ask you something," Safi said. "Where would you be if you weren't here now?"

"Probably not too far from here, strangely enough. I told you I was a GRACE monitor didn't I, along with everything else? I was lined up for that Chile trip before this came along, but I might have come out this way, depending on what I found. It's the shifting ocean currents from this part of the world causing all the problems there right now. What about you? What would you be doing?"

"Still flying, though I don't know where. It's getting harder to find jobs these days."

"I forgot you were a pilot. What got you into that?"

"My father. He was a flyer too. For as long as I can remember it's all I wanted to do. I learned to fly when I was fifteen, did engineering at the Air Force college, and I was with them for five years after that."

On first meeting, Safi hadn't struck him as the military type at all. Even now he knew more of her background she seemed too mild and soft spoken to have coped well in that environment. In her case, however, her obvious self-discipline and organisation were the telltale signs, rather than any outward show of toughness. Whether she was tough on the inside was a different question. Somehow he thought she probably was.

"What made you leave?" he said.

"I'd just finished a tour flying TAVs — excuse me, Trans Atmospheric Vehicles. It was the same plane my dad flew, thirteen years before. Nobody gets two chances at flying something like that, so I decided to go."

"Those were the U-155s, right?"

"Yeah, you've heard of them."

"And did you ever see any action?" Even as he spoke Max was doing the maths in his head: ten years had passed since the world was so close to GRACE that the China Block's refusal to back down meant military action against its member states seemed the only option. Safi would have been in her mid twenties when it happened, when what could easily have been the opening skirmishes of World War Three took place.

"Yeah, I did," she said. "Three times, all single-orbit bombing runs. We'd dip into the mesosphere over Sumatra then guide the ORAMs onto the Jakarta heavy industry zone. Sixty seconds later we were powering out and heading home."

"I'd love to go up there. Ever since I heard my dad talking about the things he was designing and what planet or moon they were going to end up sitting on, I've wanted to see it for myself. I know you can buy tourist flights now, all the way to the Moon if you're rich enough, but even a trip to the station would be a stretch."

"I know what you mean. I saw enough on those flights to know I wanted to see more, so I looked for a job in civil space-flight. That's how I ended up on the Earthrise program, but as an engineer."

Max looked up and noticed the Moon for the first time, high in the northern sky.

"So where's your bit then?" he said.

"My bit?" she said, looking over her shoulder. "Oh, I see. Okay, you see that roundish area near the edge?"

"Yeah, I see it."

"Well, that's Mare Crisium, and the base is about halfway up, near the right hand side. You should know that, you can see the lights on a new moon. But we were based to the north of there. About fifty miles north."

"Do you think you'll ever go back?"

"I'd love to, more than anything, but I doubt it. I've already seen more of it than most people get to see. I was lucky, Niall made sure I never forgot that."

"Niall — he was your boss up there?"

"Kind of," she laughed. "We were going to get married once we got back to Earth. But yeah, he was in charge of things. It was his team."

"And how long ago was this?"

"Seven years. That's how long it's been since the accident."

"So what happened?"

Safi took a deep breath before answering. "They, ah, they were getting ready for an EVA, prebreathing oxygen while they suited up. They'd been sealed in there for an hour almost. As they were putting their suits on, there was a short somewhere in the room. Just a spark from a panel someone hadn't wired up properly, that's all it took. It was — it was over pretty fast."

In fact it had taken twelve seconds from beginning to end, Max would later read: the first glow of the flames as the insulation caught light, the unmistakable sight of plastics and foam composites being consumed, and finally, the searing white inferno as even solid metal began to burn in the pure oxygen atmosphere. Only when the outer skin burst under the pressure and threw the flames out into the vacuum did the fire stop. But through it all, one image had persisted over all others. It was the same image that had haunted spacecraft fires since the very beginning: that of a gloved hand beating on glass, with the flames rearing up behind it.

"I never forgot what we were trying to do up there though, how important it is to give ourselves this capability, us as a race that is."

"And Niall was the one who started it?"

"John von Neumann started it, but Niall was the first to try to make it a reality. Until now."

"And that's why you're here?"

"Of course, I jumped at the chance. Even before Victor's offer came along I was writing papers, documenting what we'd managed to achieve. I had to be careful where I sent them — there are more than enough Olivers out there, ready to call us crackpots — but I was looking for any opportunity to try again. That's how Victor found me. Niall's the one to thank though. It was his vision. There was so much we could have achieved." She stared off into the distance, seemingly lost in memories.

"What would you have done if the accident hadn't happened? If you'd been able to stay up there?"

"If we'd carried on with the work?" She turned back to face Max. "If we'd been able to turn our facility into an autonomous replicator, the way we'd planned to, and if we'd left it to run, the industrial complex that grew out of it would cover one twentieth of the visible side of the Moon by now."

"And that's a good thing?" Max asked, incredulous.

"I don't see why not," she said. "There's nothing else up there. But the Moon was just an experiment, we would have stopped after three replications. The asteroid belt was our real target. We were trying to design seed pods, about a hundred tonnes each, that you would launch at the biggest objects in the belt. The factories that grew out of them would be reprogrammable from Earth, so you could just radio up the plans for anything you wanted built and leave them to get on with it. Even the ships that brought the products back would be built for free. And the low gravity would mean the factories could send out new seed pods, to spread themselves from one rock to another. Within a hundred years the mere idea of being short of materials or power or food would have been something from history. It would be a whole new age for humanity: the stone age, the industrial age, the replicative age. And it's going to happen too. We may not have got that far when we tried, but it's going to happen one day."

"Just because it's inevitable doesn't mean it's right," Max said.

"That's true, but it will solve more problems than it creates. There's no doubt about that."

"How can you be so sure?"

She looked up and to the side as she answered, the way she always did when recalling memories. "My father told me something once. I think he was joking when he said it, but it's stayed with me ever since. He said that out of all the things people have done, out of all of humanity's achievements that we're all so proud of, the only thing we've ever really done is take things that were already there and move them around. Like the Pyramids: they're impressive, but all they did was dig up some stones and rearrange them. And the biggest cities in the world are just rock and metal that were hauled out of the ground and put together in the right order. Even space travel, and sending probes to other planets, that's just moving things big distances instead of short ones."

Max couldn't help smiling at the observation. It certainly put things into perspective.

"But this," she continued. "This is something different. Here we're taking inanimate matter, and giving it the power to arrange itself. We set it going, but from then on it's self-sustaining. And if we do it so that we can control it, then we get the physical world working for us for a change, instead of having to work against it. Order out of disorder: that has to be a good thing, doesn't it?"

Max thought for a second. "It reminds me of what the old seventeenth century scientists used to think, that the difference between living things and dead matter was some kind of supernatural force. They thought that only high order creatures like horses and humans could reproduce, and that low order animals like frogs and worms would just appear spontaneously out of mud and water. Even two hundred years later, people were still putting electricity through wet clay to try and make insects appear. Order out of disorder, animate out of inanimate. I wonder what they'd have thought if they could see what we're doing here."

"It's hardly the same thing," Safi said. "It's not as if we've made something that's alive."

"That's a matter of opinion."

They went to bed after that, Safi in the single cabin below deck, Max on one of the padded benches up top. She'd wanted to toss a coin for it but he insisted.

She was halfway down the stairs when she stopped and turned as if about to say something. They stood frozen in place while she hovered hesitantly, seemingly unsure whether to share what was on her mind. She snapped out of it after a couple of seconds; whatever it was, it seemed she'd thought better of it.

"I'll see you tomorrow, Max. Sleep well."

Just for a moment, the discomfort had been thick enough to feel it in the air. "Sure," he said, wondering what the hell it might have been. "Sleep well."

* * *

The next morning, Max was the first to wake up. He got himself some food from one of the storage lockers, then went to see how the replication was progressing.

The new machine was already recognisable as a copy of its parent. The rear five percent of the thing was almost complete, including the manipulator arms that would connect the sections together when it was creating its own copies. Max leant over the side to get a closer look at how well these parts had been built. They were the first mechanical parts, the first real challenge for the process, and as far as he could see everything had been built correctly, including the physical and electrical connectors that mated each watertight unit to its neighbours. The arms' rotating joints were the most difficult, and even those looked good.

"How's it going?" Safi asked from behind him. He hadn't heard her coming up onto the deck.

"Pretty good. We won't know until it's switched on but I think it's working out."

"Great. Funny how it looks a different colour in the daylight."

Max hadn't noticed up until then, but the structure of the thing was definitely a different shade of green to its parent. In addition the surface was slightly mottled, as if the quality of the materials refinement had varied from one section to another.

"Ross said we could expect things like this though," Safi continued. "There's always going to be a few impurities in the cellulose mix. Depends what flavour of algae it picks up."

"Yeah, I hope that's the only difference."

"It will be. We've got another two hours before they expect us back at base. I'll give them a call, make sure our relief crew is ready."

* * *

The next ten days came and went, with the replication process kept under continuous surveillance. At every stage its progress was compared with the plans and simulations to make sure it was behaving as expected. No one was certain exactly how long it would take, but the estimates were repeatedly fine tuned as the new Prospector got closer to completion. They only knew for sure when the last of the vessel's sections began to appear in the layering chamber, which gave them approximately five hours to go. And this time they weren't so lucky with the timing, as it became clear that the activation of the new machine would take place in darkness. And so, as Max, Safi, Ross and Victor watched on their screens on the island, the observers on the boat turned their floodlights onto the two Prospectors and waited for the moment of activation.

When the final piece was slotted into place and the machine came to life, it behaved just as its predecessor had, aligning its sails to what little wind there was, and slowly moving off toward the collection site it had chosen for itself. Then the first Prospector, its task for now complete, turned the other way and steered a course toward the island, while the observers on the boat manoeuvred themselves to keep out of both machines' way. In spite of the lateness, the operations room was as full as it had been when the first Prospector had been activated, and the sight of the new arrival heading off to do its duty sparked a round of applause from the onlookers. Even Max felt a sense of pride at what he was seeing, which surprised him. He guessed Safi must have been feeling the same thing.

Then everyone's attention switched back to the first craft, as it prepared to complete its first operating cycle by delivering the cargo it had been carrying. It took fifteen minutes to reach the drop site, and all that could be seen of the delivery was the Prospector steering a wide arc through the site before heading back out into open sea. But if everything had gone to plan, and so far everything else had, somewhere on that shallow seabed was the package it had left behind.

Finding it took another ten minutes. Later, when deliveries were being dropped off continuously, automated minisubs would literally rake them in off the seabed, but for this first one a pair of ESOS divers were sent out to retrieve it. The crowd moved down to the lab where it would be brought in, and waited for it to arrive.

When it did appear, Ross took over to handle the processing, another job that would be automated later on. The object itself was a thin flexible strip, like yellow plastic, about three inches long and half an inch wide, with electrodes at each end. One end was weighted to allow it to stay put when dropped to the seabed. Between the two electrodes were a set of uneven stripes, as if different coloured inks had been soaked into the material and allowed to smear along its length by different amounts. One of these bands of colour had a slight purple tint, and this, according to Ross, was where the gold lay.

Carefully he scraped the material off the strip onto the sterile surface of the workbench. Against the white background the stuff looked almost black, a tiny pile of black powder in the middle of an expanse of white. No one was saying a word as Ross worked, gathering the material together for the next stage. He even laughed when he looked round and saw the intense expressions on everyone's faces. "Relax, guys," he said. "I'm the one who needs to be concentrating." Then he dropped the powder into a ceramic container, placed it in a small electric furnace mounted in the wall, and shut the toughened glass door. The bricks lining the tiny cavity were glowing orange from the heat, and there was a brief flash of flame as some impurities were burned off. When the remaining material had melted, he took it out and poured it onto a ceramic mat, where it solidified almost instantly into a small sphere less than a millimetre across. And then, at last, there it was, and this time the colour was unmistakable. Their first delivery of gold, no bigger than the first grain of rice on Shere Khan's chessboard. But like that grain of rice, it was the first of many.

Ross picked it up between his finger and thumb and held it up for everyone to see. Then Victor stepped forward and took it carefully from him. "Take a look people," he said. "This is why we're doing this. This is why we're here."

Chapter 7

It was amazing, Max thought, how quickly they got into the habit of doing absolutely nothing. Compared to the relentless activity of designing and building the first of the Prospectors, the job of overseeing their operation was positively relaxed. Most days would involve an hour or two in the operations room watching the Prospector population at work, followed perhaps by a visit to the processing centre to see the finished product mounting up. So far the collection wasn't huge, but it was big enough to need locking away. Other than that, their time was their own.

The island's beaches were a great attraction for all the inhabitants, especially Ross, whose knowledge of sports and beach games seemed endless. And Victor was happy to let him organise the ESOS workforce into leagues and tournaments if it was good for morale and helped pass the time. The nearest inhabited island was over two hours away by boat, so they had to make the most of what was around them.

Max, Safi and Doug Chowdry were resting at the top of one of the island's remoter beaches when Ross wandered over and joined them. Doug had come out just three days earlier, at Max's invitation, so that he could see for himself what he'd helped to produce. Safi and he were sitting on the sand facing out to sea, but Max was off to the side, teaching Gillian how to throw crude wooden spears into a dead tree trunk he'd chosen as a target. He'd found a piece of driftwood shaped like an old spear thrower, and he'd soon remembered the knack of launching the long wooden darts, using their flexibility and elasticity to amplify the force of his arm. In the right hands it could bring down a bison at fifty feet, or so his anthropology teacher had claimed when she'd taught the class how to use them. The gouge marks in the tree were certainly a good indication of their power.

"You're getting pretty lethal with that thing you know, Max," Ross said when he reached them.

"I used to be better. We had competitions at college, I was usually in the top three."

"What's it called again?"

"It's an atlatl. That's what the Aztecs called them."

"Cool. You'll have to show me how to use it, in case I ever run into Oliver again."

Max laughed. "I think you'll be joining the queue for that one." Then he gathered up the spears that he'd thrown and paced back out for Gillian to have a try. Ross sat down next to Safi and Doug.

"How long do you reckon those things will be running?" Doug was asking. Off in the distance the drop site was visible and a steady procession of Prospectors was sailing through it, dropping their cargoes as they went. They were unmissable now; Victor had belatedly realised that employees' families could never be kept out of the secret once the things were operating in force, and had signed the entire island onto the non-disclosure agreement. Gillian hadn't had the nerve to tell him she already knew the whole thing.

"We think we've got another four months," Safi said. "Then we can wind the program up."

"Geez," Doug said. "It's going to get crowded out there."

"It already is."

Even as they spoke, another two vehicles appeared on the horizon and started to curve in toward the drop site.

"So what are you guys going to do all that time?" Doug said.

"I'll be needed in the operations room," Safi said. "And we're planning to capture one of the later generation machines to check it over. I'll be needed for that too. I don't know about anyone else though."

"We may not be sticking around here much longer," Max said, as he and Gillian finally sat down. "I was in line for some survey work before I came here and I had some pet projects worked into the itinerary. I may use this downtime to go work on those."

"That applies to both of you I guess?"

"Yeah, me too," Gillian said. "I'm starting to feel as if I've made the most of being here, in terms of my artwork that is. And the treatments are pretty much done too." She ran her hand over her upper arm as she spoke, where the implant had been sitting for over a month now, a small hard lump just under the skin. "Time for nature to take its own course."

"So you'll be off counting bugs in swamps again, Max?" Doug said. "I thought you'd grown out of that kind of thing."

"Just trying to get back to my roots, Doug. You know me."

"True. But don't you have your own little food chain to study now, from the comfort of your office chair?"

"I do, but real life is far more interesting."

Ross shifted his position to stretch out on the sand, and propped himself up on one elbow facing the others.

"You never know, Max," he said, grinning. "Cambria may have developed its own intelligent life while you were away. Even now they might be waiting for their creator to return, wondering where you've got to."

"Intelligent? No, not much chance of that. If we ran it for a few million years, maybe then. But the way it's going these days, I doubt it."

"Really?" Ross said. "You've got some pretty complex behaviour in there already, from what I've seen. Doesn't that count as intelligent?"

"No more than the contents of the nearest anthill," Max said. "The social interaction within each species is impressive, but don't read too much into it."

"But what about the predators and the food chains, all the hunting strategies that have emerged? You can't say that's not an achievement."

"An achievement? Sure, different species, different behaviours, all competing with each other, all wiping each other out as if that's the only way they can stay on top. Some achievement." If he was trying to hide his views on the subject, he'd failed.

"I thought you'd be glad to see that kind of complexity," Ross said. "After all, it was meant to happen that way, wasn't it?"

"No, it wasn't meant to happen, not like that anyway. We wanted to see complex, social life forms developing, but not the organised carnage that's going on now. It's as if we took all the right ingredients, put them together, and suddenly all hell broke loose. It's almost as if the rate of evolution is itself a stable, evolved system, and trying to speed things up artificially will always be a mistake."

In fact Max could still remember the day the first predator had appeared, about three years into the project. At first it had looked almost comical, that lone creature striding round the landscape, picking up rocks and mechanically smashing them down on any other creatures it came across, all because of a random fluke in its behaviour rules. It had looked like some kind of sick, gratuitous cartoon. The first victims hadn't even tried to move away, but had simply stood there unaware of what was happening to them until it was too late. In the end each one became a free meal for its killer. Predatory behaviour wasn't bad in itself, but that creature had been the first step in the path that led to modern day Cambria. It had become the fittest, so survival would follow. Its descendants would share in its fortune.

"But it's not real life, Max. Whatever happens it's only a figment in some computer somewhere."

"It is for now," Max said, glancing briefly out to sea. Nobody answered him, but Safi saw where he was looking and stared back with a quizzical frown on her face.

Doug however was looking thoughtful. "What if you did leave it going until something intelligent appeared, no matter how long it took? Would they know they were only in a game on some computer? Would they be able to figure out that their world wasn't real life?"

"I'm not sure they would," Max said. "After all, how do we know?"

Doug laughed. "That's a good question."

"Anyway, that's assuming that intelligence is inevitable," Ross said. "I'm so not sure it is."

"How do you mean?" Safi said.

"Well, life on Earth has been around for nearly four billion years, and it's only in the last million or so that anything intelligent has been here. I think we're a fluke. Life was getting on quite happily without us, and we evolved against the odds."

"That's a popular view," Max said. "The amount of energy it takes to run a brain our size is huge, and we're born with fewer survival instincts because we learn so much later on. Intelligence is more of a drawback than we like to think."

"So if I asked you guys about life on other planets, you'd say the chances were pretty slim?" Doug said.

"Do you mean intelligent life, or anything from microbes upward?" Max said.

"To be honest, I think the chances of both are pretty slim," Ross said.

"How come?" Max said.

"Think of all those years people have been pointing dishes into space looking for signals, and still nothing, and all those people who said Europa had to have life because there was water under the ice, and look what they found there."

It had been over twenty years since the first lander had been despatched to the icy moon of Jupiter, its robotic microsub melting its way to the vast ocean beneath. It had found stalactites of ice measuring kilometres in height, complex rock formations round volcanic undersea vents, salinity levels that would make the Dead Sea look like tap water — and no life.

"That was disappointing," Safi said, "but it's not conclusive."

"So if you were looking for life off this planet, what would you look for?" Doug asked her.

"If I was looking for *intelligent* life, I know exactly what I'd look for," she said, turning to face out to sea. "I'd look for those." Then she pointed the way she was looking, out toward the Prospectors on the horizon.

"You'd look for robotic boats?" Ross said, confusion on his face.

"I'd look for replicators. They're a sure sign that something intelligent has been at work."

"Why?" Ross said.

"Think about it. All the time and money that's been spent sending probes to other planets. Why not just send one that can copy itself? The same principle as those things out there, but for exploration rather than production. It travels to a new star system, spends some time exploring, replicates itself using the materials it finds, then the machines split up and head off to the next two stars. Soon you'd have a wave of exploring machines spreading out through the galaxy, each one beaming its findings back home."

"Sounds like a good solution," Doug said.

"It is. And any intelligent race that appears will have the same idea, they're bound to. Even if the things spent a hundred years at each star, and moved at a fraction of the speed of light, the galaxy would be teeming with them within a hundred million years. If intelligent life had ever existed away from Earth, we'd see the evidence for it right here. Their probes would have been here long ago."

"Yeah, Fermi's paradox," Doug said. "'If they're anywhere, they'd be everywhere.' But would we recognise them if we saw them?"

"We would, I'm sure. If you knew what to look for, it would be obvious."

"Then why isn't anyone looking?"

She smiled. "Well, maybe they are," she said.

"Of course, you're forgetting the dozen or so intelligent species that we already know about," Gillian said.

"Such as?"

"Whales and dolphins? They're just as intelligent as we are, only in different ways. Just as social, just as inquisitive."

"Yeah, that's true," Ross said. "I actually saw some dolphins the other week, swimming round the Prospectors. *They* were being pretty inquisitive. One of the boats had just finished its rep cycle and was about to split, and they all hung around it to watch. It was weird."

"Where did you see this?" Safi said.

"Out in the shallows, near the drop site. I was trying out some of the underwater gear."

"With Victor's permission of course."

"Of course. He said I could help myself as long as it's not being used. Looks like ex-military stuff, most of it."

"Sounds like fun. So is there much to see out there?"

"Plenty of life," he said. "Corals, fish life, that kind of thing. You can come out and see it for yourself if you like."

"Yeah, I'd like to do that. When's a good time?"

"We can do it today if we go right now. I think the tide's okay at the moment."

"Okay, let's do it."

Ross stood up, ready to go. "You guys coming too?" he said, turning to the others.

"Sure," Max and Doug said together. "Do you want to come?" Max asked Gillian.

She shook her head. "I'm not in the mood for adventures today. You guys have fun though."

"I'll see you back home?"

"Or here."

They got up and knocked the sand off their legs, then headed back along the beach, leaving Gillian alone.

* * *

The diving suits were like miniature survival systems, containing breathing gear, short range intercoms, and even navigation systems. Anyone wearing one could survive underwater for up to four hours at a time, depending on their depth and breathing rate. Max's face mask had smelled musty and damp until the fresh air had begun to flow, and it had taken a good few minutes to adjust the straps that held the watertight seal in place. But once they were ready, and the four of them had waded out into the sea next to the harbour, the experience of swimming freely underwater made it all worthwhile.

At first all they could see was sand as they swam out away from the beach into deeper and deeper water, but once the surface was thirty feet or so above their heads the first scenery came into view. Ross was leading, with the other three in a line behind him. He kept looking back over his shoulder to keep an eye on Doug and Max, but he knew that Safi had used equipment like this before in her air force training so needed little supervision. At the same time he kept everyone talking over the intercom so that he'd know if any problems emerged. In reality he was being over cautious, Max thought. Even though it was the first time Max had worn a system like this, it wasn't his first time underwater by any means, and his confidence in this environment had returned quickly.

Ross stopped them briefly to take a first look at the life that was laid out before them. Almost every colour imaginable was to be found somewhere, either in the fish swimming in and out of the corals, the plants and animals rooted to the seabed, or the corals themselves, some shaped like leafless trees, some like huge fans almost ten feet across. Max recognised almost all the species on sight, including his own favourites, the clownfish: bright orange in colour, no bigger than his hand, and seemingly playful and inquisitive of anything new that swam past, though he knew from experience that they would take a bite out of any hand that got too close for comfort.

Most of the life lay between this depth and one hundred and twenty feet, Ross explained. Any deeper and the sunlight was too weak; any shallower and the buffeting from the waves and tropical storms would break the fragile structures into pieces. Then he led them further down, diagonally across the slope, so as not to descend too quickly. As Max swam he could hear various mechanical noises coming from the equipment on his back as the breathing set adjusted to the increasing pressure. By the time they levelled off, over seventy feet of depth was registering on the display inside his faceplate. There they paused, hovering over the corals, and watched the sea creatures coming and going.

The light here was noticeably darker, and the colours seemed slightly muted, as if some parts of the spectrum hadn't got through at all. As Max looked up and to the left, he noticed a group of ten or twelve jellyfish, undulating along in the slight current. Beyond them, the water took on a definite green colour as the sunlight was filtered by the blooms of algae that now invaded the once pristine tropical waters, evidence of the shifting oceanic currents that had been — and still were — the main culprits behind the imminence of GRACE.

When the Prospector design work had still been underway and Max had seen the figures for how much solid material was held in solution in the sea, he'd found it difficult to comprehend just how huge the numbers involved were. All those tonnes of magnesium, aluminium and silicon seemed hard to equate to the seemingly empty waters of the ocean. However, as he looked round himself at this depth, at the shafts of light coming down like pillars from the surface, he could almost visualise the huge stockpile that surrounded him. He ran his hand through the water in front of his face and tried to imagine how much material had just slipped through his fingers, how much iron, how much copper — and how much gold. Why was it that gold had such an effect on people? It was more than just the value. There was something about the colour, the beauty of it. And to think that he was literally swimming in the stuff, if only he could get hold of it. He held his hand right up to his face to see if he could catch some, but every time he closed his fingers it seemed to slip away. If he looked really closely, he could almost see it glistening in front of him.

"Max, you okay?"

Max came to with a start at Ross's words and realised he'd almost tipped upside down. He dropped his hand away from his face and oriented himself toward the others. "Yeah, just looking at something," he said, shaking his head to clear the blurring from his eyes.

"Okay, good. Let's carry on."

It was Jacques Cousteau who had named it, "The Raptures of the Deep", the intoxicating effect of pressurised air giving the same response as a mild anaesthetic. It wasn't the first time Max had felt it; those divers who said they'd never experienced it were simply too badly affected to notice. Once Max had cleared his head he felt fine, but he kept his eyes moving all the same, so as not to fixate on any one object.

They swam for another twenty minutes, following the sixty foot contour and taking in all the sights along the way. Then they came to the edge of the ravine that led from the harbour and out to sea. All Max could see of it was a steep cliff face, dropping down into even darker water beyond.

"We don't want to go down there," Ross said. "It's a bit deep I think. And there won't be much to look at."

The others agreed, so they followed the edge of the ravine back toward the shore.

They were about halfway back when they heard the clicks and whistles, instantly recognisable, and seemingly all around them, then noticed the dark shapes coming at them out of the gloom.

Then they were upon them: five or six dolphins, flashing past at impossible speeds, parallel to the coastline. No one had time to say anything as they passed. Only one of the dolphins stopped to look at the four intruders, a youngster with dappled grey skin. It paused for about two seconds before heading off to follow the others. "The day we can swim like that," Ross said once they'd gone, "that's when we'll really belong down here."

The seabed gradually rose as they approached the shore. They were just entering the shallows when one of the speedboats from the complex passed overhead, the rumbling drone of its engine giving the first sign of its presence. Then the boat itself appeared as its shadowy silhouette went over them, speeding away from the island. The violent swell of its wake broke the otherwise calm surface.

"Wow, he's really going for it," Doug said. "I wonder what the hurry is."

Less than thirty seconds had passed before a second one went over, again leaving the island behind and powering out to sea.

"Must be some kind of race," Ross suggested.

Soon the water was shallow enough to stand, so they took off their fins and waded up the beach. They were only a couple of hundred yards away from where they'd gone in. The breathing sets weren't heavy, but in the strong sun they were feeling hot by the time they got back to the complex. They were just putting the sets away in the workshop area when Victor dashed in, looking agitated.

"There you are!" he said. "Where have you all been?"

"Out in the sea," Ross said. "Why, what's the matter?"

"They're getting out, the boundary's failed! We've lost fifty of them already! You need to come with me, now!"

The others exchanged glances, then followed him up to the operations room on the top floor. They felt out of place standing there in their swimming gear, but it was clear they didn't have time to get changed. Victor led them over to one of the display screens and told them what had happened.

"The first one went about twenty minutes ago. It sailed straight over the buoy line as if it wasn't there. The tripwire system picked it up of course, but then more of them went. Somehow they're ignoring the boundary."

"What about the boundary itself? Is that still working?" Max asked urgently.

"Yes, that's the strange thing, most of them are staying inside. We don't know what's causing it. If the others go too, then —"

Max cut him off. "And how far have they gone, the ones that have got out?"

"They don't move very fast, maybe three miles at most for the first ones."

"All in the same direction?"

"No, look at the screen. Almost every part of the boundary has been affected. They're going out in all directions."

"How many boats have you sent out after them?"

"Three so far, we're calling in the crews for the other two."

"And they've got the right equipment on board to tow the things back?"

"Yes, but there's no time to tow them one by one, all they can do is disable them and leave them dead in the water then round them up later."

"Assuming they don't drift too far," Safi said.

They listened in for a few minutes as the boats hunted down the rogue Prospectors, radioing back and forth between themselves and the complex every time a new one was spotted. The displays in the operations room showed which parts of the boundary each one had crossed, but there was no way of finding their current position. Only the boat crews could do that.

"We need someone in the air," Max said. "Someone to co-ordinate the boats."

"I've asked Garrett to do that," Victor said. "He'll be here soon. An extra pair of eyes might be useful if you want to join him."

Max thought for a second. "Sure, it's better than hanging round here. Let me get changed, and I'll meet him on the helipad."

He rushed back down to the workshop level to pick up some coveralls and a lifejacket, then he went out to where Garrett was getting ready.

"You got us playing hide-and-seek today?" Garrett said, opening the helicopter's door.

"Looks like it," Max said, climbing in.

They took off and flew low, out over the ocean. Their course took them right out over the box, almost from one side to the other, and at every point along the way at least one Prospector was in view. Some of them were stationary, in various stages of replication, but others were on the move, either repositioning themselves within the box or heading back toward the drop zone. Their wakes were clearly defined and Max could easily see how they were manoeuvring to spread themselves out while avoiding collisions. There was no communication between them, just the same simple rules built into each one, obeyed repeatedly throughout the population. At first Max couldn't help marvelling at the achievement that this sight represented, but then he reminded himself why he was having to take this flight at all. Obviously, somewhere along the line, something had gone badly wrong.

Once they'd reached the eastern edge of the box they began to follow its perimeter. Max looked out into the open sea, using binoculars to check anything that caught his eye. Only two minutes had passed before he spotted his first target, the twin sails of a Prospector jutting up from the horizon. Garrett guessed it was about two miles away so Max broadcast its position to the nearest of the boats. He saw the boat heading off in response, rushing underneath them to go and make the rendezvous.

He saw more and more rogue Prospectors as they continued round, each one taking its seemingly random course toward freedom. He also saw how the boat crews were disabling each one they came across, disconnecting the power in a reversal of the action that had brought each one to life. With their control systems out of action, their aerofoil sails would just spin freely like weathervanes, providing no propulsion at all. Disabling each one took only minutes, but as more and more Prospectors crossed the boundary, it soon became clear they were losing the race.

The transmissions from the boats and the complex were getting more urgent now, as the number they had to deal with got larger. As Max flew along the boundary, it seemed there were just as many Prospectors on the outside of the line as on the inside. The only clue as to which side was which was that some of the vehicles on the outside had been deactivated, but there were plenty of them still in motion, and the furthest ones were now over five miles away. Then another transmission came through, a voice that Max recognised as Victor's.

"All boat crews, all boat crews. Do not use the power supply cut-off to deactivate the machines. It's taking too long. Use the fire axes to cut the power lines, and move on to the next one as quickly as possible. Spend less than two minutes on each one. Just get them all stopped for God's sake!"

Max almost thought he could detect a note of panic in that last statement. He didn't know exactly how many vehicles they were looking for now, but it was obviously a lot more than when they'd started. How on earth five speedboats were supposed to catch them all was beyond him.

By now they were flying a few miles outside the boundary, since spotting the ones that had strayed the furthest had become a priority. At one point they passed over a group of eleven or twelve Prospectors, seemingly racing each other to leave the islands behind. The boat that was dealing with this section of sea had been joined by another faster boat, which had been assigned to give help wherever one wasn't enough. Max could clearly see the two crews, almost ramming each Prospector in an attempt to get alongside quickly enough, then scrambling over with the axes from the boats' fire-fighting kits to hack furiously at the power switch access panels. Each dead Prospector was soon surrounded by a wake of green debris where their sides had been cut open.

Max was just wondering how far from being able to cope they really were when another transmission from Victor came through his headset, and this time it was meant for him.

"Max, we need you on the west side of the box, about four miles out. It's urgent."

"We can be there in a few minutes. What's the matter?"

"One of them is heading for the shipping lanes. We're expecting traffic there today, so it has to be stopped. But there's no time to send a boat after it."

"What do you expect me to do? We can't tow it from a helicopter."

Max was sure Victor hesitated before answering. "Someone needs to board it and use an override kit to turn it round. We can get a boat out to it later, but someone has to bring it back in, at least some of the way."

"And by someone, you mean me?"

"You're the only one in a position to do it, Max. It's not going fast, you won't be in any danger. Just get on board and steer it round, then we'll send someone out to you when we can."

Max couldn't believe what he was being asked to do. Garrett had heard the whole conversation and was looking over at him expectantly.

"What do you want to do?" Garrett said.

"I don't know. Let's take a look at this thing at least."

They headed back toward the box, then crossed it again from east to west. Similar scenes of mass slaughter were taking place on this side of the perimeter as the boat crews did their best to immobilise their targets. But for every Prospector they'd stopped, at least three more were still active. No wonder they couldn't be spared to go four miles for just one of them.

They carried on in a straight line as Garrett used the helicopter's navigation system to follow the course Victor had given them. This Prospector must have been one of the first to escape to have got this far, and had only been spotted thanks to an eagle-eyed crew member on one of the boats they'd just passed. The sun was in their eyes flying in this direction, so it was hard to see into the distance, but Garrett and Max spotted it almost simultaneously. Its wake had been bent into a meandering series of S-bends by the ocean waves, but the vehicle itself was pressing on regardless, sailing purposefully into the distance on its chosen course.

"There's your ride home," Garrett said when they'd caught up. "Are you sure you want to do this?"

Max looked at the vehicle below them and for a moment had second thoughts. The only reason Victor was so keen to get it back was because of his fears of what might happen if it fell into the wrong hands. The gold they were collecting would be next to worthless if others could copy the process. But Max was probably just as eager as Victor to see the thing stopped, even if his motivations were different. He decided to go for it. "I'll be okay as long as you can keep us steady," he said. "If I fall in, the lifejacket will keep me safe."

Garrett flew down alongside the Prospector, twenty feet to its right and just three feet above the surface. Then Max released his harness, took off his headset, and twisted round to face out of the door. The air from the rotors battered his face as he leant out, and the sea below them seemed to be flashing past at an impossible speed. It hadn't looked this fast from higher up. He told himself that only their low altitude made it look that way, but he still didn't feel safe. However he didn't have time to change his mind. In one smooth motion Garrett drifted over to the left, then back to the right, while Max jumped out onto the Prospector at the point of closest approach.

He had to struggle to keep his balance, and lunged out with

his left hand to grab any part of the craft he could get hold of. In his right hand he was holding the override kit he'd taken from the helicopter's cabin, and the temptation to drop it and steady himself with both hands was overwhelming. The craft was rocking violently from the force of his landing, and even though Garrett had moved away, the helicopter's downdraught was throwing up sea spray, stinging his eyes.

He tried to shift his position to get a better footing, but he couldn't keep his eyes open for more than a few seconds at a time and was doing everything by touch. He knew he was standing on top of one of the craft's flotation tubes, and he could feel that the surface was wet and slippery beneath him, but as long as he could keep a firm hold on the superstructure and time his movements to the motion of the craft, he thought he'd be okay.

He felt like he'd moved about six feet along the length of the thing when suddenly his feet went out from under him and he tumbled down the side of the tube and into the water.

The next few seconds were chaotic. Somehow he'd managed to grab hold of something on the side of the tube, and was being dragged alongside. Even with the lifejacket his head was barely above the waterline, and if he tried to raise his head to take in air, the water was forced up his nostrils and down his throat. The panic was rising in him as he tried to breathe, turning his head as far to the side as he could to reach the air, coughing and retching saltwater the whole time. He was having to breathe in time with the rocking of the vehicle, which by now was even more violent, and the fear of drowning was strong in his mind. Somehow, however, he knew he couldn't afford to let go.

The override kit was still with him, but he knew that he'd need both hands to get back on board. He managed to take one large breath, then he shut his eyes, tucked his head down under the water, and threw the thing as hard as he could, forward and to the side. He was aiming for the top surface of the Prospector, but he had no way of knowing whether he'd hit it or not. Then with both hands free to hold on, he grabbed whatever handholds he could and pulled himself up about a foot out of the water. He was having to pull continuously to keep himself up against the force of the flow, but at least here he could breathe. His arms were aching and trembling from the effort, and he knew he couldn't stay like that for long, so he pulled himself up even further then made a grab for the top of the tube. It took five or six heaves to get him on the top surface, holding on desperately while he got his strength back. It felt like every muscle in his arms and shoulders was in pain, and the exhaustion and the seawater he'd swallowed were making him want to vomit. He was dimly aware of the sound of the helicopter, still flying alongside but not so close now. He knew he should signal to Garrett that he was okay, but somehow he couldn't move. Whole minutes went by as he lay there regaining his strength.

Eventually he got up onto his hands and knees and twisted round to look for Garrett. The helicopter was off to the side, keeping its distance, and he could see Garrett looking at him in concern. Max waved at him briefly to show he was all right, then started to look round for the override kit. It had landed just inboard of the flotation tube he was straddling, so he crawled back slowly and picked it up. He could still feel himself slipping on the wet surface of the craft, but now he could see where he was going and he knew to take it slowly.

Once he'd collected the override kit he sidled up along the top surface of the tube until he found the interface point where it plugged in. The rocking motion had subsided now and Max felt more sure of himself. He straightened up, opened the back of the small handset, and unfolded the bundle of cables to connect it to the Prospector's control system.

There were almost a dozen wires that had to be plugged in, and the attachment points looked like wormholes in a piece of infested wood. A diagram printed on the front of the unit showed which wire went where, but he had to stop and think a couple of times to make sure he got it right. It was almost as if the positions of the holes had shifted slightly compared to the way they'd been designed on the first machine. Looking round him he could see that wasn't the only difference. Most of the features of this Prospector seemed to be distortions of the original, not significantly different, but enough to show that things hadn't been copied correctly. He'd wait with interest to see exactly what had happened here.

Then, with the craft under his control, he commanded the rudder to the left and steered round one hundred and eighty degrees to face back toward the box. The wind was from the side, so he played with the angle of the sails until he felt he had the best speed he could get. He was no sailor, but at least this would get him home.

Once Garrett was sure Max was safe, he headed back toward the island. Now Max was on his own. He did his best to find a comfortable position on top of the craft, and settled himself down for the journey back.

* * *

A long three hours passed before Max approached the island. His course had taken him straight back into the box, and he'd spent most of the journey dodging other Prospectors as they drifted all around him, seemingly at random. Sunset wasn't far away, but eventually one of the ESOS boats came out to greet him and tow him the rest of the way. Max asked the crew what the latest news was.

"We got them all," one of them said. She looked exhausted. "We're rounding up the dead ones now."

"How many did we lose?" Max asked her.

"Over two hundred," she said.

And as they approached the harbour, Max saw for himself just how many had been involved. The Prospectors that had been towed back were being tied up and the small harbour was almost full of them. A narrow corridor had been left to allow boats to come and go from the complex as they brought in more to add to the collection, and the gashes in the sides of each one showed the ferocity of the treatment they had received. It was far removed from the painstaking and meticulous work that had gone into their design.

"Victor and the others are in the workshop bay," Max was told by the boat driver. "They've pulled one out of the water to strip it down. I think Dr. Biehn has taken charge."

So Safi had volunteered to lead the investigation. She was probably the best one for the job, Max thought. He, on the other hand, had no interest whatsoever in seeing one of the machines that had almost killed him, or in facing Victor and the others. All he wanted to do was sleep. He decided to leave them to it and went straight home. Gillian was already in bed and he took his place next to her without waking her up.

* * *

The autopsy, as they'd named it, yielded some interesting results. Once they were together again, in the workshops, Safi took them through what she'd discovered.

"We cut this section out of the controller," she said, holding up a flat rectangular object about two feet in length. It was the base of one of the chemical storage tanks, but thanks to the efficiency of the printing process a dense web of circuits and control components was embedded within it. "It looks good at first sight, but look down here at these seven conductor tracks."

Once she'd pointed it out it was obvious: seven lines of conductor, all running parallel, had been shorted out by an eighth track scrawled across them from one side to the other. It was like taking the back off a computer, picking seven wires at random, and connecting them together with a soldering iron.

Erratic behaviour was the least they could expect.

"So that's where the problem was," Victor said. "Now, why did it act the way it did?"

"It had effects all over the place," she said. "The main one was that the navigation system was corrupted. That's why it went straight through the boundary. The delivery process was disabled too, for bringing gold back to the drop site. But material collection and replication were unaffected, and, as we found out, it could still move itself around."

"And all two hundred had the same fault?"

"Exactly the same. Take a look at this."

She walked over to where the Prospector was sitting on the trailer and took another section of superstructure from the floor. The vehicle had a gaping hole in one side where its insides had been exposed, and the piles of components scattered around it suggested that it had been hacked apart fairly mercilessly but Max knew that Safi and her team would have been nothing if not painstaking in their investigations. Then she walked back over to where the others were standing and showed them what she'd picked up: a disk about a foot in diameter, the same dark green colour as the rest of the structure but with a reddish brown coating. She was careful to hold it by its edges.

"You'll recognise this," she said. "It's where the instruction set for replication is stored, the blueprints it uses when it copies itself. The magnetic coating looks good, but I wanted to check if the contents were okay so I ran it through a decoder. And I found something interesting: the exact same error is on here, coded into the instructions. And it's the same for all of them."

"So all the Prospectors that got out are related," Victor said.

"That's right. The first bad one must have been made about eight generations ago. Ever since then the fault has been sitting there unnoticed, getting copied every time they replicated."

"But why did they all go at the same time?" Ross said. "Some of them must have been over two months old."

"It was a delayed effect," Safi said. "That short circuit made the navigator's timing signal feed into the path selector. It meant that the prioritisation of the nav commands was no longer constant, but varied with time. When the timing signal on the boundary transmitters clocked over to zero yesterday, the priorities reversed completely: doing a U-turn at the boundary went low, and biasing the planner toward high-yield waters went high. They sailed over the boundary as if it wasn't even there."

Max hadn't said a word up until this point. "So let's get this right," he said. "The Prospector that built that first bad one carried on making more bad ones, with exactly the same fault?"

"That's right."

"And if just one of them hadn't been caught, it would have carried on replicating itself, and the machines that it built would have been made the same way too?"

Safi thought for a second. "Yes, that's true as well."

Max picked up the controller board from the machine and looked at where the mistake had been made. Compared to the neat, ordered arrangement of the other conductors, the seven track blunder that had affected it so badly was hard to view as an improvement. However from the Prospector's point of view, an improvement was exactly what it was. With no delivery cycle to slow it down, and no boundaries to hold it in place, it and its descendants would have had the whole ocean open to them.

Max looked out of the workshop loading bay, at the harbour and the sea beyond. "What would have happened if we hadn't caught them in time?" he said, without taking his eyes off the scene.

"Nothing, probably," Victor said. "We would have got them all eventually, and that would have been that."

"And if they'd started to replicate outside? If there were even more to deal with?"

"Then we'd have got them back as well, just as easily."

Max turned back inside and faced Victor. "Easily? I almost

died getting that last one back. You do know that, don't you?"

"I appreciate what you had to do, Max, but I don't think you were in any real danger."

"You weren't there, Victor, you didn't see what happened." The others were looking uncomfortable. They'd probably heard every word from Garrett while Max was being dragged alongside the Prospector. Max wondered just what Garrett had said.

"But you're safe now, and that's what counts," Victor said. "And now we've fixed the problem we can carry on with our work. Let's get on with it." He turned to leave the workshop.

"You really can't see how dangerous what you've created here is, can you?" Max said.

Victor turned back round, surprise on his face. "Dangerous? I don't know what you mean. It's a boat that sails around and sucks up seawater. What could it possibly do that's dangerous?"

"I can't even imagine," Max said. "And that's what scares me. You've let something loose here that you can only just control, and you still can't see the implications. Do you know how close you were to not getting them back at all?"

"But we did, Max, so it's alright," Victor said.

"No, it's not alright. You had a close call this time, and you think it's all okay just because you caught them early. But you can't see what might have happened, what might still happen."

"Max, — it's alright."

Max felt angrier than he thought himself capable of, as if every fear he'd had about this project had suddenly become real. Victor however was just smiling back at him blandly, as if trying to placate him. Doug cut in to try and defuse the situation.

"Guys, take it easy. You caught them and that's the important thing. All you've got to do now is keep an eye on the others and make sure you catch any problems early."

Max was still unhappy, and it obviously showed.

"Max, we've got a lot to thank you for here," Victor said. "If it wasn't for you we would never have got this far. And if it wasn't for the work you did on the navigation and boundary systems, we might never have got these machines back at all. You should be proud of what you've contributed."

"But it was the navigation and boundary systems that failed in the first place," Max said. "Don't you see what that means? It doesn't matter how careful you are in designing something like this, because it's the design itself that starts shifting once the copying errors kick in. Nothing you can put *in* that design will ever be sacred. If something like this can happen, no matter how careful we are, then maybe the whole thing is a mistake. Maybe I should have left you to it when I said I would. Or never got involved at all."

"And what would that have achieved?"

Max tried to imagine what would have happened if he hadn't agreed to take part. Would they still have got the Prospectors working without his help? In all honesty they probably would, eventually. And would the machines have been more likely to fail like this if he hadn't seen it done his way? The answer to that was probably yes as well. It didn't make him feel any better though.

"It makes no difference now anyway," he said. "I'm not going to be part of this any longer."

"Max, what are you talking about?" Safi said. She looked concerned.

"It's time I left," he said. "I was planning to leave the island soon anyway, but after this — I don't think I want to be involved at all. Victor, you can pay my department up until today if you want, or whatever. Just give me a week to sort out where I'm going and then I'll be gone."

"Max, why don't you sleep on this, give it some more thought?"

"I've done nothing but think about this from the moment I heard what you were planning. No, this is enough. I hope it all works out for you, I really do. But I'm not going to be involved. Good luck."

Part II

Chapter 8

Anna Liu had a decision to make. For months she'd been putting out feelers, priming her trawlers to look for any other informants who could help her where Tyrell had failed. She had those three names to work on too, those mysterious new employees who had been spirited out of their homes and lives and into the depths of some ESOS facility. And then, just as it seemed that none of those lines of enquiry would give her what she needed, the name at the top of her list had surfaced: Max Lowrie, large as life, dropping straight onto the grid five thousand miles from where she would ever have expected to find him.

Breaking cover was never something to do lightly. But considering how much he must know — and the things that he didn't know but she could tell him — he was possibly the most valuable asset she could have.

It was time to make her introductions.

* * *

"You shouldn't look back you know, Max, you did the right thing leaving."

"I'm not looking back, just — looking."

Max hadn't been aware of Gillian joining him on the rocky seashore. He'd been lost in thought for five minutes almost, his rock hammers and other tools scattered around him as he gazed out over the Pacific, his work temporarily forgotten.

"Just looking?" she said. "What? In case one of those things comes after you? We're thousands of miles away you know, it's hardly likely."

Max laughed. "I know, it's not going to happen. I still catch myself checking though." And on one occasion, just after they'd arrived here, he'd almost convinced himself he could see those distinctive twin sails appearing on the horizon. A trick of the light it must have been, or a yacht far in the distance. It had got his attention at the time but didn't worry him anymore. And nor did the intimidation that had stopped him coming here all those months ago. Roy's arrest wouldn't stop all those other zealots from taking exception to his work, but if he was the one behind the recent threats then it was enough of a reprieve for Max to feel safe in picking up his plans. He'd flown himself and Gillian out here at ESOS's expense, not even clearing it with Victor first. Victor hadn't been in a position to complain.

"Come on," Gillian said. "We've both got work to do. Looks like you're nearly done with this one."

The sea was calm today, for this part of the Chilean coast, but a cool wind was blowing in off the water and the storms of the previous night had made their mark on the cliffs behind them. Fresh rock falls were scattered all along the length of the beach, exposing the final resting places of sea creatures that hadn't seen daylight in hundreds of millions of years, a thought that never failed to amaze Max. The spiral ammonite that he'd found was one of the best he'd ever seen, and a few more careful taps would be all he needed to separate the rock in which it was bedded from the main body of the boulder. There was nothing new to learn from a fossil type he'd seen hundreds of times before, but the shape of the ammonites still fascinated him. Everywhere he'd travelled he'd found them, that simple, mathematically precise spiral, repeated again and again, all over the world.

"Do you know there are creatures out there right now that look almost identical to the way this thing did when it was alive?" he said.

"Yes, I know, nautilus shells, that kind of thing."

"But that's four hundred million years with no major anatomical changes, as if evolution just can't make them any better. They're incredible."

Gillian nodded.

"When Darwin was in Argentina he found remains of larger animals, horses especially," Max continued. "If you went up to the top of those cliffs and dug there, you'd probably find the same thing. But they died out, and nothing like them was seen here again. Not until the European settlers brought horses with them a few hundred years ago. Then they spread like wildfire, down through Peru and Argentina, stripping the grasslands bare, along with the European cattle. It was a disaster. That's how it happens when things change too quickly, new species suddenly appearing or being introduced artificially. It never works out well. But in the time it took a whole species to disappear then reappear, these little ammonites just carried on at their own pace, hardly changing. That's the way it's meant to work."

"So if an ecosystem is forced to change too quickly, it always ends badly?" Mentioning adaptation and change was probably the closest she'd ever come to admitting Max's view of the world.

"Yes, pretty much."

"Like Cambria?"

"Exactly like Cambria."

Until then they'd been alone on the beach, but then they heard voices behind them. A group of children had appeared, presumably from a school nearby, led by their teacher. The children were obviously local, but the teacher seemed paler, more European in appearance. They passed by close to where Max and Gillian were sitting, then headed off toward some rock pools further down the shore. Some kind of nature lesson, Max decided. As the teacher went past she glanced over at Max and Gillian, but otherwise didn't acknowledge their presence.

Max carried on easing the fossil away from the rock. Then he heard a voice behind him.

"What is that?"

One of the children, about eight or nine by the look of him, had broken away from the group and come over to see what Max and Gillian were doing. They both looked round at him at once.

"Hello there, who are you?" Gillian said.

"What is that?" the boy repeated, ignoring Gillian and looking instead at the fossil.

"It's a seashell," Max said.

"Why is it in the rock?"

"It was there when the rock was made," Max said, hoping he wouldn't be asked for answers too difficult to explain to a child.

"Who made the rock?"

"Nobody made it, it made itself. This used to be the bottom of the sea. This rock was just mud, then it got squashed, hard."

The boy frowned in puzzlement, thinking for a long time. "When?"

"Millions of years ago," Max said. "That's when this animal was alive. It died, then it fell into the mud."

Just then the teacher appeared, looming over the boy. She asked him something in Spanish, too quickly for Max or Gillian to understand. He answered nervously, obviously explaining why he'd wandered away from the others. A few more words were exchanged between them, again little of it making sense, except for the phrase, "millones de años", from the boy.

"Well you shouldn't listen to him," the teacher said sternly, suddenly switching to English. "He doesn't know what he's talking about. Come away and don't go near him again." She led him away, looking at Max and Gillian suspiciously as she did so.

"She obviously meant us to hear that last part," Gillian said once the woman had gone.

"It's a shame, that kid was bright," Max said. "His English was almost perfect."

"Yeah, I wonder what her problem was."

Max knew. He'd often wondered how the brightest members of the population would have coped back in the Dark Ages, those who in the modern world would have been natural-born scientists or mathematicians. Those people must have existed all through history, even if the level of civilisation around them wasn't advanced enough to make the most of their talents. Back then the most intellectual job a person could get was copying bibles out by hand. He'd always marvelled at the waste that represented. To see it in the modern world was even worse.

"So what would you have said to him, if he'd asked you?" Max said.

She obviously guessed why he was asking. "I'd have said it was a four hundred million year old seashell that got trapped in the mud," she said. "But that doesn't mean that it, or anything else round here wasn't made by God. Satisfied?" She gave a wry smile.

"Not really, but at least you're not trying to tell me it got washed up in Noah's flood."

She smiled and shook her head as if she didn't want to get into a discussion. "Come on, let's go," she said.

* * *

They were back in their hotel room when Max's omni signalled a call from an unknown number. It looked like a north eastern US griddex, close enough to Washington for Max to immediately assume it was Victor. He didn't answer it straight away, but let it ring off instead while he decided what to do.

"God, what does he want?" Gillian said when he told her. "Are you going to call him back?"

For a moment, he seriously wondered. He'd left the island at the first opportunity, three days after he'd said he was going, three days of Victor trying to persuade him to back down and stay put. As far as Max was concerned it wasn't even an option and with the treatments complete he knew Gillian wouldn't be desperate to hang around either. He'd called Indira even as he was packing, telling her he'd almost been killed, company negligence on a near-fatal scale. Victor had given in at that point, knowing UCLA would make moves to end the contract if he didn't do it first. In a way Max had expected Victor to call with another angle ever since. It was almost tempting to see what he'd try.

"No, I'm not going to call him back. He'd only try to hook me in again. Let him sweat."

The calls, however, continued, every hour, on the hour. When Max blocked one number, they would come from another, one time from France, another from Morocco, one even from Chile itself. That was a sure sign of ESOS involvement, he thought: routing calls from one place to another to make interception harder, an attitude to counter espionage which in the current industrial climate only just verged on paranoid.

The attempts stopped, mercifully, at ten that evening. It was when they started again at nine the next morning that Max decided he'd had enough. Gillian was still in bed when the renewed calls began so he left her to sleep and took the omni out onto the balcony. And that was when he realised just how wrong his assumptions had been.

When no picture appeared he initially thought the call had failed to connect. Then the voice began. She was Oriental by the sound of her slightly accented English, her voice a mixture of softness and sternness that gave few clues as to what she might look like, or even how old she was.

"Dr. Lowrie," she began. "We have not spoken before, but recent events have made it advisable that I contact you. I represent a group of interests who are willing to place a high value on the information you possess concerning the activities of the ESOS organisation. As a consequence I would like you to consider an arrangement, one which will be lucrative for both of us."

"Who are you?"

"Think of me as an intermediary, Dr. Lowrie, someone who can make sure you are more than adequately rewarded for passing on what you know."

Slowly, Max was getting his head round the situation. "You want me to sell out on them, is that it? Are you some kind of spy? Who are you working for?"

"'Spy' is such a dirty word, Dr. Lowrie. I prefer the term, 'Information Broker'. The end result is the same though: you tell me what my clients want, and I make sure you're paid."

Max couldn't believe she was being so blatant about it. "And who are these clients? Other companies? China?"

"I think it is best if those details are treated with a certain level of discretion. I'm sure you will understand."

"Then why do you expect me to help you? Do you really think I'll sell out just because you make me an offer?"

"No, not just because of that. You see, there are things I can tell you, as well as things you can tell me. Things which you would derive great benefit from knowing."

"What do you mean?"

"Let me just say that in case you feel any loyalty toward the ESOS organisation, that loyalty should be viewed in the light of the methods they used to recruit you."

Max didn't get time to ask her any more. Suddenly the projection was no longer blank; a message had appeared, a copy of an internal ESOS communication, sent from Victor Rioux's office to a department listed as "Human Affairs", and dated over a year and a half previously.

You will be aware of the priority that Control is placing on the SRS project. The Pacific pilot scheme must be seen to succeed before the Site Five investment can be made to pay off. Given our slow progress in developing a working technology demonstrator, the latest recruitment effort is seen as being key to that success. Having studied the skill set available within the external research community, a shortlist of high priority names has been drawn up. Details below.

Dr. Safi Biehn:

Given her prior experience, Dr. Biehn is an obvious candidate. You will recall we originally considered bringing her on board from the start. However the recommendation that she stay unaware of the full extent of the programme still stands. The lessons we learned from her previous effort are proving too useful; her ties to the surviving members of that team make it likely that the rewards of this endeavour would have to be shared. Needless to say, this division of loyalty would not be in the company's best interests.

Prof. Oliver Rudd:

Has demonstrated skills in multi-disciplinary systems design which extend far beyond the marine-tech specialisation of our own research group. Skills are not as unique as those of our other candidates, but Prof. Rudd is known to be seeking employment with some degree of urgency. Personal financial considerations make acceptance of offer a strong likelihood.

Dr. Max Lowrie:

Another prime candidate, given his proven track record in applying his techniques to previous innovative programmes. Effectiveness and versatility of those methods make him potentially the most important candidate, with the ability to augment the skills of all other research participants. However given his existing commitments, refusal to comply is judged to be a likely initial response. Recommend active measures to secure agreement. Sure you'll have plenty of ideas at your disposal.

Victor.

More text then appeared, word for word copies of the letters Max had received, interspersed with messages between ESOS senior management as they discussed the best ways to intimidate him and Gillian, up to and including those final threats that had so effectively seen him abandon the South American trip.

Max sat back, stunned. The woman's voice continued in the background, but he didn't hear a word. All along, it had been ESOS. It had been Victor. Not just the hook with the island clinic's fertility rules, but the letters too. An innocent man had been convicted for sending those threats, and all along it was an ESOS ruse to scare him into taking the job.

"What are they doing?" the woman was saying. "What is this Pacific project, and this 'Site Five' project? Now you know what they did to you, all you have to do is give me the details and you will make ten times what they would ever have paid you."

Max still couldn't speak, his mind was in turmoil. Was this genuine? It certainly seemed to be. Everything the message had said about Safi, Oliver and himself, fit what he knew. It also fit the nature of the project, but this woman clearly didn't know what the project even was or else she wouldn't be asking. No one could fake those partial details unless they had the full facts as well. This was real. ESOS had played him like a fool, and by the sound of it, Safi too.

"The answer's no," he said eventually. "I'm not going to spy for you. I've had enough of being someone else's puppet. Don't call me again."

He broke the link, waited a minute or so to see if she would try calling back, then went back inside to wake Gillian. His hands were shaking even as he nudged her awake.

"I've just had a call," he said, once she'd rubbed the sleep out of her eyes. "There are some things I'm going to have to do. But I'm going to tell you everything first. And it starts with those letters."

* * *

"Safi, are you alone right now?"

"Yeah, I'm at home. Why, what's the matter, Max?"

"I need to talk to you privately. Can you set encryption on your omni?"

"Sure, what's this about?"

"I'll tell you when we're secure."

She looked confused, but did as he said. The picture blanked as they both set the appropriate call parameters, then Safi reappeared, sitting on the sofa in her villa back on the island.

"Max, what's going on? You look like you haven't slept in days."

"I've slept, but I'm not sure when I next will. I had a call this morning, and, well, I'm glad you're sitting down."

"Okay, why?"

"They screwed us, Safi. They screwed us both. You know those threats I was telling you about, when Gillian left the island? It was Victor all along. It was the company."

"What? No, Max, that can't be right."

"It's how he got me to take part in the programme. He wanted to scare me out of any other job I might have taken over this one. And it worked. And they've been keeping you in the dark too: something from your previous work, something they're using now on another project."

"Max, are you sure about this?"

"Absolutely. Look at this."

He forwarded the messages the woman had shown him, then waited the minute it took for Safi to read them. He hadn't known what reaction to expect, but he knew that there would be one.

"Son of a bitch. Son-Of-A-Bitch. Is this real? Where did you get this from?"

"Someone was trying to get me to sell out on the project. I don't know who she was, someone from the Far East by the sound of her. She showed me this to try to persuade me. I'm pretty sure it's genuine."

"You told her no I hope."

"Yeah, I said no. God only knows who she's working for but anything I gave her would probably end up in China at some point. But I'm not going to leave this. It sounds like there's this other project running, either in parallel with what we did or following on from it, and whatever it is, that's the *real* programme. We were just hooked in to give them a head start. Now they're busy somewhere else working off the back of what we gave them, and they're planning to keep the profits. Jesus, I've just realised — everything we took from Doug, the whole printer set-up — that's the only reason we got the thing working at all. If ESOS are using that technology, they're exploiting him as well."

"Son of a bitch," she said again. "Clever. Real clever. Don't spy on people who might achieve more than you, employ them instead but make them think their little set-up is the whole picture. So who was in on this? Was Ross part of it too?"

Max considered the possibility. He'd always thought himself a pretty good judge of character, and somehow, genial, grinning Ross, himself a relative newcomer when they'd joined ESOS, just didn't seem capable of it. Max had long ago learnt to trust his gut feelings.

"No, I think Ross would be as surprised by this as we are."

"How sure are you?"

"I can't prove it, but pretty sure. Why?"

It was Safi's turn to stop and think. "I want to know how big this really is. Ross is probably in a better position than anyone to get to the bottom of it. Tess too, now she's working for the company. They could be the biggest assets we have in opening this whole thing up, so we need to know we can trust them. Because if this turns out to be real, well —"

Max knew where she was heading. "Then we settle it in Turin."

* * *

For the past twenty years the public domain patent system had been a thing of the past, the risks of openly publishing techno-logical advancements being just too high now that China and its Pacific-Asian satellite block were striving for industrial and scientific supremacy. The closest thing to a closed society since the old North Korean regime, and too self-sufficient to be swayed by sanctions or blockades, any technological advantage would be seized on by companies and agencies effectively immune from prosecution. Nowadays western companies held their designs in sealed patents at the Turin registry, with any intellectual property disputes adjudicated in closed session. Sometimes companies kept their research entirely confidential, relying solely on their own internal security to keep new methods, techniques, even whole projects hidden from the world at large. Similar companies were even grouped together for purposes of dispute resolution, the so-called, Capability Blue groups, an exercise in damage limitation if ever tit-for-tat litigation got so out of control that limited sharing of data was the only viable solution. As a result, industrial espionage, and the profits to be made by engaging in it, had multiplied year by year.

Max ran over the options in his head as he went out into the hotel gardens. He had to help Doug out, that much was clear; they hadn't worked together for years until the Prospector project, but Doug was a decent guy running a small company off innovations which he alone had the right to profit from. He needed evidence though, hard physical proof that Doug's methods were being exploited elsewhere; Turin courts wouldn't settle for anything less. But whatever it took, Max wanted to do it. ESOS had made him think his life was being threatened, almost killed him for real, and nearly wrecked his marriage along the way, letting an innocent man take the blame for crimes they'd committed. And Victor himself seemed to be behind it all, pulling the strings. Max briefly considered going back to the island, feigning some change of heart, to get close enough to Victor to do whatever came to mind at the time. That wasn't the way though, it could only end badly. Evidence, that was what they needed. When Safi called back, then he could make a plan.

He got to the bench where Gillian was sitting, having gone out there to get some fresh air and get her head round what Max had told her earlier.

"So what's happening?" she said.

"Safi is looking into it, trying to find out what they're really doing. She's going to get back to me some time today or tomorrow. But I realised when I was talking to her: if they're using what Doug gave them and not sharing the profits, this could be a very big deal. Turin judgements can see companies bankrupted if they lose out badly."

"Is that your main concern? Doug's company secrets?"

"No. It's a real concern, but what they did to us is worse. They're going to pay for it. Getting justice for Doug is important, but I'm going to make sure it hurts them so much they can't ever do this again. I'm not going to let them get away with it. No one is going to go through what we went through."

* * *

It was toward the end of the next day when Safi's call came in. Max hadn't left the hotel all day, staying within easy reach of the room so he could take it privately. He was in there on his own when she finally got in touch. When his omni linked up he saw he was in a three-way call: him, Safi, back in her home on the island, and Ross and Tess in theirs.

"Max, hi," Ross said, the most serious Max had ever seen him. "Look, I hope you haven't got the wrong idea on this or anything, but I have to tell you, I was nothing to do with any of this, not those letters, not the way you were pulled in, nothing. I didn't even know we had a separate project going on. It seems to be some kind of compartmented programme."

"It's true," Safi said. "Those ESOS messages still had their routing data intact. They were tagged with a high-order recipient list; even if they got forwarded off-list by mistake, they'd be unreadable. And pretty much everyone we were working with — including Ross — was on the no-go list. It was Victor and ESOS HQ who cooked this one up, all by themselves."

It confirmed what Max had suspected. "It's okay, Ross, I was pretty sure you'd be on the level. I think they knew that too, which is probably why you weren't made part of it."

"Cool, thanks, Max. From now on, I'm here to help."

"So, what do you have for me so far?"

"Well, we know who your mystery caller was," Tess said. "I can even show you a picture of her. Max Lowrie, meet Anna Liu."

Ross and Tess's side of the image was replaced briefly by a head shot of a young Asian woman, dark eyes and pale skin, framed by a short cropped bob of jet black hair.

"She works for an information agency based out of Singapore," Tess said, switching back to the room view. "They're a pretty ruthless bunch to be honest, usually the first ones people go to if they want some serious spying done."

"And how do you know this?"

"I called in some old contacts. Remember this used to be my line of business too. She's got a long standing interest in technical intelligence, and the call she made to you is exactly her style."

"And this is the kind of thing you used to do?" Max said, incredulous.

"I did, but always within the law. Call me old fashioned but I'd rather be described as a journalist than a spy. But these people are different, especially Anna. She's a dangerous woman to get involved with."

"So what she told me is true?"

"Unfortunately, yes. I've got a few tricks of my own up my sleeve, and now I know where to look I've been able to put a pretty good picture together of what we're really mixed up in."

"This other project then, what is it? And where is it?"

It was Safi who answered. "It's being run by a different group within ESOS, based out of Frankfurt, Germany but still run by Victor. And it's another large scale replicator programme, aimed at mineral resource extraction."

"Sea based?"

"No, I think we can be pretty sure it's on land."

Max thought quickly; where would there be the space to run something like that? Some kind of desert, clearly, somewhere far from habitation.

"So where is it based? And how do we get the evidence we need?"

"Well, I had to call some old friends of mine first, to see what they could do," Safi said. "They live and work near to this new site, and I was hoping they could get the information we need on our behalf."

"And?"

"They couldn't help. It needs someone with direct technical involvement to judge what's relevant and what constitutes an infringement. It's going to need a personal visit, from some or all of us."

"Are you sure? Why not just follow Turin rules, challenge ESOS to show they got these techniques independently? That's how the hearings work isn't it?"

"But this isn't like a normal Turin investigation. We're not looking at ESOS stealing outright from Doug; they can show they licensed the technology fair and square. The issue here is further utilisation, the fact they've taken it on to bigger things. We can't argue that out in a courtroom unless we've got hard evidence. And to get that we need to go there."

"Okay, so where? And when do we start?"

"Well, it took a bit of arranging but I think I've got it sorted. You see it's not just your friend Doug they're exploiting. You were right; there's every sign that some old colleagues of mine are in the firing line too. You remember what I told you about how big replicative technology could be if it really took off? How it could be a new industrial age? ESOS see it that way too, and they're going for the big time. They want to be the first and only ones to control this technology. It's huge what they're planning, even this other project is just the start, and if we can prove they've got there fraudulently then the payout could be one of the biggest ever seen. Big enough that my old company has agreed to support us and fund the travel. Which I think you'll agree is pretty generous."

"Yes, but travel where? Where the hell is this place?"

"Well that's the question, isn't it?" Ross said. "Let's just say you two may be the luckiest pair of bastards I've met in a long time."

"What do you mean?" Max said. Safi was smiling and he couldn't work out why.

"They're on the Moon," she said. "They've taken one of the Earthrise research sites, the same way we did. And whatever it is they're building, it looks like they've got it working. I'm going back Max, and you're coming too."

* * *

When he told Gillian she sat with her head in her hands for a full minute.

"Max, you can't go. I know I said you were right to act on this but it's dangerous, even now. People die up there."

"It'll be safe," he said. "I'll be staying in the base, not out in the middle of nowhere. It'll be like those vacation trips rich guys take. I'll come back, I promise you."

"Just make sure you do," she said. "Make sure you do."

* * *

They left the day after Safi's call, cashing in the flight warrants Max had helped himself to when leaving ESOS. They flew direct to Los Angeles, where Max's journey would begin.

The flights and transfers to Mare Crisium had been booked and paid for already, leaving him just six days to get ready for the trip. The medical tests alone took four days as his blood was probed and tested for contagious diseases and his health was checked to ensure he was fit to take the journey. By the time he was ready to go, only one day remained.

They spent the last night at a hotel near the airport. The flight was early the next morning, so they got up at five then rode to the terminal, where Max checked in. Then they headed for the international departure lounge, finally reaching the barrier that only Max could pass through.

"Well, this is it," Max said.

"I wish you weren't doing this," Gillian said. "You could have said no. Safi could go alone."

"I know, but I have to do it. If I could do this without going in person, I would, but I have to be part of it, and that means going there."

"But is it worth risking your life for? You've almost been killed once already."

"I love you," he said. It was a way of ending the debate, but he meant it, and hoped it showed.

"I love you too," she said. Then she hugged him and left, without turning back. Max watched her go, then turned and went through the barrier.

* * *

He saw Safi immediately, waiting on the other side. She smiled warmly when she spotted him; she must have got there early, true to form. The lounge area was busy even at this time of day, as the hundreds of international travellers passed the time in the shops and restaurants. Safi was standing next to a pillar, out of the main flow of traffic. He walked over to her and put his bag down on the floor.

"Hello stranger, how are things?" she said.

"Good, thanks. How long have you been here?"

"Only half an hour. There's some coffee shops on the upper

level if you want to get a drink."

"Yeah, that would be good."

Once they were seated, Max looked around at the people milling in and out of the cafés.

"I wonder how many of these people are going to the same place we are," he said.

"Thirty, exactly," Safi said. "It's a full flight today, same as usual. I checked."

"I've always thought it's strange the way they operate from here, just like it was a regular flight to Europe or somewhere."

She nodded. "It is strange. I guess it does count as an international flight though, if you think about it."

"I suppose it does."

"So how have you been? It's a while since I saw you."

"I'm fine. Or I was until a week ago."

"Yeah, I could kind of say the same thing myself."

"Does Victor have any idea you're here?"

"No. As far as he's concerned I'm taking a short notice vacation. There's a squadron reunion at Edwards Air Force Base around now, it was a convenient excuse."

"I don't know how you could face him to tell him. I wouldn't have."

"Well, I'll be out of there soon enough. Ross and Tess too. They're only staying because it would be too obvious if they suddenly left."

"Yeah, what a mess."

They sat in silence, checking the airport infocasts for the boarding time. "Listen, do you mind if I get on with some work while we're waiting?" Safi said after a few minutes.

"No, not at all."

"Good," she said. "I've got behind with this and I won't get much time later on." She set her omni projecting a keypad and screen onto the table top, then reached down and pulled an ancient looking paper document from her bag on the floor. Its orange cover was torn and faded with age, with the word "NASA" printed across the top.

"NASA? That must be old," Max said, taking it off her. "What is it?"

"It's a conference paper on replicating systems, from back when people first started trying to design them. I'm writing a report of my own, and that's part of the research. Look through it if you want, it shows just how old some of the ideas really are."

"Who's asked you to do this?" Max said, leafing through the pages.

"It's for Obispo, my old outfit from before. They reckon once we've sorted ESOS out, they might get back into this line of research. It would be good if they did, I'd prefer to see them get the credit than ESOS."

"And what are you writing?"

"It's a summary report, listing the ways you could use replicators in space environments."

"No different from what Victor's doing now you mean?"

"Obispo were first remember. Only the accident slowed us down. Anyway, space is the natural environment for replicators, it always has been. If you want to build them or look for them, that's the place."

"Look for them? How do you mean?"

Safi faltered for a second, as if realising she'd said more than she'd meant to. "I, ah, I've got some other work underway right now," she said.

"Doing what?"

She still looked unsure about telling him. "Okay, have you heard of the SRC, the Space Research Council?"

"Yeah, I've heard of them."

"Well, they've got an archive of space probe imagery like you wouldn't believe, decades old, a lot of it from the asteroid belt. There are probes there even now, searching out ore deposits that could be mined someday. But they use automated search algorithms to analyse the data, and there's something they should be looking for that I reckon they could miss."

"You mean replicators, don't you? You're looking for replicators." And in that moment he was back on the beach, sitting in a line with Safi, Ross and Doug, talking about life on other planets and Fermi's paradox and how to spot the signs of an intelligent race spreading through the cosmos.

"Exactly," Safi said. "I'm not saying they're there right now, in fact they're probably not. But if they've ever been there, the signs will still be visible. I've bought the rights to tap into the SRC archive, and I've had some search routines of my own coded up. They're working on it right now, even as we speak. When they find what they're looking for, they'll tell me."

"And how do you know what to look for?"

"Traces of mining or excavating. Any replicator will need to dig for its materials. The marks they leave behind are going to stand out, whatever they look like."

"You sound pretty confident you're going to find something."

"I'm more than confident, I'm certain. Just do the sums, Max. Try to estimate the number of intelligent races that have ever existed in the galaxy over the past few billion years, then work out what proportion of the stars would have been visited by the replicators they built. There's no doubt about it, we're going to find something one day."

"So the whole time we were on the island, you were doing this as well. Why didn't you say anything?"

"I want to keep it to myself until I get something worth talking about. It'll make things easier this way."

She seemed to be implying that Max should keep it quiet too, though he was uncertain as to the need for secrecy. He decided to leave the subject there and continued to look through the document in his hands. He paused at a page that Safi had marked.

"Now that one's interesting," she said, seeing where he was

looking. "That replicating factory they're showing there is pretty much the way Anchorville was laid out. It's amazing how advanced their designs were, even back then."

"When was this written?"

"Nineteen-eighty-two," she said. "But it took over half a century before we could put it into practice."

Max looked at the black and white diagrams in the book, the conceptual lunar replicators laid out like huge factory complexes, their attendant robots going about their various jobs. "So is this what ESOS are building too?" he said.

She shook her head. "Unlikely. The details are pretty sketchy but we know they didn't take this factory approach. It may be more similar to the Prospectors we built on the island. We'll have to wait until we're there before we can be sure."

"And we're just going to invite ourselves in and show ourselves around?"

"Pretty much, yeah. These research sites are huge, they're difficult to guard. Plus I know some people up there who can help us out with transport."

"Why does no one else know about this if those sites are so easy to explore?"

"Well, if it's anything like Anchorville was, it won't be listed as 'Top Secret Self-Replicating Factory', it'll be something more generic like 'Resource Optimisation Facility'. That's the one we used."

"And what do we do when we're there? Take a look round and then come home?"

"We do as much as we need to do to get the evidence: pictures, samples, whatever."

"With a bit of sabotage thrown in for good measure?"

She smiled. "You're joking, right?"

"Yes, I'm joking, but only just."

Thirty minutes later the boarding call came over the PA system.

"I guess this is us," Safi said, jumping up and collecting her things. A change had come over her as soon as she heard the call. She was smiling broadly and hurriedly putting things in her bag, as if impatient to get going. "You okay?" she said. "You look nervous."

"I'm okay," Max said. "Come on, let's go."

They took the moving walkway out to the gate, moving through a long glass tunnel that led away from the terminal building. The sun had been up for just under an hour, but its full brightness had yet to break through the early morning haze. The sky above them was pale blue and speckled with cloud.

"In two hours' time we'll be above all that," Safi said, craning her neck back.

Then at last they got to their gate, and saw what was waiting for them. For most of the journey from the terminal they'd been surrounded by rows of parked aircraft, the ubiquitous Boeings and Airbuses, ranging from five to fifty years old. None of them however looked anything like the craft that was sitting at the final gate. It slowly came into view as the tunnel took them round the last corner.

"There it is," Safi said when she saw it. "There it is."

The Spirit of Nevada was almost the size of the 777s parked alongside, but looked more like a stretched version of the old space shuttles that Max had seen on display in Florida. It had the same black and white heatproof tiles as its ancestor, the same swept triangular wings, and the same thick windows round the cockpit. The passenger windows running down the sides were one major difference however, as was the engine pod on top of the rear fuselage, holding the turbojet engines that would take it through its first forty thousand feet of altitude. The three huge rocket engines that would take it the rest of the way were at the back, behind the fuel and liquid oxygen tanks that would feed them. The fuel tank was already loaded with kerosene, but the oxygen tank was empty, for the time being at least. The fact that it was empty not only made the craft safe to take off from regular airports: the missing weight was the only reason it could take off at all.

They waited for ten minutes at the gate, standing by the windows, looking at the craft along with the other passengers. Most of them would be taking this trip for the first and only time in their lives, Safi explained. The development of vehicles like this one was supposed to make access to space affordable, and compared to the early days of space tourism the cost had dropped by a factor of a hundred. However the price of a return trip was still more than most people would pay for all the houses they'd ever own in their lives, and with GRACE controls affecting earthbound flights so badly, these trips had to be rationed as well. Few had been as lucky as Safi herself, making the journey into orbit countless times in the course of her career.

"How many times have you been up now?" Max said.

"Eighty-something I guess, but most of them were with the Air Force, strapped into a U-155. I've only gone up in one of these things once before."

And considering how that trip had ended, Max was surprised to see her so eager to get back in one at all. However if there was one thing he'd learnt about Safi and her previous experiences it was that space travel and exploration were probably among the greatest loves of her life — and even "love" may not have been a strong enough word. It must have been the lure of a new frontier, an environment where humans hadn't evolved to survive so had to ensure their own survival for themselves. He'd occasionally met divers and mountaineers who showed the same attitude: they loved what they did in spite of the danger, and when they were reminded of the danger, even if it affected them personally, it only made them love it more.

The call to start boarding came soon afterward, as the ground crew down on the tarmac finished their checks and preparations. As they walked down the embarkation ramp, Safi looked down at the boarding card in Max's hand.

"They've given you the aisle seat, haven't they?"

"Yeah, looks like it. Why?"

"I'll let you swap with me and take the window. This is one view you won't want to miss."

"Are you sure? I don't mind if you want to take it."

"I've seen it plenty of times already. Go on, I even made sure we were on the left hand side."

"Why's that?"

She smiled mysteriously. "You'll see," she said.

The cabin was tiny, only four seats across, with a narrow centre aisle and no room to stand up. Once strapped into his seat, Max peered out through the window at his side. It was like looking through a tunnel bored into the skin of the craft and showed clearly just how thick the layers of structure and insulation really were. All he could see were reflections of the inside of the cabin as the light bounced around between the five or six panes that made up the window.

"They'll turn the cabin lights off before we leave," Safi said. "You'll see things better then."

The take off from the airport was just like any other, with the obligatory safety briefing as they taxied out. Just how useful the lifejackets and escape slides could be on a trip like this was debatable, but Max guessed they had to be there. Once their turn came to depart, the plane started its take-off run, slowly gathering speed as it rolled down the concrete. It must have used the entire length of the runway as it struggled into the air on its undersized jet engines before heading eastward into the desert, climbing all the way.

Almost an hour later the announcement came that they were forty thousand feet above the Arizona desert, waiting to meet up with their target: the cryogenic tanker plane that would provide the missing oxygen they needed to complete the ascent. It had come all the way from Kirtland, New Mexico, just to link up with them for ten minutes of their flight. Max tried looking for the tanker as they lined up with it, but he didn't manage to see it. The first signs of its presence were the muffled mechanical sounds as the refuelling boom made contact with the inlet port some way behind them. For the next ten minutes the planes flew in tandem as thousands of gallons of liquefied oxygen were pumped across, making their own craft heavier and heavier all the time.

"They'll be lighting the centre engine in a minute," Safi said. "Then things are gonna get noisy round here." She was grinning as she spoke, clearly back doing something she adored. "You're gonna just love this, Max."

Within a minute they heard the first of the rocket engines firing up, as the weight of the plane became too much for the jet engines alone to handle. The muted roar came at them through the structure of the plane, entering Max's body through his seat rather than his ears. As the tank got closer and closer to being full, the vibrations increased, until Max found himself blinking to clear the blurring in his eyes.

Then the noise suddenly increased again as the final two engines were lit. He looked across at Safi to ask if that meant they were ready for the final push, but all she was doing was sitting with her eyes closed saying, "here we go, here we go," again and again under her breath. He guessed that meant they were and turned to look back outside. Then things started to happen quickly.

First he heard the sound of the hook-up to the tanker being broken as it pulled its fill line away from their plane. Then he heard the engines rise in pitch even more, as their plane used the brute force of its rockets to fly under and ahead of the tanker. There was no time for the other plane to delicately manoeuvre out of the way here; every second that was wasted would use up gallons of precious fuel and oxygen that both craft had laboured to carry this high. Instead, all their plane could do was open up the throttles while the tanker hauled itself away from a collision. And then, for the first time, Max saw it: the converted cargo plane peeling away from their own trajectory, banking impossibly steeply for something so large, with the early morning sun glinting off its bright white fuselage, the sky-blue "Kirtland LOX" logo painted down the side, and a trail of freezing vapour streaming from its refuelling boom.

In seconds it was gone, lost behind them as their own speed increased. By now even Max's teeth were shaking as the noise and vibration grew. He could hear one of the women passengers behind him shouting, "Oh my God!" over and over in terror, but she was almost drowned out by Safi's shouts and cheers. "This is it!" was all he could make out from her before her voice was lost in the cacophony.

As the noise increased, so did the acceleration, pushing Max further and further into his seat, until he felt as if he was lying on his back looking up at the ceiling. He tried to lift his head to look straight ahead but it wouldn't go, so instead he kept it where it was, facing the window. Even his breathing became difficult, as if a hundred-pound weight was sitting on his chest. He concentrated instead on the view outside; he couldn't see the ground, but the sky was divided into definite bands of light and dark by the rising sun, and he could see the plane's climb angle creeping closer to the vertical. Then, as the lighter bands disappeared and the darker bands got darker still, the overall colour of the sky went from blue to navy, and finally to black.

Safi was yelling with excitement, and Max could feel it too, though he couldn't have made a noise even if he'd tried. Instead, all he could do was grip onto the armrests of his seat and ride it out. He suddenly realised that Safi's hand was squeezing him back, but he didn't know how long it had been there. He was starting to feel the same fear as the woman behind him, as if he was on a roller coaster ride that had gone off the rails but hadn't hit the ground yet and gripping Safi's hand seemed to be the only reassurance he could get.

The ascent went on for whole minutes, deafening and shaking them in their seats the entire time. Then at last the plane manoeuvred, rolling and pitching out of its near vertical climb in a series of slow, deliberate rotations. Max could see the patches of sunlight and shadow moving round inside the cabin as the plane's orientation changed. The force and noise from the engines was still just as loud as before, but now he could hear Safi shouting to him, "Max! Max! Look outside now!" He did as she'd said, straining to move his head closer to the glass, and then he suddenly realised why she'd wanted him to see this sight. Laid out beneath him, sliding across his window like some fantastically detailed map, was the northern Gulf of Mexico, and directly below, at least two hundred miles straight down, was the Mississippi delta, the branches of the river feeding into the Gulf like fingers of land and water. The sight was breathtaking; he'd seen pictures from space before, but this was different, this was with his own eyes. "Oh my God," was all that he could say.

And then, eight minutes after they'd left the tanker plane behind, the engines suddenly went quiet. Instead, gasps and cries filled the cabin as the passengers suddenly felt the same thing at once, one of the most unnatural sensations a human being could ever experience. To Max it was like driving a car off a cliff, starting to fall, but never reaching the bottom. He felt as if his whole insides had just risen up inside him, as prickles of fear and disorientation spread across the tops of his legs and down his back. He turned to face Safi, finding to his alarm that the rest of his body tried to turn the other way instead. He gripped the armrest and faced her properly, waiting for her to say something. She just looked at him and grinned, breathing heavily.

"What a rush," she said, finally releasing his hand.

Max had no sense of time over the next few hours. He could have been staring out of that window for whole days on end as the world passed by beneath them, or it could just have been minutes. The plane was spinning slowly as they orbited, spreading the heat of the sun evenly over the airframe, and once every rotation the harsh light would stream in through the windows on Max's side causing him to look away and shield his eyes. The colour of the sunlight had surprised him at first, and he'd even heard someone in the cabin saying, "My God, it's blue!" the first time they saw it. It shouldn't have been such a surprise though; with no atmosphere to scatter the shorter wavelengths and give the sky its distinctive colour, they could see the sun in its true form, a radiant ball of electric-blue light.

The sheer size of the Pacific Ocean was another surprise that he should have been prepared for. Every time they crossed it, the surrounding landmasses would be completely hidden by the curvature of the Earth, leaving nothing but clouds and blue water below them. For almost half of every orbit, occasional chains of islands were the only solid ground in view. Max tried spotting places he recognised, expecting it to be like looking at a map with the names taken off, but in reality it was far more difficult.

At first he couldn't work out why that small circle of islands looked familiar, with the slightly larger one toward the southern end. Then it hit him, and he almost kicked himself for not recognising it sooner. He was about to point it out to Safi, but then he noticed something else, and it made him gasp in amazement. Inside the circle, the water was a whole shade lighter than outside. He knew straight away what he was looking at: the combined action of millions of robotic boats, churning up the water as they milled around endlessly leaving foamy white wakes behind them. He was amazed just how visible it was; they certainly hadn't anticipated it. If anyone saw it from up here, all they'd need would be a high-res camera with enough magnification and they'd probably make out the individual boats. For all he knew, maybe someone already had. He kept his eyes on the islands as they vanished behind the plane.

The announcements from the cabin crew kept them informed

as their low Earth orbit took them toward the May station, where they would disembark. The huge modular station, with its research facilities, communication relays and orbital hotel was easily the largest space structure ever constructed, with a near constant flow of visitors like themselves arriving and departing every day. The link-up itself was carried out smoothly and almost noiselessly. The only sound was the faint hiss of the control jets as the autopilot guided them in over the last ten metres, followed by the sound of the docking ring latching into place.

The two cabin crew were the first out of their seats to help the passengers through the cabin and up the tunnel into the station. Max was glad to see he wasn't the only one having difficulty moving around in this environment. Only Safi seemed to be completely at ease, floating horizontally over the seats, keeping herself steady by pushing lightly against the seat frames below her. They went through the tunnel one at a time, then waited in the large module on the other side. Like all parts of the station it was heavily padded, and painted dark and light on different surfaces to suggest a floor and a ceiling and help people orient themselves. Even the fittings and switches were the same way round, to reinforce the idea of up and down. Most of the passengers were directed straight ahead through the far wall and into the main part of the station, but six of them, including Max and Safi, had to go up through the ceiling into an access tunnel, and eventually to another docking module, where their next ride was waiting.

It was as Max floated through the final tunnel that he suffered his first moment of real disorientation. He'd formed a fairly good mental picture of how the modules and tunnels were laid out, and was quite comfortable with the idea of floating up and down between rooms as well as moving forward. However, when he got his first view of the inside of the lunar transfer vehicle and saw how what he'd convinced himself was a horizontal tunnel actually came in through the roof of the thing, he lost all sense of which way up he really was. For a few terrifying seconds he could see himself hanging upside down over the seats of the lander, with nothing to support him or stop him falling. All he could do was grab onto a cable duct running alongside and turn to face the wall, waiting for the feeling to pass.

Once he'd reoriented himself he carried on, dropping into the craft and moving away from the hatch so Safi could follow behind him.

"You got a case of the shakes there, didn't you?" she asked him.

"Just for a moment. I couldn't tell which way up I was."

"Inversion illusion, everyone gets it. You okay now?"

"Yeah, a lot better thanks."

"Good, let's get strapped in. I think they want to move us pretty soon."

In terms of external appearance, the lunar landers hadn't changed much since the day of the old Apollo-era LEMs. Aerodynamics were of no concern, weight however was. Only the cabin had solid walls, like a fifteen foot cylinder lying on its side, with the pilots' seats looking forward out of one end cap and the passenger windows down the side. The rest of the vehicle was all struts and space frames, holding the spherical fuel tanks running alongside the cylinder's lower half, and also forming the four landing legs which arced outward and downward to the pads, fifteen feet below. The excessive ground clearance was there for a reason, to enable the unpressurised cargo pod, the same size and shape as the cabin, to be cradled between the legs. The downward facing engines were at the four corners, each one topped by a gantry-like outrigger, holding the small pitch, roll and yaw thrusters at their tips.

The interior was bare and cramped, with canvas seats and a wire mesh floor, and no divide between the passenger area and where the two crew sat. The only closed-off area was the toilet, tucked into a rear corner of the cabin. Somehow, Max realised, they would have to spend the next three and a half days crammed in here.

Twenty minutes later they left the station and gently manoeuvred away, freeing up the docking port so that other arrivals could use it. The view of the huge structure was spectacular as they pulled back, like a branching three-dimensional network of gleaming white cylinders studded with lights and windows. They even saw another space plane, *The Spirit of Queensland*, noiselessly approaching from beneath them and linking up to the docking port they'd just vacated. Max could vaguely see the faces of people in the station's habitation modules, pressed up against the glass to watch its arrival and their own departure. He wondered just how many people spent their whole time up here simply staring out of the windows, hardly sleeping or eating for fear of missing something they'd never again get the chance to see. A good few he guessed, and he could understand why.

They spent the next half hour just hanging in space, waiting for the right moment to push away from the grip of the Earth. When the time finally came, the craft tipped over parallel to the ground, then fired its engines to take it from orbital speed up to escape speed. The noise from the engines was nowhere near as fierce as it had been on the way up and Max actually found himself enjoying the feeling of being pressed down into his seat as the acceleration took hold.

"Goodbye, Earth," Safi said as the world slid past beneath them. "We won't be so close to you for a while."

Almost six minutes later the engines stopped and weightlessness returned. The Earth didn't look to be any further away, but now every second was adding whole miles to the distance. Max suddenly felt a pang of separation, knowing that they were locked into a course which was taking them forever further from their home planet and everything they'd left behind.

"Don't worry, we're not gone for good," Safi said, as if reading his mind. "You hungry? I think they're going to break out the supplies soon."

Max hadn't had time to notice himself getting hungry, but almost five hours had passed since he'd last had any food. "Yeah, I'll try and eat something," he said.

He soon settled down to a routine of just sitting and staring out of the windows as the day went on. The craft had set itself slowly spinning, the same way the plane had, dispersing the sun's heat over its surface in a "barbecue roll" as the pilots had called it. Safi had quickly fallen into conversation with the pilots, swapping stories from her own flying career and her previous trips into space. She also got talking to the other four passengers, all technicians and astronomers heading for the radio observatory on the lunar far side. The cargo pod beneath the craft was theirs, packed with equipment for a long overdue upgrade to the antennas and dishes built into the craters.

"How come you're landing at Crisium?" Safi asked one of them. "Why not go to the far side directly?"

"Too expensive, we were told. It's all scheduled transfers nowadays, whether we like it or not. Means we've got a three day road journey ahead of us though."

"You taking the North road?"

"Yeah, that's right."

The North road wasn't a road in the normal sense, just a series of radio beacons marking the route between Crisium and the far side observatory, picking its way through the craters and mountains that lay in between. One of the main jobs of the Crisium base was to act as a staging post to the observatory, one of the requirements that had dictated its location. Max didn't envy the technicians their journey though, or the conditions they'd face when they got there. The far side was the perfect place to shield a radio telescope against interference from Earth, but the distance to the nearest civilisation meant that the living was basic to say the least.

Safi spent the next few hours sitting with them, then floated herself over and joined Max again. He was still up at the window watching the view, and already the Earth looked smaller and more distant.

"You're quiet," she said.

"Just taking everything in." The things he'd seen and experienced in the last eight hours were starting to overwhelm him and he knew there was more to come.

"It sure is an amazing sight," Safi said. "You've got plenty of time to take it in, you know, we're not even halfway yet."

"That's okay, I'm in no hurry," he said. He turned away from the window to face her. "So what are you going to do once this is all over and ESOS is behind you?"

"I'll be back with Obispo probably, where I should have been all along. If they restart their own research I'll want to be in on it."

"Why did you leave in the first place?"

"After the accident? I could have stayed, but the programme was effectively dead, and I needed to get away. Luckily I've always had my commercial pilot's licence to fall back on. But getting back into the replication field was what I always wanted. And being back with Obispo again, getting real results out of this technology, these could be pretty exciting times."

"Exciting isn't the word I'd use."

She frowned at him. "You shouldn't be so worried, Max. I know things didn't go entirely to plan back there, but new technology never does. It's a learning process."

"And some lessons come harder than others."

"But think of what we can gain by doing this. You must see it."

He didn't answer; there wasn't much more he could say on the subject.

"Oh, and you might like to know," Safi said. "Victor's in

danger of getting his fingers burnt by more than just us. We found a bug in the transmitter room, not long after you left."

"A bug? Who was doing it?"

"No idea, but it was someone on the island. It's only a short range device, one tiny component inside one of the encryption servers pulled out and replaced with a copy. It looked the same and worked the same, but it had a whole data transmission system built into it. Victor's been going wild trying to figure out who it is. He even thought it was you at one point."

"How did you find it?"

"It kept malfunctioning and causing interference on the comms. The repair guy unearthed it."

Max thought back to the conversations he'd had through that link and the audio and video problems he'd suffered. The realisation that followed made him jolt so hard in his seat he almost floated straight off it.

"I know who it was," he said. "It was Oliver."

"Oliver? Are you sure?"

"Absolutely." The facts were falling into place, following up his gut reaction like one piece of a jigsaw after another. "Someone got hold of the threat letters and sent them to Gillian. Someone had access to them, and the motive to pass them on, and it happened just days after I had that row with Oliver, about Isaac Rourke helping me on the nav system."

In fact he could even remember Oliver's words: *Don't think this ends here, Lowrie. People who cross me end up regretting it.*

"My UCLA boss told me about the last of those threat letters down that link. It was never even mentioned anywhere else, but it was among the ones Gillian got sent. If Oliver heard the whole conversation he'd know just how to get back at me."

So Gillian's mysterious informer was Oliver. Tyrell-B, apparently of UCLA, was Oliver. It all made sense.

"But if he thought we were wasting our time with the Prospectors, why bother bugging us in the first place?" Safi said.

"Maybe he figured if we were stupid enough to believe it, others would be too. Stupid enough to pay for it as well."

"That's not really enough to go on, Max."

"It makes perfect sense to me. Do you remember how Oliver chose that office right next to the terminal room, when we first arrived? It can't be a coincidence. Everything fits — my boss mentioned the threats in that call, she mentioned the fact I hadn't told Gillian yet — anyone listening in would have known just how to hurt me the most. And if they could access UCLA servers, which whoever sent that message to Gillian must have done, they could get hold of the full set, every threat I'd ever been sent. The day we had that meeting about the nav system, that time during the rains: that was when Gillian went, she'd already gone by the time I got home. Oliver must have known what was waiting for me the whole time we were arguing with him."

Safi wasn't yet convinced, but seemed to be taking it seriously. "Okay, it's possible I guess. And remember, the Prospectors weren't the only project running on the island. There are all sorts of secrets tied up in that place."

"Maybe he's done it before, other places he's worked. It would explain how his career got so far, 'knowledge is power', and all that." The image of Oliver Rudd moving from job to job bugging every place he worked was easy to visualise for Max. It seemed to fit. "I'll bet UCLA is one of those places too. That'll be how he got the scans of those letters, if he left himself a backdoor. And the address he messaged Gillian from too."

"You know, it could even explain that Anna Liu woman contacting you when she did as well. If she was the one buying the information off him, she would have needed another informant once Oliver had left."

"You're right, it fits everything. Oliver and Anna Liù, what a partnership."

"What a loser more like. Nothing to contribute, everything to gain. Still, he's gone now. We don't need to worry about him anymore."

"Is there any chance he's got his hands on the technology though?" Max had a sudden image of Oliver passing the techniques they were so desperate to protect to anyone who wanted to buy them.

"No, he left before we knew how to crack the problem, before you brought Doug on board. And that bug wouldn't have helped him once he'd left; he'd have to be within half a mile of the place to pick up what it caught. As far as he's concerned we're still tying ourselves up in knots trying to do the impossible."

"Good. Because if he's as deceitful as he seems then I'd hate to have him know we got it working."

"I bet he'd be kicking himself if he did."

"Yeah, but not for long. It's what he'd do after that that worries me."

"I wonder if we should tell Victor? See his reaction?"

It was certainly tempting. "No, I think I'd rather let him sweat."

Max tried to get some sleep after that, once Safi had reminded him to strap in first. It was difficult though after what he'd just realised. He sat in silence, mulling over the likely sequence of events while everyone else on board slept.

The Earth was a lot smaller in the window when they passed the halfway point, and the Moon was already dominating the view on the other side. They were heading for a point just off the edge of the Moon's disk, and once they got there, just five minutes' worth of thrust from the vehicle's engines was all they would need to slow them into lunar orbit.

In the end only half an hour separated the orbital injection from the de-orbit burn that would send them dropping to the surface, but that time was still enough to watch the whole lunar landscape pass by, sixty miles beneath them. It looked like light grey plaster to Max and only the sharply defined shadows showed the true shape of the ground with its rounded hills, mountain peaks, and circular craters. Each pass took them straight over Mare Crisium, their eventual landing ground, and every time they went over Max struggled to see some sign of the base. He couldn't see it at all until Safi pointed out a tiny smudge of darker land near the eastern edge. It wasn't the base itself, just the disturbed soil extending almost a mile around it, where over a decade of human activity and traffic had stirred up the dirt. Only in complete darkness could the base be seen directly, when its lights were no longer swamped by the sun.

Three orbits later they got the signal to descend and make their approach. The engines were fired once again, but this time they wouldn't stop until they were on solid ground. The craft began to slow, and as the speed that was keeping it in orbit vanished, it started gradually to fall toward the Moon. At first the engines were fired along the direction of motion, purely to lose speed, but as the descent rate increased the craft pitched over toward the vertical and began to support itself on its own thrust. Max had a clear view of the ground as their orientation changed, until finally they were upright, moving slowly forward at almost constant height. He still had no idea how high up they really were, until suddenly the ground came into focus, and what had looked like a two-dimensional pattern of light and shadow became a real, three-dimensional landscape. Then the first man-made objects appeared, red and white open-framed towers way below them, holding the dishes and antennae that were guiding the landing craft in. He tried looking ahead through the pilots' forward-facing windows, but it was hard to make anything out so he turned back to the side instead, and suddenly the base was there, all two square miles of it, safely isolated from the landing site by a good mile of empty ground. A few blasts from the control jets stopped the craft's forward motion, and then it settled slowly downward, kicking up dust with its exhaust. The landing was a perfect one, gentle and almost silent, and as the engines were shut down for the final time, the dust clouds outside immediately settled to the ground as if nothing had happened.

"Okay folks, we're here," one of the pilots said. "One sixth gravity, so don't bang your heads when you get up."

They vented what little fuel remained out into the vacuum, then once the tanks were safely dry, a truck from the base arrived to tow them over to the docking ports. The ride seemed to take ages, but Max spent the whole time studying the base as they drew closer. He'd seen it on television so many times that he knew pretty well how it was laid out, but as with everything on this journey, seeing it with his own eyes was different. Safi was leaning over him to look outside too, pointing out the structures that she remembered from her last visit.

"Those are the original modules off to the left there. Can you believe they're built out of sandbags? The inner layer is airtight, but all they did was bag up the dirt and pile it over."

"Everything's built underground now, right?"

"More or less, yeah, they've got decent earth moving gear nowadays. You can pretty much guess the age of each module by how far down they managed to sink it. Lunar soil is a good radiation shield if it's thick enough, but it takes a lot of digging."

In fact the most recent additions were just vague mounds of soil, sheltering the labs and living quarters inside.

"How do people cope without windows?" Max said.

"There are viewing areas spread around. You wouldn't want to spend your whole time in unshielded sunlight though. It's pretty harmful if you get too much."

Finally the tow truck got them as far as the base. The docking adapters were like large pressurised tunnels, articulated to swing out over the landers and clamp onto the hatch at the top. They heard the attachment taking place, followed by a faint hiss of air as the pressures were equalised. Then one of the pilots opened the hatch from inside and grinned up at someone above him. "Welcome to Crisium." Max heard a voice say.

Climbing the vertical ladder through the hatch was easy with one sixth of his normal weight, once he'd passed his bags up ahead of him. Then the six passengers were led along the tunnel and into the reception area. There were no large open spaces inside the base, just a network of cylindrical modules laid on their sides but the lighting and colours had been designed to make them seem as open and airy as possible. Even so, it wouldn't be a place for the claustrophobic.

The docking tunnel led into another tunnel, then eventually to a meeting room where they were given a safety briefing by a base representative. Most of it was common sense — no open flames, no toxic chemicals — and Safi probably knew it backward, but she listened intently nonetheless. Then, eventually, they were allowed through into the main body of the base.

They came out into a corridor, one of the main thoroughfares of the settlement, with people passing by almost continuously. Down at one end they could see one of the viewing areas, with a small crowd gathered up against the thick glass staring at the low grey hills to the east. Most of them were dressed casually, in jeans and t-shirts, drinking coffee out of plastic cups. If it wasn't for the view outside they could have been anywhere. Safi immediately ran over to join them and pressed herself up against the large window.

"Just the way I remember it," she said, as Max joined her.

Ever since Max had set out on this trip he'd seen people doing nothing but stare wide-eyed at the scenery, and he'd done it enough times himself. "Magnificent desolation", was the term one of the old Apollo astronauts had used, and it still fit this scene of undulating ridges and crests, cold and barren but captivating in its stark beauty. He wondered whether a day would ever come when people got bored of these sights and started to take them for granted. Safi, at least, certainly hadn't.

"There should be someone here waiting for us," she said,

looking round. "A friend of mine from when I was here before." She scanned the faces in both directions, then suddenly stopped and smiled at a man standing off to the side. He was tall, with long messy hair and a dark grey beard, and he was smiling back at her broadly.

"Safi, my old friend," he said with a heavy accent. "How are you?"

"I'm good, Ariel," she said as he walked over to her. "Just fine."

They hugged for a couple of seconds, then he took her by the shoulders and looked into her eyes. Max saw him mouth the words "You okay now?" and Safi nodded rapidly. He must have known her around the time of the accident, Max guessed. She would have left soon afterward.

"Let me introduce you," Safi said. "This is Max Lowrie, excuse me, *Dr.* Max Lowrie, we've been working together lately. And Max, this is Ariel Zamir. Ariel is a permanent resident here, he runs the transport and life support infrastructure and he'll be helping us with logistics."

Max figured Ariel was Russian from his accent. He was lean, but strong looking in spite of it. "It's good to meet you," Max said, holding his hand out. Ariel however just looked at Max, scanning him up and down as if weighing him up. He eventually did put his own hand out, though he seemed reluctant to do even that, then briefly shook Max's before turning to face Safi instead.

"I've got some space for you in one of our hab modules," he said. "Not luxury, but good enough for a week or two."

"That's fine, we can live rough if we have to," Safi said.

"Follow me then," he said, setting off down the corridor with Safi beside him. Max followed up behind, wondering if he'd imagined what had just happened.

"When can you get us out to site five?" Safi said.

"Tomorrow afternoon, I should have a rover ready by then. Does your friend here do EVAs? Or is he just another tourist?"

"No, but he can learn. You'll be okay in a spacesuit won't you Max?"

"Sure," Max said. "As long as it's eight-hundred millibars or above. I don't want to spend more than an hour prebreathing."

That was the limit of Max's knowledge on the subject but it was enough to catch Ariel off his guard. He looked round quickly at Max, seemingly surprised that he knew anything at all about spacesuit function and design, then looked him over again, more warily this time. "That's okay then," he said cautiously, and continued walking.

Max and Safi were given bunk beds in a module close to where Ariel worked. The beds were narrow and hard and the space was limited, but the designers had done all they could to fit as many comforts in as possible. The water from the dispenser tasted metallic however, and the shower could only be used once every six hours, though Max had decided to use both facilities as little as possible. He knew enough about how the recycling system worked in this place, and where it got its raw materials from.

He spent the first few minutes unpacking the things he'd brought then he settled down on the top bunk to relax. Ariel appeared a few minutes later and took Safi to one of the rest areas to talk. This time he hardly even looked at Max, it was as if he simply wasn't there. Max, however, decided against saying anything; he would ask Safi what the problem was another time. Instead he waited until the two of them had gone, then looked round for something to read or pass the time with. On the table next to the bunk was the old NASA document Safi had shown him back at the airport. He reached over and picked it up.

More than a dozen page markers were inserted into the report at various points, all neatly stuck in with their coloured tabs protruding at perfect right angles. The pencilled notes that filled the margins were similarly neat and precise, in spite of the tattered state of the rest of the book. One section seemed to have received more attention than any other however, and that was the one titled "Applications": the potential uses for fleets of replicating machines, both on Earth and off it. And as Max read both the text of the report and Safi's comments beside it, he could almost begin to see why she was pushing the subject so hard.

Mining and manufacturing on a scale never dreamt of in human history was, it appeared, merely the most trivial of the possible applications. Terraforming of whole planets could follow if required: the manipulation of entire planetary climates and atmospheres to turn lifeless rocks into Earth-like habitats. Self-replicating space probes — the wave of exploring machines Safi had described back on the island — those would be even easier. And finally, even stellar-scale macro-engineering projects such as Dyson spheres could become a reality, the constituent materials of whole solar systems, processed and assembled to form habitable surfaces completely surrounding their parent stars.

Max paused at that point, trying to remember where he'd read about the idea before. Wasn't there a story, written decades ago, about a voyage to explore a Dyson sphere with as much surface area as millions of Earths? Or wasn't it a ring, built around an alien star, as far from the star as the Earth was from the Sun? At the time, building such a thing had seemed too far-fetched to even be worth considering, but within Safi's notes, in calm, level-headed language, was a detailed description of how replicators could finish the job in less than two hundred years. With machines that spread exponentially, it seemed that no job was too big to attempt.

Safi came back an hour later and started unpacking her own things.

"Ariel says we can do what we want tomorrow morning and he'll message us when we're ready to go," she said. "He thinks it'll be easy to get to where ESOS are operating."

"And what do we do then?"

"We'll see how it goes."

"Fair enough. As long as he trusts me not to put a pressure suit on back-to-front or anything stupid like that."

Safi smiled. "Ariel's okay, he's been here from the start, that's all. It was a tough environment when they first set this place up. You just have to earn his respect. If you've never worn one of these suits before, I'll make sure you're okay with it."

"Thanks," he said.

Chapter 9

Max called back home once they were unpacked, as he'd promised he would.

"I'm here," he said. "We finally made it."

"So what's it like?" Gillian said. The delay was noticeable; no amount of communication gear could beat the speed of light.

"Cramped. I've seen it on TV before but there's no preparing for how narrow all these tubes are. It smells too, like fireworks, old gunpowder. Must be something in the soil or the dust. People bring it in on their boots when they do EVA and the smell just doesn't go away."

"Sounds lovely. So what are you going to do next?"

"Safi's got an old friend here and she's called in a few favours. We've pretty much got the run of the place. Once we get the call saying things are ready, we head out to see what we can find. How are things back home?"

"It's tough. Max, I've got to tell you, knowing Roy was innocent is just cutting me up here. Are you sure we can't say anything?"

"Not just yet. If we let on that we know who was responsible, everything I'm doing up here might be jeopardised. Wait until I'm back, then we can act. It won't be long."

"It's already been long enough. My sister's fiancé is in jail for something someone else did. And why? Why make it look like Roy did it at all? Why did they need a scapegoat?"

"To get me to come back after you left, that's all it could be. Victor must have panicked when he realised why you'd gone, so he did the first thing he could think of."

"But why did he keep sending those things at all? After you'd gone to the island?"

"I don't know. Maybe he thought it would look suspicious if the letters stopped too suddenly. Who can know how minds that

216

sick work? At least people who write those things for real are doing something they think they believe in."

A flashing SeleCom icon appeared in the corner of the display, telling them their time was almost up.

"Look, it's not easy booking these link-ups, I think the Earth-Moon relay is tied up pretty much all the time, but if I call you back in two or three days? How does that sound?"

"Make sure you do," she said. "And come back safe."

* * *

The message that told Max and Safi they were ready to go came the next morning, far earlier than expected. Safi had just started showing him round the rest of the base when suddenly her omni chimed with an incoming message, taking them both by surprise. She opened it up and checked the display.

"He's all set, we're going early. You ready?"

For the first time since setting out on this trip, Max felt reluctant to go, though he couldn't tell why. He certainly wasn't afraid of going outside; he trusted himself and the technology around him too much for that. Something else was bothering him though, some nagging memory of what had happened last time he'd gone out into the unknown. He ignored it and decided to press on.

"I'm ready," he said.

* * *

Five people occupied the pressurised rover that they took from the base; Max and Safi themselves, then Ariel and two of his colleagues from base infrastructure, Harris and Damon. Harris was the older and stockier of the two, by a long way on both counts, though they were both relatively new to the base and Safi hadn't met either of them before. Damon was lightly built with sharp, angular features. Even his nose and eyebrows seemed to have been constructed with a protractor.

"This rover was in for motor repair, but we finished early," Ariel told them. "We have it for the next three days. Will you need transport after that?"

"It depends what we see," Safi said.

The research site that ESOS were using would be easy to find; all they had to do was follow the service line that led from the base. There were twenty lines in all, one for each site, like shiny, gold foil tents, housing the air, power and water ducts that allowed each satellite settlement to survive. They came out of the base running parallel, but then fanned outward and headed for the horizon. Each one had crossing points at regular intervals, like wide metal ramps spanning the lines.

They found the one marked as leading to site five, then crossed the intervening lines and began to follow its course northward. There were so many vehicle tracks running alongside it that it almost looked as if the soil had been ploughed over. Occasionally the tracks would veer away from the line then rejoin it further on, following the contours of the land as it rose and fell. Boulder fields were also scattered around the landscape, strewn with rocks up to ten feet in height.

For the first half hour another of the service lines ran alongside theirs, but then it split away and headed off to the right, into the distance. Safi moved over to the right hand side of the rover at that point, and stared out of the window as if searching for something.

"What can you see?" Max asked her.

"Nothing," she said quietly. "Site six is over there, that's all. That's where we were."

Max didn't ask her any more about it.

"We're inside their perimeter now," Harris told them from the driver's seat soon afterward. "You don't want these guys to know you're here, right? Can I suggest we move away from the service line, off to the east?"

"Sure," Safi said. "Take us a few miles east, then head north again, toward where they're operating."

They made the turn, then moved off over virgin soil, leaving fresh track marks behind them.

"Aren't we going to leave a trail like this?" Max said.

"Then what do you suggest?" Ariel said testily. Max didn't bother replying.

"It can't be helped," Safi said to him. "This whole area is criss-crossed with tracks anyway, a few more won't hurt."

In spite of the grey monotony of the surrounding terrain, Max couldn't take his eyes off it as they covered the distance. Seeing pictures back home hadn't prepared him at all for the effect the sight was having on him. The closeness of the horizon was the most unnerving thing; just with his own eyes he could clearly see that they were moving over a ball of rock, far smaller than the Earth. He tried to extend the contour of the ground in his imagination, taking it beyond what his eyes could see, visualising the way it curved away and eventually met up with itself on the other side as if he could gauge the size of the whole surface just by sight. It looked a lot smaller than he'd expected.

"It seems so small when you're on it, the Moon I mean," he said.

"It's bigger than you think," Safi said. "It's too big even to count as a moon, strictly speaking. We live on a double planet, a bigger one and a smaller one, orbiting each other. It shouldn't be called, 'the Moon', at all."

"Really? That's surprising," he said.

Suddenly they felt the rover turning off to the left and speeding up, jolting over bumps in the ground as it accelerated. Ariel stood up from his seat and leant over to see what Harris had spotted.

"What can you see?" he said.

"Over there, next to that rise. Looks like an antenna, a relay or something."

By now they'd all stood up to look out of the front windows, holding onto the seat backs and handholds as the rover moved forward. They were soon right in front of the structure that Harris had spotted. It was like a small radio mast, eight feet tall, with a pair of antennae and a flashing beacon at the top.

"Can you figure out what it's sending?" Ariel said.

"Steady repeated signal, no information content," Harris said, reading figures off a display at his side. "It's on a frequency they're cleared to use for telemetry."

"You want to look closer?" Ariel asked Safi.

"No, I don't think it would tell us much. Unless you do, Max?" He shook his head. "Okay, let's leave it," she said. "Head north, see what we find."

Their route was now taking them closer to the centre of the site, where the ESOS personnel would be living and working. Max felt the tension within the vehicle rise as the need to stay watchful increased. Then the rover stopped suddenly, and Harris peered out ahead of them.

"We've got company," he said.

Off in the distance, something was moving. It looked like a vehicle of some sort, dull grey in appearance, but it was too far away to judge its size or shape. It seemed to be moving backward and forward across the face of a low ridge, travelling around a hundred yards each time. Damon reached behind his seat and found some binoculars, then held them up and adjusted the focus.

"It's not a rover," he said. "It's too small. Looks like some kind of robot. And it's towing something."

"Here, let me see," Ariel said, leaning forward between the two front seats and taking the binoculars. "That's a robot. No mistake."

"You reckon it can see us? It may be transmitting."

"I can only see one antenna, low gain. Doesn't look like it's built to transmit pictures." He turned round to face Safi. "What do you want to do? Go over and look at it?"

Safi had her turn peering at it, frowning into the eyepieces for a good ten seconds. "Well, we came here to see what's going on," she said. "Let's go and see what it is."

Harris got the rover moving again, then took them slowly toward the robot, looking out for any reaction from it as they approached. There was none. He stopped when they were about a hundred yards away, then they watched as it kept on moving, seemingly oblivious to their presence.

"It's strip mining, look at it," Max said. Now they were this close it was easy to see what it was doing. The course it had taken over the side of the ridge was clearly marked by a deep furrow where something under its body had dug into the soil as it zigzagged back and forth. Most of the soil was being pushed back out again through a duct at its side, but presumably whatever materials it was collecting were being separated out and stored in the trailer behind it. Even with the trailer attached it was barely ten feet long.

"I want to get out and take a look up close," Safi said.

"Are you sure it's safe?" Ariel said, keeping his eyes fixed on it.

"It hasn't reacted to the rover," Safi said. "We'll be safe. Come on, Max, this is your job too."

They got up and moved to the back of the rover, where the suits were stored. Five of them were attached to the walls there, sized for the five of them in the cabin. Safi went over to the bag she'd brought and pulled out some brightly coloured triangles of fabric, then went over to the suits and started attaching them to the shoulders.

"ID patches," she said. "Red and white okay for you?"

"Yeah, they're fine," Max said. They looked like the Japanese flag in reverse, large white dots surrounded by red. Safi's ones he recognised from the film clips she'd shown back on the island:

bright saffron yellow, with no other pattern or design. It was some kind of superstition among people who worked in space, he seemed to remember, keeping the same patch colours for life. Then she took out another pair, blue and white in colour. She folded them up and put them in a pocket on her own suit without saying a word.

Getting into the suits was relatively easy. The backpack of each one swung open like a hatch, allowing them to climb straight in through the back. The lower gravity certainly helped too. Once he'd been sealed in Max felt the pressure rise slightly as the suit tested itself for leaks, then a green light lit up on the control panel on his left forearm. The smell inside was of pine, some kind of freshening agent to make it feel less claustrophobic. It was stronger than it needed to be though, almost overpowering.

"This is a basic four-hour suit," Safi told him. "Just like the tourists wear. It's all automatic, so don't worry about the controls or displays, I'll keep an eye on them."

"And don't over-exert yourself either," Ariel said, checking all the straps and fittings on the outside, yanking them hard to make sure nothing was loose. It almost felt as if he was trying to pull Max over. "These things fog up when you sweat. And you *will* sweat, okay?"

"Sure," Max said. It felt like he'd just been told he wasn't fit enough to even be there.

They stepped into the airlock leaving the other three in the main cabin. Prebreathing oxygen to purge their bodies of nitrogen wasn't required when operating from the rover as the oxygen level in the cabin already matched what they would get inside the suits. Ariel shut the inner door on them, then Safi hit a couple of the controls on the wall and set the vacuum pumps running. Max felt the suit inflating around him as the pressure in the airlock fell; he could hear the material stretching and creaking as it began to take the strain, then the lining flushed cold and then warm again as the backpack's conditioners drove argon gas into the insulating layers of the suit. Once enough air had been lost from the airlock, valves opened to vent the rest out into the vacuum, then the outer door unlatched itself. Max was standing closest to it.

"After you," Safi said.

He pulled it open, blinking as the harsh light flooded in, then stepped out onto the small rear platform and down onto the ground. He moved away to give Safi room to get out, and turned to take in what lay around him.

The Sun was high in the sky, and would be for whole days to come as the Moon slowly spun on its axis. The glare of the sunlight was intense, and he soon had to reach up and pull down the gold plated outer visor of his helmet. Then, and only then, was he able to look up into the sky and see for himself the sight that had captivated everyone who had ever travelled to this place.

Just above the southern horizon, hanging in space, was the Earth. From here it looked small enough to cover with his thumb but somehow, packed onto the surface of that blue and brown sphere, the whole of human history had taken place. Only for the last hundred years had people been able to leave it behind, turn around, and take it all in with one glance. Max counted himself lucky to be among them.

It was hard to tell which part of it he was looking at now; most of it seemed to be in darkness and only a thin crescent of land and sea could be seen. It could have been the tip of South America that was visible, or it could equally well have been Africa. However, even as the Earth went through its phases, from new to full then new again, its position in the sky never changed. As the Moon kept one face permanently pointed at its parent, the position of the Earth as seen from Mare Crisium stayed fixed over the horizon. It was this effect that had given the twenty sites of the Crisium research project their name: Earthrise.

"Come on, Max! Let's go say hello to this thing!" Safi was bounding away from the rover, almost hopping from foot to foot in a series of long slow jumps. She was laughing as she went, obviously loving every minute of it now that she was outside. It occurred to Max that he'd never really seen her look happy until they'd taken this trip and left Earth behind. Maybe, somehow, she was meant to be here, he thought. He broke himself away from the view and tried to walk after her, but soon found himself moving the same way she was just to keep up. The unfamiliar motion was surprisingly tiring, as rarely used muscles woke up within his legs.

"Okay, let's see what we've got here," Safi said.

The robot was coming toward them as they approached it, adding another straight line to the parallel rows it had already made. They kept off to the side as it went past them, watching it closely as it motored along on its large wheels. Its colour was almost the same as the soil it was moving over.

"It's built out of basalt," Safi said. "The same trick we used."

"Basalt? You mean rock? How come?"

"It's the one thing you've got most of round here. You can melt it down and mould it, just like metal. You can even make it flexible if you spin it into fibres. Look at the tyres."

Max looked closely at the wheels as the back end of the trailer slowly went past. They were made of a woven mesh of the same grey material as the rest of the thing, flexing slightly with its weight. "Clever," he said.

"That's our first bit of evidence," she said. "Using lunar basalt in this many ways was an Obispo idea. We were the first to make it work and now they've helped themselves to it."

Interesting, she was calling Obispo "us" and ESOS "them", Max thought. It hadn't taken long for her to finally settle her loyalties.

She reached into a suit pouch at that point and brought out her omni, the slim silver bracelet looking somehow incongruous in her bulky, gloved hand.

"Is that thing okay out here?" Max said.

"Sure, it's vacuum hardened. I had it custom built." Somehow that didn't surprise Max at all. His own was still round his neck under his suit, and probably wouldn't last five minutes if he'd brought it out here. "We need pictures after all," she said. "That's what we came for isn't it?"

She started walking alongside the machine, levelling the omni at it, having presumably set some video or photographic function running. She went in close a couple of times too, getting detailed shots of the tyres and the various mechanisms that seemed to support the wheels. Then she ran round to the front of the machine, overtaking it easily, and stopped right in its path.

"Safi, be careful," Ariel's voice came over the radio link.

"I'll be fine, I just want to see what it does."

The robot got within five feet of her, stopped for a second, then turned off to the side and neatly bypassed her before continuing on its original course.

"Collision avoidance sensors on the front," she said. "Thought so. I told you I'd be okay."

They examined the machine for the next five minutes as it slowly dug the dirt, moving down the slope the whole time. As soon as they looked up close at its surface they could see how it had been constructed. The stepped appearance of the layers it had been built from was familiar to both of them.

"And there's our next proof," Safi said. "Your friend Doug would be very interested to see this."

"I think he would. Let's get some shots of that too."

"Strange though," Safi said as she took the pictures. "It doesn't look as if it can replicate. It's just a mining machine, unless it's way more complex than it looks."

"So we're not looking at a Prospector with wheels then."

"I guess not."

Suddenly Damon's voice came across from the rover. "Can

you see inside the trailer?" he said. "See what it's collecting?"

"No, it's sealed," Safi said. "There are some attachment points at the back though. Looks like it's meant to dock onto something and unload."

"So where does it go when it's full?"

"Home, I guess," Harris said.

Just then, almost as if it had heard them, it broke away from the straight path it had been steering and headed up the incline, straight over the pattern of lines it had previously laid down. They watched it as it reached the top of the ridge then disappeared down the other side.

"I think it's going back where it came from," Max said to Safi. "We should follow it."

"Are you sure? With this machine, pretty much every bit of proof we need is right here, even if we just take pictures."

"It's not a replicator though. It's the core technology we need to find evidence of, not just some peripheral bit of machinery. Come on, let's go."

It took around five minutes to climb back inside the rover and get through the airlock. They opened up their inner visors, but didn't bother getting out of the suits. "If we see anything else we'll only want to go outside again," Safi said. "Just don't get dirt onto any of the panels."

They caught up with the robot easily as it moved off to the north. Alongside the wheel marks it was making was another track, presumably the one it had left on the way down.

"If we follow those marks we can get there ahead of it, wherever it's going," Max said.

"Sure," Harris said. "Better than following it at this crawl."

The tracks led them north for another half hour. If they'd stayed next to the service line then they would have reached the ESOS buildings by now, according to Ariel. As it was, they'd missed the settlement completely, passing it by way off to the side. The number of wheel tracks they were seeing had increased significantly, small ones like the one they were following, plus some larger ones, clearly made by rovers like their own.

"We should be careful here," Ariel said. "It looks like they come through here sometimes."

They carried on further, seeing more and more tracks coming in from the sides and taking the same route as them. Harris slowed down almost to a standstill as they went over one low hill after another to ensure they weren't taken by surprise by anything that might be on the other side. Then, as they reached the top of one of the slopes, he brought them to a halt and looked out through the binoculars.

"Is that what you're looking for?" he said.

Directly ahead of them, in the floor of a wide valley, was what looked like a cross between a chemical refinery and a grove of palm trees. Low cylindrical structures dominated the scene, different heights and widths all nestled together, with pipes and ducts connecting them. They all had flat circular roofs, but on top of some of them were narrow vertical girders, sprouting up and heading into the sky. Each one branched outward at the top into a collection of broad, flat surfaces, tilted toward the sun. To Max they almost looked like leaves.

"I bet those are solar panels, those things at the top."

"I think you're right," Safi said. "Shall we go and look?"

"Let's wait first, see if anyone is around."

"Max is right," Ariel said. "It would be wise to wait." From Ariel that almost sounded like glowing praise.

They waited and watched for over ten minutes, looking out for rovers or other signs of human activity. All they saw was four mining robots like the one they'd left behind, coming in from different directions then backing up against a hatch on one of the buildings for a minute or so before heading off. "I guess that's how they unload," Safi had said. Watching the robots also gave them a chance to judge the scale of the place. It wasn't large at all, maybe three hundred yards across, and twenty feet tall at its highest point. None of the structures seemed to have airtight doors or windows in them.

"We can assume nobody lives in there," Ariel said. "What about transmissions?"

"Very few," Damon said. "Certainly no voice comms or high data rates."

"Good, it's safe. Let's go."

They warily drove down the hill and parked off to the side, away from where they'd seen the mining robots unloading. Ariel, Harris and Damon decided to come out too this time, so they climbed out of their seats and started to suit up at the back. Then they went outside.

The overwhelming impression they got when they saw the place up close was of a city in miniature, a city populated by robots. The mining machines they'd seen already were just one variety of what must have been over a dozen different types, most of them operating within the boundaries of the structure. Some of them were mobile, shuttling around the hardened surfaces that joined the cylinders, carrying parts and materials, while others were fixed in place, barely visible through gaps in the walls as they carried out what looked like manufacturing tasks. None of them were any larger than the mining machines they'd already seen.

"I know what this place is," Max said as realisation dawned. "It's an anthill, a termite nest. These are the workers."

"You may be right," Safi said. "It would explain why they can't replicate themselves."

"So how *do* they replicate?" Ariel said. "That is what they're meant to do, right?"

"I don't know," she said.

"If this is an anthill, maybe we should look for the queen," Damon suggested.

Max looked in toward the centre. "Don't bother," he said. "I think I've found it."

Right at the core, visible through gaps in the surrounding structures, was the largest of the cylindrical blocks, like a wide gas tank sitting on its end. The outer surface wasn't continuous, but instead was peppered with gaps and spaces, those near the ground providing access for the mobile robots that were moving in and out of them. Max was crouching down to get the best possible view through one of these gaps, trying to make out what was happening inside. The other four gathered alongside to see what he was seeing.

The inside of the structure was in near darkness, but light from gaps in the roof gave enough illumination to guess what it contained. The details were hidden, but within the shadows some kind of mechanism could be seen moving rapidly back and forth over a shape that they recognised as one half of a mining robot, lying on its side.

"It's a 3D printer," Safi said. "Just like we used, just like on a Prospector. That's how it builds the robots. Told you."

"Listen, people," Ariel said. "If you don't want us to be discovered here then we shouldn't stay too long. We need to work quickly, then go."

"You're right," Safi said, standing up straight. "If we take pictures of everything, then we can look them over back at the base. Everyone agreed?"

Max and Safi spent the next twenty minutes walking round the perimeter, Safi filming everything they saw, pointing her omni into any gaps or spaces that might contain anything interesting. When they got back to their starting point the five of them returned to the rover and got out of their suits. They drove round the perimeter once more, then retraced their route back to the base.

Chapter 10

A message to call Ross had arrived while they'd been gone, via Ariel's office comms as Safi had arranged. Ariel took them to a private room, then left them alone as they set up the secure call. Ross's familiar grinning face appeared on the screen when the connection got through.

"Hi, you two, how are things?"

"Hi, Ross, we're good," Safi said.

"So what's it like to be back there?"

"Amazing, just unbelievable."

"I bet it is. You guys are so lucky, I wish I'd been able to go too. How about you, Max, how are you finding it?"

"It's incredible, this place is breathtaking," he said, and he meant it.

"So what can we do for you, Ross?" Safi said.

"Oh, just giving you an update. Things are okay at the moment, the weather's pretty hot, the food's pretty average, the simulation group are winning the atlatl spear throwing league I started in your honour, Max. Oh, and I thought you might want to hear the news; Victor sank all the Prospectors yesterday."

Safi seemed to almost choke. "He did what?"

"He's worried people are taking an interest in the island. Ever since that bug was found he's been checking and rechecking every angle in case someone somewhere is acting on what they saw. It wouldn't take much to figure out what we were doing, so he had the control room send the deactivation signal early."

"Wow. I guess that proves the Prospectors were only a pilot. If they were the main event, Victor would never cut production that quickly. So where were you when he did it?"

"He called us in to see it. He sent the termination command through the boundary transmitters, then we just sat back and watched them sail home."

"Did they all come?" Max said. The chance of aberrant behaviour was still his number one concern.

"Every last one," Ross said. "Do you want to see them? I'll send up some of the footage we took."

"Sure, go ahead."

Max and Safi set the film clip running as soon as it arrived, then watched as the entire Prospector population, by now numbering over a million, swarmed in toward the island. Crowded together with no gaps between them they formed a continuous mass almost nine miles across. The shots were taken from the air, presumably from Garrett's helicopter, but despite the bright sunlit waters and postcard views of the island there was little to the place that Max missed. He didn't miss the Prospectors either; seeing them now reminded him just how sinister they looked, like blind lumbering creatures, dark and menacing in appearance. He was glad to see them disappear beneath the surface as they scuttled themselves and sank from view, piling up at the foot of the huge underwater cliff that ringed the island. It was good to be rid of the things.

"When are you going to blast them?" he said.

"We've already done it," Ross said over the pictures. "You'll see it at the end of the film. The pile was almost a thousand feet deep, but they're well broken up now."

So the Prospectors no longer existed, Max thought, their materials had been returned to the same sea they came from. In a way he wished he could have been there to see it himself, or even pressed the button to set the explosives off in person. The detonations didn't look huge on the surface, but down on the seabed they must have pulverised those fragile machines that hadn't already been crushed by the pressure or sunk into the mud. The avalanche of debris from the cliff itself would have covered what was left. "I wonder what future archaeologists will think, if they ever dig up the remains?" he said when the clip had finished.

"I don't know," Ross said. "I guess we've given them something to think about."

* * *

The next morning Max and Safi got together again to run through the pictures she'd taken the previous day. Ariel was working that morning, which gave them half a day to decide on their next course of action.

"Well, I was wrong about those things at the top," Max said, as her more than capable camerawork played out on the viewing screen. "They look more like mirrors than solar cells."

"You're right," Safi said. "I'll bet there are generators and furnaces inside those blocks there. The mirrors must follow the sun round, and focus the light down inside. More than enough power."

"In that case I think I can see how the place is laid out now. The miners bring the raw materials in here, and these blocks must be where the stuff is processed."

"Yeah, look at what's coming out on that conveyor. It's almost like metallic powder. Must be magnesium. I guess those tubes must be taking other materials."

"And it all feeds into the centre, where the printer is."

"Simple really."

"Yes, but remember, the robots are doing most of the hard work. There must be some pretty complex machinery inside those blocks. Even the mining robots are pretty sophisticated, considering how they're made."

They watched for another few minutes, then Max suddenly saw something and got her to rewind a few frames and pause.

"That's interesting," he said, pointing out one of the structures on the screen. "Look at that block, over on the far side. It doesn't look as if it's been finished."

"I see it," Safi said.

The block Max had spotted was near the perimeter of the buildings, but the wide hole in its side was only visible when looking at it across the centre from the other side. And unlike the other blocks, this time the interior was perfectly visible. It looked as if some kind of half built manufacturing robot was inside it, waiting lifeless for the components that would make it complete.

"I get it," Safi said. "This place is self-extracting. It's building itself, growing outward one block at a time."

"And the more machines it builds, the more materials it can process, and the more it can spread."

"Exactly."

"But it can't grow forever. It looks like the printer at the middle is the only part that can actually make anything. What does it do when it reaches its limit?"

"I don't know, we haven't seen enough yet. We need to get out there again, see it up close."

"Are you sure? Aren't these pictures enough?"

"No, they've given us as many questions as they have answers. We don't want to miss anything out. Let me call Ariel, I'll tell him what we want to do."

* * *

They drove out again later that day, this time with Damon in the driving seat, and went straight to the site they'd explored the day before. They waited again to see if anyone else was around, then parked up alongside and got into their suits.

"Wow, look how it's changed," Safi said once she was outside. She'd gone straight to the spot that gave the best view of the block they'd seen in the pictures, and already it seemed to be almost complete. The machinery inside it filled its interior right to the top, and many of the missing outer panels had now been put in place. They even saw one of them being installed, as a small, wheeled robot, carried it over from the printer block and pushed it into position. The panel seemed to latch into place, without the need for any screws or fixings.

"I was right, it's growing," Safi said.

That however wasn't the only change. Harris called them over to where he was standing, and pointed down at his feet.

"Look at the ground, where we were standing yesterday. Something's been busy while we were gone."

It looked as if the hard paved surface that connected the cylindrical blocks had been extended outward, covering some of the footprints that they'd made the previous day. The hard slabs were perfectly flat, but rough in texture.

"Sintered basalt," Safi said, kneeling down to look at them. "These must be made in the furnace, basalt powder fused together by heat. Just like we did. I guess it's getting ready to put another building here."

Just then Max saw some movement out of the corner of his eye, and turned to look over his shoulder.

"Look out, Safi, there's a miner coming in," he said.

Safi moved to the side to let the machine through, then they watched as it went through its now familiar routine of backing up to the unloading bay and waiting for its delivery to be extracted. It was only there for about twenty seconds before it moved off again. However, what happened next took them all by surprise. Just as it was turning to head back out into the wilderness, two new robots emerged from one of the buildings and put themselves in its path. The newcomers were much smaller than the miner but were equipped with a fierce looking array of cutting tools on their fronts. As the miner came to a halt they drove over to it and started methodically cutting chunks off its structure, one on each side. Before the miner had a chance to move, its wheels had been completely shredded. Max, Safi and Harris looked on in amazement as it was reduced to pieces no bigger than a fist. The two robots then started to bulldoze the remains toward one of the structures.

"Now why did they do that?" Harris said.

"Must be for recycling," Safi said. "Getting the materials back. But if this place is growing you'd think it would need more miners, not less. Strange."

"Is it worth seeing if that happens again?" Max said. "We could get some pictures of it if we're quick enough."

"Yeah, good idea," she said, reaching into her suit pouch to get her omni. Then she tried another pocket, and another, and finally the thigh pockets. "Damn it. Now why would I do that?"

"Do what?"

"I left my omni back at base, in the hab module. Do you guys have anything with you?"

"No," Harris said.

"Nothing here," Damon added. "Maybe there's a camera in the rover."

Suddenly Ariel's voice came through their headsets, calling them over from the far side of the site. "We have something new here," he said.

They moved round and joined him where he was standing.

"Look at those marks," he said. "They're not like anything I've seen before."

"They certainly weren't there yesterday," Max said.

Leading out of the complex, heading off into the hills, was a collection of tyre tracks. They were bigger than those left by the mining machines, but smaller than those of a rover. Several sets were visible, some coming and some going, as if the same vehicle had gone away then returned several times in succession. Ariel bent down to examine them, then stood up again and looked out into the distance.

"Some new kind of machine," he said. "Something we haven't seen before."

"Well, let's go see where they lead," Safi said.

They got back into the rover, then followed the tracks out over the low, undulating hills that made up the local landscape. Only ten minutes had passed when they spotted their target in the distance. Damon brought them to a halt so that they could watch.

The robot was bigger than the mining machines they'd seen but seemed to be built along similar lines with its low, broad profile and its six bulbous tyres. However the array of arms and manipulators at the front was new, as was the rack on top of it, loaded with various pieces of machinery. It had stopped in the middle of a wide flat area between two ridges and was busy building something out of the parts it had brought with it. Max and the others watched from their vantage point as the construction took shape.

"It's making another printer, you can see the shape of it," Safi said. "It must be building another site from scratch."

"So those nests don't just grow, they can reproduce as well," Max said. "I should have guessed that would happen."

"What are those things, piled up around it?" Ariel said, pointing out of the window. Surrounding the new machine were eight or nine mounds, as if bars and rods of different materials had been stacked up for safe keeping.

"I don't know, they remind me of haystacks," Safi said. "Some kind of materials store?"

"That must be what it uses to establish itself, before it can make its own mining machines," Max said. "The yolk of the egg. It would make sense."

"Do you want to take a closer look?" Ariel said.

"Sure," Safi said. "Let's go."

Damon set the motors running to take them down the slope, then released the brake to let them move off. Then he suddenly put it back on again and scanned the instrument panel, concern on his face.

"Something's wrong here, we're overheating."

"I can smell burning," Max said. "It's coming from the back, under the floor."

"Right, suits sealed," Ariel said urgently. "We need to vent."

With the high oxygen content in the rover, the merest suspicion of a fire had to be dealt with quickly. Fortunately all five of them were still in their suits, so once their faceplates were sealed, Damon opened the vent valves and sent the cabin atmosphere out into space. Max could still detect the burning smell in the air around his face. He hoped his suit's breathing system would filter it out quickly.

"What was that?" he said.

"The motors," Harris said. "That's where they're installed. This rover was brought in with electrical problems. They were signed off as fixed."

"It's completely dead now," Damon said from the front. "Must have shorted out."

"So we're stuck," Safi said.

"That's right."

Max decided not to ask what they should do now. He knew they would be thinking about it already without him prompting them, so instead he waited. Ariel looked sternly at the floor, thinking hard.

"We need to follow standard breakdown procedure," he said eventually. "There's no alternative."

"Are you sure?" Safi said. She didn't look happy with the decision. "Why not call the base?"

"I'm sure. Whoever we talk to will just route the message back up here anyway. Damon, make the call."

"What's the standard procedure?" Max asked Safi.

"We send a distress call on the emergency channel, then whoever's based nearest comes to pick us up."

"But the nearest settlement is —"

"Exactly. Damn it, Max, this was all going so well."

* * *

The response to the SOS call came quickly, barely a minute after it had been sent out. The ESOS operative who spoke was clipped and business like in the way he dealt with them but Max could easily hear a note of confusion in his voice when he read back the position they'd given. However the emergency channel wasn't the right place for him to ask what they were doing there; those explanations would have to wait until they met their rescuers face to face.

"There's no point lying," Safi said when the call was finished. "We can't just pretend we got lost. They'll figure out why we're here."

"Well I'm not going to just sit and wait," Harris said. "We might as well go outside and see if we can fix the damage before they get here."

Ariel nodded. "You're right. Let's see what we can do."

Ariel and Harris worked solidly on the underside of the rover for half an hour as they waited, with Damon and Safi helping them as required. Max just stood off to the side feeling spare. They didn't want to repressurise the rover in case a fire broke out, so he stayed outside and watched as the pile of parts and tools slowly built up around the vehicle.

They'd almost given up on repairing it when the two open topped rovers appeared in the distance, kicking up swathes of dust as they bounced over the hills like beach buggies. Max was the first to spot them. He and the others turned to face them and waited for them to close the gap.

The rovers pulled up next to their own, then the driver of the lead one got out and walked over to them. They could only see his face through his visor once he was within ten feet of them. He looked at each of them in turn as they waited expectantly, and only then did he speak.

"You should come with us. Get onto the rovers, now please."

His accent was German, like the ESOS man who had taken their original call; Safi had said this branch of ESOS was run from there. They did as he said without saying a word, climbing awkwardly onto the two vehicles. Then the rovers moved off, back the way they'd come.

The ride was bumpy and uncomfortable as they took the hills and ridges at speed. Max clung onto the handholds in the first rover, wedging himself against the seat to avoid being thrown out. Like the others though, he didn't say a thing. Eventually they came to the ESOS settlement, a small collection of pressurised modules like the main Crisium base in miniature. The rovers parked on the end of a row of similar vehicles, then the drivers climbed off them and headed for the nearby airlock.

"I guess we follow them," Max said.

They climbed in after their rescuers and waited while the repressurisation cycle took place. Then finally they could open up their visors and see each other face to face.

The two men who had come for them were both tall and stern in appearance and they were looking at Max and the others with suspicion. They directed them to get out of their suits and led them through into a workshop area. Everything apart from the clothes they were wearing was taken, including omnis, watches, anything that might contain a means of communication. Then the men spoke briefly in German before one of them left the room. He was only gone for two minutes, and he didn't come back alone.

The man who came back with him was short and freckled, with a thin, pointed face and long red hair, tied back in a ponytail. He walked straight over to Safi, and held out his hand to shake hers. When he spoke, it was with a mild German accent.

"Dr. Biehn, or can I call you, Safi? You have no idea how pleased I am to meet you. And Dr. Lowrie," he said turning to Max, "it is also a pleasure to have you with us. I am only sorry that it took such bad luck with your transport to bring us together. But please, you should feel welcome. All of you."

"Thank you," Safi said cautiously. "And, who — ?"

"Oh, of course, I am sorry. My name is Joel, Joel Flieger."

"Well, Joel Flieger," Ariel said. "I am sure you want us to go as much as we do. When will we be able to continue back to the base?"

"Our long-range rover is in use at the moment, but we will be able to transport you back soon enough. But please, we should use this opportunity to get to know each other better. I was not expecting to meet in person the two people who have made possible everything that I am doing here today."

Max and Safi looked at each other briefly. For him, Joel's words were hardly an accolade, and he didn't think she would be appreciating the praise either.

"So, please come with me," Joel continued. "We should go somewhere more comfortable to talk." He led them out of the workshop and through a corridor to a rest area. Max didn't see any choice other than to follow.

The rest area was fitted out simply, with nothing but a few padded benches and a drinks dispenser. The ceiling was low and the lighting was harsh and electric. They were just about to find themselves seats when someone else walked in, from the other end of the room. Safi gasped when she saw who it was.

"I don't believe it," she said. "Not you."

"I'm afraid so," Oliver Rudd said, smirking slightly. "I would ask what you're doing here but I'd imagine the answer is fairly obvious. Someone else paying your wages these days?"

Max felt his hands forming fists, an instinctive move, despite never having had a fistfight since he was ten years old. But seeing this obnoxious, overbearing moron, in front of him again, who he now knew to have almost wrecked his marriage to Gillian out of nothing more than spite; for a second, hitting Oliver Rudd in the middle of his face was all Max could think of. He managed not to, pulling himself back from the brink instead, then turned to Joel.

"Listen, Joel, I don't know what he told you to get back in with the company, but he's dangerous. Just ask Victor about the bug he found on the island: that was Oliver. He was stealing from you the whole time, and the things he gets, he sells them to anyone who wants them, and not just other companies. China, the whole Eastern block, anyone; he's probably done it his whole career."

Joel motioned for Max to calm down. "Don't worry, Dr. Lowrie, we are well aware of Professor Rudd's extensive portfolio of contacts. In many ways that is one of his strengths. We take a pragmatic approach to our research here, as I'm sure you will understand."

"So you don't care that it was him spying on you, just so long as what he stole from other people before that is more valuable?"

Joel didn't answer, but shrugged noncommittally.

Oliver was leaning nonchalantly against the doorframe, apparently unconcerned that his criminal activities were being openly discussed as if he wasn't even in the room. "What do you plan to do with them?" he said to Joel.

"Assist them in every way, of course," Joel said. "They may be here illegally, but our prime responsibility is their safety. Once the transport has returned, we can help them get back to the base." Then he turned to face Safi and Max. "But before then, of course, I need to ask you some questions. You must understand that we need to know everything that you saw and did while you were travelling within our territory. Your presence here can only be an act of espionage and when you are prosecuted it will be important that we are all working from the facts. I hope that does not offend you in any way."

None of them answered.

"Good! I should however start by congratulating you on your outstanding achievements in the South Pacific. I personally was extremely impressed with what you accomplished there, especially in those far from ideal conditions. Tell me, when you settled on the three dimensional printer as your primary manufacturing tool, how did you adapt the laydown mechanism to cope with the variable viscosity powder flow? The notes I was passed gave only some of the details. We have had many problems with this issue."

Again, no one spoke. Joel looked hurt.

"Please, Safi, as one engineer to another, you must understand my interest in this matter. To work on something as original and innovative as that is an opportunity you must have been proud to take. I, for one, consider this project to be the highlight of my career."

"So that mechanical termite nest out there is a highlight?" Max said.

"Indeed, it is," Joel said, brightening. "And I see you noticed where we got our inspiration, well done. We deliberately based our design on insect populations. Oliver, you never told me how observant and intelligent your colleagues were!"

Oliver shifted slightly in discomfort. Max just felt patronised.

"However," Joel continued, "we prefer to call them colonies. I am sure you will appreciate the advantages over the design that you used. Your Prospectors were a great achievement: a single robotic device, capable of independent self-replication, incredible. But the colony approach is far more, ah, flexible, I'm sure you will agree."

"What do you mean, flexible?" Safi said. To Max, Joel was giving the impression of somebody who liked to talk about his achievements and he guessed Safi had picked up on it too.

"Why, in terms of continual reconfiguration, of course. You don't think we just designed the simplest system we could then set it running, do you? No, adaptive redesign is the key, endless reinvention."

"And what does that mean?" Max said.

"Every machine in a colony has a specific job," Joel said. "The diggers, the refiners, the pavers, all of them do specific tasks for the good of the whole. But their design is not fixed. Every time the colony builds itself a new machine, it uses the successes and failures of previous machines to modify their construction. Even when whole kilometres away from their parent colony they can use radio links to tell it which of their design features should be changed. Those machines that have performed best are used as the basis for future designs, and those that have performed worst, well," — he made a cut throat action across his neck — "they are recycled."

"Like evolution, but within a single lifetime," Safi said thoughtfully. Max looked over at her in alarm; she almost sounded as if she was impressed.

"Exactly," Joel said. "But guided evolution, not the messy random process that you will be familiar with. The colony can deliberately adapt its own design even as it grows, to maximise its success. So if it decides that some new type of material is needed it will work out how to build new refining machines for the job, and if a miner comes back with a richer grade of ore, it designs new miners to hunt out similar reserves. A perfect system."

He looked round at them all, smiling proudly. Max however felt differently. The "messy random process" Joel had just described was one he'd spent his life studying, marvelling the whole time at what it could produce. This seemed more like a recipe for anarchy.

"And how long has it been running?" Safi said. "How long has it taken for that colony we saw to grow?"

"We have been in operation for almost six months now," he said. "But that colony you saw? Near where you were picked up? Those ones are very recent, a few weeks at most. They haven't grown at all. The one we built first however, now that *is* a sight." He stopped suddenly and looked thoughtful. "Oliver, do you think we should take our guests on a tour, to show them what we have achieved?"

"Are you sure that's a good idea?"

"What harm can it do? One call from us and once they return to Earth they will be arrested as soon as they land. Nothing they learn here can ever be put to profitable use. No company will touch them. We have nothing to lose by being civil."

Oliver shifted again. "Alright," he said. He looked at Max and Safi. "I hope you're ready for this," he said, as a smile slowly spread across his face.

Chapter 11

"I can't believe Oliver managed to get his job back," Safi said as they were driven away from the ESOS buildings. She'd sat next to Max on the same rover they'd arrived in, and they'd set their suit communicators to a private channel so that the driver wouldn't hear them. "And not just his old job; he got in up here too."

"Victor must see him as a calculated risk," Max said. "It's the only explanation. Oliver must have heard about the Prospectors working and come crawling back with a sackful of other peoples' innovations to sell."

"And Victor decided to let him in on the full deal?"

"Well, Oliver's proved himself pretty formidable at gathering information. Joel as much as confirmed it. Depending on how Victor sees things, that could make him more valuable rather than less. Keep your friends close and your enemies closer, as the saying goes."

"Yeah, maybe having him inside the tent pissing out is better than having him outside pissing in."

Max looked over at Safi and tried not to laugh. Normally a paragon of new world politeness, that was the closest thing to a profanity he'd ever heard from her. "Maybe," he said. "Still, it doesn't look like Oliver's enjoying the ride. Don't they have health screening for a reason up here?"

Safi looked over at Oliver on the other rover and laughed. His overweight body was almost wedged sideways in the seat, whereas everyone else had managed to sit down properly. They couldn't see his face, but it was unlikely that he was having a good journey.

"Looks comfortable," she said. "Serves him right."

The rovers went on, following a well-travelled route past mile upon mile of strip-mined lunar soil before eventually stopping at the base of a hill. The patchwork of parallel furrows looked out of place, like ploughed-over farmland where no farm could possibly be. Joel twisted round to face Max and Safi from his seat next to Oliver.

"We are here," he said. "Now please, prepare yourselves."

Then the rovers started moving again, taking them round the side of the hill, and showing them for the first time what was lying on the other side.

"Oh my God," Safi said when she saw it. "Oh My God."

If the colony they'd seen before had looked like a clump of palm trees, then this one was a forest, a forest of giant redwoods. Gone were the squat cylinders that had made up the previous site, and the clumsy angular frameworks that had held the solar reflectors. Instead they'd been replaced by elegant, sinuous structures, with thick solid bases like huge tree trunks, blending into curved frameworks of struts and girders, growing and branching upward with thousands upon thousands of solar collectors at their tips. The comparison with a forest canopy was unavoidable, as the hundreds of structures that were present managed between them to capture every bit of sunlight that fell on the site. The area that they covered must have been two miles wide, and the largest ones stood over two hundred feet tall. Max could find no words to describe what he felt as they approached the place. Only Joel broke the silence.

"Welcome to the jungle, people!" he said, laughing.

As the rovers took them closer, Max started to see movement, both on the ground and in amongst the branches. Hundreds of thousands of robots were visible, swarming in and around the structures, ferrying the parts and materials necessary to keep the place maintained and to let it spread. By now it was large enough to fill his entire range of vision, but they still had some distance to go before they would reach it.

"Nothing you can see here was designed or built by human hands," Joel told them. "Isn't that amazing? Evolution at work!"

"And this is all one colony?" Max said.

"Yes, though now I would call it a super colony. It has developed the capability of using multiple printers in addition to its original core block. The rate at which it can test new designs is currently measured in hours, not days. Adaptation will soon reach geometric proportions."

At last they reached the outermost parts of the site. The structures here were only half built, and even as they watched, new parts and components were being brought in to complete them. Despite this they still towered over Max and the others, some with their insides laid bare to the vacuum. Max climbed off the rover as soon as it came to a halt, then walked over to one of them and looked inside.

"What can you see?" Safi said as she joined him.

"Hard to say, I can't make much sense of it." The tangle of mechanisms, wiring and tubing was hardly easy to decipher. How they had been made on the other hand was immediately obvious. "It's been built in a printer though, then slotted together. Just like Prospector parts."

"That's no surprise. It looks like they put the layers down in powder form, then sinter them together. Clever. But wow, will you look at this place, Max." She'd stepped back from the thing and was now craning her head back to look up to the top. "It's huge!"

Max didn't say anything, but instead looked between the structures, trying to see the interior of the place. The nearest ones were brightly lit on their sunward sides and in deep shadow on the other, but those in the interior were completely dark. The gloom was almost impenetrable.

"Come on," Joel said walking past them. "Let's go inside, there is more to see."

He strode off confidently, entering between two of the trunks while Max and Safi followed cautiously. Oliver and the two rover drivers went in behind them, presumably where they could watch them more easily.

"You'll need your suit lights in here," Joel said. "And watch where you put your feet."

They switched on the lights in their helmets and looked down at the ground, walking in the pools of light projected around their feet. The place was eerie, and due to the vacuum, completely silent. The movement around them however, was continuous, as countless small robots moved along the narrow walkways which linked the structures and braced them against one another. Every so often someone's beam of light would race upward as they looked into the darkness above, trying to get a better look at something high off the ground, or in Max and Safi's case, just to take in the enormity of what they were seeing. When Max looked up he had to stop walking altogether, to avoid tripping over the tangle of pipes and ducts that ran at ground level like tree roots. Instead he stood still and tried to study the canopy of reflectors above him. Then he turned off his light and waited for his eyes to adjust to the darkness.

There was some light at the top, after all. Ever so slightly, gaps between the leaves were letting in sunlight, outlining the shapes of the branches that made up the canopy. The branches were still recognisable as engineering structures, with their open framed design and zigzag bracing, but the overall shape was far more organic as the branches twisted and divided to cover the whole area. Safi had stopped to look too, perhaps wondering what had captured Max's attention.

"Those are optimised structures," he said. "When we design bridges and buildings by simulated evolution, we always get shapes like that. Maximum strength from the minimum material."

"That is to be expected," Joel said, joining them. "If you design things the way nature does, you get the same results nature does. Come on, we should keep going."

They carried on, keeping a steady pace through the dark grey forest. As with everything they'd seen, the main structural material was the local basalt rock, ground into powder then fused into shape. Even the robots had the same dull grey appearance and Max was starting to wish for a change of colour. The shapes of the robots, though, were immensely varied, as different designs were put through their paces to see which would work better than others. Some had four wheels compared to the original design of six, whereas others had eight or even more. Some, however, had none at all.

"Look at that component transporter!" Joel called out, pointing up at something on the side of one of the structures. "See how it is moving! It has invented legs!"

The machine he had indicated could clearly be seen climbing up the outside of one of the trunks without needing to use the walkways. The load it was carrying was held firmly to its back by jointed arms, curving out from its side. It looked almost insect-like.

"And I always thought legs came before the wheel! Incredible!"

They watched it for a minute or so as it climbed up the trunk and was lost from view. Then Max took advantage of the pause to ask Joel a question that had been in his mind ever since they'd come to this place.

"Tell me something," he said. "What does this colony actually do? Apart from just expanding itself?"

"Do? It does nothing! It lives to grow!"

"Then, what's the point?"

"It is a resource, a store of materials and wealth. Crops and trees don't do anything apart from grow, but we still cultivate them on Earth to take what we need from them. Think how much valuable metal and other resources are locked away in this construction, having literally pulled themselves out of the ground for us. It's unimaginable!"

Max looked round slowly, taking in what Joel had said, and

he had to admit that it was true. All those lunar mining projects that had struggled to break even, and yet this stockpile of purified trace elements was literally growing by the day, with no human effort expended whatsoever.

"I'm impressed," he said, surprised at his own reaction.

"Thank you," Joel said, and he sounded sincere. "Thank you very much. I hope in that case you will not mind if I make a slight confession."

"What do you mean?" Max said.

"I must admit to having, ah, borrowed slightly from one of your own research projects when we decided upon the name for this place."

That wasn't all that he'd "borrowed", Max thought. "Go on," he said.

"Well, we see this project as representing an explosion in the abilities of robotic systems to adapt themselves to their surroundings, an explosion in the variety of function and design that is possible. You will of course be familiar with the equivalent period in our own evolution: the Cambrian explosion on Earth, when hundreds of new life forms appeared from just a few simple ancestors. The subsequent evolution of life on Earth owes everything to the events of those few million years. For that reason, we couldn't think of a better name for this place than, Cambria."

It was a name that brought back memories for Max, and few of them were good. However it also reminded him of something else: of another question he'd been meaning to ask Joel but so far hadn't. He couldn't believe it had slipped his mind.

"Joel, there's something else I want to know about these robots."

"Of course, go ahead."

"The ones that work outside the colony, like the miners, and the ones that set up new colonies. How do you control where they go? How do you keep them where you want them?"

"Oh, that is easy," Joel said, as if he'd been expecting a harder question. "We have a chain of transmitters marking the boundary of our operating region. All robots are built to recognise the transmissions and turn away from them. It's the same method you used. Simple."

Joel was smiling. Max just looked at him in disbelief. "Please tell me you're joking," he said.

Chapter 12

Max was silent for the rest of the tour. As soon as he was on the rover for the return trip, he motioned Safi to switch her radio back to the private channel.

"Can you believe how stupid those people are?" he said. "Didn't they learn anything from what happened to us?"

Safi didn't reply at first. She looked as if she was trying to choose her words carefully.

"Max, please don't take this the wrong way. I haven't forgotten what happened to you, but you've got to try and see beyond that. Don't tell me you weren't blown away by what you saw just now."

"Blown away? It's an achievement, true, but that doesn't mean it's not a mistake."

"But you were impressed by it, Max, you even said so yourself."

"That was before I realised what a time bomb they're sitting on. They've blindly thrown this thing together to get it working as fast as they can, and they haven't even thought about what the implications are. They're idiots."

"What implications? In the space of six months they've outstripped every mining project that's ever been attempted here. Those are the implications. These people aren't idiots, they're geniuses."

"Even with Oliver on their side?"

"Oliver is the same loser he always was. This place is most likely running in spite of him, not because of him. But Joel Flieger and the others, I reckon we could learn from them."

Max couldn't think of anything else to say that wouldn't start an argument. She was letting her technical fascination get the better of her, seeing other people's answers to problems she'd faced just months before, but he wished she could see past it. He didn't reply, switching his suit back over to the main communication channel and listening in on the chatter running back and forth between the drivers. He couldn't speak German, but at least it was something to listen to. Suddenly Joel cut in, calling over to the two of them.

"Max, Safi, I've been told that there was a brand new colony being set up near to where you broke down, less than a day old. We are going to check it out. It is not far out of our way."

"Okay, fine," Safi said, even though the rovers had already started turning.

As Joel had promised, the journey to the place they'd abandoned their rover didn't take them far off their original course. However, only the navigation systems on the ESOS rovers gave any indication of exactly where they were heading. The landscape itself gave no clues whatsoever. Max was still looking out for any landmarks that he recognised when the rover itself came into view, sitting forlornly on the low ridge where they'd left it. They drew level with it as they headed for the new colony that had been established in the valley beyond. They'd almost gone straight past when Safi noticed that something wasn't right.

"That's weird," she said. "All our tools are gone."

She called to Joel to get him to stop the rovers, then she got off and went to investigate. Max went with her and saw immediately what she meant. Next to the rover, where Ariel and Harris had left the tools and parts they'd been working on, there was now nothing but stirred up soil. A lot of it was from their own footprints, when they'd been trying to fix the rover themselves, and the rovers that had recovered them had churned up the soil as well as they'd sped in to the rescue. However, nothing gave any explanation as to how their tools had simply vanished. Then Max spotted some familiar looking wheel tracks, running up and over the ridge and heading off on the other side.

"These are miner tracks," he said. "One of them has been

through here."

Joel joined him and examined them. "Yes, you are right," he said. "It must have come through after you were picked up."

The shape of the tracks was harder to make out right next to the rover. It looked like the machine had doubled back on itself several times, as if trying to cover the whole area. At least that explained where the missing items had gone.

"I think you need to get yourselves a new toolbox," Joel said, laughing. "Come on, we will send someone out later on to tow your rover back. But first, let's go down and look at this colony."

They spent about half an hour looking over the new structure, seeing how the haystack-shaped store piles were being used by the core of the thing to create its own mining and processing infrastructure around it. It had developed considerably in the time since Max and Safi had last been there and already the outline of its first set of buildings was visible in the hard, paved surface it had laid down. Oliver suddenly seemed more reticent about letting them see the thing up close, as if he'd shown them enough to boast about but didn't want them to learn too much. Max, however, didn't think he needed to see any more, so just stayed off to the side and watched. Eventually they got back onto the rovers and moved off toward the ESOS settlement.

* * *

One of the ESOS personnel took Joel off to the side when they returned and spoke to him privately while Max and Safi waited by the airlock. Max couldn't hear what was being said but when they'd finished Joel came straight back over to them, an apologetic look on his face.

"Max, Safi, I am sorry, we were planning to get you back to the base today. However, our long-range rover has been delayed."

"Delayed?" Safi said. "Why?"

"It is carrying out tests near to one of the colonies and has had to stay an extra day. But we will take you tomorrow instead, I promise." He was already leading them away from the airlock.

"You can't take us any sooner?" Safi said as she followed.

"No, I am afraid not." He took them the short distance to the rest area, then motioned them to go inside where Ariel had been waiting with Harris and Damon. He didn't go in with them, but instead left the five of them alone.

"Have you heard what's happening?" Ariel said as soon he saw them. He looked agitated.

"He told us they can't take us back until tomorrow," Safi said. "Is that what you mean?"

"They gave you that story as well then. I think there is more to it though."

"Like what?"

"Some kind of call came in while you were gone, then they all disappeared into the control room for an hour. We were just left on our own. It sounded like they were arguing."

"That's strange. The guy Joel was talking to earlier looked unhappy about something. Maybe we should ask them what's going on."

"We should do more than just ask them," Ariel said, immediately on the offensive. "We have work to do at the base. Tomorrow is too late, it has to be today. We need to make them understand that."

"We're in a difficult position though, Ariel, I'm not sure we can start making demands of them. Remember why we came up here in the first place. To them we're trespassers and yet they're giving us guided tours. I think we're lucky they've treated us as well as they have done."

"Maybe that Joel has," Harris said, "but only because he's taken a shine to you both and he likes to show off. We've been kept in here like prisoners while you were gone."

"Okay, okay," Safi said. "Let me talk to him. I'll see what he can do."

She went back out into the corridors of the settlement, then returned a few minutes later with Joel in tow.

"Right, how long are you going to keep us here?" Ariel said.

"Please, please," Joel said. "As I said before, as soon as our transport is available, we will recover your rover then take you and it back to the base. You must understand that we can't do any of those things with our short range vehicles."

"We understand that," Ariel said, "but we need to go today, all of us. What can your other vehicle be doing that is so important?"

"Another task has unexpectedly taken priority. The crew of the rover have had to stay out a day longer than they planned."

"And what exactly are they doing?"

Joel paused, as if composing his answer. "They are monitoring the control signals sent between the colonies and their robots," he said. "The Cambria colony just recalled all of its mining robots. It is nothing serious, but we want to find out why it has happened. That is all."

"Why would it recall its miners?" Max said. Something had struck him as significant about what Joel had just said but he couldn't work out what.

"I don't know, probably to recycle them," Joel said. "It must have decided on a new design. That is the only reason I can think of."

"Okay," Max said, doubtfully. Joel, however, was already starting to back out of the door.

"I must return to my work," he said as he left, "but I promise, you will be taken to the base tomorrow."

Max sat in silence for a long time after Joel had left. Ariel was still complaining about the treatment they were receiving but Max wasn't listening to him. Instead, he was looking at the floor, deep in thought. The others were busy talking among themselves and seemed to have forgotten he was there. Suddenly Max sat up straight, and cut Ariel off in mid sentence.

"Ariel, I need to ask you something."

"What?" Ariel said, shocked by Max's interruption.

"Do they keep guns in a place like this?"

"Guns? What — you want to force these people to take us back?"

"That's not what I mean. I'm looking for something that could be used as a weapon, even if it wasn't built as one, like a cutting laser or a riveting gun."

"No, nothing like that. This is a research site. Why would they have guns?"

"Then what about explosives?"

"Maybe blasting charges for survey work or trench digging. They're strictly controlled though, stored away from the main buildings. Why, what do you want them for?" He was looking at Max in confusion. Safi was looking at him as if he'd gone mad.

"We may need them," Max said. "I think there's going to be —"

"Going to be what, Lowrie?" Everyone looked up to see Oliver standing in the doorway. "Going to be hell to pay when your little attempts at spying land you in the shit?"

"Going to be trouble, I was about to say."

"Well you're right there. Industrial espionage is a serious matter. Don't think you're going to be let off lightly just because Joel likes the look of you. I'm going to make sure that you receive the strongest possible treatment. You realise that this is a criminal matter?"

"No more criminal than you bugging the island and selling it to Anna Liu," Safi said.

"I don't know what you're talking about," Oliver said. "And I challenge you to prove otherwise."

"Then how do you explain what you're doing here?" Safi said. "You must have realised we got the Prospectors to work, or else why come crawling back?"

"I crawl for no-one. In case you were wondering, Victor came to *me*. I was the principal engineer on that project, and he offered me a posting here because he knew this was where my skills would be better used."

"Really? You got here on merit? I find that hard to believe."

"Some of us *are* good at our jobs you know."

"No, Oliver, I don't know what you told Victor, or anyone else to get this job, but you didn't get here because you're any good. All you've got to offer is what you stole from other people. Joel as good as said so."

"Huh, I wouldn't listen to a word that little idiot says. His capacity for lunatic ideas is almost as large as yours. And that's saying something."

"What, lunatic ideas like machines replicating themselves? Something you said was impossible but we managed to achieve?"

"If you call those floating death-traps of yours an achievement, then I feel sorry for you. What about you, Lowrie, are you proud of what you built back there?"

Oliver certainly knew what buttons to press. Max couldn't answer yes, but he wasn't about to say no either.

"I'm proud of sticking with it, Oliver, instead of jumping ship when the work got too hard."

"Jumping ship? You can call it that if you want to. Though I think when the revenues start to flow we'll see who made the right decision, don't you?"

"Is that the only reason you came to see us?" Safi said. "To gloat?"

"No, I came to inform you that for some reason Joel has decided to house you in the accommodation block for tonight. If it was up to me then you'd be out in the vacuum by now, but there you go. I would take you there myself but I'm growing sick of the sight of you. Just wait here until someone comes for you. Oh, and keep your eyes away from our work. You don't want to land yourselves in any more trouble." With that he left.

Chapter 13

The next morning Max woke suddenly. At first he was only dimly aware of what had woken him, but as the sounds of running feet and raised voices in the corridor came into focus in his mind, he quickly realised that something wasn't right. He sat up and looked round the module, trying to work out what was going on. Safi, Ariel and Damon were awake too, sitting up in their bunks, looking at each other in confusion. Harris however was nowhere to be seen.

"What's happening?" Safi said. "What's all the shouting about?"

"I don't know," Damon said. "And where's Harris gone?"

Just then Harris appeared in the doorway, silhouetted by the light outside.

"Ariel, I think you should see this," he said.

"Why, what's going on?"

Harris looked back at him gravely. "Things just got interesting."

They got up and dressed quickly, then followed Harris out into the corridor. He took them to what appeared to be a control room for the colonies, explaining to Ariel what he'd already seen as they went.

"It looks like some new type of robot has appeared, unlike anything they've had before. The drivers who were meant to be taking us back have been following a group of them. But now they've started — well, see for yourself."

They went into the darkened control room then moved away from the door and hid themselves at the back, seemingly unnoticed by any of the personnel inside. A large display screen was on the far wall, showing a low quality video feed taken somewhere on the lunar surface. It was from a handheld camera, presumably held by one of the crew of the ESOS rover, working outside in the open. They recognised the location at once.

"Oh my God," Safi whispered. "That's our rover."

Or what's left of it, Max thought. By now only the lower half was still recognisable. The upper half was almost gone, and what was left was being systematically dismantled by the four robots gathered round it. Superficially they looked the same as the miners they'd seen already, but these ones were much larger, and were fitted out with the same cutting and crushing tools they'd seen in use at the colony. As they watched, whole sections were being torn out of the rover's pressure hull and reduced to fragments, then piled up ready to be hauled back to the colony. It stood to reason, Max thought. Instead of strip mining the soil, they'd found a ready-made source of materials, just waiting to be carved up and taken away.

"I knew it," Max said. "That one that took the tools, it must have detected the same materials making up the rover. That's why the miners have been redesigned."

"Incredible," Safi said. She must have spoken too loudly however, because just then Oliver turned round and saw her. Then he noticed the others and his mouth fell open.

"What the hell are they doing in here?" he shouted. "Get them out, keep them out of the way!"

"I prefer to stay if you don't mind," Ariel said, stepping forward. "That's our vehicle your machines are destroying. I think we have the right to an explanation."

"You lost your rights when you first set foot here. I would be a little more co-operative if I were you. Now go!"

Joel was also in the room, sitting at a console at the front. He sprang up and came over to Ariel.

"You must go, please. Let us handle this. We know what we are doing."

"You're doing nothing!" Ariel said. "Base property is being destroyed and you're doing nothing to stop it!"

"Please, we have enough to handle here. Let us deal with

everything else then we can talk about your rover."

"Everything else?" Max said. For some reason something sounded significant about that. "What do you mean, everything else?"

Joel didn't answer, but instead looked off to his side, at a large display screen on one of the other walls. Max followed his eyes and looked the same way. It showed a map of the research site, with the settlement on the southern boundary and the colonies arranged to the north of it. The Germanised word "Kambria" marked the colony they'd been taken to the day before, but for some reason all the colonies surrounding it were marked in red, flashing as if in alarm. Then Max realised what it meant.

"Those other colonies, they're being attacked too aren't they?" he said. "The Kambria machines are breaking them up as well."

Joel seemed reluctant to answer. "I think that is what we are looking at, yes."

Max, however, knew exactly what he was looking at. "Predators," he said.

At that moment the voice of one of the rover crew came over the video link, saying something in German that Max couldn't understand, but sounding as if he was calling for attention. Everyone in the room simultaneously looked to the front and saw what had appeared on the screen.

Off in the distance, beyond the remains of the rover, more robots were approaching. There were five or six of them, moving in a group, and all built to the new design. The crewman holding the camera backed away from them as they drew near, opening up the picture and revealing the ESOS rover parked off to the side. It was a standard pressurised design, and, Max noticed, looked almost the same as their own one had.

"Joel," he said, his voice level but urgent. "Tell your men to get out of there."

"What?"

"Get them out of there, now. Can't you see what's going to

happen?"

Joel looked uncertain for a second, then he seemed to under-stand. He went back to his seat and spoke quickly into the micro-phone. Again Max couldn't understand what was being said but the communication went back and forth several times, almost as if Joel was having to talk the crew into leaving. It didn't sound as if they were convinced.

This time there was more urgency in Max's voice. "Get them out of there, Joel, before it's too late!"

A few seconds later however, it was too late. The first of the robots arrived, going straight past the remains of the first rover and heading for the ESOS one. It rolled up to the nearest corner of the vehicle, extended a pair of cutting tools and began to slice into the metalwork supporting one of the wheel arches. Only then did the crew take the threat seriously, shouting and exclaiming down the audio link. Max and the others saw the picture on the screen lurch as the camera was thrown to the ground and the two crewmen ran forward to challenge the machine. They were only just visible in the picture as they kicked and swung at the robot, trying to break its grip on their vehicle. By now however, others had arrived, effectively surrounding the rover and cutting into it on all sides. Suddenly a blast of gas and vapour was seen, as the rover's pressure hull was punctured and the cabin air rushed out into the vacuum. Max hoped that no one had been inside. If they had been though, then it would probably have been quicker for them than what happened next.

The scream was so loud that everyone in the room recoiled at once. From the grainy pictures on the screen it looked as if one of the crewmen had got too close to the cutting arms of the robot and had lost his own arm in the process. All that could be seen as he fell to the ground was a dark mist spraying from his severed suit as the air inside shot out, taking droplets of blood with it. His scream stopped almost immediately, but only because there was no longer any air in his suit to carry the sound. The onlookers in the control room watched, horrified, as the body on the ground continued to turn and writhe for at least five seconds more as the machine cut into it. All they could hear were cries of revulsion from the other crewman as he tried to force the thing away.

Then the machine turned on him, he at least had the sense to run. He bounded away from it, round to the back of the rover and into the now airless cabin. Almost at once the rover began to move, trying to reverse away from the robots that were attacking it, but it soon became clear that the damage it had sustained was too much for it to cope with. The left side of the vehicle was rising and falling as if one of the wheels had been buckled and a large gash was being cut in the soil as part of its damaged super-structure dragged along the ground. It struggled on however, steering erratically past the camera, as the robots turned and followed it out of the picture. By now all that could be seen on the display was the body of the first crewman, motionless at last, but on the audio link the second crewman could still be heard, breathing heavily as he fought to get the vehicle under his control.

Joel tried to talk to him but the replies he got were limited. As far as Max could see, the only hope for the man was for another rover to be sent out to rescue him, assuming he could keep ahead of his pursuers. That question was answered quickly though, when shouts of anger and exasperation from the crewman made it clear that the rover had ground to a halt for the final time. What happened next was less clear, though how it ended was only too apparent. They heard the crewman's breathing getting faster and deeper, as if he was struggling with something, perhaps trying to get out of the vehicle to escape on foot; they heard the muffled impact of soil under his boots as he ran from the rover, seemingly for his life; and last of all they heard the same final futile cry for help that showed that his attempts too had failed.

As before, the cries were cut short almost immediately. For

whole seconds there was silence in the control room as those who'd heard what had happened just stood and stared at the screen in disbelief. However, even as they did so, and the echoes of the crewman's voice faded in his mind, Max knew that the robots would be communicating with their home colony, and what was more, he could almost imagine what they would be saying. "Sometimes the resource will move," the message would go, "and sometimes it will move fast. Build the machines so that they move faster."

He looked at the map display again, at the warning lights flashing on the stricken colonies, and suddenly he had a vision, of a wave of destruction spreading out from the Kambria colony, as dozens or even hundreds of machines went in search of new feeding grounds.

"We need to leave," he said. "Evacuate this place, now."

"Why should we evacuate?" Joel said. His face was white and he was trembling from shock.

"Those things have learned that there's more to gain from attacking us than from digging dirt," Max said. "Our vehicles, our buildings, everything that keeps us alive; they're all targets now, including this place. They've become predators, and we're at the bottom of the food chain."

"Food chain? What are you talking about? That's nonsense!"

"No it isn't, Joel, you even said it yourself; if you use nature's methods, you get nature's results. Well they have done. They've become hunters."

"But we're protected by the barrier. They can't reach us."

"The barrier counts for nothing. Ours was breached, and yours will be too. The only question is when. We have to get away from here, before it happens."

"No, we're not leaving. It would be ridiculous."

"I can't say it any other way, Joel. We have to go, now!"

Oliver stood up and walked over to them. "I don't think you're in any position to tell us what we should be doing, do you? I think we've heard enough from you, all of you. Now as I said before, get out." He called over one of the other ESOS personnel. "Take these people back to the accommodation block," he said. "And this time, make sure they stay there."

Ariel didn't look as if he was prepared to co-operate, but Max decided it was probably the best idea. "Let's go," he said. "I think we need to talk."

* * *

Back in the accommodation module, Max was the first to speak.

"Right, this is serious, we don't have much time. Ariel, what are our chances of getting out of here and taking one of those rovers?"

Ariel didn't answer, but looked at him uncertainly. Then he turned to Safi, as if seeking her approval as to whether the things Max had said were worth listening to. Max just hoped she'd seen enough to convince her.

"I think," she said eventually, "I think Max is right. We need to go, whether the people here want to come or not."

"Then let's do it soon," Harris said.

"But where would we go?" Damon said. "One of those open-top rovers won't get us back to the base, even on full charge."

"No, but we can open up some distance," Max said. "Did you see on that map, how far those machines had spread? That was in less than twenty-four hours, and they're going to get better, and faster. They're learning all the time. I think this place has less than a day left. If we head back down toward the base, we can send a distress call, then someone can come up to meet us halfway."

"And if we — if we run into any of those things?" Safi said. The look on her face showed that the events of the past ten minutes were still fresh in her mind.

"That's why I was asking about weapons. If we run into

trouble, we'll need to fight back."

Ariel thought for a second, then turned to Safi.

"Safi, do you really trust this guy?" he said.

"Yes, yes I do."

"Okay then," he said, as if that was all the answer he needed. "Let's go."

They got up and started to head out of the door, Ariel in the lead. Until that point Max had forgotten about the man standing guard outside the module, but he didn't get much chance to wonder what they were going to do about him. As soon as the man turned to challenge them, Ariel struck out at him with a controlled blow to the temple, sending him crumpling to the floor, unconscious. They practically had to step over him to get into the corridor.

The passageways were almost deserted now, and the few people they did see on their way to the airlock seemed to be too preoccupied to give them any trouble. However, when they got back to the workshop area that led into the airlock itself, they found two more personnel inside, suited up and getting ready to make their own way out. Ariel didn't even hesitate, but instead went in and walked straight up to them. At first Max thought he was going to use the same move on them as he had on the previous man, but it seemed he had a different plan this time. He walked up to the first one, then without even giving the man time to react, bodily lifted him off the ground with one hand and hung him up on the storage rail where the rest of the suits were kept. Max was impressed; even with the lower gravity, lifting the man and his suit one-handed would have been like lifting a fifty pound weight on Earth. The second man tried to fight Ariel off but was encumbered by the bulky suit and soon received the same treatment. Within ten seconds both of them were suspended two feet off the floor, struggling to get themselves free.

"That's what we do to new recruits on their first day at the base," Ariel said as the others followed him in. "Then we see how long it takes them to get down. Isn't that right, Damon?" Damon laughed weakly.

The two men were now shouting and thrashing and were in danger of attracting attention, so Ariel turned to face them again and punched them both in the stomachs, just enough to wind them and keep them quiet. Then, again, with no hesitation, he walked along the suit rail to where their own suits had been hung and started to get the five of them down.

Max suited up in silence, trying not to look at the two ESOS men, who were now putting far less energy into their attempts to get free. He was amazed how unemotional Ariel had been about attacking them, as if it was a means to an end but nothing more. However if it helped them get out of the settlement, then he wasn't about to complain.

Once they were ready and had sealed each other's backpacks, they climbed into the airlock, closed the inner hatch and set the vacuum pumps running.

"Ariel, won't it show up on their consoles that the airlock is being used?" Harris said as the air was drawn out.

"It will," he said. "Hopefully, they'll just assume it's our two friends out there."

"What if they use their suit communicators? They can still reach the controls, even hung up like that. Shouldn't we have put them out of action?"

"If that happens, we'll just have to deal with it."

They continued to wait in the airlock while the vacuum pumps did their work, keeping a look out through the window in the inner door in case anyone came into the workshop. For safety reasons the controls in there would override the ones in the airlock, so if anyone did appear then their chances of escape would be gone. The pumps however were running slowly and Ariel, for one, decided he wasn't going to wait for them.

"This is taking too long," he said irritably. "Let's open up now."

He reached over to the airlock controls and hit the switch for the dump valves, opening the air lines that sent the remaining atmosphere rushing outside. A fog of white vapour appeared in the airlock as the pressure plummeted, then got sucked outside just as quickly. Once the outer door was unlatched they quickly scrambled out and headed for the rovers.

"How many people are based here again?" Ariel said. "About twenty-five, right?"

"Yeah, I think so," Harris said.

Ariel looked at the five rovers that would be left after they'd helped themselves to one and nodded to himself. "It's enough," he said.

They went up to the nearest of them and Damon pulled the recharge cable out of its battery pack and threw it out of the way. They were just about to climb on board when a sudden change in light level made them stop and look up.

The floodlights that had been illuminating the rover bay were now dead, plunging the shaded side of the building into near darkness. They quickly exchanged glances, then Max went back to the outer door of the airlock and looked through the thick glass panes at the room beyond. All the lights and control panels in there appeared to be dead as well. It was as if every sign of power or artificial lighting had just gone out. Then, just as suddenly, the light reappeared, though far less bright than it had been before.

"What just happened?" Damon said.

"I don't know," Ariel said. "It looks like it's switched to emergency power. I'll take a look."

Ariel went off to the side of the module then round the corner into the sunlight. They could see him looking into the distance. "It's the same everywhere," he said. "It must be the service line."

By now the others had walked over to see for themselves. From here they could see most of the length of the settlement and as Ariel had said, the few lighted windows which were visible were all dimmed, as if running off back-up supplies. However, the service line itself, visible at the far end of the settlement, was showing no light at all. Even when the sun was up it had some illumination of its own, purely to mark the crossing points, but now these were gone completely.

"Are you thinking what I'm thinking?" Harris said. He looked at Max as he spoke.

"Yes, I am," Max said. "They must have got out already, then gone south and found the service line."

Max pictured the map in his mind again, visualising the areas known to be occupied by the Kambria machines. The north and west were already taken, and if the machines had somehow cut round to the south then that meant they were surrounded on three sides. It was lucky the machines hadn't stumbled across them already.

"Does that mean they're on their way here?" Harris said. "They could follow the service line straight to this place."

"Probably, though the line should keep them busy for a while. It must be the single richest supply of materials they've found so far. But if they work the way I think they do then they're going to call in reinforcements to help them break it up. The place will be crawling with them."

They looked into the south, at the service line stretching off into the distance. There was no sign of any activity there, but it wasn't hard to imagine what might be happening just over the horizon.

"That was the way we were planning to go," Damon said.

"Well we can't go there now, can we?" Harris said.

"So what are we going to do?"

No one answered, until Ariel finally spoke. "I have an idea," he said. They all looked at him expectantly. "We fly out."

"Fly? What do you mean?"

"Who's at base right now out of the lander pilots? Whoever it is, we call them, get them to bring a lander up here."

"It's Jack," Harris said. "He got in this morning."

"Good. If anyone can get us back to the base, he can."

"Who is he?" Max said.

"Jack Rogan," Harris said. "One of the transfer pilots on the geo-lunar route. He's the best, too. An open field landing like this will be no problem for him."

"Sounds like our best option," Damon said. "Let's call him."

"Well, whatever we do," Ariel said, "we shouldn't do it standing here. Not if those things are on their way. Let's get driving, then arrange a pick-up somewhere else."

They started to pile onto the rover with Harris in the driving seat. It seemed to have been kitted out for survey work, with long flexible marker posts like slalom flags bundled together under the rear seats. They didn't look heavy, otherwise Max would have considered pulling them out and ditching them.

"Ariel, how long do you expect it to take for Jack to get out to us?" Safi said.

"It takes over an hour to get a lander fuelled up and ready," Ariel said. "We may be waiting two hours, or more."

"In that case we certainly can't wait here," Harris said. "Let's move." He set the rover in motion.

"Wait a minute," Max said. "We need to know where we're going. If we just drive out into the open, we won't stand a chance."

Harris brought them to a halt again. They'd barely moved twenty feet. "So where then?" he said.

"We need to head east," Max said. "That's the only safe direction now. But we need to assume those things can catch us in a chase. This rover won't be too fast with five of us on board. We need to get somewhere safe, that we can defend."

"Defend?" Ariel said. "Like where?"

"I don't know," Max said. "You people are the locals here, where do you suggest?"

At first no one answered, then Safi spoke. "I know a place," she said. "Site six, Anchorville."

"Is that place still there, after all these years?"

"Yeah, it's still there, just empty. But it's big, and solidly built, and we can get up off the ground. We'll be safe for a few hours at least."

No one seemed to have any better ideas.

"Let's do it," Max said. "We're going to need protection though. Any idea where those blasting charges will be stored?"

"I don't know how this place is laid out," Harris said. "I saw some unpressurised huts when we were driven in here, they might be the hazstore."

"Let's try there then."

They drove away from the settlement, toward the huts that Harris had mentioned. As they were driving, Damon looked back over his shoulder at the ESOS buildings they were leaving behind.

"I'd have thought they'd have come out after us by now," he said. "We spent enough time talking back there."

"I think they're busy working out where their power has gone," Ariel said.

"They're going to have something else to keep them busy pretty soon," Harris added.

"Maybe we should contact them," Max said. "Tell them to head east, if they do decide to follow us."

"They'll work out where to go for themselves," Ariel said. "They're stupid but not that stupid. Though even if they did follow us, what would they do then? There isn't room for thirty people in a lander, not wearing suits."

Max couldn't think of an answer to that one. He didn't think there was one.

"Plus, it's their fault those things exist," Ariel continued. "Let them deal with them."

They soon got to the huts and saw the familiar explosive warning marks on the outside of one of them. Ariel climbed off first, then took a hammer from the rover's toolbox and broke the hut's lock clean off its door. Then he went inside, joined by Harris and Damon, and started loading up the remaining space on the rover with boxes of explosives. They shifted two boxes each, then went back to their seats and strapped themselves in.

"I've tied them down as tight as I can," Harris said once they were back on board. "They're not going to fall off. The weight will slow us down though."

Safi leant over from the back seat and looked at the rover's control console. "Harris, are you using the manual traction controls?" she said. "You'll get more speed out of it if you do."

"No," he said. "It's all automatic on the bigger rovers. I don't drive these open tops much."

"Mind if I take over then?" she said, climbing off and moving round to the front.

"Sure, if you want to."

"Can you drive these things, Safi?" Max asked her as she swapped places with Harris.

"Drive them?" she said with a gleam in her eye, "I used to race them."

Then she set off, throwing dust out from beneath the tyres as she put the settlement behind them.

As soon as they were underway, Ariel extended the long whip antenna that would let him transmit to the main base and tried to reach Jack Rogan. He used a private channel, talking for at least five minutes before switching back to the common channel and telling the others what he'd found out.

"They know something's up," he said. "Earthrise control have registered that site five's service line is down but they haven't made contact with them yet."

"What about Jack?" Harris said. "Can he come for us?"

"He can, but he's had a hard time getting a lander. I had to tell him everything that's happened here. He's going to meet us at Anchorville though, in two hours' time."

"Let's go then!" Safi said, putting on another burst of speed.

They drove on, heading east under Safi's far from leisurely driving. She was enjoying every minute, taking the hills and rises at almost full throttle, and every time they cleared the crests Max would feel his stomach rising up inside him as the feeling of weightlessness returned. The impacts that ended each jump were violent as well, causing him to clamp his jaws together to avoid damaging his teeth. All he could do was hold on tight and trust her driving.

"Safi, remember we're carrying explosives here," he called at one point.

"Insensitive munitions," she said. "They're drop-tested to worse than what I'm giving them. Stop worrying, Max!" Then she laughed, in spite of the danger they were in, and opened up the throttle even more.

The shortest route east took them back into the original operating area of the colonies, though as the boundary itself now seemed to be meaningless, they didn't see any advantages in going the long way round. Max watched the moving map display over Safi's shoulder as they went, and matched it up in his mind with the places he'd seen other colonies being attacked. This was their point of closest approach to the Kambria colony and if the trouble had spread south, then this was where they were most likely to meet it.

He was just about to tell Safi to keep her eyes out when suddenly she slammed on the brakes, sending the rover into a weaving, four-wheel skid across the dirt as she tried to keep it facing forward. "Come on, damn it!" was all they heard from her as she struggled with the controls, losing speed the whole time. When eventually they did come to a halt, they were facing almost sideways and were covered from head to foot in dirt and dust that their wheels had sent flying. Max cleared his visor and checked everyone was okay, then looked into the east to see what had made her stop so quickly. What he saw next made his jaw drop.

A few hundred yards ahead of them was another machine, hard at work destroying yet another colony. The colony was small, obviously a new one, with only its central block and a few half-built smaller structures surrounding it, but otherwise no different to the ones they'd already seen. The machine however was unlike anything they'd seen before.

Two streams of thought, running simultaneously, went through Max's mind when he saw the thing standing there. On the one hand, the scientist in him tried to rationalise the way it looked, to work out the reasons for its appearance based on what he knew about how these machines were built and how their designs could adapt. On that level at least it made sense. He could see how using legs rather than wheels would give the best speed in this low gravity environment, and he could see how having four of them arching out of its body like spider legs would give the best compromise between speed and stability. He could see how turning the cutting tools into a pair of agile front limbs made the job of dismantling other colonies and machines more efficient, and he could also see how grouping all the vision systems and receivers into a single unit at the top of its body would help it sense its surroundings. However, even as he looked at it, and saw how its component parts and characteristics helped it to do the job it had to do, the other part of his brain still couldn't quite shake the thought that this was some kind of enormous mechanical monster, almost arachnid in its shape and appearance.

This was what Kambria had created. In the day or so since the discovery of the broken-down rover had signalled that human artefacts gave a better yield than lunar dirt, and the in the few hours since the attack on the ESOS rover had shown that speed as well as strength were needed to bring in the harvest, this was what that two-mile wide factory had decided to build and send out. The simulated evolution codes that could cover a thousand generations in a matter of hours, the problem solving algorithms directing and steering the process with frightening precision: this was the design they had produced. To see the response appear so quickly was chilling.

"Do you think it can see us?" Damon said.

"I don't know," Ariel said. "But if it looks this way then it will do."

"I don't want to move too fast," Safi said. "Let's get out of here slowly, then go round."

She started to back up gently. There was a boulder field to the south, and if anywhere was going to give them cover then that was it.

They'd moved about thirty feet when a light on their communication panel lit up, showing that the rover's transmitter had suddenly become active. It was probably updating its navigational fix, or carrying out some other purely automatic function, but it was obviously enough for the machine's sensors to detect. It turned its head to face them, looked at them for no more than two seconds, then backed away from the section of the colony it had been working on and started to walk toward them.

"Oh shit," Harris said, as the machine began to move.

At first Max thought they would be okay as the machine slowly came closer. Maybe it wasn't as fast as it looked, maybe those long jointed legs were there for a reason other than speed; it almost looked as if all they had to do was drive fast and they'd be okay. Then the machine began to accelerate, changing its slow ungainly walk into a series of long, leisurely jumps, first off one leg then off another, seemingly in no hurry at all but covering tens of feet with each bound. Max reckoned its top speed must have been double its current pace if not more.

"Right, we're going," Safi said, turning off to the side and speeding away from it. Max looked back over his shoulder to see what it would do next. As he had feared, it soon showed it had more reserves of speed available as it increased the length and the pace of its strides, spending whole seconds off the ground between each one. They were heading out into the open now, almost back the way they'd come, and Max didn't see any chance of getting away from the thing if it managed to close the gap further.

"Safi! Take us back to the colony! That boulder field will slow it down!"

She understood what he meant straight away and took them in a wide curve back toward their original heading. Max looked behind them again to see how close the machine had got. It was less than a hundred feet away now and was closing rapidly, its four legs stretching outward to keep its body and sensors balanced between each leap. He'd seen identical behaviour in running robots that he'd helped to design, giving a computer nothing more than the laws of physics and a design job to complete and seeing what solution it found. The fact that those designs were currently being vindicated by the performance of their pursuer was hardly much comfort.

When the rover began to slow down Max turned around in alarm, initially thinking they had run out of power or broken down. Then he saw the large rocks passing by on either side as Safi took them in amongst the boulders. Some of them were over twenty feet in height, craggy and pockmarked by millions of years of micrometeorite impacts. As soon as they had rounded the first one, the machine was lost from view behind them. She still kept the pace up though, driving first left then right, losing them among the scattered rocks and outcrops.

"We can't hide from it in here you know," Harris said as they made their way deeper into the rock field. "It can still follow us through the gaps."

"True, but it can't go quickly," Max said. "This will buy us time."

"As long we don't run into a dead end," Safi said. "This may have been a mistake."

The boulder field did almost look like a maze now they were inside it. Their tyres could handle rocks up to a foot in height, but the impassable ones formed definite channels and pathways. Safi seemed to be driving almost at random but the map display on the rover console gave enough information to retrace their steps. Ariel, however, seemed to think they would be better off without it.

"We should turn the navigator off," he said. "It's got us into enough trouble already. If that thing out there can detect our transmissions, it will only give us away."

Whatever radio reception capability the first machines had been designed with, whether for boundary sensing or communicating with their colonies, those designed after the rover attack had clearly adapted them for hunting.

"What about our suit transmitters?" Max said.

"Those too. Plug yourselves into the rover, we'll talk along the wires."

They each hooked themselves up to the rover's communication loop, then turned off their personal radios. Once their communications were safe, Ariel was the next to speak.

"I think we should lay a trap for our new friend there. If it homes in on transmissions then that's what we should give it. With a little surprise of our own thrown in."

No one had to ask what he meant. Only the details needed to be agreed.

"Can we do without the emergency beacons on our suits?" Damon said. "If we take them off they'll make good decoys."

"We'll only need one," Ariel said. "We'll use mine. Harris, were any of those charges on remote detonators?"

"No, they're on timers, all of them."

"This could be tricky then. Get me one out, let's see what we can do."

They were still moving round inside the boulder field, heading roughly eastward the whole time. By now, however, they'd slowed down enough for Harris to reach back over to the boxes they'd brought and pull out one of the cylindrical blasting charges. It was the same length as a drinks can but twice as wide, with thick, foil-coated insulation round the outside. The timing device and detonator were contained in another, much thinner cylinder which slid into the main charge down its centreline. Ariel assembled the two components, then took the small emergency beacon off the chest pack of his suit and tied the whole thing together into a ready-made booby trap. Vac-tape and bungee cord seemed to be the main constituents, part of the ubiquitous rammel carried by all space-based professionals.

"It's done," he said. "Let's see how it likes this."

"We should get out into the open again," Max said. "If we use it in here we won't know how long that machine will take to find it. We need to time it right."

"We'll go back to that colony then. Take it out at the same time. We plant this thing, rig the timer to give us one minute, then we get back here and hide."

Safi took them north again, this time without the aid of the navigation display. As they emerged from between two of the larger rocks they saw the colony not far away, with just a quarter of a mile of ground in between. The machine was no longer in sight.

"It's still here," Ariel said. "I can feel it. I don't know if it followed us in though. Let's move."

Safi took them back over to the colony, accelerating back to almost full speed. Every second they had over the machine was valuable, and she knew without being told that there was little time to waste.

It was only when they got within fifty feet of the colony that they realised the mistake they had made. The machine was there, as it had been all along, having returned to the easier pickings of the colony rather than chase them through the rocks. Only the bulk of the structure's central block had hidden it from their view.

Safi's reactions seemed to be the fastest of the five of them. Before the others even had time to speak she'd turned the wheel, hard over to the right, away from the colony and toward the outlying fringes of the boulder field. All they could do was grip onto the handholds, struggling to stay in their seats as she turned into the corner at almost full speed.

Time seemed to slow down for Max as the rover took the turn. At first he thought they were going to make it as the low-slung suspension flexed and twisted to keep all four wheels on the ground. He even had time to wonder what they were going to do next, whether they would go back among the boulders, or out into the open to risk another high-speed chase. They were about halfway through the turn however, with the vehicle skidding at almost ninety degrees, when he realised that something altogether different was about to happen. Rocks, more like loose rubble but some larger ones too, were now passing under the chassis of the rover. Oh my God, he thought, if we hit one of those we're going to go over. And then it happened.

The rock hit the front left hand tyre almost side-on, slamming it to the side and wrenching the steering wheel out of Safi's hands. She grabbed it back, fighting for control as the left wheel ploughed into the soil and the right hand side of the rover started to lift. From that point on there was no hope of recovery. All Max could see was the horizon gracefully rotating as the vehicle rolled onto its side and the blur of rocks and boulders came up to meet them. Then the protective bars enclosing the top of the rover hit the ground, kicking up a flurry of soil and stones, and suddenly the full violence of the impact could be felt. Five, six times they rolled, each collision hitting them like hammer blows as the safety cage began to collapse under the strain. They were on proper boulders now, big ones, capable of causing real damage whether the cage was there or not and for one instant, Max was sure they weren't going to get out alive. He closed his eyes and waited for it to end.

They came to rest upside down, with only the crushed metal tubes of the roll cage between them and the ground. Max opened his eyes and saw a large rock right in front of his face, about two inches from his visor. Any closer and it would have shattered the glass.

He tried calling to the others but got no reply. The low humming that he usually heard from the communication loop was gone too. He could see movement, though, as the other four tried to pull themselves out from under the rover. At least they were still alive, he thought. He released his harness then twisted round to try and slide out on his side. It was hard work pulling himself past the twisted metal without ripping his suit, but eventually he made it. Only then did his thoughts return to the machine.

It was already coming toward them, leaving the colony fifty feet away and walking slowly in their direction. In another few seconds it would be on them.

"We need the bomb!" Max called, but again got no reply. The cable that had connected him to the communication loop was now hanging by his side, and there was no way they could even have heard him. Instead he looked over at the front of the rover where Ariel had been sitting with the device in his hands. Ariel wasn't yet out of his seat, but was lying on his back, halfway out of the rover, desperately trying to pull himself the rest of the way. He seemed to be looking for something too, straining his head from side to side and running his hands over the ground as if searching by touch. It had to be the charge.

Max looked round quickly. They'd covered over fifty feet of ground as they'd rolled and there was no telling when Ariel had lost his grip on it, or how far it had been thrown. Then he spotted it, lying off to the side, with the sun reflecting off its foil cover. He ran over to it, almost falling over as he pushed back against the soil, then in one move he slid to a halt and grabbed for the thing, balancing himself with one hand while reaching down with the other. He was now facing back toward the rover, where Safi and Harris had also managed to get themselves out. Damon was on his way out too, but Ariel still appeared to be trapped. Safi and Harris were bending over him trying to help him out and didn't seem to have noticed that the machine was only seconds away from reaching them.

"Safi! Look out!" he shouted, but yet again there was no response; even if he turned on his suit transmitter, everyone else's was still switched off. Then he had an idea.

He activated his own communicator and started yelling at the machine itself.

"This way! Here! Here!" he yelled. There was no way it could understand him but the transmissions might be enough to get its attention. He pulled the activation toggle for Ariel's suit beacon on the charge and saw the red flashing light that showed it was sending out its signal. The beacon was a long-range high power device, unlike the communicator, and might have more of an effect. Then he ran back the way he'd come, not aiming for the rover, but trying to pass by close enough to distract the machine and draw it off toward the colony.

It was only when he saw the machine change course and head toward him that he realised he had no idea how to set the timer on the charge. The machine was coming for him now and unless he could destroy it himself, he knew it would take him. He ran faster, sweating with the effort as a growing patch of mist began to form on the inside of his visor, clouding his vision.

He looked down at the device in his hands as he ran and tried to make sense of the controls. It appeared to be a mechanical timer, better than electronics at coping with radiation he figured, and hopefully simpler to operate. In fact there were only two controls on the thing; a safety switch and a dial marked out in minutes. The maximum time setting was one hour, but the ten-minute mark was labelled as the minimum, as if ten minutes was the shortest countdown that could be set. It made sense for safety, but in this situation it made the thing almost useless. It wasn't what Max wanted to see. Yet again he felt his stomach clenching with fear, as if their last chance for survival had suddenly been taken away.

Then he realised; there had to be a way of making the thing go off sooner. Ariel and the others must have known how the timer worked. If they were planning to use it, then they must have known a way to fix it. He looked at it again and suddenly had a flash of inspiration. He turned the dial to fifteen minutes, flicked the safety switch from "SAFE" to "ARM", and forced the dial back past ten, down past one minute, finally leaving it just one click away from zero. Then he turned, saw the machine closing in on him, and threw the charge as hard as he could.

It landed just in front of the machine. The machine stopped, reached out with one of its manipulator arms and picked the device up to examine it. Max however kept running. The nearest of the colony buildings was only thirty feet away, but nearer still was an isolated rock just three feet tall. Max got to it, threw himself to the ground behind it, then curled up with as much of his body in its shadow as possible.

The explosion was silent in the airless lunar environment, but could easily be felt as its force rippled through the ground. The only thing Max heard was a single low-pitched thud as the vibrations from the blast came through the ground and up into his body. He could see the effects though, as a spray of soil and loose rocks passed straight over him and out into the distance before splattering back down to the ground. It looked as if over a ton of material had suddenly been sent flying, maybe more. He waited a few seconds until everything seemed to have stopped, then he crawled out from his hiding place to see the effect the charge had had.

The machine was no longer there. Only parts of it could be recognised, and most of those were some distance from the site of the explosion. The place where the charge had gone off was marked by a shallow crater, with nothing but bare rock showing where the dirt had been blasted away. The colony buildings had suffered shrapnel damage as well, and some of them looked as if they'd been hit by machine gun fire. They were further away than Max had been and much further than he would have been able to run if the rock hadn't been there. He counted himself lucky.

Then he looked back toward the rover. Ariel was out now and the four of them were lifting the vehicle up to roll it back onto its wheels. It looked as if it had been through a bomb blast of its own, though the crates of explosives they'd tied on and the survey poles it had come with all seemed to be intact. Once it was upright they turned their communicators back on and started to assess the damage.

"Guys, I'm sorry, I don't know what happened," Safi said. She sounded shaken.

"Don't be," Ariel said. "You weren't to blame. You had to drive fast and you had to turn fast. None of us knew that thing was going to be there."

That seemed to be enough to settle it. "Thanks," she said. Then she saw Max standing by the crater and came over to join him.

"Max, are you okay?" she said.

"No, I'm not," he said. He was exhausted and was shaking so badly his legs could barely support him. He felt sick too, and his mouth was parched. "That thing nearly had me."

"I know. You did well, though. Very well."

Max managed to smile.

"Come on, let's look at what's left of this thing," she said, heading off toward some of the larger pieces of wreckage. She picked one of them up and turned it over in her hands, then did the same with several others. She seemed fascinated by them.

"Do you really want to get that close to it?" he said. "Even in pieces?"

"Sure, now that it's safe," she said. "I want to see how it worked. Those were some pretty amazing moves it was pulling. Did you see the way it ran?"

"Yeah," Max said. "I saw."

The pieces were like intricately carved chunks of layered stone, with fine metallic lines running through them. Safi put the piece she was examining down and continued looking around her. "So what else have we got round here?" she said, stepping through the debris. She was heading toward the colony and also toward Max's rock. Then she stopped and looked over at the rock itself.

"That's interesting," she said, under her breath.

She walked up to it and looked closely at its top surface, even though there didn't appear to be anything there. All Max could see was the remains of one of the colony's material stores, the haystack-shaped pile smashed and scattered by the blast. However, it was obvious that something had captured her attention.

Just then the rover pulled up, battered but still driveable. Damon jumped off it, leaving Ariel and Harris in their seats.

"My God, will you look at this," Damon said, taking in the destruction around him. "You sure know how to make a mess, Max."

"Yeah, I think I'll arrange to be a bit further away next time I set one of those things off."

"That's a good idea, I just hope you don't get the chance to try. Listen though, we need to get going, and soon."

Suddenly Safi's voice cut in. "Hey, come over here and look at this," she said.

"Look at what?" Damon said as he and Max started to walk over. Safi was still in the same place, apparently staring at bare rock.

"What do you think that is?" she said, pointing at something on top of the boulder. They bent over to see what she was looking at.

Sticking out of the rock, almost vertically, was a metallic spike about two inches long. It was needle-thin for most of its length, with a slightly bulbous section near the bottom end. It seemed to be bedded into the rock, though they couldn't tell how far in it went. Max was surprised it had caught her eye from so far away.

"It's part of the machine, it's got to be," Damon said. "Thrown out by the explosion."

"But it's gone right into the rock," Safi said. "Solid rock, and it isn't even bent. How could that happen?"

"I don't know, that thing went up with quite a bang. Strange things can happen in explosions. It came pretty close to hitting you though, Max. Lucky the rock was there."

Safi still didn't seem convinced. "But it's vertical," she said. "It came downward, not outward."

Just then Ariel's voice joined them from the rover. "Safi, guys," he said. "We need to hurry, please!"

"Sure, on our way," Damon said. "Come on, let's go." He headed back toward the rover with Max following him. Safi came last, reluctantly, but not before taking one last look at the spike. Max was sure she glanced up into the sky as she left it.

They got onto the rover quickly, Safi again swapping with Harris for the driving seat. She didn't seem so shaken or distracted now and was soon up to her usual speed. Then the ground levelled out, and thirty blissfully uneventful minutes passed before they crossed into site six and saw their destination ahead of them.

Chapter 14

"I never expected to be back here again," Safi said as Anchorville came into view.

So this is the place it all started, Max thought. Somehow it had looked bigger in the pictures, but it was still an imposing structure. A lattice of upright pillars and horizontal girders formed the main bulk of the factory, hundreds of yards of it stretching into the distance, topped for most of its length by an array of solar panels and reflectors. The intermittent canopy cast dark shadows over the interior, full of indistinct shapes and huge pieces of machinery, now sitting idle.

"They've stripped the place down since I was last here," Safi said as she drove them alongside. "It looks so creepy now."

It was certainly eerie, Max thought, almost as eerie as the Kambria colony had been but in a different way. That place had been alive, full of sinister, inhuman life; this place however was dead, and had been for a long time. The angular pillars and braces almost looked like some kind of ruined temple, inhabited only by shadows. The repeat pattern of the outer framework sailed past them as they drove down its length.

Safi slowed down as they approached the far end, where the inhabitants appeared to have lived. Max remembered seeing the window lights of the modules in the videos she'd shown, though, these too were now dead. Then he noticed one of the smaller modules, down at ground level, its skin seemingly peeled open from inside. Safi turned and took them toward it.

"This is where it happened," she said, coming to a halt. She sat and looked at it for a few seconds, then she got off and walked over to it, stopping just ten feet away. Max and the others joined her but didn't go any closer. They could see where the skin had ruptured and could also see the effects of the fire that had raged inside it, though it looked like everything it had contained was now gone. A plaque had been added to the outside, however, with three names engraved on its surface; M. Connor, V. Wren, and at the top, N. West.

"Their ashes are here too," she said. "In the soil. We all said that's what we'd want if anything happened."

"Did you know all of them?" Max said.

"Yes, I did," she said, "not just Niall. All of them." Then she stood in silence for a moment more before walking away, heading off toward where the other modules were grouped.

She stopped when she got to them and looked upward. They were stacked three levels high against the bulky framework of the structure, with pressurised walkways linking them on the inward side and an open stairway, like a building's fire escape, bolted to the outside. She went to this stairway, climbed the first few steps, then turned back to face the others.

"We can get up high here," she said. "Keep a lookout. We'll see if anything comes our way."

"Good idea," Ariel said. "Let's take the charges up as well, just in case."

They unloaded the rover and carried the boxes of explosives up the three flights of stairs, to the wire mesh platform that circled the upper level of the site. It would have been built to provide maintenance access to the solar canopy, Max guessed, but it also made a good vantage point for them to sit and wait for rescue. They based themselves at the corner next to the stairway, then sat down on the boxes next to the safety rail. It must have looked like some kind of bizarre veranda party.

"Has anyone else ever used this site?" Max said once he was comfortable.

"No, not at all," Safi said. "The place was closed down for the investigation. It's been in legal limbo ever since. For eight years."

"And the second factory?" he said, indicating off to his side. "Is that as far as you got with it?" In fact all that he could see of Anchorville's own half-built replication was the same vague, skeletal shape he'd seen in Safi's videos. It didn't look as if it had progressed much after those pictures were taken. Only getting this high had made it visible at all.

"No, that's as far as we got. We never realised the shutdown would be for good. That was hard. We'd already proved we could make this place replicate. We could have carried on. We should have done. That's what Niall would have wanted."

"How can you say that after what we've seen?" Max said.

"It isn't the same," Safi said. "It's not the same at all."

"What isn't the same?" Ariel said.

Neither Max nor Safi answered. It was an old argument by now and neither of them wanted to run through it again. Instead the five of them sat there in silence until, eventually, Ariel stood up and started to walk away from them.

"I'm going to keep a look-out," he said. "You can help me if you want." Harris and Damon both immediately got to their feet and followed him wordlessly. Max and Safi were left alone. They were silent for a long time.

Max looked up at the Earth as he sat there. Somewhere down on that planet was Gillian, possibly looking right back up at him. The last time he'd spoken to her he'd promised he'd come back safe. That was looking less likely by the minute.

"You would have liked Niall, I think," Safi said suddenly. "You would have had a lot in common."

"You think so? How come?"

"He was meticulous, he worked the way you work. He was cautious too; I think you would have liked some of the things he said. He believed in this technology but he believed in us controlling it, not the other way round."

"As if that would ever be possible."

She looked out into the distance, toward the ESOS site. "This wouldn't have happened if he'd been running things. He'd have kept it under control."

Max shook his head. "If there's one thing I've learnt from my job, it's that life can never be controlled. Barriers and boundaries are never as strong as you think they are. Life spreads, and it always finds a way to survive."

She turned back to face him. "Is that really what we're looking at here? Life?"

"Yes, it is. No different from any forest or ocean on Earth. The fact these things are made of stone and metal is just incidental. They're as alive as you and me."

"I did wonder why Victor had brought a biologist onto the team. It didn't seem to fit, even though you're a math guy as well. Maybe he knew you had more to offer."

"I doubt it. He certainly didn't like the things I was saying."

"Niall would have though. You should have met him. You remind me of him a lot." She looked him in the eye. "I think, maybe that's why —"

Ariel's voice suddenly cut over her, calling from the other end of the structure.

"Safi! Come over here now, both of you! And bring the boxes!"

Max and Safi looked at each other, then jumped up together and hurried over to where the other three were standing, taking two of the boxes as they went. Ariel, Harris and Damon were pressed up against the railing, looking into the distance.

"Something's coming this way," Ariel said.

Max could see it straight away, though at first it wasn't clear what he was looking at. It was no more than a blur of dust on the horizon, caused by something — or more than one thing — approaching at high speed. Within seconds however the objects had drawn close enough to be identified.

"Rovers," Harris said. "It's ESOS, it has to be. But there's only three of them, where are the others?"

"I don't know," Ariel said. "Though I think we are about to find out."

The three rovers reached Anchorville and sped alongside it to the same stairway that Max and the others had used. They stopped and fifteen people got off, lifting a sixteenth off the back of the last one. Whoever it was, they weren't moving.

They started up the stairway in a tight group, while Max and those on the platform moved round to meet them. Finally the first of the ESOS personnel reached the top and walked swiftly over toward them. Of the five, Max was the closest.

Max couldn't see the man's face until he was almost on top of him, but by then it was too late. He walked up to Max, livid with rage, and pushed him back against one of the canopy supports. He was shouting but his suit must have been on a different channel because none of the sound reached Max's ears. All Max could do was try to stay upright and fend off the blows as he was pushed back again and again. Then Ariel appeared and grabbed the man's arm, while one of the other ESOS men took his other arm. Between them they managed to pull him back and Max could stand up straight again. He felt bad about being caught off his guard.

"Das ist genug! Das ist genug!" they heard Joel shouting. He'd stepped forward from amongst the group and switched his suit to the correct channel. "That is enough! We are not going to do this!"

"Then ask them!" the first man shouted in heavily accented English. He'd been let free on one side and retuned his own communicator, though Ariel still held him on the other side. "Ask them why they left us, why they stole our rover! We could have escaped, all of us!"

"And what would you have done if we'd stayed?" Harris said. "Left us behind? We only took one rover, we left enough for you."

"No, you didn't!" the man shouted, now trying to get free from Ariel's grip. "We were too slow, we couldn't go fast enough. Do you know what you've done? We lost nine men back there!" Then he stopped struggling, though Ariel still held on tight. None of the other ESOS personnel had spoken or come forward, but they had almost encircled Max and the others, their expressions harsh.

"We tried to escape," Joel said, once the first man had calmed down. "All of us. We got on the five rovers, but we were overloaded. They caught us easily. Two vehicles were destroyed."

"But what would have happened if we'd stayed?" Max said, repeating Harris's question. "We would still have taken up one of the rovers for ourselves when we did go. Or would you really have left us there?"

"If it was up to me, we would have done," Oliver said. He'd been among the last to climb the stairs and had been leaning against the rail at the back of the group ever since. It looked as if he'd only just recovered from the climb.

"In that case we did the right thing by escaping, didn't we?" Ariel said.

"You attacked our people, you stole our property and you left us to die," another of the ESOS men said. "How can that be right?"

"You created those things in the first place," Ariel said. "You live with the consequences." Then he walked away, back to the lookout post on the opposite side.

They split into two groups after that; the ESOS personnel staying by the stairway, while, Max, Safi, Harris and Damon joined Ariel. By now the injured ESOS man had been carried up the stairs and laid down on the platform. His suit didn't appear to be punctured, but it had taken some external damage and he still wasn't moving. Joel went over to him briefly then joined Max and the others at the far end. They stood in a loose circle next to the railing, all except for Ariel, who was looking out into the distance with his back to the others. Joel was the first to speak.

"I am sorry about what happened just then," he said. "We have had a difficult journey. Nine of us died. It was only because they stopped to feed on the first two rovers they attacked that the rest of us were able to escape at all. I am glad we found you though. We knew you would come here. We could even follow your wheel marks once we got away from the colonies.

"When did you finally decide to leave?" Max said.

"Our buildings were attacked. They came up the service line, stripping it as they went. Once they got to us we only had minutes to escape. We would have done too, if we had been able to drive fast enough. There is a new machine, faster than anything we've ever seen. It is — monstrous. That is the only way I can describe it."

"We've seen one. We ran into it on the way here."

"How did you escape?"

"We destroyed — *killed* it. With explosives."

Joel nodded. "Clever. I saw you had taken some of our blasting charges. I wish we had had time to take similar precautions. I never thought they would get through the barrier so quickly."

"So how did it happen?" Safi asked him. "How did they get out?"

"Easily," Joel said, shaking his head. "Only miners and replicators are fitted with boundary sensors. These new machines, however, are not a new design of miner. They are based on reapers."

"Reapers?"

"They work inside the colony, breaking down other machines and recycling the materials. Kambria must have decided to use them for gathering materials, rather than miners. They were never intended to travel far from the colony itself and never designed to recognise the boundary. A regrettable mistake."

"You create life, you should expect it to live," Max said.

"That is true," Joel said.

"Speaking of which," Ariel said. "I believe we have company." He still had his back to them, facing into the west. "They are coming."

As before, a distant cloud of grey dust was the first sign that something was approaching, though this time it was clear that a far greater number was on its way. Even as the nearer ones came into focus, more appeared behind them, rising up from beyond the horizon and racing toward the Anchorville stronghold.

"Machines," Harris said. "Just like the last one. Dozens of them." He turned to Joel. "You idiots had your transmitters live the whole way here, didn't you?"

"Yes, we had to," Joel said. "We had to communicate."

"You've led them right to us!"

"In that case we should prepare ourselves," Ariel said. "Bring more explosives down here. And spread people round the whole perimeter, quickly!"

Joel ran off at once to organise his own people, while Max and the others stayed at the corner nearest the approaching machines. By now they had halved the distance from the horizon.

"Help me get these things set up," Harris said, already unloading charges and detonators and slotting them together. This time there was no point adding transmitters or decoys; from the top of Anchorville the best they could do was use them as grenades. Max, Safi and Damon knelt down and started assembling the units into piles of ready-made weapons. Glancing down the length of the structure they could see the ESOS personnel doing the same thing with the other boxes, under Joel's direction. Then the first of the machines arrived.

"Give me one, fast," Ariel said. Max stood up as he handed the charge over and suddenly saw how quickly the machines had covered the distance. Three of them were at the front, heading straight for the near corner of the structure. Ariel took the charge, armed and zeroed the timer, then threw it as hard as he could toward the machines. He lunged forward into the safety rail with the effort, bending the barrier with his weight as he fell against it.

The charge hit the ground about thirty feet from the bottom of one of Anchorville's pillars and exploded almost instantly. The machine that Ariel had aimed at was another twenty feet away. The blast sent it flying, peppered with shrapnel, but had a similar effect on the base of the pillar. Whole sections of latticework fell outward, severed from the main body of the support. They even felt the explosion fifty feet up on the platform.

"I can't throw far enough, not wearing this suit!" Ariel said. "The pillars are too wide!"

Looking down over the railing, Max could see what he meant. The bottom of each pillar flared outward like a buttress. If Ariel couldn't throw far enough to miss them then it was unlikely anyone could.

"We nearly got hit as well," Damon said. "Those fragments are flying for miles."

Then they felt another jolt coming up through the structure, then another. They looked back at once to where the ESOS personnel were standing and saw them throwing their own explosives over the side where more machines had now arrived. They could hear shouts and yells as the blasts got their targets but it was clear that the damage being inflicted on Anchorville was just as great. Safi ran down toward the ESOS positions, looking over the edge of the railing as she did so.

"Stop! You're weakening the structure!" she shouted. Two more blasts were set off before anyone listened to her. It was Joel who finally stopped the attack, calling in German for it to end. He ran over to Safi.

"What are we supposed to do?" he called. "This is all we have!"

"I don't know," she said. "But we're doing more damage than they are like this."

Max was still at the western end of the structure. He looked over the edge at where the remaining machines had now arrived, well over thirty of them. With no hesitation at all they had got to work on the lower portions of the framework, stripping the metal components and fittings away from the fused basalt girders. It looked as if they only had minutes to go before the structure they were standing on would become unstable.

They needed something else, he realised, some way of fending off the machines without risking their own survival. Then an idea struck him. In any other circumstances it would have seemed like madness, but looking round he could tell that no one else had any better plans. If they only had minutes to live then anything was worth a try.

"Wait here," he said. "I'm going to get something."

He ran off, heading down the length of Anchorville until he reached the steps, then began jumping down them three at a time, grabbing the rail for support between each leap. The ESOS men he'd passed on the way watched him as he went, presumably wondering what he was up to, though only Safi called after him. "Max! Where are you going?" she said, but he didn't answer her. Instead he carried on down to ground level and ran over to the rover they'd arrived on. The nearest machines were just a hundred feet away but didn't seem to notice him. He went up to the rear seats of the rover then bent down and pulled out the bundle of marker poles from the survey kit he'd noticed when they first took the thing. He also took the long narrow spade that was used for planting them, then ran back to the stairway and started climbing.

This time Oliver was there to greet him, recognisable by his sheer width if nothing else. He stood at the top, blocking Max's way. "Where do you think you're going, Lowrie?" he said as Max climbed the last few steps. Max however didn't have time to stop. Instead he slipped past Oliver, almost pushing him out of the way in the process, and ran back to the far end of the platform.

Ariel had another charge in his hands when Max returned. It looked as if he was about to throw it over.

"What are you doing?" Max said.

Ariel looked at Max briefly, seemingly in irritation, and carried on with arming the timer. It was Damon who answered.

"There's nothing else we can do," he said. "We can't just stand here and wait for them to bring the whole place down."

There wasn't time to argue, Max decided. Instead he moved along the platform to where there was more room and set the marker poles down in front of him. Ariel had already thrown the charge over the side and Max found himself instinctively turning away in case any fragments came his way. He felt the force of the explosion hitting the structure, then he carried on working. First he took the spade and banged it repeatedly against the metal floor until the end of it had bent round like a lip. Then he picked up one of the poles and laid it on top of the spade, with the sharp end pointing forward and the other end slotted into the lip. Finally, he gripped the whole thing by the handle of the spade, held it high above his right shoulder, and let loose.

It was an action he had practised many times in the past. As his right arm came forward like a javelin thrower, he let the free end of the spade arc outward, effectively lengthening his arm by almost two feet. The pole moved forward too, but held back by its own inertia it began to bend in the middle as Max propelled it forward by its back end. Even the spade itself flexed slightly, so fast was the motion. Then, just as the force of the stroke reached its peak, the spade and the pole sprang back again, releasing the energy stored in them and adding their own contributions to the speed and force of the throw. The pole shot away from Max, faster than his eyes could follow, and flew down toward the machines beneath him.

It hit one of them right in the centre of its body, burying itself almost a foot inside the thing. The machine staggered, then fell over onto its side, its limbs thrashing as if still trying to run. Safi and the others had been looking at Max in amazement but now all eyes were on the machine, as it writhed across the ground, burying itself in the dust.

"Jesus, what did you just do to it?" Damon said.

"It's an atlatl, an old hunting weapon," Max said, already preparing the next spear. "Prehistoric probably, but it still works against these things."

The next two shots were misses, but at the third attempt he hit another of the machines. This one was hit in the head and once it had fallen, it didn't move at all.

"Nice work," Harris said. "Reckon you can get the rest of them?"

Max looked down at the poles at his feet. There were barely two dozen of them left, though by now more than forty machines were swarming round Anchorville, breaking up its lower supports.

"Do any of those other rovers have poles like these?" he said. "I didn't get time to look."

"I don't know," Damon said. "Let me go and check." He ran back along the platform until he could spot the rovers below him. "I can see some!" he said. "Wait there!"

He carried on along the length of the platform, heading for the top of the stairway. He was about halfway along when two more explosions rocked the structure, as one of the ESOS groups resumed their attacks on the machines. The group was right next to where Damon was running and had obviously decided for themselves that risking the explosions was better than doing nothing. Damon staggered briefly against the safety rail as the platform shook, then carried on. Safi started running after him, shouting at the ESOS group as she did do.

"Stop! You don't need to use those!" she called. "We've got" Then she stopped dead.

The whole section of platform, over fifty feet in length, had just collapsed right in front of her. It went down slowly, much slower than it would do on Earth, but there was still no time for those standing on it to react. First it bowed in the middle as the pillar supporting it gave way, then it folded up completely, sliding off the neighbouring pillars and plunging fifty feet to the ground below. In the space where seven people had been standing, now there was nothing. Most of them had been from ESOS. One of them had been the injured man they'd carried up the stairs. One of them had been Damon.

Safi ran to the edge and looked over. "Oh my God, they're still moving," she said. "They're still alive!"

Everyone else was on the scene in seconds, the remaining ESOS men on one side of the gap, and, Max, Harris and Ariel on the same side as Safi. Down below was in chaos. Of the seven people who had fallen, two were lying motionless. One of them was face down, and it was clear that his faceplate had been shattered by the fall. The other five were moving, but only two of them were on their feet. They could tell from the shoulder patches that Damon was one of them.

Harris and Safi were shouting to him, but the communication channels were clogged with shouts and calls from other people. In amongst the yelling they could hear groans and cries from those still lying on the ground. Then the first of the machines arrived.

Four of them came at first, cutting and grabbing at any metal parts they could find, stripping out the refined materials that were their ultimate objective. For the men on the ground, that included the suits they were wearing.

The first to die was one of the ESOS men, lying in a heap amongst a pile of twisted metalwork. If he even saw the machine approaching, he wasn't able to avoid it. Those above however could easily see as the machine cut into one of his legs, his arms and his other leg suddenly flailing in pain and panic as he realised what was happening to him.

Max got the spear thrower reloaded just as the man was being dismembered. With only the slightest pause, he raised it up and took aim at the machine. Safi was standing on one side of him and Ariel was on the other. They both moved outward to give him more room. Max reached back and flung the spear down, almost vertically. It hit the machine dead centre.

The machine stopped, jerked once, then fell over onto its side, motionless. For the man on the ground, however, it was too late. The machine had already cut away most of the metalwork he was lying on, shredding whatever parts of his body happened to be in the way. All that could be seen of his legs and lower half was a mess of suit material and dark brown matter, the remains of his flesh, freeze-dried by the vacuum. His hands clenched and unclenched in spasms as what was left of his body went through the last few seconds of its life, but there was no sound at all; inside that depressurised suit, even his final scream was denied him.

It was no different to what they had seen happen to the rover driver on the video link, but somehow this was far worse. Max turned away at once, clutching for the safety rail, trying to keep himself standing. Something far more pressing than staying upright was now on his mind though: he was going to throw up, and if he did then he was as good as dead. He would block the breathing hoses in his suit and suffocate in seconds.

He gripped the rail, squeezing his eyes shut, and tried to slow his breathing. He could feel the oxygen supply being blown over his face and he tried to empty his mind of everything except the pine-scented coolness of the gas and the humming of the fans. However, he didn't manage it for long. Whatever was happening on the ground below him, it appeared that the machines were now taking fresh victims, and this time every detail could be heard.

The sounds coming through his headset were indescribable: one wailing scream after another, grown men shrieking and crying, barely knowing what was happening to them except that they were about to die, and in amongst it he could hear his own name too, being shouted out again and again. It was Safi's voice, and Harris's as well, shouting at him to get back to the edge, to carry on taking out the machines and save whoever might be left. All Max wanted however was for the noise to stop. If he could have reached inside his helmet and ripped the headset away from his ears then he would have done. In reality though, he knew what he had to do. He forced himself away from the railing, then went back to the edge and looked down. And what he saw below him was like a vision of hell.

Ten machines were now on the scene, taking advantage of the sudden windfall of high-grade metals and materials. They were frantically cutting up the pile, hacking through anything or anyone that got in their way, while the two people who were still on their feet did their best to fend them off. Damon and the other man could be seen hitting one of them with lengths of girder that they'd found among the wreckage but with little real effect. Then Damon picked up another piece of debris, sharp-tipped where it had broken off its support, and stabbed the machine through its side. It looked as if it had taken all of his strength to do it, but that at least had more of a result. The machine shuddered, then lashed out with its legs, rolling away from them across the wreckage as its limbs flailed and jerked at random before finally coming to rest. There were still more machines to deal with though, as one after another arrived at the site of the collapse.

On the other side of the gap more ESOS men were now running back toward the stairs having decided to help those on the ground rather than just watch. Max, however, was on the wrong side of the divide so wouldn't have been able to get down even if he'd wanted to. He was secretly glad that he didn't have to make the choice. Instead, he stayed where he was and did the only thing he could do. He picked up the first of the remaining poles, fitted it to the thrower, and launched it down amongst the machines. Then he did the same again, and again, hurling them down as quickly as his strength would allow.

The machines were crowding in tightly now and he was

hitting them more often than he was missing, but he still couldn't aim too close to the men in case he got the wrong target. As a result, the machines that were doing the real damage were carrying on unhindered and the screams of the men they were hacking into were getting louder every second. Damon and the other man were doing their best to fight them off, and were having some success too, but against the numbers they were facing there was little hope. Before long even Max couldn't help them anymore, as the last of his spears was used up. The pile of dead machines he'd created was impressive, but nowhere near enough.

It was Safi who first realised they should give up. The three injured men on the ground were now as good as dead whatever was done for them, and by putting themselves in danger, those who were still on their feet would only add to the body count. Just by wearing suits made of metal and plastic they had made themselves targets for the gathering instincts of the machines.

"Damon!" she called. "Get out of there! Get everyone out of there!"

There was no answer, but they could tell he'd heard her. He backed off from the nearest machines, climbing part way up the rubble pile, and looked around him at the field of wreckage and human bodies being carved up on all sides. He must have decided she was right, because then he looked round again, as if searching for a way out. However his way to the stairs was now blocked where other machines had moved in to take their share of the scrap pile. The only way Damon could go was into the structure itself.

Safi saw and called to him again. "Head inside!" she shouted. "There's an access ladder to the canopy! At the far end!"

Again there was no word from Damon, but he seemed to understand. He ran up the rubble pile then down the other side, into the main body of Anchorville and out of their view. The ESOS man he had been fighting alongside went with him.

Those who had gone down to join the fight however were now doing exactly that, with their fists alone in some cases. They were attacking the machines from behind which gave them some advantage, but every time a machine turned to face them, anyone who took it on would be overwhelmed. Again the sounds of their deaths flooded the radio channels and this time there was nothing Max could do to help. Sickened, he reached down, knowing that he shouldn't but unable to stop himself, and turned his communicator off altogether.

Cocooned in a sudden bubble of silence, even time itself seemed to flow differently. He was now detached from the scene below him as the swarming machines inundated the men trying to disable them. He hadn't noticed until now, just how haphazard the machines' fighting was, as if the colony that had built them hadn't yet had a chance to learn from previous fights against humans, but he could easily see how lethal they were when they did go for a human target. He wondered how long it would take them to learn better tactics, given their rate of development so far, and how invincible they would become when that happened.

Suddenly a movement caught his eye off to the left, and he looked up quickly. Another section of platform, this time on the far corner, had just collapsed, silently sinking from view behind the intervening framework. Whatever was happening on the ground there was out of sight to him, but it was obvious that even more machines must have been there the whole time, eating into the pillars and eroding their supports. He had no idea how many they were facing now, but it must have been almost a hundred. How so many had appeared out of Kambria so quickly was unbelievable, as was their ferocity. Max saw Safi and Harris turn suddenly, their eyes drawn by something happening behind him. He tried to do the same, but before he could get round, Ariel had grabbed him by the shoulder and yanked him backward, almost pulling him off his feet in the process. Max shouted out as he staggered back, briefly forgetting that he couldn't be heard, but then he saw what they'd seen: another section of walkway, just two feet from where he'd been standing, slowly caving in on itself and dropping to the ground. Now all that was beneath their feet was an isolated platform, supported by just two of the pillars, with the four of them standing at the top.

He could feel the pillars swaying as he, Safi, Ariel and Harris looked round. All the ESOS personnel were on the other side of the first gap, a distance of fifty feet, too far to jump but in an infinitely safer position. The only thing linking them was Anchorville's solar canopy, the fragile structure that roofed the site and whose edge was at head height to the platform. It looked as if that was their only way across, and the only way to do it would be to traverse, hanging by their arms, over the carnage below.

Ariel seemed to have had the same thought. Max couldn't hear what he was saying, but his intentions were clear enough. He went over to the canopy support, grabbed it to test its strength, then held on tight and lifted his feet off the platform. It looked like the effort was intense; although the lower gravity made him and his suit just one sixth as heavy, getting a good enough grip on the ledge through thick spacesuit gloves must have been almost impossible. Max kept his distance while Ariel clumsily swung away and took himself out over the gap.

He'd covered about ten feet when it looked as if couldn't go any further. Every time he shifted his grip it looked like a struggle and he was already having to pause between each move. They saw him hang there briefly, legs kicking, while he tried to summon the strength to come back again. The return journey was even slower than the way out, but he made it eventually, his face screwed up with pain from the effort of holding on.

As soon as he was back on the platform he started looking round again, trying to come up with some other way of getting them to safety. Max couldn't see any way out, and it didn't look as if Ariel could either. He was looking round almost in desperation, his eyes wide and his movements random — until suddenly he stopped. At first Max couldn't tell what had happened. Ariel had simply frozen, his head to one side and his eyes defocused, as if something momentous had just occurred to him. In fact they had all done it — Ariel, Safi and Harris — all suddenly straightening, changing their postures as if realising the same thing at the same time. Then Max knew.

Safi even had her hand to her helmet, tilting her head to get a better signal. Something had happened on the radio channels, Max realised, and he was the only one missing it. He reached down to turn on his communicator, and a voice erupted into life in his ears.

"What the hell?" the voice was saying. It sounded American, and old too. "What the hell is this?"

"Jack! It's Ariel!" a more familiar voice called. "Where are you? We can't see you!" He, Harris and Safi were looking round now, scanning the whole perimeter, but only looking upward.

"I — I'm approaching from the south. I can see — Jesus, what am I seeing here? I'm gonna land, where are you guys?"

"No! Do not land! Repeat — do not land!"

"Then what do you want me to do?"

Ariel paused, and turned to the others. "We're going to have to jump for it guys," he said. Then he spoke again to the lander pilot. "Jack, we are on the south side of this structure, up high at the edge of the roof. Can you hover next to us?"

"I can hover for three minutes, no more," came the reply.

"Okay, do it!"

Then for the first time Max saw the lander, coming down from high in the sky, its spidery legs tipped with flashing beacons as four jets of expanding gas, almost colourless, shot out of its downward-pointing nozzles. It descended even more, its upper structure and windows coming into view as it reached the same fifty-foot altitude that they were watching from and began to advance toward them. Clouds of dust were being swept up by its engines, while short blasts of gas from its small control jets were also visible, keeping it balanced on the invisible columns of flame that were supporting it.

Ariel was talking Jack in the whole time, giving simple "up-down" and "left-right" commands to guide him to the right point in space. By now the lander was barely fifty feet away but Ariel called it even closer, telling Jack to fly lower as he did so, so that the top of the craft was level with the platform. It was now so close that one of the front landing legs was between the two pillars but Ariel called it in even more, until the roof of the thing looked almost close enough to jump to. That, it turned out, appeared to be the plan.

"I'm going to go first, to see if we can make it," Ariel said, already stepping up onto the railing. He didn't look as if he was prepared to waste any time talking about it. Instead he braced himself for the jump, then in the same move he leapt forward, arms wheeling to keep his balance as he crossed the gap.

He hit the lander on the edge of its roof, causing it to lurch forward with the force of the impact. The lander came even closer as a result, almost colliding with the upright pillars as a flurry of activity from the control jets tried to keep it level. All Ariel could do was hold on, hanging by his arms with his legs dangling over the forward-looking windows of the craft, until eventually it stabilised. Then he pulled himself up, the effort evident over his radio link, before finally getting a foothold on part of the cabin and turning to face them.

"You can do it!" he called to them, edging sideways to make room. "Just jump! Max, you go next!"

Max knew that if he hesitated now then he would never go. Instead he copied Ariel's actions, getting one foot up first, then stepping up all the way, not pausing long enough to have to balance there but instead crouching down and leaping forward in one go. He felt himself falling forward as he crouched, but he knew that he could jump fast enough to avoid a drop. And so, without even thinking about it, he suddenly found himself suspended in space, arms outstretched, with the dark grey ground passing by fifty feet below him. Then he looked up and saw the roof of the lander approaching and reached out to grab anything that he could get his hands around. It must have been some kind of antenna assembly that he caught. It bent alarmingly as his body crashed onto the vehicle but it was enough to support his weight. His right arm was almost dead from the repeated effort of throwing the spears but he willed the muscles to work for him again as he pulled himself up and found some support from the body of the craft. He was careful how he moved too; his lower legs were level with the front of the cabin and the pilot's windows, either of which he could easily put his foot through.

"Is there any way we can get inside?" he asked Ariel once he'd steadied himself. He knew there was no airlock on these vehicles, just docking ports for other pressurised vehicles or buildings. If the craft had landed then the pilot would have been able to suit up and depressurise the cabin to let them in. With that option removed they would have to spend the whole journey clinging onto the outside of the thing. It wasn't a prospect that he was looking forward to.

"No, no airlock," Ariel said, confirming Max's fears. "We stay like this, we have to. The accelerations are all under one-g, we'll be okay."

Max tried not to think about what that would be like. Instead he hung on while the lander pitched and swayed again, this time as Harris made the leap. The pilot seemed to be getting used to the jumps now, anticipating each one by a fraction of a second and reducing the effects of the impact. Harris grabbed the same antenna array that Max had, bending it almost beyond recognition as he made his grip secure. Then he moved over to make room for Safi.

She was the lightest of the four of them, and probably the fittest too. She covered the distance easily, catching hold of the structure with both hands and barely disturbing its hover at all.

"I'm going to get these guys too," they heard Jack saying, "but I don't have much time left." Just hovering near the surface of the Moon was using fuel at the same rate as ascending into orbit. Max wasn't sure how long that gave them.

Jack took the lander sideways, toward where the ESOS men were standing. They began jumping almost at once, the ones who had stayed at the top, plus some who had returned from the ground level. There were seven of them in all, jumping two at a time and grabbing whatever parts of the lander that they could. One of them ended up on the lower section of the craft, the tubular framework that enclosed the fuel tanks and engines, while the next one grabbed one of the landing leg struts, wrapping his arms and legs round it as if he was climbing a palm tree. The next one hit the cabin, near to where Harris was hanging on. They could see even before he joined them that it was Joel. He looked at them briefly, then tightened his grip and held on in silence.

The man who jumped after Joel wasn't so lucky. He'd jumped from further to the side, making a grab for the starboard outrigger, one of the long metal arms which held the control jets away from the craft's centre of gravity. The lander rolled sideways with the force of the collision, the jets themselves blasting wildly to get the vehicle back under control. It managed it, but at a high price for the man. He must have been facing right into one of the jets when it fired. All that could be seen was his suddenly limp shape falling away from the outrigger, his faceplate blown inward and his body decapitated by the force of the jet.

Now, however, something else could be heard over the radio channels: a calm, female voice, almost like a recording, talking over the chaos in placid, business-like tones. "Warning, fuel setpoint thirty seconds," was the first they heard of her, the steadiness and composure of her voice a strong contrast to the screaming and shouting that even now was continuing. It was the lander's flight control system, Max realised, telling the pilot how much longer they could hover and still get back to the base. Thirty seconds wasn't long. The three men still on the platform would probably be okay, but the handful who had stayed on the ground, including Damon, would be another matter. The sounds coming over the communicators showed that some of them at least were still alive.

"Everyone on the ground, get up here!" Max called out. "Damon! We don't have long!" He heard some shouting in German, but he couldn't tell who it had come from. Damon's voice couldn't be heard at all.

Almost immediately the next warning message came, identical to the first one but this time giving them just twenty seconds to go. The men on the platform had obviously heard and understood it as well. Two of them got up onto the railing, their efforts to scramble up even more frantic than those who had gone before, and launched themselves at the lander. The lower structure was now the only place with room to take them, and this was where they aimed themselves. They hit the bulky framework together, pushing the lander back away from Anchorville, hanging on by their hands and desperately trying to pull themselves up. Now only one person remained on the platform.

Max looked up, expecting the man to already be jumping, and saw to his dismay that it was Oliver Rudd.

Oliver stood there, gripping the railing in terror. Max could see his face clearly, his watery eyes as wide as saucers and his cheeks shaking with fear. The ten second warning came and went as he stood, rooted to the spot. It looked as if he wasn't going to move at all. Then, with what must have been less than five seconds to go, some kind of inner resolve seemed to come over him. With sudden determination he started to clamber up the railings, struggling to get to the top one even though it was only at waist height. There he paused, still trembling with fear, with one foot on the top rail and the other on the next one down. Pausing was a mistake, however, as he suddenly found himself having to balance at the top, arms swinging wildly as he tried to remain upright, somehow not willing to step the rest of the way up but not wanting to step down either. It was then that they ran out of time.

"Warning, fuel setpoint zero, fuel setpoint zero," the same calm voice informed them.

"I've got to go!" Jack called from the pilot's seat.

"Can't you wait? Just ten more seconds?" Joel said, breaking his silence. The radio channel as a whole had become unusually quiet in the last few seconds, but now people were shouting again, this time at Oliver, trying to get him to jump. Some sounded like they were encouraging him; others were just shouting at him.

"No can do," Jack said. "We go now, or none of us make it."

Then he increased the thrust of the engines, evident to Max from the vibrations coming through the lander's structure. The dust clouds beneath them became thicker too, and he felt a firm but steady downward pull as they began to accelerate upward. It looked as if Oliver was going to be left behind. Oliver however seemed to have different ideas.

Max watched in amazement as Oliver finally got the last shreds of resolve together. He stepped up to the top of the railing, still looking unsteady, and threw himself upward and outward toward the departing craft. The lander had risen by about five feet since Jack had opened up the throttles, but Oliver was still trying to jump for the top of the thing. As a result, he missed.

The craft heaved and swung yet again as Oliver crashed into the lower structure, immediately below where Safi was hanging on. The remains of Anchorville were now directly below them, and framed against them was Oliver Rudd, clinging on with all his strength as the lander's acceleration became more and more intense. Max could see Oliver's face even more clearly now, his eyes still wide and his face still white with shock as his legs kicked uselessly in the empty space below him. It looked as if all he could do was hang on by his arms and stare up at the others. Then, suddenly, a change came over him. If it was possible for his face to show any more terror, then that was what it did, but this time it was mixed with something else: pain. His face screwed up as he hung there, his head arching back in his helmet as some indescribable agony took hold of him. At first Max thought he'd broken his arm in the jump, but as Oliver's left hand let go of the structure and clutched at his chest it became obvious what was happening. He was having a heart attack.

He was hanging by just one hand now, sounds of anguish coming from between his gritted teeth, and it was clear he wouldn't be able to stay like that for long. They all watched, horrified, as the fingers of his right hand began to slip off the strut that he'd been holding onto. His hand was level with their ankles, but there was no way they could let go and reach down to him against the upward acceleration of the lander. Then, just as Oliver lost his grip altogether, his left hand swung out and made a grab for the only other thing he could get hold of: Safi's leg.

If she'd been expecting it then maybe she would have been able to hold on. As it was, the sudden shock of having to support Oliver's weight as well as her own, coupled with having one of her feet pulled out from under her, took away any chance she might have had of keeping her grip. It was Max who saw her falling first. He lashed out sideways to try to catch her arm as she was pulled off the structure. Ariel tried the same from the other side, but they both failed. All they could do was watch as she fell away from them, Oliver still holding onto her leg, dropping through the exhaust from the lander's nozzles and down toward the ground below. They were now over two hundred feet above the surface and the fall took ten full seconds, their bodies wheeling and turning the whole way, their screams blasting into the ears of everyone who was listening. They hit the top of Anchorville right on its edge, severing the canopy support and falling straight through it to the ground below. The silence from their communicators was instant.

Max couldn't even move his head, let alone speak. Ariel however was shouting, loud.

"Go back down!" he yelled at the pilot. "Go back down and get her!"

"I can't," Jack said, his voice shaking.

"Do it for God's sake!"

"I can't! We have to carry on! We're in a program now, this thing's flying itself!"

Then, just to prove his point, the engines cut themselves out, putting them on the ballistic freefall trajectory which would take them the rest of the way back to base.

"They're dead anyway," Jack added. "You wouldn't have been able to do anything." Ariel didn't answer, and nor did anyone else. Max just looked down as Anchorville receded, disappearing from sight among the dust clouds and the mist forming before his eyes.

The rest of the journey passed almost in silence. Those who did want to talk tuned themselves into private channels. All of them were from ESOS. Max, Ariel and Harris were silent. The lander was in weightlessness now as the laws of physics took it on a shallow parabolic freefall toward its final destination at the Crisium base. The engines wouldn't be lit again until they were coming in to land.

At their highest point they were over twelve miles above the lunar surface and the view was incredible. Max, however, was incapable of taking it in. He held on loosely and watched impassively, as the barren desolation passed by beneath him, too numb even to feel the vertigo that his brain was telling him he should be experiencing. She was dead, and he hadn't been able to save her; and even though the knowledge of that fact was filling his mind completely, the realisation itself just kept on coming, as if he was feeling it for the first time.

It was then that he saw the Anchorville service line, miles below, and for some reason it seemed to hold his attention. For not only could he see its sharply defined shadow, standing out from the jumble of hills and craters, not only could he see the sunlight, glinting off its surface where it met the ESOS line they'd driven along the day before; there was something else there too, and when he realised what it was, it made his blood turn to ice.

He could see them — the machines — not as individuals but rather as a swarm of destruction, crowding round the two lines. It was easy to spot the parts they'd begun to strip down, and the parts they hadn't yet got to. What was also clear was that tearing up the lines' remaining length was only a matter of time: and that included what lay at their end.

"Ariel," he said, his voice hoarse. "We may have a problem."

"What?" Ariel snapped.

"The machines, the ones that followed the service line, they're following it in both directions."

Ariel thought for a second, realising the implications. "Oh my God," he said. "The base."

"The base," Max repeated.

Chapter 15

"Jack — call the vehicle control centre," Ariel said. "Tell them to get all landers prepared for flight. And tell them to evacuate the base."

"Evacuate? You mean everyone?"

"The whole thing. And it needs to happen fast."

"But with only five landers? For two hundred people?"

"We'll take as many as we can. It's all we can do. Just — make the call."

The pilot had obviously seen enough to not need any more persuasion. "Okay, I'll do what I can. Stand by."

Jack dropped out of the open channel to make the call. They were now on the downhill half of the flight, with less than two minutes remaining until they landed. The pilot came back onto their channel less than a minute later.

"I told them, but they took some convincing."

"Are they getting people out of there?"

"Yes, but prepping landers takes time. They — they're going to try. Look, we're going to need this lander too if we're taking everyone. I'm going to land right next to the base so we can get more people on board, but the tanks will be almost dry. I need you to organise people, get us loaded before we refuel. Can you do that?"

"I'll do it," Ariel said.

Even as he spoke the base came into view below them. They were descending at almost forty-five degrees, with the lunar surface visibly coming up to meet them as gravity took them down. If they didn't slow their descent, they would hit it at the same speed they'd blasted away from Anchorville.

"Hold on everyone, we're going for the burn," Jack said.

The feeling of weight returned as the engines came to life. Max held on tight as the lander pitched back, burning off its forward as well as its downward motion, before righting itself for the final approach. And as the view of the ground returned, Max looked down, seeing not the landing site beneath them but the base buildings instead, barely fifty yards away, being blasted by the dust storm that was gushing out from under their engines. He could see faces too, up against the windows of one of the viewing areas, watching on in amazement as the lander, people hanging off it on every side, came down so close to the modules. They couldn't have had any idea what was happening.

As soon as they were down those people clinging to the outside started to climb off. Four other landers apart from their own could be seen, linked up to the docking tunnels but otherwise sitting idle. Ariel jumped down and started running, heading along the line of vehicles, giving out instructions even as he went.

"Follow me, and head for the airlock next to the last tunnel," he said quickly. "We need to go inside, then back through into the lander again. Harris, get someone from flight control prepping these other ones, they need to work faster than this. I'm going to work the hatches from the top. Once we're fuelled, we go. All agreed? Good. Max, you stay with me."

"I can't," Max said, as they reached the ground level airlock. "There's something I need to do. It's important."

Ariel paused and looked at him briefly but didn't ask him what he'd meant. Maybe he'd guessed, Max thought, though he himself had only just realised what he had to do. Ariel merely nodded, and headed into the airlock. Max squeezed in with the rest of them and waited for the atmosphere to return. Then, for the first time in almost four hours, he was able to tilt back his visor and get vaguely fresh air onto his face.

Once inside they quickly found their way back into the embarkation module where the articulated docking adapters led into the base. The area was deserted and the tunnels leading to the other landers were in darkness. Ariel went over to one of the spare tunnels and waited for the automated tow truck to hook up to their own lander and bring it over. At the same time, Harris went off into the base, searching for other personnel.

Max also left the group, but in another direction. He went without saying a word, and found his way back into the main corridors of the base. As he went he passed the same viewing area that their landing had been watched from. The same people were still there, though this time it was him that they were staring at, with his dirt-stained suit and wild, sweat-soaked hair. He didn't look back, but instead carried on down the corridor toward the habitation module where he and Safi had stayed.

An alarm started sounding as he went, but he barely heard it. All he could think about was what had happened to Safi and how little he'd really known her. Did she even have any family? She hadn't mentioned any, apart from air force stories about her father. Max didn't even know if the man was still alive. The only other person he'd heard her talk about was her old colleague and fiancé, Niall, and she was in the same place as him now.

But one thing of hers did remain and if he could retrieve that, then maybe he could salvage something from this journey. Because although she'd only had her omni with her the first time they'd gone out, the pictures and commentary she'd recorded might well be the only surviving evidence that those machines' precursors were designed by human hands, by ESOS. If the base and the research sites were about to be wiped off the map, her omni might well be the only way of demonstrating what had really started this.

He was still getting the same strange glances from the people he passed, but now the alarm had added a touch of panic to the way they were looking at him. They could tell something was wrong, but the full story obviously hadn't got round yet. He briefly thought of trying to warn them, telling them what was going to happen, but he knew even without trying that they would only look at him like a lunatic. A call over the P.A. would

315

be the only way to do it, the only way to get people moving quickly. For the moment, however, Max had other things to do.

He got to the room they'd shared and burst inside. It was exactly as they'd left it. He quickly started searching through her things, feeling guilty about upturning the neatly piled and folded clothes and possessions but with no time to do anything else, before finally finding what he was looking for at the bottom of her bag.

It was only when he was back in the corridor that he realised he hadn't retrieved anything of his own. It didn't matter though, there was nothing there that he couldn't replace. Instead he hurried onward, back toward the landers.

There was an announcement being made at long last, a voice he didn't recognise saying something about a chemical leak, nothing to panic over but still serious enough to call for an evacuation. Max wondered who had thought it up: Ariel, or Harris, or someone else from the base support staff. It was certainly better than telling the truth, or more believable at least. Keep calm, people were being told, but keep moving.

The people Max saw in the corridors were looking genuinely worried now however, and had started to guess that his appearance in the base had something to do with whatever was happening. Several of them tried to catch him as he went by, to ask him what was going on, but he didn't stop to talk. "Just get to the landers!", was all he said as he rushed past them.

Many of the inhabitants seemed to be doing that already. The corridor leading to the docking adapters was now filling up as people moved toward the embarkation area. The passageway was only wide enough for three people to walk side by side and none of them seemed to have the same sense of urgency as Max about getting out of there. He had no idea how far away the machines were but some kind of intuition was telling him there wasn't long left. He could feel the tension building up inside him, making him want to run through the crowd, shouting at them to move faster, but he knew that if he did then he would only cause a panic. The base was home to over two hundred people and a quick look ahead and behind showed that barely half of them were making the move.

He got to the viewing area that overlooked the landers and pushed over to the side so that he could see the progress. Their lander was now linked up and lights were visible in three of the others. He carried on, up to the embarkation area. Base personnel were there now, directing people down the docking tunnels. They seemed to be packing them into the landers tightly as well, sending as many as possible into each one. Anyone trying to take luggage with them was being told to leave it behind and a large pile of bags and other possessions was building up against one wall of the module. In Max's case the bulky suit he was wearing would probably be more of a problem. He went over to one of the base workers and asked him to help him get out of it.

The man looked at him uncertainly for a second but didn't seem to want to ask why he was still wearing it, or why he looked to be in such a state. Instead he went round behind Max and unlocked the backpack, then swung it away and held the suit steady while Max climbed out. The look on the man's face, and those people around him, gave some clue as to the smell that had come out with him. Max ignored them.

He carried on down the length of the embarkation module, looking around for anyone he recognised. Only two of the landers were being boarded and the stream of people that Max had joined was being shepherded toward the nearer one. The other landers, including the one they'd escaped from Anchorville in, must have been either full already or waiting for these first ones to be filled. Max briefly thought of trying to get back into the original one, assuming that Ariel and Harris would be there too, but there was nothing to be gained by sharing the same ride away from the base. His only priority was to leave and if the people he'd just fought alongside were in different vehicles then it made no difference. He decided to stay in line, following the crowd down into the craft.

There were twenty people in there already when he dropped into the cabin. The vehicle was only built to take eight, but with the cargo space beneath the cabin empty, the weight would not be a problem. Only seats were in short supply. Max worked his way into one of the corners and wedged himself against the wall while yet more people came down the docking tube. By now they were packed in shoulder to shoulder. Most of them seemed to be engineers and researchers, on the Moon to do a job and experienced at living with the conditions there, but despite their professionalism they were still looking scared. There was very little conversation going on in the lander but what Max did hear suggested that people knew something more serious than a chemical leak was behind the evacuation. As before however, he kept his mouth shut and silently wished for the vehicle to get underway.

Then events took a turn of their own.

He felt it in his ears first, a slight drop in pressure, like riding a fast elevator up a tall building. Other people had felt it too and he could see them exchanging glances, looking even more worried than before. "What the hell was that?" someone said in the tunnel up above them. Rapid, subdued conversations started almost at once, around him and above him, and although he couldn't make any of it out clearly, the same word seemed to figure in all of them: depressurisation. Yet again, Max felt a sudden realisation taking hold of him, gripping his insides. He knew the base modules were connected by pressure doors, designed to clamp shut if the skin of one of them was breached or punctured, and he knew that it was designed to happen almost instantaneously. He also knew that no matter how fast the doors were, the effect of a depressurisation taking place would be felt throughout the entire base. It meant there was only one explanation for what had just happened. The machines had arrived.

The last man down the ladder was wearing pilot's overalls, and he at least was moving quickly. "Something's going on up there folks," he said, jumping straight into the flight seat. "We need to move fast. I'm going to fly over to the fuel dump, so hold on tight." He was already flicking switches and activating the lander's systems even as he spoke. The luminous display screens lit up his dark, lean features as he turned this way and that, checking instruments on either side. First they heard the hatch closing, then the sounds of the docking tunnel disconnecting from the top of the craft. The pilot could be seen craning his neck to look upward out of the windows, waiting for the tunnel to swing safely out of the way. Then he set the engines running on minimum throttle, made a final check over his shoulder that everyone was ready to go, and turned up the power.

They rose quickly, immediately rotating to face the fuel store, and pitched forward to fly toward it. Max's view from the back of the cabin was limited but he could still see the low soil-covered mounds of the underground fuel tanks as they got closer. Normally the landers would be towed over here by truck then towed to the take-off site but it looked, to Max's relief, as if their pilot at least had realised how little time they had. Even though the tanks were supposedly dry there must have been just enough coating the sides to get them this far. They made a hard, rushed landing in front of the refuelling point, then the articulated fuel lines unfolded from the pump housings and came out to meet them. They linked up automatically, by now out of Max's sight, and started to transfer their contents across.

It was then that the first of the machines was spotted. A group of three people, clustered up against the right-hand window, suddenly reacted together to something they had seen. "What in God's name is that thing?" one of them said, pressing his face up against the glass. At first no one else seemed to pick up on what was happening but as those people by the window tried to comprehend what they were seeing, it became clear that something out of the ordinary was going on.

"There's something out there, next to that building!"

"Where? I don't see it?"

"In the distance, where the service lines come in!"

"What the hell — ?"

By now the other passengers were jostling for position, trying to see what they were talking about but Max already knew what must have been going on. The only relief came from the knowledge that the base buildings themselves were now almost a mile away, but he also knew how fast those machines could move. He put his head back against the cold metal wall of the lander and closed his eyes, trying to block out any sign or sound of what he knew must be happening and what could come their way at any second. It didn't work.

"Jesus Christ! It just — what the — ?"

"There's more of them! There, and there!"

"They're cutting into the — oh my God that's where —"

Max couldn't tell exactly what those three or four people were seeing but he could hear enough to realise how bad it must have been. Other people in the lander were now shouting, almost screaming at them, trying to get them to say what was going on, but whatever was happening before their eyes must have been too much to put into words. In a way Max was glad not to hear it. Instead he waited, calling on anything he thought might help, as if willing the fuel to flow into the tanks before the machines came their way. Then, at last, the fuelling process was complete. Max heard a warning tone from the pilot's console as the fuel lines prepared to retract, and looked over to see how close to setting off they actually were. The pilot was looking off to the right, his eyes wide and his mouth hanging open, but he responded to the tone immediately, breaking his eyes away from the scene to get the lander ready for its final lift-off. This time he didn't bother looking back at the passengers but instead started up the engines and took them straight to full throttle, taking off vertically and turning to face the west where their ascent would take place. Max felt his weight suddenly increasing as the lander thrusted upward, though with people crammed in on all sides there was no chance of falling over. Then the pilot switched the craft over to autopilot, letting its own systems orient it for the start of the climb, and Max felt the slow, measured rotation as their trajectory immediately broke away from the vertical, pitching over to build up horizontal speed even as they rose. And it was then, roughly ten seconds after they'd left the ground, that Max saw with his own eyes what the other passengers had been seeing the whole time.

If they'd departed from the take-off site instead of the fuel store and flown out over the safe, empty ground of the ascent corridor, none of it would have been visible to them. Instead, having taken off right next to the fuel silos, their flight took them within three hundred yards of the base, giving a low level flypast of the buildings, the machines, and everything else that was laid out below them. And this time, looking forward through the pilot's larger windows at the front, everyone got to see.

The view lasted just seconds but in that time the fate of the entire settlement was sealed. Most of the base modules were already wrecked, lights dead in viewing ports, ragged slits in the bare metal revealing blackness where just minutes before there had been light. Even the intact ones were being overrun, their soil coverings dug away to expose them to the vacuum. And it was then, just as the view slid below the bottom of the window and out of sight altogether, that another of the modules was breached, right before the passengers' eyes. It was the corridor leading to the lander bay, the one route to safety the remaining base population had left.

They saw the initial blast of air and vapour, the torn shreds of the outer skin peeling back like paper. They saw the cloud of insulation from around the inner skin erupting like a snowstorm.

And in the midst of the cloud, like rags in a hurricane, they saw dozens of tiny shapes, all different colours, wheeling and tumbling in the gale of depressurisation as they poured out onto the lunar soil. The shapes rolled across the ground, then stopped and did not move again.

Max looked away and shut his eyes, just a fraction too late. It made no difference; the sight was lost from view anyway. He hadn't been the only one to see it either, or to recognise what had happened. This time though there was no noise in the cabin, no cries or shouts, just silence, and the smell of fear and revulsion, dead and clammy. Max opened his eyes once and looked at the ceiling of the cabin, purely to give his mind some other image to dwell on, then he closed them again and kept them closed for a long, long time.

* * *

He spent the next two days like that, only opening his eyes when necessary, trying to block out the sounds and smells of the strangers who were crowding him on all sides. They left him alone however, much as they seemed to be leaving each other alone. Even those who knew each other had little they could communicate through words. The pilot was the only one who spoke much, usually talking to Earth, trying to arrange to dock with the May station and then get taken down to the surface. He also tried the Crisium base, as if hoping that someone there could hear and respond to him, though there was no reply. The only contact he did make was with another of the landers, which had taken off just after their own and was now following their course a few minutes behind. The passengers could only hear the pilot's side of the conversation but he gave them the message that another twenty-five people had been rescued. It meant that barely a quarter of the base population had escaped. He then went round the cabin taking names, so that people on Earth would know who was and wasn't coming back.

"Lowrie," Max said when he was asked. It was the only time he spoke.

* * *

Even with his eyes closed he didn't sleep. The rest of the journey was spent awake, but dead on the inside. Even the image of the Earth filling the window did little for him when they finally put themselves into orbit, lining up with the May station for the transfer back down toward home. He followed the others as they slowly left the lander, going straight into a space plane attached to a neighbouring adapter. He had no memory of being assisted or guided, but he supposed someone must have been there to help them. No one from the other lander was here; they would be put on another plane he was told, that one landing in Brisbane. Max could only assume that Ariel, Joel and Harris were among them. Then, with no more delay than was necessary, the plane he was on pulled away from the station, backed off by several miles and fired its motors to slow down for re-entry. The spectacular pink glow of the plasma sheets gushing off the heatproof skin left him unmoved, as did the view of the Pacific Ocean beneath them as they descended toward Los Angeles. On the ground he just walked where he was pointed, as most of them did, before finally emerging into a sectioned-off zone of the arrivals area where a crowd of relatives was waiting. Gillian was there too. She held him tight, and he held her too, though slowly, as if the fatigue had made even that too much of an effort. She led him to their car and drove him home. At the house he went straight upstairs, taking a shower only because Gillian told him he should. Details seemed inordinately vivid for some reason: the colour of the tiles, the smell of the soap, the sound of the water hitting the floor. He was still standing there in a stupor when Gillian came in and guided him to the bedroom. She sat next to him as he lay there, looking at the familiar surroundings of the room and trying to reconcile it all with the places he'd been and the things he'd seen just days before. It was impossible. Then the exhaustion became too much, and he finally fell asleep.

* * *

Max knew as soon as he woke that he had been asleep for a long time. It was only when he turned on the TV and saw the date that he realised how long it had really been. He had slept for a day and a half, solidly. Even now, moving was still an effort, as if the fatigue hadn't truly left his body. He didn't try to sit up, or even to call out to Gillian, but instead started switching through the channels, hoping to regain some strength in his body by letting his brain wake up first.

The destruction at Crisium was still dominating the news, he wasn't surprised to see. Interviews with other survivors were being shown, some of whom he recognised from the journey home, plus pictures of the attack itself, taken by fixed cameras at the base and beamed back to Earth even as it took place. The worst shots had been edited out, but the machines could still be seen as clearly as he'd seen them himself and by now there couldn't have been a person on the planet who didn't know what the things looked like. What they were though, no one seemed to know.

Something Max wasn't prepared for, however, was the real extent of the damage. He knew the main base was gone but the other Earthrise research sites — twelve of them inhabited — had all been destroyed too, as had the North Road transmitter chain leading to the far side observatory, and the observatory itself. A cargo truck which had been following the road had also been attacked, he heard. It took almost a minute for him to realise that those were the same people he and Safi had shared the transfer flight with when they'd first arrived. The plague that had started in Mare Crisium, the Sea of Crises, had quickly spread beyond those flat lowlands, taking over any man-made artefacts it could find along the way. It meant that now, for the first time in over twenty years, there was no human presence anywhere on the Moon. It was the same uninhabited rock that Max had looked up at as a child. Then he corrected himself; uninhabited was the wrong word entirely.

Gillian came into the room at that point and walked over to the bed. She must have heard the sounds from the TV. She sat down and asked him how he was. He muted the volume and sat up.

"I'm okay," he said. "Just tired."

"I know you are," she said. "But you're safe now." Then she paused. "I — I heard about Safi. I'm sorry, Max."

"Thanks," he said. "She was strong, and smart too. She shouldn't have gone like that. How did you know about her?"

"Someone called for you yesterday. He told me what happened up there, some of it anyway. He left you a message too. It's stored on the home account. Do you want to see it?"

"Yeah, sure."

"I'll get you something to eat too, you must be starving."

Max lay still for a minute or so after she'd gone, then turned to the bedside terminal and looked down the list of stored messages. The topmost one was just twenty-four hours old. Max set it playing; he hadn't known who to expect, but he certainly hadn't expected to see Ariel.

"Max, your wife says you are still recovering, but I hope you get this soon. I'm glad you made it back, and I hope you managed to do what you had to do before you left. We will all miss her. Harris is with me now, but it looks as if Damon didn't make it. That Joel character came back with us though. I think he will have some explaining to do. There's going to be an inquiry of course, and they'll probably call you in too, so I expect I'll see you then, but it may not be for some time. I just wanted to say, thank you. You faced up to those things well. I was glad you were with us. Goodbye."

They hadn't looked like easy words for Ariel. Max was genuinely honoured. It didn't make him feel any better though. Ariel's words had reminded him just how few people had managed to survive, and all that was going through his mind was the times when he'd got away and other people hadn't. The collapsing walkways at Anchorville, the jump to the lander, the evacuation at Crisium: all those times when he was saved but others weren't so lucky. He almost felt responsible for them. "Survivor guilt", he'd heard it called, but putting a name on it didn't make it any easier.

Fifty people got out, and I am one of them, he thought. Fifty people who had no reason to think when they got up that morning that they would be lucky to survive the day, and yet barely ten of them even know what happened. Is that enough to stop the same thing happening again? Or is it always going to happen? Just how long will it be before someone's well-intentioned dabbling succeeds in creating life once again?

Life — no longer could anyone doubt that that was what they were dealing with. And all it had taken to start the process, to turn dead matter into living things, was the ability to reproduce. It was like the electric current that brought Frankenstein's monster to life, except that no lightning bolts or supernatural forces were required. Just put the right materials in the right places, and you will have machines that can copy themselves indefinitely, evolving over time, whether you want them to or not.

It really was that simple, he thought. The atoms, the chemicals that every living thing, including himself, was built from had existed for billions of years and would do for billions more. It was just the way they happened to be put together for these few decades that allowed him to exist, as a person. Arrange them to the right plan and you could build a bacterium, or a fly, or a human. Or you could build a machine that would sail around pulling gold out of seawater. Or, if you wanted, you could build a colony of robots that would grow and spread, replicating themselves first out of lunar dirt, then out of anything else that crossed their path. There would be no need for any mystical "life force", and no need even for God. The laws of physics would be enough.

No need for God, he thought, and wondered what Gillian would think of that.

Then he remembered something, something that had been clear as day at the time, but which had since left his mind completely. He remembered standing in the lander, waiting for its fuel tanks to fill so that they could take off and leave the destruction behind once and for all. He remembered wishing and hoping for the refuelling to finish, knowing that there was nothing he could do to make it happen faster and that for once his survival was in someone else's hands. And he also remembered what exactly had gone through his mind as he'd stood there, eyes tightly shut. I can't die here, he had thought. We've got to get away. *I've* got to get away.

God wouldn't let me get this far just to kill me.

He had thought it clearly, and what was more, he had believed it.

He tried to shake the idea from his head. It was a natural reaction after all, to call on God for help when life was in danger. It bore no relationship to his real beliefs, his real ideals. Somehow, though, he didn't manage to convince himself. He tried instead to think what Safi would have said if she'd been there too, but that only brought back bad memories — and one memory in particular. In fact, that final image of her falling from the lander was so predominant that even her face was beginning to fade from his mind. He was almost starting to forget what she looked like.

It was mad, he told himself; he'd only been with her a few

days previously, but already he could only picture her in vague, indistinct terms. It was almost as if his mind was trying to block out that last memory of her, but everything else about her was going too. Nothing was left: her body, her possessions, by now all of them would be part of that still growing colony.

Then he remembered, not everything of hers had gone. He got out of bed, went over to where his clothes were piled up and reached into the pocket of his trousers. Her omni was still there, and he'd brought it back for a reason.

Her whole life would be stored in that little bracelet's memory cells: all her pictures, all the films she'd watched, the music she liked, the messages she'd sent and received, everything she'd ever bought, everything she'd ever worked on. However, it would be her most recent entries that would justify the risks he'd taken in going back for it.

He activated the unit and looked at the top level of its storage. Personal and private data were further down and he wouldn't dream of trying to look there unless the colony recordings weren't obvious, but as it turned out he didn't need to. The pictures and video clips were there, right at the top. He opened a couple up to check they'd recorded okay. It took a while to get used to her omni control conventions; like his, selections were made by tracing shapes and letters in the air next to it, but she'd set hers up differently. He soon figured it out, though, and reviewed what she'd been able to capture. He hoped it would be enough; short of having an 'ESOS' logo stamped on every machine, this was probably the best evidence he could wish for.

Then he noticed something else in the top level storage. The report — the document she'd been working on before the flight — that was in there too, along with all its accompanying notes and drafts. As a recipe for how to create life from rock and metal he was tempted to delete it there and then, but he knew that would be wrong. He opened it up instead, purely to see how far through it she was and what she'd really written, and whether there was any other person or organisation more entitled than himself to decide what to do with it.

How to build replicators, and how to look for them. Those two threads seemed to run right through what she'd written so far and looking at her notes, Max could finally see the connection between the two. For not only was this a construction manual, a how-to guide on making self-replicating machines from scratch; she was also laying out, in some degree of detail, what people should look for if evidence of replicators from elsewhere was to be found. The only question was where to look for the signs. And it seemed that, for her, the airless, low-gravity environment of ore-rich asteroids had been the obvious choice. And what was more, she'd expected to find those signs herself, within decades if not years.

Max was just scrolling through the pages now, his eyes wandering over the words in front of him. It was then that something else caught his eye, some word or phrase that must have meant something to his subconscious, but which was still hidden from the rest of him even with the text in front of his face. He backed up and began to read the section from the top, this time slowly, taking in every word.

It was something about building replicators for unfamiliar environments, how to maximise their chances if it wasn't known what kind of gravity, radiation levels or chemical resources they would be surrounded by. There was a proof, mathematical at first, but then summarised in the text, showing that machines whose components were of a similar scale to the basic blocks of raw material surrounding them would be by far and away the most likely to succeed. They would replicate more easily and their design would be easier to tailor to whatever job they were intended to do. There was only one way to genuinely achieve this, she had decided, and that was to build machines at the molecular scale. In this way they could take in and filter the parts they needed directly from their surroundings, with no complex chemical extraction or processing required, then put them together to make whatever they were asked to make, including copies of themselves. She had then laid down a plan, more of a rough template than a finished blueprint, of how such a machine could code its own design using chains of atoms and molecules, then pull in more of those molecules to grow and reproduce according to what its design code told it. A machine of this type, running on chemical reactions rather than motors and mechanisms, would be the easiest design to optimise for the widest range of operating environments. *In fact,* she wrote, *with a sufficiently versatile coding scheme for growth and replication, and the ability to replicate with minimal processing of incoming materials, machines of this type would represent the ultimate in replicative efficiency. For not only would the shape and function of these devices be infinitely variable; in the extreme case, even their internal functioning need not be set in stone.*

Max put the omni down and closed his eyes. *Set in stone,* his mind was repeating to him again and again, *set in stone.* Then he opened his eyes and sat up straight. An image had just appeared to him, or rather two images, of two entirely separate objects in two entirely different places, that had no business whatsoever looking the same as each other but that still somehow did. One of them he'd seen over twelve months ago; the other, just three days.

He got up quickly, almost staggering as the blood left his head, then he cleared his senses and started to get dressed. What were the chances? he asked himself, pulling his clothes on. What were the chances of something like that falling into his hands so easily? And after all the time and effort that she'd spent looking millions of miles away from Earth, when all the time the proof was all around her? She was even part of it herself. There would have to have been thousands of the things, of course, millions more like, but to find one after all this time; he might even have picked it up and held it in his hands; just how likely was that?

He left the room and headed downstairs. Gillian was on her

way up carrying a tray, but he passed her by and ran toward the door.

"Max, where are you going?" she called after him.

"I have to go to work," he said, stopping briefly and looking back at her. "There's something I've got to do."

"But Max!"

He got into the car and drove himself to UCLA, still trying to clear the sleep and fatigue from his head, then parked up on the street and ran inside, down toward the basement labs. He found the room he wanted and went in, still running. John Olson was there, but Max didn't even give him time to react.

"John, those x-rays you sent me of the rocks, where are they?"

"The scans? What do you want those for? Max, are you sure you should be —"

"Just show them to me. I need to see them."

John paused slightly in indecision, then went over to one of the terminals and brought the images up one by one. Max recognised them from the files John had sent him on the island but on the larger screen of the terminal they were much clearer, much more defined. There was one in particular he was looking for though, and when it flashed up in front of him he reached over and froze the screen.

"Is that what you're looking for?" John said. "What's so special about it?"

Max pointed at part of the image, at one of the shapes bedded into the rock — a narrow line, about three inches long, slightly bulbous toward one end — and said, "That is."

John peered in close to the screen, as if trying to discern it from the crystalline deposits surrounding it. "What is it?"

"Split it along that seam and I'll show you."

John still had no idea what Max was getting at, but didn't seem to want to question him. Instead he checked the catalogue number for the rock in the picture, then took it from its storage box and carried it over to one of the benches along the side wall of the lab. There were tools there, hammers, diamond saws and chisels, plus other rocks from the collection, lying in pieces where they had already been broken along the natural faults separating the layered bacterial mats that had formed them. John put the rock in a clamp, looked at the scans again to check the location of the seam and split it in two.

Max stepped forward and picked up the two halves, turning them so that the cut surfaces were uppermost. And there, lying amongst the calcite and trapped sediment of the ocean floor it had fallen onto, was a three inch long needle, sharp at each tip and rounded in the middle, its shape slightly disguised by the mineral growths that had formed around it, but otherwise as smooth and pristine as the day it was made, whenever that was. What it was made for was another mystery, but, Max at least thought he could guess.

Chapter 16

They were out at New Venice beach, near Gillian's gallery, walking along the seafront as the cold November wind came in from the west. Few other walkers were out but Max had only just got back from the Crisium enquiry board, and having to relive those events one more time had made him want to breathe safe, fresh air at every opportunity.

"So let me ask you the question you've always asked us poor, stupid, Christians," Gillian said. "If life here was started by some intelligent creator, what created them?"

It was a good question, Max thought, and in the circumstances a fair one. "Somewhere, at some time in the past, life really did start by chance. The Karman-Lowrie number is only an estimate, but it gives an idea of how often it must happen, how many planets you would need for one spontaneous emergence to occur every billion years. But wherever it did happen, we know something intelligent grew up as a result. And when it decided it wanted to spread out into the cosmos, it hit on the best method imaginable of turning as many of the planets around it as possible into habitable environments. They probably fired those things out trillions at a time, hoping that some small percentage would hit somewhere viable. Isotope analysis of the needle's surface suggests it was in interstellar space for up to ten thousand years before it even reached Earth. It could have covered tens of light-years before it got here, hundreds even, with its cargo of bacteria in deep freeze the whole time."

Gillian still didn't seem to believe what he was telling her. "I just never thought I'd hear stuff like this from someone like you. I thought you were a Darwin man, through and through."

"I still am, and I always will be. The way different species and life forms developed from those beginnings is purely down to evolution and nothing else. Darwin got it right, and no one will ever take that away. It's where Earth's first precursor life forms came from that was the big unanswered question. And this seems to be the answer."

"It still sounds like you're changing your mind to me."

"Not really. Even Darwin considered this question, but he got nowhere near this answer of course. In "The Origin of the Species", he talked about the creator 'breathing life into many forms, or into one', but letters he sent to his colleagues often talked about life starting in 'some warm little pond', with just 'ammonia, salts and heat' to drive it. Whatever planet *they* grew up on, that's probably how it happened. It just didn't happen that way here."

"And you think those bacteria are like what you were doing? Like what ESOS was building?"

"Yes. What we call Archaean cyanobacteria, were actually replicating machines, chemical replicators, built for planetary terraforming. DNA based life is just too unlikely: Sheldon Karman and I worked that out ten years ago but we were never willing to face the implications. Those things had to be artificial. That needle was packed with them, all sorts of species, but most of them died out as soon as they were released. The cyanobacteria though, they're the ones that took hold. Every bit of free oxygen in Earth's early atmosphere was thanks to them. Someone wanted Earth to have a cosy oxygen-rich environment. We were being seeded for a reason."

"But by who?"

"I don't know, but whoever they were they never followed it up with a personal visit. The seeds they planted here took over and did their own thing. And that's what we are. Everything that's ever lived, in the whole history of Earth's evolution, came from those beginnings. Replicating machines evolving out of control."

She shook her head, as if still trying to digest the story he was feeding her. "No way, Max. I can't explain what you found in that rock, or why it looks like that needle you saw on the Moon, but you can't tell me this is the simplest explanation?"

"It makes a lot of sense to me. It's like we've found a whole new cycle of evolution, acting on a timescale of billions of years. Within each cycle, species grow and adapt the way Darwinian evolution takes them, but whenever something intelligent figures out how to build replicators, they end up making way for their own creations. It's going to happen to us too. It's already started."

The Moon wasn't visible from where they were but Max had seen the news reports of the accelerating growth currently underway, telescope images of that growing dark patch centred on the place he knew Kambria lay. It had made Victor's defence at the enquiry all the harder, knowing that the effects of what he'd built would be visible to the naked eye within weeks. Corporate negligence on an exponential scale; Max was no lawyer, but it was probably a legal first.

"I take it you know how people will react when you tell them all this," Gillian said. "Space aliens seeding Earth, like some cosmic-scale science experiment."

"We're taking it into consideration. No one else looking at those samples has found anything similar, so it'll be a UCLA announcement. I'm going to have to brace myself for the backlash though. Do you think you'll be ready for that?"

"I think so."

"There's no walking out on me this time you know."

She didn't answer straight away, but smiled instead, walking in silence with her hand to her stomach. She was already starting to show.

"She'll be the first generation to be born knowing we're not alone, and where we really came from," Max said. "Some people will find that hard to get used to. They're going to blame me before they blame anyone else."

"I know. But I'll be here, I promise."

"It's going to be a very different world you know, for us as well as her," Max said.

"I think it is," Gillian said. "I think it is."

COSMIC
EGG
BOOKS

If you prefer to spend your nights with Vampires and
Werewolves rather than the mundane then we publish the books
for you. If your preference is for Dragons and Faeries or Angels
and Demons – we should be your first stop. Perhaps your
perfect partner has artificial skin or comes from another planet –
step right this way. Our curiosity shop contains treasures you
will enjoy unearthing. If your passion is Fantasy (including
magical realism and spiritual fantasy), Horror or Science Fiction
(including Steampunk), Cosmic Egg books will
feed your hunger.